LUCY

Come Home

LUCY

Come Home

Dave and Neta Jackson

CASTLE
ROCK
CREATIVE
Evanston, Illinois 60202

© 2012 by Dave and Neta Jackson

All rights reserved. No portion of this book may be reproduced, stored in a retrieval system, or transmitted in any form or by any means—electronic, mechanical, photocopy, recording, scanning, or other—except for brief quotations in critical reviews or articles, without the prior written permission of the publisher.

Published in Evanston, Illinois. Castle Rock Creative.

Scripture quotations are taken from THE HOLY BIBLE, King James Version, Cambridge, 1769. Public domain.

"God bless the corners of this house," an Irish blessing, anonymous. Public domain.

"Pass Me Not, O Gentle Savior," written by Fanny Crosby, 1868, first printed in *Songs of Devotion*, by Howard Doane (New York: 1870). Public domain.

"Softly and Tenderly Jesus Is Calling," Will Lamartine Thompson, in Sparkling Gems, Nos. 1 and 2, by J. Calvin Bushey (Chicago, Illinois: Will L. Thompson & Company, 1880). Public domain.

"'Tis So Sweet to Trust in Jesus," William J. Kirkpatrick and Louisa M. R. Stead, 1881. Public Domain.

Publisher's Note: This novel is a work of fiction. Names, characters, places, and incidents are either products of the authors' imaginations or used fictitiously. All characters are fictional, and any similarity to people living or dead is purely coincidental.

ISBN: 978-0-9820544-3-7

Windy City Stories
by Dave and Neta Jackson

The Yada Yada Prayer Group Series

The Yada Yada Prayer Group, Neta Jackson (Thomas Nelson, 2003).

The Yada Yada Prayer Group Gets Down, Neta Jackson (Thomas Nelson, 2004).

The Yada Yada Prayer Group Gets Real, Neta Jackson (Thomas Nelson, 2005).

The Yada Yada Prayer Group Gets Tough, Neta Jackson (Thomas Nelson, 2005).

The Yada Yada Prayer Group Gets Caught, Neta Jackson (Thomas Nelson, 2006).

The Yada Yada Prayer Group Gets Rolling, Neta Jackson (Thomas Nelson, 2007).

The Yada Yada Prayer Group Gets Decked Out, Neta Jackson (Thomas Nelson, 2007).

Yada Yada House of Hope Series

Where Do I Go? Neta Jackson (Thomas Nelson, 2008).

Who Do I Talk To? Neta Jackson (Thomas Nelson, 2009).

Who Do I Lean On? Neta Jackson (Thomas Nelson, 2010).

Who Is My Shelter? Neta Jackson (Thomas Nelson, 2011).

Lucy Come Home, Dave and Neta Jackson (Castle Rock Creative, 2012).

Yada Yada Brothers Series

Harry Bentley's Second Chance, Dave Jackson (Castle Rock Creative, 2008).

Harry Bentley's Second Sight, Dave Jackson (Castle Rock Creative, 2010).

Souled Out Sisters Series

Stand by Me, Neta Jackson (Thomas Nelson, 2012).

Come to the Table, Neta Jackson (Thomas Nelson, December 2012).

For a complete listing of
books by Dave and Neta Jackson visit
www.daveneta.com and www.trailblazerbooks.com

Prologue

1942

BELCHING BLACK SMOKE AND STEAM, the *Grand Trunk Western* bore down on the train station in Lapeer, Michigan, with a series of jerks and ear-splitting squeals. But not all the squeals originated from the train's undercarriage where the rusty brakes gripped the huge metal wheels.

The young elephant in the menagerie boxcar squealed too.

The moment the train shuddered to a stop on a siding, the air exploded into new sounds: men shouting, metal doors sliding open, horses stamping, and flatbed trucks gunning their motors as they pulled alongside the train cars to unload the gaudy carnival wagons, animal cages, support poles, electric wiring, and mountains of heavy canvas that would soon balloon into numerous tents.

The Carson Brothers' Carnival of the Century had arrived.

"Bo" Bodeen jumped down from the sleeping car where he'd been bunking with some of the carny crew, a black-and-white mutt close on his heels. The lanky, good-looking youth with wavy black hair combed straight back from his tanned forehead barely noticed the banner draped across the front of the station—*WELCOME TO LAPEER DAYS! Annual Summer Festival Since 1902!* He ran along the tracks toward the flatcars loaded with the jumble of machinery for the midway rides. Already he could hear his father barking orders at the roustabouts. "Get those straps loose!... Where in tarnation is the rest of the crew?... Pull those cables tighter!... Drop that motor, Buster, an' it's comin' outta your hide!... Easy! Easy! This ain't a junkyard, ya know!... Mickey! Pick four rousties and load those carousel critters onto the next truck ... Bo! 'Bout time you showed up. Get that dog out of the way! Tie him up somewhere. And tell that gilly-truck driver to back up and pull closer to the carousel boxcar!"

Bo wasn't worried about Jigger. The starving stray pup he'd found a year ago somewhere along their route in Ohio was a survivor and nimble as a cat. Bo jumped on the bed of the gilly truck in question and guided the truck closer to the boxcar carrying the prancing wooden horses for the popular carousel. Down the line he saw the long metal beams of the Big Eli Wheel being offloaded onto another truck. All in all, Bodeen Midway Rides—which his father had contracted to travel with the Carnival of the Century for two years—boasted a grand total of seven rides. The newest one in the Bodeen lineup was the Ridee-O, one of the fastest thrill rides on the carnival circuit to date ... and Bo was determined to prove he could be the ride foreman who operated it.

An hour later, drenched with sweat in the heavy August heat, Bo yelled, "Jigger! Get in, boy!" He and the dog hopped into the cab of one of the gilly trucks as the loaded caravan lumbered down the main street of Lapeer to the big vacant lot where the carnival was being set up.

The grease-stained driver sneered at his passengers. "Your pa ain't shot that dog yet? S'prised he lets him hang around. Thought all the critters on this here show s'posed to work fer their livin'."

Bo ignored him. Half the population traveling with the carnival, performers and roustabouts alike, had made friends

2

with the dog. "Why'd the Chief sign on to play this Lapeer Days festival, anyway?" he said, gawking at the fluttering flags lining the main street and stalls set up for selling local produce and crafts. "Thought the Carnival of the Century preferred its own dates."

"You askin' me?" The grimy truck driver snorted. "Don't know an' don't care. 'Long as they keep this show on the road an' keep ahead o' that letter from Uncle Sam."

Bo cast a quick glance at the driver. Hard to tell his age … maybe thirty, thirty-five, but still eligible for the military draft that had already nabbed ten or twelve crewmen, plus three performers since the attack on Pearl Harbor last year. The carnival had done ten towns since the last weekend of May, and mail was slow and sometimes took weeks to catch up to them.

The world was at war, after all.

Bo tried not to think about it. He wasn't yet eighteen, and neither were a dozen or so other young gazoonies traveling with the carnival who'd been taken on because of the shortage. And right now they had maybe four hours to get all the rides, concession stands, sideshow tents, entrance arch, fences, show ring, generators and light poles set up and running before the carnival opened at five o'clock that evening. His pulse quickened. He loved the running chatter of the Talkers enticing the crowds into the string of sideshows, the sticky smell of cotton candy, and the strings of lights glittering overhead as dusk fell.

"And tonight," he murmured into Jigger's floppy ear as the truck ground to a stop on the carnival lot, "if I'm lucky, I'm gonna take over ol' man Cooper's job and run the Ridee-O."

THE LATE AFTERNOON SUN BORE DOWN on the old Dodge sedan jostling its way over the rutted dirt roads, baking its inhabitants like potatoes poked into the coals of a campfire. Dust swirled through the open windows of the ancient car—a beauty in its day, but now held together by little more than baling wire and a prayer. A fine layer of grit settled into the ears, eyes, and hair of the family of nine—five children packed into the backseat, plus two more up front between their weary parents, with most of their worldly possessions strapped to the top, back, and running boards of the old jalopy.

Lucinda Tucker, crammed into the corner by the right rear window with a sleeping toddler on her lap, pushed ten-year-old Willy's sweaty bare leg away, only to have it come pushing back, stickier than ever. "Get *off* me, Willy!" the fifteen-year-old hissed. "You gonna wake Johnny."

"Get off me, yourself," grumbled the boy. "You the one takin' up mosta the seat, you an' your big butt."

"That's *enough*, William Tucker." The children's mother spoke sharply from the front seat. "You respect your sister."

Willy stitched his mouth shut but gave Cindy a poke in the side with his sharp, skinny elbow.

Cindy gritted her teeth. The heat … the dust … having to come back to the sugar beet field … it was all too much. "Pa! Can ya stop the car an' let me walk the rest of the way?"

Lester Tucker didn't answer, keeping a tight grip on the steering wheel as the car lurched this way and that over the hardened ruts. The road was barely visible through the dust-covered windshield.

"We're almost to the camp, Cindy." Her mother sighed wearily, wiping the back of her hand across her brow. "We can all get out and stretch then."

The camp … ugh! As if the tumbledown shacks of the migrant camp were something to look forward to. Why'd they have to leave the blueberry picking anyway? It was still early August. Blueberry

4

season wasn't over for another three, maybe four weeks. At least she could pop the juicy berries into her mouth from time to time, a sweet treat that made the long hours pulling the berries off the bushes somewhat bearable—unlike chopping weeds or pulling up the squat sugar beet plants at harvest. *Nothing* broke the tedium of having to bend over till her back felt as if it might never straighten out again. Ever.

The towheaded girl hung an arm out the window and leaned her chin on it, hoping to catch a breeze in spite of the dust, making sure she was shading the sleeping toddler on her lap. It had all sounded so good last April when that fast-talking factory man from Lapeer County had talked up the exploding sugar beet industry in Michigan to the desperate Dust Bowl farmers in Arkansas, Oklahoma, and Texas whose farms had failed during the perilous 1930s. "Plenty of work! Need workers all season! Good pay!" All Pa had to do was sign a contract that the Tucker family would stay the whole season—planting, thinning, weeding, harvesting.

Swirling grit thrown up by the bald tires stung her eyes, and Cindy pulled her head back inside the stifling car, untangling her windblown hair with her fingers. *The whole season ... huh.* Pa said he should've known what that meant for a single-crop farm. Each phase of work was separated by weeks of downtime, for which they did not get paid, and they'd had to move from county to county, finding crop work wherever they could get it. Digging potatoes while the ground was still cool. Beans in late June. Blueberries in late July. But the sugar beet boss man thought he knew how to get his workers to come back when it was time for the next all-important cycle.

He withheld part of their pay until the *end* of the season ... or perhaps he was counting on them *not* coming back so he could keep the money.

The overloaded car—rattling with the attached galvanized washtub, pots and pans, wooden boxes, Ma's old ladder-back rocker and junior-sized guitar, and all their other worldly possessions—turned off the rutted dirt road and onto pavement as they approached town. The migrant camp sat in a swampy area a couple of miles beyond Lapeer, which loomed ahead of them through the dirty windshield. They headed north along Main Street, breathing in relief from the unrelenting dust. "Maybe we should stop by the store and pick up some bread and a quart of milk for the babies," Ma murmured. "Long as we're in town."

Pa grunted. "Can't we make do with what we got?"

"Lester, the young'uns ..."

"I don't know. This engine's way out of kilter, but I'm aimin' to get there 'fore it quits."

"But couldn't we at least drop—"

"Ma! Ma! Look yonder! They got a carnival come to town!" George, seven, scrunched between his father and twelve-year-old Tom in the front seat, was pointing past his father's nose.

"Where?" Willy launched himself away from Cindy and poked his head out the other backseat window, practically lying across Maggie's lap, the second oldest girl, who'd been holding little Betty. Betty let out a squeal. Johnny woke up and started to cry.

But the fussing of the two youngest Tuckers was the only sound inside the car as it rattled along Main Street toward the once-vacant lot. Everyone else gaped at the Big Eli Wheel with its rocking seats sticking high up into the air, and the ballooning tents being staked and tied down. Men in sweat-stained A-shirts erected a fence around the lot, leaving only a space for an archway facing the town and a ticket booth standing on a platform off to one side outside the fence.

Then Willy found his voice. "An elephant! I seen an elephant! I did! I did!"

Several youthful voices started clamoring at once. "Can we go to the carnival, Pa? Can we, huh? Huh, Ma?"

The car lurched forward, picking up speed. "You kids know we cain't afford no carnival." Pa hunched tighter over the steering wheel, nursing the noisy old car along. "'Sides, we gotta unpack tonight and get up at first light to start work in the field."

"But, Pa …!"

"Ever'body's in the field tomorrow—'cept your ma an' the babies."

"But, Pa …!"

"No 'buts.' Now shut up." The car chugged past the carnival lot toward the dirt road that would take them to the migrant camp.

Cindy twisted her head and looked out the back window. A youth about her age—maybe a few years older—was helping to put up the fence. A black-and-white dog tumbled about nearby, chasing a stick the older boy threw from time to time.

Oh. Longing rose up in her throat. It would be so much fun just to wander around the carnival for one night. Just one night! Forget the dust. Forget the leaking shanties they called "home" all season long. Forget the backbreaking work and burning sun. Forget the despair in her father's eyes. For just one night …

"We didn't get the bread an' milk, Lester," she heard Ma say quietly.

Pa hit the steering wheel. "Well then! One o' the young'uns'll just have ta walk to town an' get it, now, won't they?"

Cindy had known who that would be the moment Pa said it. At least she got out of unpacking and setting up. Kicking stones along the road, she grumbled most of the two miles back to town. It was Pa's fault for forgetting. Why didn't he go back? He could even have driven … if the car could still make it. But as she got closer, the flags above the carnival tents changed her mood. She'd take a little detour on the way back, maybe catch a glimpse of some of the animals or a trapeze girl in her sparkly tutu.

By the time Cindy was returning with her groceries, orange still streaked the western horizon, and electric lights blazed on the Big Eli Wheel as it lifted riders into the cobalt sky of early evening. She crept around the end of an animal wagon parked outside the temporary fence. The smell was definitely not horse. Maybe cats, perhaps big cats! Through the bars, in the far dark corner ... could it be a lion? Cindy took one more furtive step, then tripped over something long and heavy. She went sprawling, landing on the paper bag of groceries, which was the only thing that saved her from planting her face in the dirt. She picked herself up and hurried away before someone caught her snooping around. That's when she realized the brown bag was growing damp. Her mom wouldn't like that. She saved paper bags. But milk was oozing from the split corner of the carton. She upended it to save as much as possible and tried to dry off the loaf of Wonder Bread and small package of baloney as she hurried down the road, past a large white farm house with its even larger barn, and turned down the lane to the migrant camp.

She found her way to the family's shanty and saw that Pa had already pulled the car close to the front door and strung a canvas between its top and the cabin's roof to create a breezeway so the car could act as a second room—a place for the boys to sleep—Tom and Willy on the seats and George on the back floor.

Cindy stepped into the shanty where a kerosene lamp lit the room that would be home for the next few weeks. Her mother sat in her ladder-back chair in the corner nursing baby Johnny, rocking back and forth, and softly praying her evening prayer for the family.

God bless the corners of this house
An' all the lintel blessed.

Cindy rolled her eyes. Oh, yeah. *Bless the corners of this house …* One puff would blow them over.

Seeing her come in, Ma briefly put a finger to her lips, then reached down to gently stroke the back of three-year-old Betty who lay on a tattered blanket beside her.

An' bless the hearth an' bless the board,
An' bless each place of rest.

Bless the board, huh? Cindy put the bread and lunchmeat on the bare wooden table and quietly searched until she found a tin pot to put the upside-down milk carton in before more leaked out. And as for *each place of rest,* well, if sleepin' on the floor would give any rest, that would certainly be a blessing.

An' bless each door that opens wide
To strangers as to kin …

The door swung open, and her father stood there, tall, gaunt, and tired … even before he'd picked sugar beets for one day. His sweat-stained fedora was pulled low over one eye. He looked around, stepped over to the table, and frowned.

"Lucinda? What's the meaning of this?"

What peace there'd been was gone, replaced by the question she'd never been able to answer.

Chapter 1

ITHOUGHT IT WAS PA SHAKIN' ME AWAKE from one of my carnival dreams.

"Mmph ... huh? *Ouch!*" I blinked until the pale face came into focus. *Oh, yeah, the library woman!* Too young to know not to yank an old woman's shoulder 'cause she might have arthritis. "Uhh? Whatcha want?" But I already knew. She always pretended to be helpful—"*Can I do something for you?*" ... "*Are you looking for a book?*" ... "*What do you like to read?*"—when what she really meant was, "*No hangin' out in here!*" As though it wasn't a "public" library! I closed my eyes and let my head drift down onto my folded arms again.

"Lady, I told you. You can't sleep in here. This is a library. It's for patrons who are reading or checking out books."

"So how am I s'posed to check out books if I ain't got no library card?"

She rolled her eyes. She probably knew I didn't have a card because I didn't have a Chicago address. But why couldn't I just stay there and relax? I wasn't bothering nobody.

"Lady! If you don't leave, I'll have to call the police."

Grr! The po-lice. Why did people always say they were going to call the police? Was my past stamped all over my face like a

10

permanent tattoo? "Don't get yer panties in a knot, missy. I ain't breakin' no law sittin' in this here chair. But …" I threw up a hand in surrender. "… don't want to give you no heart attack, 'cause then I'd hafta call an ambulance for *you*." With a groan, I hefted myself out of that nice padded chair. "Jus' lemme use the facilities an' I'll be movin' on—" Wait … my cart! I peered this way and that between the stacks. "Hey, you! Where's my cart? It was right here, next to this chair 'fore I dozed off."

The prissy young woman headed back toward her desk. "Hey, my cart! Somebody's done stole my—" A hacking cough cut off my words, and I leaned over, hands on my knees as I tried to get my breath. But it wouldn't stop. I needed a drink of water … no, I needed to find my cart! I headed down the aisle. "Has anybody seen my cart?"

"Lady! Shh! This is a library!" The librarian was following me again. "Nobody has stolen your cart. It's not allowed in here. We took it outside." She pointed toward the front door.

"You *what?* You … you took my cart an' jus' left it out there? Where any Joe Blow could make off wit' it?"

The woman shrugged and turned away. No wonder the kids were going wild these days, if adults had no more respect for private property than that woman had. I hustled toward the front door, feeling like a metronome when I tried to walk faster than my hips allowed.

There it was!

"Hey! Hey, you kids! Get away from my cart! That ain't yours!"

A boy about five was standing on the back of my shopping cart, reaching inside.

"Look out! You gonna tip it over!" But I was too late. It crashed to the sidewalk, spilling my extra clothes, water bottles, a loaf of day-old bread and three apples I'd rescued that morning.

The kids ran off, but there went my worldly possessions, scattered to the wind. Speakin' of the po-lice, where were the cops when you needed 'em? I bent over to pick up my stuff, and the exertion soon had me sweating and coughing again. I wiped my forehead on my sleeve and then looked at it ... pink sweater—well, it used to be—over flannel shirt, over thermal underwear. I could take it off and not be so hot, but then it was easier to carry clothes when they was on you. And besides, it was only April. It'd be gettin' cold again this evening.

Once I'd retrieved everything and stuffed it in my cart—I'd reorganize later—I headed north, slowly enough to keep my cough at bay. Clouds were gathering, thick ones, white and puffy on top, but the bellies of those in the distance were gray and streaked from the bottoms like some meteorological cat's claw had snagged them. You learn to watch the weather when you've lived in the rough as long as I have, and it wouldn't be long ...

I made it six blocks north to the Double-Bubble Laundromat before the rain. But that cough doubled me over again—I really ought to get it checked out. When I came up for air, I peeked through the window: no Ramon in sight. Good! I went in and plopped down in one of those orange, molded plastic chairs near the dryers. But I shoulda known. There's no rest for the weary. As soon as Ramon came out of the utility closet, he began shouting. "What you doin' in here, Lucy? I know you ain't dryin' no clothes. Now move on. Don't be hangin' out in here."

"Ain't these chairs for your customers? What makes you think I'm not drying my clothes?"

"'Cause, you not been washing anything, that's why. Besides, the only dryer that's goin' is number three, and it's got my cleanup towels in it. See that sign? 'No loitering!' That means you."

I just sat there, lookin' around. "You know, Ramon, the first time I was in one of these establishments, I was just a little girl.

12

It was afore we come north. The drought had hit, and we didn't have enough water on the place to wash our clothes, so Ma took us in to town to the 'wash-a-teria.' Yep, that's what they called it, a wash-a-teria, but it weren't automatic. No siree Bob. Had to do it all yourself—"

"What're you talkin' about? Do I look like *Bob*? Now you git!" He shooed his hand at me. "Go on!"

"Ah, come on, Ramon. Look outside. It's gonna rain any minute. I can't get wet again."

"*Ay Diós*, I don't do the weather, but if you get wet, *then* you can come back here and dry your clothes ... for a buck, four quarters in that little slot! Move on, now!"

I rose slowly, shooting Ramon as many daggers as my rheumy old eyes could fire. "Someday you gonna be the one who needs a place to sit, and they gonna chase you off too. Then see how you like them apples!"

Outside the Double-Bubble, I looked both ways. I was tired, tired in body and tired in spirit. People always hassling me. It was time to retreat to someplace where no one would bother me. I hobbled to the corner and turned east toward the lake.

As the afternoon's light faded and the first sprinkles began to fall, I wedged my shopping cart between two large bushes in the park near the walk-through tunnel that sneaks under Lake Shore Drive to the beach. Then I upended one black garbage bag over my cart to keep off the rain and split another one in half to wrap around my shoulders like a cape. I took as deep a breath as I dared and kneeled to crawl back under the bushes where no one could see me ... I hoped. But the cough attacked me again. If I kept sleeping rough, I'd never kick this cold. It'd been houndin' me all winter.

I felt my forehead, trying to figure whether the fever had returned. Could mean pneumonia if it had, I s'pose. But there weren't much I could do till I got to the county clinic on Tuesday. 'Course, there was always the ER, but they were so mean there. And 'sides, you might catch somethin' worse while you was waiting … and waiting … and waiting.

For now, weren't nothin' I could do. I pulled the plastic over my head and let the crackle of the rain landing on it lull me to sleep. Sleep's good. Gotta take it when and where you can, ya know. Who knew what the rest of the night might bring.

What it brought a few minutes later was a crash that nearly knocked over my cart and yanked me roughly back to consciousness. What!? If it was those gang kids attacking me again, I'd— But the howl of pain I heard came from a woman, who'd thudded to the ground not two feet away.

"Hey! Whatchu go kickin' my cart for?" I made my challenge as strong as I could, still thinkin' it might be some thugs, let them know they better not mess with me. But all it did was produce a coughing fit big enough to scare off anyone with "germaphobia."

In the dim light, I watched between the leaves as a youngish woman rolled over and sat up. Seemed like she was the only one there. "Sorry," came a feeble voice as she wiped her mane of wild hair out of her eyes and squinted at my bush. "Didn't see it … where are you, anyway?"

With a sigh, I pushed some branches aside and poked my head out. "Keepin' dry is where I'm at, tha's what." I tightened the plastic bag around my shoulders and stifled another cough. "Leastwise I was till Orphan Annie came along …"

Having finally spotted me, she seemed to lose interest and reached for her bare right foot.

"Uh-oh. That foot's bleedin', girlie. Here, lemme see it." I crawled out from under the bushes and grabbed the woman's foot for a better look. "Aiya. Gotta stop that bleedin' … hang on a minnit." I pulled the plastic off my cart—don't know why she tripped on it. It wasn't stickin' out that far—and began looking for a cloth to bind up the wound. A clean one had to be in there somewhere. Finally I found one, but another coughing fit took my breath away. Ah, it was getting worse. I shouldn't be out in this wet weather.

"Oh, don't bother." The woman stood up, the mop of reddish hair falling over her face. "I really have to get …" She tried putting weight on her foot.

I shook my head. Crazy woman! The foot probably wasn't broken, but I knew that cut on her foot could get infected real fast. "Oh, don't get your mop in a knot. Siddown." She sat. I grabbed the bleeding foot and began wrapping it when she jerked her leg away. "It's clean, if tha's wha's botherin' ya." She relaxed … a little, but I barely tied the knot before another cough convulsed me again, and I dropped the foot. Once I caught my breath, I said, "Now git on with ya an' leave me be," and turned back to crawl under bushes, hoping for a little peace.

"Wait! This is ridiculous. It's raining, and you've got a terrible cough. Come on with me. I can get you dry clothes and some cough syrup."

I stopped, half in, half out. Dry clothes, something for my cough? But I knew … if it wasn't on my terms, there was always a hitch. "Nah, I'm okay."

"Please, I mean it. Come on. Just until the rain stops, at least."

Until the rain stops. That'd be good, but still … The good Lord knew I wasn't too proud to take handouts, it was just that you had to keep everything on your terms. Never let those do-gooders get the upper hand. I backed out and stood up, choking back another coughing fit. The park lights had started to come on, and I studied the woman. Why not? I could handle her. I grabbed the handle of my shopping cart and headed across the park.

In a moment Fuzz Top had caught up with me, limping along and pointing toward the high-rise apartments overlooking the park, the Outer Drive, and Lake Michigan. So she was one of those rich people, was she? Well, maybe there would be something in it for me, after all.

"My name's Gabby Fairbanks. Yours is ...?"

Ha, not that easy, honey! A name has power, and I wasn't gonna give up mine without knowing the implications, not if I could help it. Keeping the initiative, I plodded across the frontage road and glanced back for directions, though by then I was pretty sure we were headed for the building with all that black glass and curved edges. Fuzz Top pointed toward its revolving doors. I bounced my cart up over the curb, grateful for even a brief reprieve from coughing.

But when I pushed my way through the revolving doors, a man in a uniform saw me immediately. I stopped. Didn't need no more trouble with the law. But as I squinted at him, I saw he wasn't the police—no gun, no badge, no mace—just the doorman. *Ha!*

Still, he had that determined look in his eye and scowled. "Hey! Get that rickety cart outta here. Lady, you can't come in here. Residents only."

Yeah, well ... whatever. It's what I should've expected, thinking I could get something from that rich girl. I started to turn when a timid voice from behind me said, "Uh, she's with me, Mr. Bentley ... Mrs. Fairbanks?" Her voice went up like she wasn't even sure of her own name.

"Fairbanks? Penthouse?" The doorman's frown deepened, but did he say *penthouse*? Ooo, this girl was money. His tone had changed. "Whatchu doin' with this old bag lady?" Then he looked down and cocked his head to the side. "Are you all right, ma'am? What happened to your foot?"

"It's all right, Mr. Bentley. I, uh, we just need to get up to the, uh, apartment and get into some dry clothes."

Money or not, I was ready to back out. I didn't need any more drama tonight. But the woman grabbed my arm and hustled me toward the elevator.

Pain stabbed me in my left ear as we went higher and higher. I swallowed, trying to adjust the pressure. Like when I was a little girl and had so many earaches. Fuzz Top was staring at me as though I was bleeding from my ear or somethin'. I wiped at it. No blood. So what was the big deal? She looked like she was dizzy or something. Poor kid. Never should have come with her. Maybe I owed her for getting me past that guard downstairs. Maybe … I closed my eyes, thinking. Guess I could've been a little more friendly. Without opening my eyes, I said, "Lucy."

It took a moment, then, "Lucy …? Oh! Your name. Thanks."

I opened my eyes. The shock was gone, but she still looked worried.

The elevator came to a stop, and the doors opened on a gleaming hallway. Had the woman brought me to a doctor's office or somethin'?

"Well, come on, Lucy." She led the way to the only door, one with huge pots on each side with flowers. Beautiful. I reached out and touched one. Fake! Figured!

"Let's get you into some dry clothes and do something about that cough." Fuzz Top opened the door with her key and led the way.

Oh, my! Oh, my! What had I gotten myself into? If that doorman downstairs wasn't a cop, he'd soon be calling one to get me out of here. We'd walked in on some kind of a high-class party. Through the archway, in the middle of an enormous living room, stood a tall man with dark hair and the good looks of one of them

17

fashion models. The sight of him shocked me. He was what my Pa might've looked like if it wasn't for all those back-breakin' years of wind and weather that etched deep lines in his face and left him as gaunt as a scarecrow. But this smooth devil held a glass of wine in one hand while he swept his other arm like he was God a-paintin' the lakefront for his two guests.

In the same instant, they must've heard us, because all three turned and stared right at us. Silence hung in the air for a split-second. Then the tall man came toward us, eyes glarin'. "Gabrielle!" he hissed between his teeth. "What's the meaning of this?"

Chapter 2

LUCK HAD NOTHING TO DO WITH WHO OPERATED Bodeen's Midway Rides. James Earl Bodeen—known as "Jeb" around the carnival—wasn't about to let anyone but himself handle the new thrill ride until he knew all its quirks, how it should sound running at maximum speed, and exactly how much grease was needed to keep all its joints and wheels and moving parts running slick and smooth. Not to mention timing the ride with the three-minute hourglass so the riders felt they'd gotten their money's worth, but not so lengthy that he ended up with long lines of grumpy patrons who'd been made to wait beyond their patience.

Which meant Bo ended up taking tickets and throwing the lever on the carousel that night for the horde of farm kids swarming into Lapeer for the opening of its annual festival. What a bore! Not that he could show it. If there was one rule a carny man lived by, it was "flash and dash"—keep that smile flashing and keep your feet dashing. Work the crowd. Generate excitement. Make them laugh. People came to a carnival for only one purpose: to have a good time. And it was the only thing that would bring them back.

"Hey, there, missy! You want to ride the silver horse? All right, up you go ... Mom and Dad! Make a memory for the whole family!

You can ride too, just ten cents!... Who's next?... Hey, there, big fella, grab that black stallion over there ... All right! Hold tight! Here we go!..."

The carousel was positioned near the front of the midway, just after the initial group of concessions and games of chance where customers could try to win trinkets and stuffed animals. It was a family-friendly ride to get the carnival-goers relaxed and in a festive mood. Though by the time the carnival closed at midnight, Bo was ready to take a sledgehammer to the steam-driven calliope pumping out the same tune over and over and over.

As the concession booths and side shows zipped up, Barbara the Bearded Lady waddled past, cracking jokes with a couple of the midgets who did tumbling tricks and clown acts. An animal handler led the young elephant that'd been giving rides to children back to its sturdy pen, alongside the cages of the rest of the carnival's menagerie, which included several chimps, an ostrich, five big cats, and a performing bear. Teams of heavy workhorses plodded past the midway. Even the pampered dancing horses had lost their spark, heads and tails hanging as they were quartered in their canvas stable. One by one, the strings of lights winked out.

Only the cookhouse—an enormous tent at the back of the lot—stayed alive during the night to be ready to feed the large crew of roustabouts and performers at first light.

Fighting heavy eyelids, Bo shut down the carousel. He'd have to pick up trash, swab down the platform, and polish the dozens of glittering mirrors Saturday morning before the carnival opened at noon. "C'mon, Jigger. Let's get some sleep."

It was a half-mile walk back to the train and the sleeping cars. Bo was tempted to find a grassy spot behind a tent and get some shut-eye ... but a flash of light in the night sky changed his mind. A storm was headed their way. He groaned. It'd better be a light rain, or the lot would be a sea of mud the next day, which always meant more work, padding the soggy ground with straw and laying planks over the worst of it. At last he crawled into one of the lower bunk tiers in the sleeping car. Jigger curled up on the floor beneath him, before the first pings of rain started to drum on the metal roof.

BANG! BANG! BANG!

Bo sat up with a start, cracking his head on the bunk just above. Someone was banging on the doors. He heard muffled shouts. "Chimps loose! Chimps loose! Everybody out!"

He rolled off the bunk, hitched up his trousers, and felt around in the darkness for his shoes. A minute later he hopped out of the car along with a dozen other crewmen. A faint gray light brightened the sky along the eastern horizon. The rain had stopped, but the sky was still mottled with heavy clouds.

The word passed from group to group of bleary-eyed roustabouts tumbling from the sleeping cars. "The chimps got frightened by the thunder!"—*What thunder?* Bo hadn't heard anything—"Must've rattled their cage doors too. One wasn't securely fastened." *Huh, some poor chuck's gonna get sacked,* Bo thought as the head animal trainer barked orders, sending two teams to comb the carnival grounds, and four teams to fan out north, south, east, and west of the lot. Two of the missing chimps had been captured already, but the biggest chimp—a copper-faced beauty named Ruby—was still at large. "And don't let me see your mugs till that big mama's back in her cage safe an' sound!" the trainer shouted. "The Chief spent a pretty penny on that ape, an' he ain't gonna take it kindly if she gets hurt."

Bo was assigned to a team combing the carnival lot. But the groggy roustabouts seemed to be poking around hit-or-miss, idly lifting canvas and peering under tents, banging on barrels, or climbing through the metal rigging of the midway rides. "Jigger! C'mon, boy," he hissed quietly and headed straight for the menagerie cages at the back of the lot. Sure enough, the door of Ruby's cage hung open. He pulled a tuft of black hair from the wire cage. "Here, boy … take a good whiff. Got it? Okay, Jigger, find her!"

Excited, the dog took off like a shot, nose to the ground, zigzagging this way and that around equipment, and disappearing behind the side-show tents. Grabbing a length of rope, Bo ran, trying to keep the dog in sight. The next thing he knew, he caught a flash of black-and-white tail disappearing around the front gate.

"Ruby's not on the lot!" Bo yelled over his shoulder, but he didn't wait to make sure the other searchers heard him. He had to keep Jigger in sight.

To Bo's consternation, the dog ran down a side street and then darted between two small houses, windows still dark in the early morning stillness. He almost caught up to Jigger when the dog paused, sniffing at the dented metal garbage cans sitting behind each house along the dirt alley … then the dog took off again, nose still to the ground, came to the end of the rutted alley, and disappeared around a corner.

But when Bo followed around the same corner, he nearly tripped over Jigger, who stood stock-still. The dog whined softly and took a step forward. Bo squinted into the dim light of morning. A black shape halfway down the block was digging into another metal can sitting along the paved side street. "Easy, boy … stay," Bo murmured and moved past the dog, creeping quietly toward the black shape, which was busy tossing out paper and cans from the garbage and stuffing bits of something into its mouth.

As Bo drew closer, he began to talk to the chimp in a low voice so as not to startle her. "Hey, there, Ruby … now why you want to eat that garbage for, eh? You got a nice breakfast of fruit and vegetables back in your cage."

The chimp raised her head and stopped pawing, watching Bo approach. Bo held out his hand with the rope and kept talking. Was Ruby friendly? He didn't know much about chimps, had only seen their handler carrying some of the smaller ones around. Was this one—?

The chimp suddenly bolted, heading for a six-foot fence across the street. "Head her off, Jigger!" Bo yelled. The dog shot across the street. The chimp leaped for the fence, but before it could get over the top, Jigger leaped up and caught it by the foot. Howling Helga! Such a squeal! Sounded like a fancy lady being terrorized by a mouse. Jigger held on. Ruby came tumbling down off the fence.

Bo was right there with his rope and dropped a loop around the chimp's head as a collar. "Good boy, good dog! Let her go now. Come on, let her go." Jigger released his grip and sat down on his haunches, one ear flopped forward, panting a doggy smile. Bo reached out a hand toward the chimp, who was huddled against the fence, whimpering. "Easy … easy, now, Ruby. You're all right. We're not gonna hurtcha …" Bo stroked the wiry hair until the chimp calmed down. Could he carry her? No, too big. They'd just take it slow.

He noticed Ruby favoring her hind leg as the trio made their way back to the carnival lot. Had Jigger hurt her? Well, he'd check it out as soon as he got her back in the cage. She'd be all right.

Cheers went up as Bo led the chimp through the main gate and headed toward the menagerie cages at the back of the lot. "Atta boy, Bo!" someone yelled.

"Yeah, now we can go get some breakfast!" yelled another, to general laughter.

Bo led the chimp back to the cage and made sure the door was latched tight. "You stay here, Jigger," he told the dog. "Make sure she stays in that cage till the Chief sees her. Got it?"

The dog whined a little as Bo headed for the cookhouse but then lay down and put his head on his paws. "I'll bring ya some breakfast!" Bo called to the dog, heading at a trot for the cookhouse. That run had given him an appetite!

BO WAS SHOVELING A SECOND STACK of pancakes into his mouth when a hard hand closed around his arm and jerked him off the table bench. "Now you've done it!" hissed his father, pulling Bo to his feet and dragging him out of the noisy tent.

Bo stumbled after his father, trying to keep his balance. "Wha ... what's the matter, Pa? Didn't you hear? I'm the one who found the runaway chimp!"

Outside the tent, Jeb Bodeen spun his son around and leaned into his face. His eyes were narrow slits under the slouch cap he wore. "I heard all right. Got a tongue-lashing from the Chief 'cause the chimp's got an injured foot! *Dog bite*, the vet says."

"But ... but, Pa! Jigger's the one who caught her! She'd be long gone by now if it weren't for my dog."

"Oh yeah? I *told* you that dog was gonna be trouble for us. Chief said he better not catch it on the premises, or he'd shoot 'im on sight. But I took care of it."

Bo thought his heart was going to lurch right up into his throat. "What do ya mean? Pa! Where's Jigger? What'd you do to him?"

Jeb Bodeen didn't answer, just turned and stalked away. "Took care of it, is all," he tossed back over his shoulder. "Now get to work! We've already lost a couple hours gettin' the equipment ready for opening." The man suddenly turned back and shook a finger at Bo. "An' don't you go lookin' fer that dog, neither. He's gone, I tell ya. Gone for good!"

24

Chapter 3

SATURDAY BREAKFAST WAS CATCH-AS-CATCH-CAN. Cindy rolled a slice of bread around a piece of baloney, grabbed the water bucket, and escaped out the door. But the shack's walls were so thin, she still heard everything.

"Fool me once, shame on you. Fool me twice, shame on me!" It was Pa's new motto. She could picture him saying it through gritted teeth like he had so many times since he'd realized how unfair the beet contract he'd signed was. "Leastwise we got here in time to get a roof over our heads, an' that Buster Doyle can't fire us like I know he was lookin' to do if we'd showed up even a day late. He'd use any excuse to keep that hundred and fifty bucks he owes us and hire new hands. Come to think of it, I haven't seen any of the old crew come back, but he's still got their wages. We done earned our money fair and square! An' I ain't never gonna let him get over on me again!"

"Reckon yer not," her ma said. And then after a pause, "But this here shack's worse'n anything we had back at the blueberries."

"That's 'cause Doyle is a cheat and a thief. Like I said, fool me once—"

"Lester! I hear ya. It's just…" Ma's voice trailed off in weariness.

"Just what?"

"Oh, never mind."

Cindy had heard enough. She headed for the hand pump at the far end of the row of shacks to fill her bucket with water. It was one of her chores, and it was better to do it early before it turned into a mudhole. The morning fog muffled the Tucker voices once she got some distance, but just as much bickering came from the other shacks. Germans and Mexicans and folks whose language Cindy couldn't even guess, their voices rasped like sand blasting against the kitchen window back home when the wind got up. Seemed like the only other people in the camp she could understand were the black people, probably came up from down South. It made her feel so very far from home in Arkansas.

A streak of black and white took her breath away as a dog ducked behind an old pickup someone had left in the middle of the street, jacked up with one wheel missing. The dog peeked out at her from behind a dangling fender, a piebald mutt with a lop ear and a white blaze between its eyes that widened and slid off the left side of its nose. It flinched as though it thought Cindy's quick hand movement might hold a rock. But as she brought the rolled sandwich up to her mouth, the dog trotted out into the open and took a wide stance, its head cocked to the side in anticipation.

"What? Ya think this is fer you? Ha! Might be my last till evenin'. Can't eat them sugar beets, ya know. Not like blueberries." She took a bite, and the dog came a few steps closer and sat down on its haunches. "Oh, all right. Here, boy!" She tore off a strip of crust and tossed it up.

The mutt leaped to grab the bread when it was still five feet in the air. He landed nimble as a cat and bounced once to twist and face her again, ready to jump for another morsel, front paws pounding the ground like a drum.

"Hey, you ain't gettin' no more." Pa's motto sprang to mind—was this dog playin' her? She watched the excited animal—so eager, so ready—and decided all he wanted was another bite. Suddenly, he stood up on his hind legs and twisted around three times in a little dance, front paws shredding the air.

Cindy stared at the creature in amazement, a smile spreading across her thin face. But when she didn't deliver another treat, the dog sprang straight up into the air and did a backward summersault, landing on its feet, head cocked, ear aflop, and mouth hanging open ... expecting.

"Wonkers! You some kinda trick dog, that's for sure! Okay, here!" She tossed him another bite, which was gone in a snap. "So what else can you do?"

As if on cue, the dog turned around once and lay down on his side, head in the dust, eyes closed. A body might've taken it for dead, 'cept for the white tip of his tail flickin' up and down uncontrollably. After a moment, he opened his eyes and looked up at her, waiting for the release signal.

"Lucinda Tucker! Where you at, girl?" The yell came from the other end of row of shanties. "Get yourself back in here and help your ma with the young'uns."

"Just gettin' water."

"Well, you needn't take all day!"

She tossed her final bite of bread in the air and went to fill her bucket. The dog seemed to know the food was gone and started sniffing around the trash burn barrel. But when she headed back to the shanty, the dog slinked along behind as though checking out where she lived. Cindy gave him one last glance over her shoulder as she went in.

THE BEET HARVEST WASN'T SUPPOSED TO START until Monday, but Buster Doyle rolled into the camp in his old pickup on Saturday morning and began blowing his horn, the signal for the workers to come see what he wanted. The Tucker family gathered around with the others as the boss got out. Buster Doyle was a short, hard-boiled man with a deep chest, a round face, and a full mustache. He wore no hat on his short-cropped, black hair. Cindy guessed he seldom wore one because his receding forehead wasn't white like that of her pa's and other farmers who worked outdoors.

"All right, listen up. Mosta you field rats don't know a sugar beet from a hole in the ground. So today you learn what's what ... that is, if you want a job on Monday. Otherwise, hit the road and find work elsewhere. I got more workers comin' in over the weekend who are itchin' to have a job."

None of the other people who'd arrived in camp by Saturday had been there earlier in the season to help with thinning and cultivating, as their family had done. And so the boss knew what he was talking about, because it was chaos that first morning with the man yelling and running back and forth between the three crews. "No! No! No! Once the plow turns up the beets, ya grab 'em like this! And get 'em all—every one—or they'll rot in the ground." He pointed to one worker. "You! Knock two of 'em together to get the dirt off, then lay 'em on this here board on the back of the wagon. But ya gotta lay 'em straight so this guy"—the boss pointed to another worker—"can chop off the greens. But you can't knick the beet or it'll bleed sugar, and I'll dock your pay. You savvy?"

Cindy figured most of the migrants didn't get it at all because they couldn't speak English.

But Mr. Doyle knew that Pa and his four older children could work well together, and so he made Pa the foreman of one crew while he tried to teach the other crews how to harvest the beets. All that meant was Pa got yelled at if the workers in his crew didn't do what they were supposed to do.

Cindy could see the muscles along the sides of Pa's jaws working when Doyle yelled at him for someone else's mistakes, and she knew he was fighting with himself to keep from decking the guy and walking off the job. But if he did, that boss man would keep his held-back wages because Pa had signed that contract to work the full season.

Pulling the beets was hot and dirty work, and Cindy was so hungry when they got back to camp that evening she was ready to eat a raw sugar beet. But thankfully, Ma had cooked up a pot of dandelion greens she'd foraged. "Thought I'd make good use of 'em before they got trampled into the ground," she said. "Sorry if they's a little bitter. Kinda late in the season." But she'd also made some skillet cornbread and sausages—one each, except for George and Betty, who had to share one.

Pa stuffed his whole sausage in his mouth and chewed for a minute, a twinkle in his eye as he looked at Ma and nodded his head. "So where'd you get these links, anyway, Harriet?"

"Boss's wife drove over, said they's startin' a camp commissary where we can get whatever we need cheaper'n in town. Had these sausages with her for samples, so I got us some."

"Whadda ya mean, *samples*? She givin' 'em out free?"

Ma looked frustrated. "No. She just put 'em on our tab."

"*Our tab?*" Pa slammed down his fork and stood up so fast he almost tipped over the sawhorse table. Betty wailed, and Cindy took her on her lap.

"Don't ya see what's happenin' here, Harriet? They're suckerin' us in again. Before those beets get harvested, we'll owe more'n we've earned, and we'll leave here without a red cent in

29

our pockets! We gotta make do with what little money we got. Stretch it ... an' only buy in town. Ya hear!"

"But the sausages was half price."

"Half price for becomin' a slave, ya mean!" Pa sat back down, shaking his head. "You don't get it, do ya?" He shook his head. "Just don't be puttin' no more on that tab, ya hear? Take the babies and walk into town when you need somethin', but don't be runnin' up no more debt."

Ma sighed, "All right, Lester. I hear ya. Now eat your dinner afore it gets cold." She stood up and took her empty plate over to the washbasin balanced on some boards between a couple of apple crates. "I don't see how that woman can run any commissary, anyway. Not the way she looks."

"What's the matter with how she looks?"

"She's with child, that's what! She don't look all that big, but she's havin' lots of pains already. The woman can hardly walk. That's why she drove over here in her shiny new Hudson. She oughta be in bed, if you ask me."

The meal continued in silence as Ma poured some water into the basin and then rubbed the bar of soap in it.

Cindy looked around the table at her brothers and sisters. Nobody wanted to be the first to break the calm after the storm between their parents. Seemed like squalls were happening morning and night ever since they'd been on the road.

Finally, she worked up her courage. "Saw a dog this mornin'. Looked kinda like our old Tippy, but smaller and shorthaired." She shrugged. "Reckon it was a stray, though."

"A stray?" The storm was over for Tom. "Can we keep it, Pa?"

Willy jumped in. "Yeah. We need a dog. I'll help take care of it."

Pa frowned at his children, but the fury was gone. "Main thing 'bout carin' for a dog is feedin' him. Whatcha gonna feed him?"

Willy shrugged. "I'll share with him."

"Me too," chimed in Tom and George.

Cindy and Maggie kept quiet.

"*Hmph.*" Pa shook his head. "That'd be takin' food outta yer own mouths. We're short enough as it is."

"Ah, Pa ..."

"No whining, now. 'Sides, we don't know for sure it's a stray. Might belong to someone. Right, Cindy?"

She nodded without looking up from her plate.

Quiet descended on the table again. But finally she tried again. "Just think about it, Pa. I know you miss ol' Tippy too."

"Yeah," George piped up. "You think about it, Pa, and I'll pray about it!"

Even Pa laughed.

"Okay, okay! Ma, why don't you leave that be an' come back to the table for a bit. Read us from the Good Book, will ya? Tomorrow's the Lord's Day. We ain't got no church, but we shouldn't forget the Good Lord's kept us this far."

Ma wiped her hands on her flour-sack apron and got her black Bible from the beat-up suitcase that held her things. She sat back down at the table and pulled the lamp toward her. "Where was we, now?"

"Jacob was gettin' hisself a wife," said George. At seven years old, he was already the most bookish in the family.

"*Hmm,* let's see ... Jacob had gone all the way back to the old country to find a wife, and he'd come to the house of his relative, Laban. So here we go ... 'And Laban had two daughters: the name of the elder was Leah, and the name of the younger was Rachel.'"

"We already read that!" George broke in.

Ma looked up. "That's right. Jacob fell in love with Rachel and made an agreement with Laban to work for him for seven years

31

in order to marry Rachel." Ma returned to the Bible, following the words with her finger as she read. "'And Jacob served seven years for Rachel; and they seemed unto him but a few days, for the love he had for her. And Jacob said unto Laban, Give me my wife, for my days are fulfilled—'"

"Wait a minute." Pa put his hand down hard on the table. "I remember this from back in Sunday school. Is this where Laban cheats Jacob by giving him his oldest daughter instead of Rachel?"

Ma scanned with her finger. "Uh ... that's right. Leah."

"And he has to work seven *more* years to get Rachel?"

Cindy couldn't keep quiet. "Wait a minnit. Why'd he have to work for a wife, anyway? That's like he's buyin' a cow or somethin'."

"That's 'cause Leah was a cow, right, Pa?"

"That's not my point, son." He held his hand up toward Cindy as though her question would have to wait. "Whaddya find, Ma?"

"Uh, lemme see ..." She was scanning the verses with her finger. "Guess you're kinda right. Laban said, 'It must not be so done in our country, to give the younger before the firstborn. Fulfill her week, and we will give thee this also for the service which thou shalt serve with me yet seven other years.'"

"*Yet seven other years*? See what I mean? Fool me once, shame on you. Fool me twice, shame on me! I hope Jacob learned his lesson."

Ma sighed deeply and closed the Bible. "Well, I think he did. As I recollect, when he finally finished his term of service and left Laban, he was a rich man and left Laban with very little."

"There you go," said Pa. "Can't let people cheat you. You gotta do for yourself, 'cause no one else'll do for you."

"'Cept Jacob was known as a cheater. We don't want to be known as no cheaters, do we?"

32

"How you know that?"

Ma opened her Bible again and flipped back a few pages. "Says right here in this little bottom note that Jacob's name means *grabber*. Don't forget, he stole his brother's birthright."

"Ha! His brother was the fool. Gave it away for a bowl of stew. You read that to us just last week."

Ma shrugged and closed the Bible again. This time she got up and put it back in her suitcase. Reading time was over for the evening.

Pa got up, too, and put his old fedora back on his head. He opened the door and started to go out, then turned back. "I still say, don't let nobody fool you. And take whatever's yours ... whatever anyone'll give you."

Chapter 4

WELL, PA ALWAYS SAID TO TAKE WHATEVER THEY'D GIVE YA, and that's just what I was doin' in that rich woman's penthouse. No tellin' how soon I'd get thrown out, but the eats was pretty good while they lasted. There were plates of fancy cheeses like you see in the deli at the Jewel and bowls of nuts—I stuffed what I could in my pockets—and trays of fruit.

"Hey ..." What was her name? Oh, yeah. "Hey, Gabby girl, where are ya? Ya got some bread an' stuff? Some 'a this here cheese'ud be good wit' some sandwich makin's, don'cha think?"

Whoops! Guess I'd called in the cavalry, 'cause that fancy-pants came a runnin' with Gabby right behind him.

"Out! Out *now*!"

Of course, he meant me! I felt kinda bad for Gabby 'cause I could see she was in deeper doo-doo than I was. He went back to his shindig in the other room, sweet-talkin' his guests with excuses for me like he wasn't in the middle of a full-blown conniption fit.

"Come on, Lucy," Gabby said. "I'll get you some real food to eat." And she led me into the kitchen. My first thought was about a bird-in-the-hand, but she soon served me up a plate of pasta salad from their fancy icebox and somethin' she called beef tips over rice from the warming oven.

"Hey, this here's pretty good. You ain't had nothin' yet, yourself. Oughta try some." I hardly got the words out before I started coughing again. The lady gave me a frown, then stuck her face in a phonebook. I knew what she was fishin' for—some way to get rid of me, nice like. And sure enough, in a minute she picked up her phone and called that man down in the lobby.

"Mr. Bentley?... Yes, it's, uh, Mrs. Fairbanks. Top floor. Do you know the whereabouts of a homeless shelter for women in the area?.... uh-huh ... uh-huh ... Is that nearby?... All right. Thanks— no, wait. Could you call a cab for my, uh, friend?... Thanks."

I shoveled in a few more bites, knowin' for sure I was on my way out now. But I wasn't gonna give up that easily, no siree *Betsy*! I looked that girl right in the eye and squinted just a little bit to let her know she'd betrayed my trust in follerin' her. "Did anyone ask *me* if I wanna go to some homeless shelter? Whatcha think I am, chopped liver?"

Looking like a wet rag-baby with her red hair all frizzed up and makeup smeared, she stared at me for a moment. Then she left the room, so I just kept eatin', takin' what I could get, never knowin' where the next would come from.

Don't know how long it was 'fore she came back 'cause I dozed off a little, standin' right there. One time I fell asleep sittin' on a bench waitin' for the El and actually fell over onto the platform. Lucky I didn't roll onto the tracks. She couldn't have been gone very long, 'cause I was still leanin' on her counter. I heard her call my name, but I took my time. It's all I had.

"Lucy, wake up. We've got to go. Here, take a spoonful of this."

I opened my eyes. She was standin' there with a dose of some kind of purple medicine.

"Cough syrup," she said. She'd washed her face. "It'll help you feel better."

I doubted that, but I swallowed it anyway and followed her out of that fancy bird's nest. I knew I'd never be back up there again, but once was enough for me to see how rich folks live. Not sure I envy them. They all seem so ... so plum out of kilter and not too happy, neither.

Down in the lobby, she turned me over to that doorman and headed back up to her perch without a glance back at me and my cart as she ducked into the elevator.

The doorman put a cap on his shiny dome—a shield from the rain, I guess—and ushered me out to the yellow cab. "So, where's she sendin' me, anyway?"

"Manna House, shelter for women."

"Huh. Been there, done that ... more'n once!"

I ALMOST DIDN'T GO IN WHEN THE CABBY let me off at Manna House. But he kept sittin' there watchin' me like that doorman had paid him to make sure I didn't run off. I was of a mind to do it anyway, 'cept for the drizzle. So I toted my cart up the steps, one by one, then waved him away as I rang the doorbell.

Inside, some girl I didn't know shoved a clipboard and a pen at me.

"What's this? I already filled out your ol' form ages ago. Just look in your files ... Lucy Tucker."

"But even if we can find it, it'd be good to update it."

"Ain't nothin' to update. I was here just two weeks ago ... or a month. I don't 'xactly recollect. Wasn't that long. Ask Mabel Turner. She can get it for ya, if it's so all-fire important that you have it." I started for the double doors into the multipurpose room. "They still servin' dinner downstairs?"

"No. Though there's probably still some leftovers. But you can't go down there until you've checked in."

I turned back to her. "Ya got a free bed for tonight?"

She nodded as she held up her finger at me like she had just one more thing.

"Then it's mine, so sign me in. Can't ya see? I'm near ready to give out here. Don't have no time for all these shenanigans."

I left my cart in the big room and went downstairs. They was all finished eatin' and cleanin' up. Just a Mexican woman with a net on her head in the kitchen puttin' away the last of the pots and pans. "You the chief cook and bottle washer 'round here?"

She glanced my way but didn't speak so I went behind the counter and opened the big ol' icebox. But the only leftovers I could see were some soggy hush puppies or Tater Tots and a big bowl of somethin' that looked like poke salad—don't ask me where anyone woulda got that 'round here—but I wasn't gonna take a chance on it givin' me the trots. Didn't see no chicken or nothin'. Probably run out of the good stuff. No matter, I'd tanked up pretty good at that rich girl's place, so I headed on up to find that empty bed.

I MUSTA BEEN MORE TUCKERED OUT than I figured—and a couple of coughing spells during the night didn't help—'cause I slept right through breakfast. By the time I got down there, they was already cleanin' up, and I was lucky to get some cold pancakes and coffee. They was usin' this new thingamajig that was supposta keep the coffee hot. You have to push the top down and it squirts out a spout. But it was only lukewarm.

I was nearly finished when I heard Precious McGill's high-pitched voice. "That's my Sabrina over there, getting whupped by little Sammy." I didn't look up but knew she was talking about the two kids playin' foosball in the adjoinin' rec room. Precious was a volunteer at the shelter, and I liked her well enough 'cause she's real, a homegirl who knows the streets. She's dark-skinned and wears her hair in these tight little braids that hang down with pink beads on the end.

I heard her walkin' my way. "Someone to see you, Miz Lucy ... Nice to meetchu, Miz Gabby. I'm gonna go catch Edesa's Bible study while I have a chance. Don't get to sit in too often, 'cause I'm usually waitressin' at this café, but this week they give me Friday off. Come on up later, if you want."

I looked up as Precious skedaddled up the stairs with somebody else's baby on her hip. And there on the other side of the table stood that rich woman who'd sent me over here. "*Hmph!*" I stuffed the rest of the pancake in my mouth, and she was still standin' there like she expected me to do something for her. "You gonna jus' stand there? Go on. Siddown." I waved at one of the molded plastic chairs. "You hungry?"

"No, I'm fine." She sat. "I ... I just came to see if you made it okay to the shelter last night. I was worried about your cough. And ... I wanted to apologize for my husband's rudeness yesterday. I didn't know he'd be home."

I stared at her. Ha! Well, that dog sure won't hunt! That's what I don't like 'bout some of these college-educated people, always gotta be making something bigger than it is. Why not just let bygones be bygones. Walk away from it. Don't look back. But she was waitin', so ... "Yeah, well. He can't help it. I shoulda known better'n ta go up ta that fancy penthouse wit' you." I coughed and tried to turn it into a laugh, change the subject, let her know it didn't matter. "Man, that was some highfalutin place you got there. Ain't never seen one o' them. An' that bathroom smelled mighty good. Didn't have no bathtub in it, though. You must be payin' through the nose for that place, an' they don't even put a bathtub in there?"

At least that got her to laugh. "Don't worry," she said. "It has two more bathrooms with bathtubs *and* showers. But I'm sorry the situation was awkward. We just moved here to Chicago, and my husband was entertaining his new business partner. And then we come in, all drippy wet, and me barefoot, bleeding on the rug ..."

"*Hee, hee,*" I chuckled. This girl couldn't quit pickin' at it, so I played along. "Gotta admit, the look on their faces was priceless." The picture of it got me laughin' for real, then, and afore I knew it, she was laughin' too. Felt good ... until I started coughin'. Her face got all worried, and we didn't need none of that, so I got up. "Well, I'm goin' upstairs to sit in somethin' more comfortable than this plastic chair. You comin'?"

I was halfway up the stairs before it clicked that Precious had said Edesa was gonna be teachin' her Bible study up there, but by then there was no turnin' back. I found a big soft chair near enough to the circle of women to not look rude and plopped down in it. The only chair nearby was another of those molded plastic ones, but Gabby was young and didn't seem to mind.

Edesa was already preachin'.   "... no accident that *Jesús*"—she was black, married to that white Baxter boy, but she talked Mexican or somethin'—"*Jesús* was celebrating the Passover feast with His disciples that night, the day we now call Good Friday ..."

Well, I'll be a monkey's uncle! I'd plum forgot this was Good Friday, not that there'd ever seemed much *good* about it to me, them killin' Jesus and all. Far as I was concerned, it's one of those things best put outta your mind. And I got quite a few of those, though they always seem to come back to haunt me whether I want 'em to or not.

"For centuries," continued Edesa, "this Jewish feast had commemorated their deliverance from bondage in Egypt, that old, old story when Moses told the Hebrew slaves to put the blood of a lamb on their doorposts, and the angel of death would *pass over* them when it saw the blood. And now Jesus, the Lamb of God, was about to sacrifice Himself and spill His blood to deliver *all* of us from death. He broke the bread that night and said, 'This is My broken body.' He filled the cups with wine and said, 'This is My blood,' fulfilling the true meaning of this Passover feast, once and for all."

"Sounds gory ta me." It slipped out before I even realized it.

"*Sí.* You're right, Lucy. Jesus' death on the cross wasn't pretty. But He took the punishment for our sins so we don't have to be separated from a holy God, either in this life or when we die—oh, praise You, *Senõr!*"

Now that done it! That pretty young woman got all choked up and had to grab a tissue to dab her eyes. But it got me thinkin' 'bout all the ways I'd become separated, not so much from God—who knew what that meant?—but from my family ... and everyone, I guess. It wasn't a warm and cozy way to live, but I'd survived when a lot of others hadn't.

"Lunch is in half an hour!" Mabel Turner's voice called from the back of the room. "Tina, Tanya, Carolyn, and Lucy ... you're on setup and serving."

Oh, no! That's what was wrong with this place. They give you no peace. All the time tryin' to rope you into the group thing when all a body wants is to be left alone.

"Hey, I got this cough," I growled, hacking a few times to prove my point. "You don't want me coughing all over the food, do ya?"

"Oh, all right. Cleanup instead."

"*Hmph.*" I made my way toward the stairs to the lower level without lookin' back at that Gabby woman. I hope she could see what she'd got me into, 'cause it wasn't pretty. But Mabel—that woman can see right through you—caught my drift. I heard her explainin' to Gabby, loud enough so I could hear: "No to summer camp. Yes to daily chores. One of the rules. Everyone needs to contribute in some way to their room and board while they're here."

"Yeah, yeah, yeah!" I threw back at her.

At least for lunch, I was first in line. If they was gonna make me work on cleanup, I'd need somethin' in my breadbasket, that's for sure. And the taco salad they dished out was pretty good. I sat by myself, but that Gabby Fairbanks horned right in and sat right across from me.

We ate, and I looked around, every place but at her. Finally, it was too much for her. "The people here seem to know you, Lucy. Have you been here before?"

What a question! I just rolled my eyes at her. But she wasn't one to give up.

"Have you lived in Chicago most of your life?"

What was I gonna do? I went to get a fill-up on punch and brought her back some cookies. If she couldn't take a hint, maybe ... I held out a cookie. "Nope."

She hesitated, then took the cookie. "Thanks."

I stood up, piling her paper plate on top of mine. "Huh. If ever'body cleaned up after themselves, wouldn't be no need for a cleanup crew." How could I send her packin'? I took as deep a breath as I could without coughing. "Well, thanks for comin' ta visit me. If I don't see ya again, been real nice." And turned away.

"Wait. Lucy. I'd, um, I'd like to see you again. If I came back—"

"Nah, don't bother. If it don't rain this weekend, I'll prob'ly be outta here."

41

She took a step around the end of the table and started to follow me toward the kitchen. "But what about that cough? You really ought to get medical help."

"Lady ... Gabby ... whatever you wanna be called. I been takin' care of myself 'fore you came along, and I intend to do just that after you leave. But if it makes you feel any better, the nurse comes here ever' Wednesday, an' I'll probably let her fill me up with that red stuff an' a bunch o' pills, if it ain't gone already by then. Satisfied?"

She obviously wasn't, but she was too shocked to say anything more, so I headed for the kitchen, lickety-split. Well, as lickety-split as my tired ol' dogs'd carry me.

Chapter 5

WHEN CINDY STEPPED OUTSIDE EARLY SUNDAY MORNING with a hairbrush, the family's bar of soap, and an old rag for a towel, she found Ma around to the side of the shanty, sitting in her rocking chair, tending a campfire. Ma added more sticks and waved a piece of cardboard to fan up the flames before getting awkwardly to her feet and wiping the back of her hand across her forehead. Her faded dress hung crookedly off one thin shoulder. She hadn't looked strong since the birth of baby Johnny.

"Whatcha cookin'?" Cindy asked.

"Just some johnnycakes."

Cindy eyed the bowl of batter on the big wood stump that served as an outside table. Leaning against it was the tin sheet Ma would use for a griddle. The only problem was the heat varied so much over an open fire it was nearly impossible to keep from burning some of the cakes.

"Got any syrup for 'em?"

"No. But don't you worry. Breakfast'll be good."

Cindy drifted off, past the other shacks to the water pump to clean up. The soap was harsh, but so much dirt had collected in her hair on the dusty trip, she just had to get it clean. Pumping until water flowed, she ducked her head under the cold stream only to have it to quit before she got a good soaking. She had to do it over and over again, especially to get the soap out. When she finally finished and toweled her hair as dry as possible, she brushed it out and wound the ends around her finger to give it a little curl. Maggie, being two years younger, still parted her hair right down the middle—when she combed it at all—letting its straw-gray strands fall to either side except for the little cowlick that stuck up right in front. But Cindy was letting hers grow out and had taken to parting it on the side. She thought her hair looked brighter, too, thanks to washing it more often. And although she'd never been to a picture show, she'd seen posters and imagined she might someday look a little like Myrna Loy in *I Love You Again.* Course, Myrna's hair was auburn, but still … Cindy could dream.

Back at the cabin, the fire had burned down enough for Ma to spread it out and balance the tin "griddle" on the surrounding stones. "Would you get the boys up for me? It'll soon be time to eat."

A movement across the dusty road caught Cindy's eye. It was that stray dog sniffing around again. "Here, boy!" She kissed the air a couple of times. "Come here. Come on, come on, now."

The black-and-white dog pranced up to her, head high, neck arched like a parade pony, just waiting for a snack.

"Sorry, boy. Ain't got nothin' for ya. But come on." She knelt down and held out her hand to pat him.

"Cindy … you hear me?"

"Yes ma'am." She looked at the car where the boys slept. "Hey Tom, Willy, George! That dog's out here again."

That got them up. They came flying out of the old Dodge like hornets from a kicked nest. "Where? Where? Where?" Pretty soon they were chucking sticks for the dog to retrieve and getting him to dance his little jig and roll over and sit up. But the dog was no fool. After playing with them for a few minutes, he just plopped his rump down in the dust, cocked his head to one side with one ear half up, and wagged his tail. Every so often he'd give a sharp bark, but he wouldn't fetch, and he wouldn't dance or do any other tricks until they went in and got some crusts of bread.

Ma was putting spoons of batter on the griddle when she realized what the boys were doing. "Hey, y'all quit feedin' that dog! Don'tcha ya know that's near all we got to eat ourselves? Feed him, and there won't be enough for the family. Now, all y'all get on over to the pump and wash your hands and face 'fore I give ya what for!"

They were out of crusts, so they headed toward the pump, all the while coaxing the dog to follow along. "You better hurry," Cindy called after them, being big sister, "or you won't get none of these johnnycakes."

Ma had saved a mess of blueberries from where they'd been picking them in western Michigan. Mashed, they were better than syrup on the johnnycakes. The family was finishing up the last crumbs—even those with burned edges—when a truck pulled up outside, blaring its horn.

"What in tarnation?" Pa slid back his stool and stood up.

The horn blowing stopped. "Tucker? You in there?" It was the boss man's voice.

Pa grabbed his hat off the nail near the door and went out.

"Willy, Tom, George! Si'down. If anything needs tendin' to, your pa can handle it."

"But Ma—"

"Don't give me no backtalk! Y'all gonna lose your noses one of these days, pokin' 'em in where they don't belong. Now, si'down."

Cindy could hear the voices of the boss man and her Pa carrying on back and forth in some kind of a serious discussion until her father called above the din. "Lucinda, come on out here."

Cindy's gut clenched. She hadn't done anything wrong, far as she knew. She glanced at Ma who only shrugged and rolled her eyes. Wiping her hands on the front of her dress without thinking, she went to the door and opened it a few inches. "Yeah, Pa."

"Come on out here. Come on, now. Mr. Doyle wants a word with you."

Cindy glanced back at Ma and then squeezed out the door, moving slowly toward Pa and Mr. Doyle. She'd never had to talk to the man herself before. Of course, she'd heard all his rants— probably the whole county had heard him complaining that everyone worked too slow and the pickers were the cause of every little problem in or out of the field. But Pa had always been Cindy's buffer, making sure she didn't have to deal with the man. But now, as she approached the boss, she saw his eyes slowly look her up and down until she wanted to run back into the shack.

"Mr. Doyle has an offer to make you."

"Uh, yeah." The man chewed the corner of his thick mustache for a moment. "How'd you like to come work for my wife? That's our place over there." He pointed over his shoulder toward the white farmhouse and barn across one of the beet fields. "Wife's gettin' on toward her time and needs someone to help her during the day. And with the beets comin' in and these yahoos not knowin' what they're doin', I gotta be out in the field nearly all the time. So whaddya say?" He looked Cindy up and down again, pausing a little too long at her bust line, a feature she wasn't yet sure was any kind of a blessing. "Oh, one other thing. My wife just started a commissary for everyone in the camp." Doyle glanced at Pa. "She was hoping it could continue, but now she can't handle it. You count money, girl?"

By age fifteen, Cindy had missed most of her schooling, what with the drought and Ma needing help with the little ones, but Pa had made sure she knew her numbers, how to add and subtract and count change. *"They'll always try to cheat you if you don't know your money,"* he'd said. So she nodded yes to Doyle's question.

"Good then. You can do the commissary too. We got it set up in a little room in the barn right next to my office." Again, he glanced at Pa. "Don't keep stock in the barn anymore, so it's clean." A movement at the corner of the Tuckers' shack caught Doyle's attention. "Hey! Is that a dog? You know I don't allow no dogs in camp."

"Ain't ours." Pa glanced at Cindy and gave her a quick *don't-say-nothin'* look.

By then, the little stray had halved the distance between the cabin and the boss man, creeping slowly forward, its head and ears low and a ridge of hair along its back spiked like a smallmouth bass. Doyle took a roundhouse kick at the dog that sent it scurrying under the Tuckers' car. When the man regained his balance and saw the frown on Pa's face, he cleared his throat. "You allow one dog, you get two, three, then dog fights and fleas, and pretty soon someone gets bit. No place for 'em in camp. Get rid of him!"

"How much?" Pa said.

"For the dog? You think I … Oh …" He looked at Cindy. "I'll pay her 20 cents an hour. That's a good deal more than a slip of a girl like her could earn pickin' beets."

"Minimum wage is 30 cents an hour, and not a penny less."

"Ah, come on now, Tucker. This ain't a factory or a department store in the city. I'm just tryin' to help you out here. Tell you what I'll do, though. She don't have to come over till ten in the mornin'. She can help out my wife through the day and get the commissary ready to open by five when the workers come in from the fields. Commissary from five to seven. She'll be home in time to eat. Can't beat that." He pointed a finger at Cindy. "Come over later this afternoon when you see I'm back from town. I'll show you around and how to run the commissary. Won't take long."

Pa crossed his arms and tipped his head back so he was looking down his nose at the boss man. "Might be an okay job for Lucinda … at 30 cents an hour?"

"Thirty—? No, no, no." Doyle's head-shaking slowed and came to a stop as he studied the stubborn look on Pa's face. "Look, I'll come up to twenty-five, but that's as far as I can go. These are special circumstances, you understand."

"Ain't nothin' in the labor law sayin' you can reduce the minimum wage accordin' to *special circumstances*, whatever that might be. It's a straight 30 cents an hour. And you pay her for this afternoon too!"

The boss threw his hands up and turned to get into his pickup. Then, with his hand on the handle, he turned back. "All right! All right! But she better do a good job, or I'll hire someone else. I'm sure there's lotsa women 'round here who'd be glad for the work."

"And most of 'em can't speak no English, neither."

"And can your girl talk whatever they speak? That German and Spanish and … and whatever."

Pa just stared at the man for a few moments, then he said straight as a train track, "Thirty cents an hour."

"Oh, *all right*. But I gotta run into town now." He got in his pickup. "Wife needs some kinda herbs for her pains." He surveyed Cindy one more time. "When you see my truck's back, 'bout noonish, get yourself on over there. Ya hear? Most likely, I'll be in the barn." He started his engine. As the pickup began to move, the dog darted out from under the Tuckers' old car and began barking at the pickup as though chasing it out of camp. Doyle leaned out the window. "And get that mutt outta here 'fore I run him over!" And then he was gone in a cloud of dust.

"I don't trust that man." Pa shook his head as he headed back to the shack. "Anybody who hates dogs … You just keep track of your time real careful, Lucinda. Mark it down on something, or he won't pay you right."

BO WASN'T TOO WORRIED ABOUT JIGGER. If his dad had just chased him off, he was sure to turn up on his own. Besides, on Saturday afternoon, Jeb Bodeen pulled Bo off the carousel and gave him his big chance to operate the Ridee-O. He coached Bo what he'd learned about using the clutch to give the ride a smooth start and then how to pop it in and out to jerk the riders around a little. "They love it, and this is one ride that'll shake some change out of their pockets, so check underneath after you close down. That's money we don't have to report to the Chief."

Bo was the proudest ride jockey on the midway that night, but when he finally closed down, picked up the change—three dollars and eighteen cents—and set out for the sleeping cars, his mind was a jumble. He was now the foreman on Bodeen Midway Rides' newest and fastest thriller, but the whole day had passed and he hadn't seen a flicker of Jigger.

He detoured through the menagerie and around some of the other wagons. "Jigger!" he called softly. "Here, boy. It's me. Where you at, boy? Jigger!" He gave a sharp whistle.

By the time he got back to the train, his certainty that Jigger would turn up on his own gave way to a creeping dread, and he made up his mind: if Jigger wasn't back by morning, he'd go searching for him. He didn't care what his father said or did. He could demote him to a gazoonie and send him to the menagerie to shovel manure all day. Bo didn't care. That dog was his best friend. He'd rescued the little fellow and fed him, and the dog had responded with complete trust, always doing his best to fulfill Bo's requests with an uncanny ability to understand what Bo told him.

He couldn't just let him go.

BUT WHEN SUNDAY MORNING CAME and Bo stumbled down the steps of the sleeping car, there was no eager, piebald little dog jumping up to greet him. Skipping breakfast, he set out looking.

The Chief had threatened to shoot Jigger if he showed up again. And Bo's father said he'd taken care of the situation. Could that mean he'd *killed* the dog himself? Bo thought about this possibility as he searched every empty tent, wagon, and truck on the carnival grounds. Still no Jigger! But Bo couldn't bring himself to believe his father had killed his dog. His father could be tough, but he wasn't mean. All he'd actually said was, *"Don't you go lookin' fer that dog, neither. He's gone, I tell ya. Gone for good!"* So what did *"Gone for good"* mean? The more Bo turned those words over in his mind, the more certain he was that his father had somehow removed the dog, put Jigger out of reach. Otherwise, he would have said that he shot him. Maybe he gave the dog to someone in town and told the person to keep Jigger penned up until the carnival moved on.

Bo spent the next two hours combing the streets of Lapeer, calling for Jigger, and listening for eager barks from anyone's woodshed or house. Being Sunday morning, there were few people about except those dressed up and headed for church, but whether it was saints going to church or sinners working in their garden, Bo boldly approached them. "You seen a stray dog 'round here? 'Bout so big, shorthaired, black and white. One ear kinda flops down more than the other?"

He was about to give up—knowing he needed to get back to the lot and get ready to open—when he saw a short man with a bushy black mustache come out of a drugstore and head for the only vehicle parked on the deserted Main Street.

"Hey mister … hold up a minute." Bo ran to catch the man before he got into his rusty old pickup and asked the question he'd already repeated so often that morning.

"Nah! Got no use for dogs!" The man waved his arm dismissively and opened the squeaky door. Then he looked back at Bo. "Wait a minute. I did see a mutt of that sort out at my migrant camp less'n an hour ago. But if that's your dog, you better get him quick, 'cause I don't allow no dogs in my camp." Then he jumped in his truck and roared off like someone was chasing him.

Bo, in fact, did jog a few steps after him, yelling, "Hey, wait a minute! Where's that camp?" Then he threw up his arms when he saw the chase was futile.

It had to be Jigger, though. Bo just knew it. Looking around for help, he ran back to the drugstore and barged in.

"Sorry, we're closed on Sunday." The druggist walked up the aisle, waving Bo away.

"But that man who was just in here—"

The man pointed to the door and shook his head. "That was an emergency. Can't help you today."

"I just need to know if you know that man who was just in here … short guy, kind of heavyset, black hair, big black mustache. You know him?"

"Yeah. Buster Doyle. Now, son, you can come back tomorrow if you need something. We open at ten."

The man put a hand on Bo's chest, pushing him toward the door. Bo nearly reacted. He was big enough now he didn't have to let anyone push him around. But he held back, aiming at what he really wanted. "Wait … he said somethin' 'bout a migrant camp of his before he drove off. You know where it is?"

Apparently, the druggist got the message that Bo only wanted a little information because he took his hand off Bo and changed his tone. "Well, sure. But what's a young man like you want with a migrant camp?"

"Lookin' for my dog. That ... Doyle, or whoever you said he was, said my dog might've turned up out at his camp."

The pharmacist shrugged and raised his eyebrows. "Well, in that case, you go north of town here, just past Fourth Street ... but then ..." He cupped his chin in his hand and got a faraway, puzzled look in his eyes. "... but then Fourth doesn't have a street sign anymore ever since Roger Fleming ran into it drivin' drunk last New Year's Eve. So let me start over." He took his hand from his chin and pointed north. "You know where they set up the carnival? Just past that, take the first dirt road to the right. Go about half a mile east. Can't miss the shacks. They're a real eyesore."

Bo grinned. "Much obliged."

Chapter 6

B O JOGGED FROM TOWN TO THE CARNIVAL. He wanted to keep going and see if Jigger was still at the migrant camp, but first he had to take care of business. When he saw how many people from Lapeer and the surrounding farms were already lined up at the gate, he knew it had to be close to noon, and he'd already missed the call.

"Hey, Rico," he said to one of the three roughies at the gate as he squeezed past them. "You on anything after you open?"

"No. I'm off till six. But then I pull an all-nighter. So what's buzzin', cousin?"

Bo grabbed his shoulder before running on. "Do me a favor, man. Come straight over to the Ridee-O as soon as you let 'em in. I need you to do somethin' for me. I'll make it up to you ... whatever you ask."

Rico nodded, and Bo ran on, around the carousel—its band organ already belting out "In the Good Old Summertime" to get the crowd outside in the mood—and to the Ridee-O. *Whew!* No one was there yet, not even his dad. He made a quick check of each of the cars, and then started the engine.

He was ready to go!

Within minutes, boys and girls, moms and dads, young couples holding hands, and screaming teenagers spread across the lot like a spring flood, and Bo had his first load. He let them go around an extra minute to build up a line of eager customers. He wanted a line long enough to demonstrate how popular the ride was but not so long as to discourage newcomers. He pulled the clutch back and forth, causing the cars to jerk for extra thrills … and the nickels, dimes, and quarters that would come rolling out of loose pants' pockets.

"How's it goin'?" His dad startled him at the side window of the doghouse.

"Great. Gonna keep 'em comin' back all afternoon."

"You do that." He watched Bo for a moment. "Be careful there how you work that clutch. You can jerk 'em around all you want, but it's either gotta be engaged or disengaged. Don't ride it, or you'll burn it out in fifteen minutes."

Bo nodded, and his father moved on to check the other rides. If all went well, it could be an hour or more before Jeb Bodeen came around again.

Okay, Rico. Get your sorry mug over here now! Bo stuck his head out the window. Ah, there he was, strolling like he was in the park, but at least he was coming.

"Yeah, whatcha need, kid?" said the veteran as he got up to the operator's booth.

"You know how to run this thing?"

"Ha!" The man spit a stream of chewing tobacco. "How could I? It's brand new, and your old man put you on it 'head of the rest of us."

"Come on, Rico. I need a favor here."

"Okay, okay. 'Course I can run it. I've operated everything else on the lot."

In a matter of minutes, Bo was out the gate and running down the road again, this time past a farm and some sugar beet fields, until he found the dilapidated shacks, old cars, and junk, just as the pharmacist had described the camp. A real eyesore!

He slowed to a walk, feigning in a more casual manner than the urgency he felt inside. He called to some kids lighting the end of sticks from the fire in the burn barrel and then waving them around to leave smoke trails. "You seen a little black-and-white dog around here?"

The kids stared at him briefly and continued their play.

"Hey, you seen a lost dog?"

Finally, the older one stopped swinging his smoldering stick. "*No hablo Inglés.*"

Bo's shoulders dropped. He'd barely learned enough Spanish on the road to get himself in trouble. "*Perro, un perro.* Uh ... uh, *blanco y negro?*"

"*Ay, sí, sí. Un perro ...*" And then the boy began speaking so fast Bo couldn't even catch one word, but the boy was gesturing toward one of the shacks. So Bo grinned and nodded—"*Gracias, gracias*"—and headed that direction.

A woman was standing with her back toward him, washing dishes in a pan on a stump beside the shack. "Excuse me, ma'am. I'm looking for a dog ..."

She turned, and Bo saw that in spite of her womanly figure, she was quite young, maybe even a little younger than he was. Blonde hair shimmered in the sun and hung in waves almost to her shoulders. Her face was open and unpretentious with full lips and high cheekbones, tanned to a warm glow. Gray eyes asked who he was without her saying a word.

"Uh, hi. I'm Bo ... James Bodeen. But they call me Bo." He glanced around. "Lost my dog, 'bout so big, shorthaired, black and white. One ear kinda flops down more'n the other." He rehearsed the description he'd been repeating all afternoon, then grinned, crossed his arms, and squeezed to flex his muscles that showed off well under his short-sleeved shirt. "Name's Jigger ... I mean my dog's named Jigger. Somebody thought they'd seen him out this way. Have ...?"

She was still gazing steadily at him. "I seen you afore. Seen ya on Friday when we was comin' through town. You're from that circus, ain't ya?"

"Well, yeah. It's actually the Carson Brothers' Carnival of the Century. But my dad, Jeb Bodeen, owns the rides, so I work them mosta the time." Proud of his recent promotion, he grinned. "Lately I've been runnin' the Ridee-O. I'm its foreman now." He paused, mesmerized by the innocence of her face. "Ever been on a Ridee-O?"

She shrugged. "We useta have a radio, but what's a *Ridee-O*?"

Bo chuckled and brushed the fingers of one hand through his dark hair. "No, you probably ain't been on one, or you'd know what it is. It's a carnival ride. We got the newest model. First one on the circuit. Like a big octopus spinning around with little cars at the end of the arms that go up and down like you're on a roller coaster. It's a real fun ride." Watching her face as she looked back at him, he nearly forgot why he'd come. "So, you seen my Jigger out thisa way?"

"Mighta." She gave him a smile that nearly stopped time. "That's probably the dog my brothers been playin' with. They're 'round here somewheres."

Bo pulled his eyes away from her smile and looked down the row of shacks. "You know where?"

"I reckon they're probably into some kinda trouble on down by the slough."

"The slough?" Bo turned his head in the direction she had nodded.

"Here, I'll take you." She wiped her hands on a threadbare towel. "It's just over yonder past the outhouses."

The girl headed down a path nearly overgrown by tall grass. "We used to have a dog back home. Called him Tippy. He was a real good dog too. Sheepdog, ya know."

"So you don't live around here?"

"Nah. We're from Arkansas. Just up here workin' the crops."

"Michigan ain't my home either. But it's okay, I guess."

She glanced back over her shoulder at him as she walked. "So where you from then?"

"Nowheres, I guess ... or you could say everywhere. That's what it's like for us carnies. Some shows go to the barn somewhere over winter, but the Carson Brothers just go down south and keep on performin' wherever they'll have us."

The grass was getting taller, and soon they were pushing their way through a patch of shoulder-high cattails. Bo broke one off, swatting it at dragonflies when they landed on top of the reeds. Finally, the grass gave way to a little clearing a few yards across.

"Tommy! Willy! Where y'all at? You still got that dog with ya?"

In a moment Bo could hear them plowing through the cattails, heading their way. Leading them when they came into the clearing was Jigger, who jumped up into Bo's arms, licking his face, and almost knocking him over. "Ah, there's my boy! Where you been, anyway? I thought I'd lost you for good."

The older of the two boys, who had reddish hair and such an excess of freckles across his nose and cheeks that it looked as if he'd smeared his face with Georgia dirt, frowned at his sister. "Who's this?"

She gestured at Bo. "Says the dog belongs to him."

57

"Hi, boys. Name's Bo, and I guess my dog got lost. But I'm grateful you been takin' care of him for me."

"How we know he's your dog?" the smaller, towheaded boy challenged. "You could just be sayin' that."

The girl gave her brother a little shove. "Well, we know he ain't ours. And he ain't the boss man's. And no one else around here been lookin' for him, so he had to come from somewhere." She looked at Bo, appealing with her eyes for him to say something definitive.

"I can see you boys been real good to him, but you saw how he jumped up in my arms." He looked back and forth between the two boys. "Hey, you know his name?"

They each shook their head and looked down at the ground.

"Name's Jigger. Watch this." He put the dog down. "Jigger, stay." He took a few steps back until his back was at the edge of the cattails. "Jigger, sit up." The dog obeyed. "Roll over … Dance … Play dead—"

"Don't mean nothin'. We was doin' those tricks with him afore you came along."

"*Hmm* …" Bo crossed his arms. "Okay, let's try this. Jigger, sit!" Bo pointed to a spot in the middle of the clearing. "Jigger, stay!" His command was sharp and clear. "Now you guys go over there, and I'll go over here, and then we'll call him and see who he comes to. How's that?"

The two boys shuffled over to the edge of the clearing.

Bo looked at the girl who stood apart. "You say when to start."

"Okay. Now!"

"Here, boy! Here. Come here!" The boys clapped their hands and dropped down on their knees, kissing their lips and whistling calls.

The dog got more and more excited, tail wagging, front feet kneading the ground. He kept glancing back and forth from the boys to Bo, but he stayed put.

"Come on, boy! Got somethin' here for you." The older boy patted his pocket.

The dog yapped and trembled all over, then uttered a strange kind of moan and licked his lips, but he remained in place.

Bo glanced at the girl and grinned. "Okay … Jigger, free!"

The dog tore across the open space and knocked the boys sprawling in his excitement.

"See, see! He came to us and not you. See. He's ain't yours. And Pa's gonna let us keep him too. I know it fer sure."

"Ya think so?" The younger boy eagerly rumpled the dog's ears.

The redhead didn't answer, but both boys continued to roll around and tussle with the happy mutt.

Bo turned to the girl, who was already looking at him with a puzzled expression on her face. Bo just raised his eyebrows and shrugged.

"Tom! Willy! Y'all better think on what just happened, and you'll know whose dog this is."

"Yeah, but—"

"Just think on it a minute, you knuckleheads. The dog did what *he* said, not what *you* said. So who's the master?"

When she looked back at Bo, he grinned at her. She sure could make time stand still—he glanced in the direction of the carnival—but he didn't have much of it. "You know, I tol' ya my name back there, but you never told me yours."

She blushed briefly. "Cindy, or … Lucinda. But I like Cindy better."

"Well, Cindy …" And she was a looker, no question about that. "Hey," he spoke softly enough so the rollicking boys wouldn't hear, "you want to go to the carnival? I can getcha in free if you want to come back with me."

"Really?" Her face lit up and then fell. "Oh, I can't. Gotta go over to the boss's place and learn how to run his commissary. Besides, there's my sister and three brothers and—"

"Boy howdy! How many you got in your family, anyway?"

"Just seven of us ... and Ma and Pa, of course."

"Wow. I got one sister, no brothers though ..." He wiped his hand across his mouth, obscuring the words as he added, "And Mom ..."

"*Hmm*." She looked at him as if waiting for him to finish.

"She took Kelsey and left when I was little. Just me and Dad now."

The thought of his father brought his dilemma back to Bo's mind. "Hey, I gotta get back, but what if your brothers took care of Jigger for a few days? Bet they'd like that."

"Whaddya mean? I thought you wanted to take him now."

"Well, I did, but ..." Bo's mind was still chewing on what to do about the Chief's threat to shoot Jigger and his dad's order to not even go looking for the dog. If he brought Jigger back now, and one of them saw him, he could lose Jigger for good and be in big trouble himself as well. "Actually, your brothers could really help me out here. It's not ... Let's just say there's some back at the carnival who don't want Jigger around right now. So, if the boys could take care of Jigger until the show pulls out at the end of the week, that'd be great." With a little time, Bo hoped everyone would have forgotten their threats to Jigger. "I could come by and pick him up just before we do the jump ... uh, leave for the next town, I mean." He looked over at Cindy's brothers, still wrestling with the dog. "Whadda you guys say? You willin' to take care of Jigger for me for a few days?"

The one with red hair and freckles gave Bo a frown. "I still say we found him. So he oughta be our'uns."

"Well, he ain't, and you know it!" said Cindy. "I think y'all oughta thank Mr. Bodeen, here, for lettin' ya play with his dog the last couple of days ... and here he is offerin' to let you play with him some more. Can ya say thank you?"

Oh, *Mr. Bodeen* was it? Now that was nice. But Bo remained quiet.

After a few moments the younger boy—the towheaded one— looked up. "I guess we could look after him fer ya." The older boy turned his head sharply to his brother and frowned, but said nothing.

"And you better not let the boss man see him when he comes around either," added Cindy. "You know he hates dogs." She turned and smiled at Bo. "I really gotta go. Gotta finish those dishes and go over to the commissary."

"So, how 'bout after that?"

"I don't know. I'd have to ask Ma. And afterward, it might be dark ..."

"Oh, I could walk you back. Look ..." He fished in his pants' pockets and came up with a dime. "Take this. It'll get you in the main gate. Just inside the gate, you'll see the carousel. Go around that, and the next ride's mine. Says "Ridee-O," plastered all across the banner. Can't miss it."

Cindy got a puzzled look on her face, then took a deep breath and accepted the coin. "Okay. But like I said, I'll have to check with Ma. If she says no, I'll give you your dime back when you come for Jigger."

"That's a deal. Hot diggity! See you later." He went over and knelt down to pet his dog. "Jigger, you stay. Stay, boy." He got up and took a few steps toward the path through the cattails. "Good boy. You stay."

Chapter 7

Later that Sunday afternoon, Cindy noticed Doyle's rust-spotted old pickup parked under the tree between his house and the barn. She stuck her head into the shack where Ma was mending one of the boy's pants. "Goin' over to see that boss man about carin' for his wife and workin' the commissary. Okay?"

"How long you be?"

"Don't know." She felt the V-neck of her dress where the material overlapped creating a tiny pocket, just large enough to hold the dime Bo had given her. It was still there. Should she tell her mother about going on to the carnival afterward? If she didn't, she wouldn't be able to stay long enough for Bo to walk her home.

"Ma, we found out who that dog belongs to." She told her mother of Bo's visit that morning and his leaving Jigger with the boys.

"You tell Pa?"

"No, but—"

"Dagnabit, Cindy. Don't you think? From what your pa said, that boss man's likely to shoot the little thing if he finds it here abouts again."

The possibility had crossed Cindy's mind too. "But it wasn't me who suggested it, Ma. Besides ..." She needed to move on

62

to her real purpose. "… that boy wants me to come over to the carnival when I get done this evening. That okay with you? Said he'd walk me home afterward if it's late." And she hoped it would be late enough for a walk under the evening sky with the stars out and the air getting cooler.

Ma shook her head and went back to stitching the pants. "Gonna cost you money to get in. You know we can't afford that."

"No, no. He gave me a dime. Said I'd be his guest, but it wouldn't cost him anything 'cause he'd get it back from the gate man later."

Ma looked up and frowned. "I don't know, Cindy. You run off doin' that, and your brothers and Maggie'll throw a fit, sayin' they deserve to go too. It'll just raise a ruckus."

But Cindy saw a twinkle come in Ma's eyes and a tiny smile tease the corner of her mouth. Ma was no pushover, but Cindy knew she'd just been saying what she needed to say. "Ma, they don't have to know where I been. Just tell 'em I went to get trained for my job."

"Well … okay. But you come straight back. Don't go nowhere else, ya hear?" Then Ma went back to mending and Cindy headed out the door before Ma could change her mind.

She was nearly to the boss man's farm when she realized she hadn't even brushed her hair. She looked back at the camp, holding her hand to her head for shade from the low sun and could see her brothers were back, playing with the dog in front of their shack. Who could know how they might complicate things if they caught on to her plan to go to the carnival? Better leave well enough alone.

Crows seemed to be having a convention in the huge elm trees over the boss man's house. Their cawing and squabbling sounded like the squeaky brakes on the Tuckers' old Dodge. Cindy kept a wary eye on them as she turned into the yard and headed toward the barn. Its end doors were wide open, revealing a tractor and some farm equipment parked in the cavernous interior.

"Mr. Doyle?" She edged into the darkness, waiting for her eyes to adjust. "Mr. Doyle, you in here?"

"Ah, there you are." The man came out of a side door, wiping his hands on a rag. "Thought you weren't gonna make it. Beginning tomorrow, I want you here on time. No strollin' in just any ol' time you please. Understand?"

She nodded. Of course she understood, but he hadn't specified a time today, just come over when she saw his truck back. She hadn't done anything wrong, but busting her chops the way he'd done threw her off-kilter from the very start. It was a bum rap!

"All right, then," he said, as though everything was hunky-dory. "This here's my office." He gestured with his thumb to the door he'd just come out of. "Used to be the tack room when we had horses. And right in here"—he opened another door beside it—"is the commissary."

Cindy followed him in.

"Got electricity out here now too. Just pull the chain hanging from this lightbulb. And over here we got the shelves of canned goods—peas and peaches and tomatoes and such. Up there we got soap and some brushes. Well, you can see for ya'self. Everything's got the price marked on it. Can you see 'em?"

"Yes sir."

"This here's an old icebox. Might sometimes have some eggs or cheese to sell. 'Course then I'd need ice, so I don't know. But over here is what you gotta look out for—these three barrels. I put sacks of cornmeal, flour, and sugar in 'em. But we got mice out here, and if you don't keep the tops tight on the barrels, they'll get in 'em. And if you let that happen, I'll have to take it out of your pay. You understand?"

Cindy nodded.

"Over here's the ledger." He walked over to a wobbly table and opened a book. "Every time anybody buys something, you gotta write down their name, how much it cost, and then to the side put a plus mark or a minus mark. Minus if it goes on their bill and plus if they happen to pay. Most won't be payin' 'cause they don't have no cash money. See?"

"Uh …" How was she supposed to tell him? "I'm sorry, Mr. Doyle, but I cain't … I mean, I never learned how to read and write."

"What the …?" he yelled. A thunderstorm brewed in his face. "You said you could do money. You led me to believe you could—"

"I *can* do numbers. I can add, I can subtract, I can make change, anything you want havin' to do with money. It's just that I can't read 'n write. Never had the chance to go to school."

"Well, what makes you think you know money, then?"

"Pa taught me." She was feeling frantic. "I can do it, Mr. Doyle. Believe me. You can even test me and see."

"I'll do just that. Wait here! And don't touch nothin'!"

He left, and she heard him rummaging around in his office next door. In a moment he came back with a moneybox, and they spent the next fifteen minutes with him yelling at her to make change for various amounts and having her add and subtract. She could do all the sums in her head, but he insisted she write down the problems on paper to prove it.

Finally, he calmed down. "Still don't know what I'm gonna do. I've a mind to send you back out to the beets for deceivin' me. You rather work the field?"

Cindy hardly knew what to say. This was more unpleasant than the hot sun, but she knew her family needed the extra money. She looked down at the floor and mumbled, "No sir."

"What? Speak up, girl." He reached out and grabbed her chin, pulling her head up, forcing her to look him in the eye. "I've a mind to call this whole thing off right now. You want that?"

She tried to shake her head, but his grip held her firm. Then like earlier in the day, he looked her up and down as he chewed on his mustache, his breathing coming a little faster. Finally, he said, "I'll give you a chance, but believe you me, you better do everything I tell you, and I mean *everything*, or you're fired. Understand?"

The voice Cindy found was barely a whisper. "Yes sir." And tears filled her eyes.

"All right, all right, now. There's no need for that. Here." He reached his arm around her shoulder and pulled her close, not to his side, but straight into him. She felt smothered, like she couldn't get her breath. And when she tried to push herself away, he pulled her all the tighter. "Now ain't that better?" He finally let go and took a deep breath. "Here's what we'll do. When someone comes in, you have *them* write their own name on the next line—better yet, make 'em print it so I can read it—then you put the numbers over in the side column accordin' to what they buy. Understand?"

Cindy nodded. Everything seemed to be her having to *understand* him. But then she tried to remind herself that he was the boss.

"Okay now. Follow me into my office. I gotta show you somethin' in there." He closed the moneybox and took it with him as he led the way.

In spite of a window that faced the farmhouse and glass panes in the door to the barn's interior, Buster Doyle's office was small and dark with bare stud walls. A desk sat under the window with a straight back chair before it, a single bookshelf hung on the nearby wall, and an old wooden cot sat off to the side with a thin, soiled blue ticking mattress. Even with its lumps, it looked more comfortable than Cindy's mat on the floor of the shack. When

Doyle noticed her looking at it, he said, "Sometimes when my wife can't sleep, I come out here for the night. 'Course, you can lay down on it, too, if ..." He paused as though caught in the spider's web of some dream. "But not when you're workin'. Understand? And lookie here, I got a light in here too." He pulled the chain.

He smiled broadly, like a Cheshire cat. "Now, Miss ... What ya say your name was?"

"Cindy."

"Cindy. Good, I want us to be on friendly terms. You can call me Mr. Doyle. Now, Cindy"—he rubbed his hands together as though warming them—"what I'm gonna show you has to be an absolute secret. Since you'll be working the commissary, I'm gonna trust you with this secret, but I've gotta have your word you won't tell a soul 'bout our secrets, not even your folks. Understand?"

Cindy felt as though the air was being sucked from her lungs. What was he getting at? But not knowing what else to do, she nodded.

"On the back side of this here stud is a nail with a key on it." He took it off and showed it to her. "It's for my desk drawers. That's where I keep the moneybox. Bottom drawer's for back wages and farm records. Don't be messing in there. Understand?"

He opened the top drawer and slipped the box in. "Okay now, that's where you'll find it. And that's where you're to put it back when you close up at night. Each day I'm gonna count every penny. Understand? And if it don't match exactly what the ledger says people paid, I'll find it no matter where you try to hide it." He looked her up and down again, making her want to put on a coat even though the day was warm and muggy. "Yeah, well ... Wanna sit down?" He gestured toward the cot. "Take a load off?"

"No." She shook her head emphatically. She just wanted to get out of there. "I ... I thought I was s'pose'ta meet your wife."

"Oh, yeah, yeah. Let's go on over. Lilly should be awake by now."

The Doyles' house was big—two stories, with four bedrooms, a parlor, and an indoor bathroom. Cindy followed the boss upstairs to the bedroom where Mrs. Doyle lay in bed. She greeted Cindy kindly enough but kept saying she could manage on her own and didn't need any help until Mr. Doyle became exasperated. "Lillian, I don't want to hear anymore of that. The doctor told you to stay down as much as possible. This girl'll be comin' every day to help you out so you don't have to get up. She's to clean and cook ..." He turned to Cindy. "You can cook, can't ya?"

When Cindy hesitated, he snorted. "No matter. You just do what Lilly tells you. If she says peel carrots, you peel carrots. If she says put on the tea, you put on the tea. Understand? You're to do everything you're told. Otherwise ..."

Cindy understood, loud and clear!

As they went back down the stairs, Mr. Doyle lowered his voice, "Don't you be worrying Lilly about anything that happens out in the commissary either. In her condition, she can't stand frettin' about anything. I mean, you'd be responsible, you know, if it riled her and caused her to ... Well, you understand?"

Doyle assigned several chores, making sure Cindy *understood*. And when she finally left the house twenty minutes later, she *understood* she was going to be the boss's slave for the rest of the beet harvest. And she didn't like him up close anymore than when he was yelling at the workers in the fields. What was worse, Pa wouldn't be around to be her shield.

But at least for this evening she was free and on her way to see Bo ... What'd he say his full name was? Oh yes, *James Bodeen*! But she liked Bo better. As she walked lightly down the road, she briefly touched the folds of material between her breasts to be sure the dime was still there that would get her into the carnival.

Chapter 8

WHEN BO CAME THROUGH THE CARNIVAL'S MAIN GATE and rounded the carousel, he saw his father standing in the doghouse operating the Ridee-O. He sucked in his breath. *Oh no! What happened?* Slowing his steps, his mind raced. Why wasn't Rico there running it? Bo had known there'd be consequences for leaving his post if his father noticed, but he'd never expected to be gone so long. To see his father pulling levers and loading people like an ordinary ride jockey meant something had gone terribly wrong. As the owner of Bodeen Midway Rides, he should be circulating around the midway, giving orders, and overseeing all the rides.

Fire sparked in his father's eyes when he noticed Bo across the line of waiting patrons. Jeb Bodeen slammed the big lever forward, sending the cars of screaming riders whirling around the little track again. "Where you been?" he yelled over the roar of the engine as the cars gained speed.

Bo swallowed. What could he say? "Uh … what happened? I left Rico here for a few minutes to run the ride."

"*A few minutes?*" He glared at his son and then turned the hourglass over … a little late. "What's the matter? You sick?"

69

"No. Just took a little longer than I expected." Bo pushed his way through the waiting teenagers and kids with their cotton candy and sickening-smelling caramel corn and stepped up to face his father. Maybe he could still talk his way out of this.

"Oh, yeah? Well, I gave Rico his walkin' papers! He nearly burned the clutch out on this thing. It was down for an hour while Johnson checked it!" His father stuck a finger in Bo's face. "You have any idea how much money you lost us this afternoon? I let you try bein' foreman on this ride because ..." He threw his hands in the air. "Who knows why I did such a fool thing? You're 'bout as useless around here as a suck-egg mule. This ride's supposed to be a cash cow. Prime location. But if it ain't running, how we gonna crack our nut? It won't even pay for itself. I'm 'bout ready to send you off to work in the WPA. So don't give me no gobbledygook, boy! Where were you?"

Bo dropped his head and clinched his lips. Anything he might say would just make matters worse. His thoughts tumbling as the screams of the thrilled riders played in the background, he searched for an answer his father would find reasonable. Suddenly, a different kind of scream penetrated his consciousness. He looked up, eyes searching. His father had heard it too. Every carny recognizes when screams of glee turn to raw terror!

There! The Big Eli Wheel that anchored the row of rides at the other end of the midway had stopped turning, and from one of the swinging seats at the top, a small girl hung, legs dangling in space, as an older girl—perhaps her sister, but not really strong enough to help—tried to pull her back to safety.

"Here, take this!" Bo's father shoved him in front of the operator's lever and ran toward the Eli.

Bo stared in horror at the spectacle at the top of the wheel. Accidents were not only tragic for the victims but could put a midway out of business or even ban a whole carnival from returning to a town. Suddenly, the screaming from the big Eli Wheel was joined by more shrieks from the Ridee-O right in front of him.

"Stop! Stop! Let me off! Those are my girls up there. Stop. Please stop! Help! Help!"

Bo cut the throttle and pulled the lever back all the way to apply the brakes. Before the cars came to a complete stop, the hysterical woman jumped out of her car, stumbled down the boarding ramp, and fell flat. Bo killed the engine and ran to her aid, but she didn't seem to be hurt and jumped up, screaming for her daughter as she ran toward the Eli.

By this time, all the rides were stopping, and the whole crowd along the midway was gaping at the girl at the top of the Eli Wheel. Bo's father began climbing the support stand and then one of the spokes of the wheel like a sailor scaling the rigging of a tall ship. But from where Bo stood, there didn't seem to be any way his father could get from the spoke he was ascending to the chair with the girls. He was going up the wrong spoke! As he neared the top, he was still ten feet away from the girls. But he had their attention and began giving them instructions, trying to calm them down and talk them through how to get the little girl back into her seat. Slowly, it seemed to work. The larger girl hooked one arm around the safety bar and was then able to inch the younger one up and up until with a final lunge she regained her seat.

"Ease 'em on down," Bo heard his father call to the operator below. But his dad was still clinging to the spoke. Slowly, as the wheel turned, his father managed to adjust his position as if one of the acrobats in the big top so that at first he was hanging on the spoke like he was chinning himself on a bar, and then he turned as the wheel turned so he descended feet first and jumped off just as the mother ran to the chair and embraced her crying children.

In a few moments, Bo could hear his father calling out to the crowd, "Everyone's okay! Everyone's safe, folks! All's well that ends well. Go back to enjoying yourselves. Hey, Lonnie, start up that carousel again. Let's have some music. Everything's back to normal, people!"

But Bo knew nothing would be back to normal for his father for the rest of the evening. He'd be facing an angry family, the carnival's Chief, perhaps even the police—if Lapeer had any police—or other city officials who'd come out to investigate whether the rides they'd allowed into their town were safe. Truth was, they were safe … and they weren't. From what Bo had seen, the incident hadn't resulted from any mechanical failure or operational neglect. But anybody could get hurt on a ride if they didn't use common sense. If legal action resulted before they left town, his dad might even need to call in the mender.

Bo's legs were shaking as he started the engine for the Ridee-O again. He opened the gate to let the next set of riders find their cars. "Wait a minute!" He reached out and caught the arm of one of three little kids who looked to be about six years of age. "You punks got someone older with you?"

"No. We don't need none."

"Yes you do. You need an adult with you." He wasn't going to take any chances.

"No we don't. None of the other rides we been on tonight said that."

"And there ain't no sign," another one said. "So who says?"

"I say so! And I'm runnin' the Ridee-O. It's the fastest ride anywhere, and you gotta have an adult with you."

"C'mon. Quit holdin' things up." Waiting patrons were getting restless. "Hey, we want to get on."

"Yeah," one of the boys said. "We paid our money, we get to ride."

"Not on this." Bo grabbed his arm and the arm of a second boy and yanked them completely out of line. Seeing his friends had no chance, the third boy surrendered, and all three walked off, cursing Bo as they left.

Bo engaged the clutch and turned the three-minute hourglass over to time the ride, taking his first deep breath. The only good thing about the near-accident on the Eli Wheel was that his dad would be so busy the rest of the day he was unlikely to get back to grilling him about being AWOL. He knew the issue wasn't over, but at least it would give his father time to cool off. Bo worked hard, laughing and joking with the people to give them a good time, hoping to crack their nut and maybe show a profit for the day in spite of the time the ride had been down. "Hey, you wanna go again? Ride three times in a row without getting sick, and I'll give you the fourth turn free." He began to relax and turned up the Flash and Dash. "Step right up, ladies and gentlemen, for the most fun you'll have all afternoon! The Ridee-O is the fastest ride on the midway! Brand new from the Spillman Engineering Corporation in New York."

But an hour later Cooper, tapped him on the shoulder. "Take a hike! Your ol' man said for me to take over." The seasoned jockey jerked a thumb over his shoulder. "Guess you're outta here."

"Where'm I supposed to go?"

Cooper stepped into the doghouse, pushing Bo out. "How should I know? Go ask him."

Bo walked away, frustration boiling in his gut. So his father wasn't letting the matter rest, was he? Well, Bo wasn't about to go look for him and bring it all to a head either. He headed for the boneyard where the carnies hung out when they weren't on duty, but then he remembered that Cindy said she might soon come by. Swinging back toward the front gate, he stayed within sight of the

Ridee-O in case he missed seeing her come in and she ended up looking for him there.

He didn't have to wait long before he saw the girl step up to the ticket booth and hand the man her dime for a ticket. She was as pretty as he'd remembered, but somehow in the throng of townspeople, she looked lost coming through the gate. "Hey, Cindy!" He walked boldly toward her. "Here I am."

There was that smile. "Hi. Thought I'd have to go find your ride first."

"Wouldn't have been hard. There it is, first one after the carrousel, just like I told you."

"Wow. That really goes fast."

The riders were squealing with delight, holding their hands in the air when they went over the humps.

Cindy turned to him, a puzzled look on her face. "But I thought you ran this ride."

"I do, well, I did, but ... Dad let me off for the evening." *That was one way to put it, wasn't it?* "But here, let me get you a turn." He led her over to the Ridee-O.

"Hey, Cooper. Put my friend here on the next round. Okay?"

"Oh." Her eyes widened. "Not by myself! You gotta come with me."

"Ah, I don't know. I've ridden lots. This one's for you." Bo would've loved to ride with Cindy as they wheeled around the corners and over humps, jostling back and forth until she was cuddled up against him with thrill and delight ... but what if his dad came along and saw him on the ride? That would be the end of the world—or at least the end of *his* world. He'd get shipped off to the WPA for sure.

"Come on, Bo." She grabbed his arm, and he flexed his bicep a little. "I got the heebie-jeebies." But she was smiling like a child on Christmas morning. "You gotta come with me."

Bo didn't think he could resist. He looked around. "Hey, Cooper! Where was my dad when you talked to him?"

"Headin' toward the office wagon with the Chief."

Relief washed over Bo. "All right. We'll take one turn on the Ridee-O, but then I want to get out of here—I mean, out of the midway—and take you to see the rest of the carnival. This is the best ride, anyway." They walked up the ramp, and he helped her get in a car just vacated by the previous riders. "Once you been on the Ridee-O, all the others are like kiddie rides." He sat down and put his arm across the seat behind her. "Hey, I know. We'll see the show in the big top."

Just as Bo hoped, Cindy squealed with delight and clung to him at the height of the excitement ... and then it was over. *Three minutes already?*

"Whew! I can hardly stand up," she said as he helped her out. His knees were shaking just a little bit, too, but he knew it wasn't from the thrill ride.

"Here, come with me." He hustled her down the ramp and across the open space to the concessions and sideshows that ringed the midway, keeping an eye out for his dad all the while.

"Ooo! What's that?" The girl stopped behind a small crowd listening to a Talker in front of a sideshow. The gaudy front showed scenes of a woman progressively turning into a raging gorilla.

"Ladies and gentlemen!" The Talker was using a small megaphone so people in the back of the growing crowd could hear. "Step right up for the most amazing biological metamorphosis known to science. You have seen caterpillars turn into butterflies, but this is more than the reverse. The beautiful Jamilia, found in the deepest jungles of Borneo appears to be a normal girl. But right before your very eyes, under bright lights that allow no illusions, you will watch her change. Her forehead will begin to recede, her eyebrows will protrude, fangs will begin to grow in her mouth, and her clothes will fall away as a heavy coat of hair grows from every square inch of her body. And in only a few short minutes she will become a wild gorilla."

The Talker's eyes narrowed and his tone grew serious. "Now for your safety, ladies and gentlemen, she is locked into a steel cage, because once she takes on the form of an ape, she attains the strength of twenty men and sometimes goes on a violent rampage."

The crowd shifted and murmured nervously.

"When you enter the exhibition, please be sure to take note of the nearest exit. We have not had an accident for some time, but should something go wrong, you will want to make an orderly escape as quickly as possible. Please try not to panic. Now, who will be first to see what few people in the world have witnessed? Step right up."

People looked at one another, but no one moved.

"Ladies and gentlemen! Step right up for the most amazing …" and the Talker began his ballyhoo all over again.

Aghast, Cindy's mouth fell open. "Does she really turn into a gorilla?"

"Of course not!" Bo watched the puzzled expression on her face. "But you want to see it?"

"Well, sure, if it's safe. Can you get us in?"

"Of course. Come on. We'll be the shill who turns the tip and brings the others in." He grabbed her hand and pulled her through the gathered onlookers, up to the ticket booth … but without actually paying any money.

"And here they are, ladies and gentlemen!" The Talker pointed at Bo and Cindy. "Our first brave souls! Perhaps they are students of science. Now, who'll be next? Remember, for safety, we can only allow a limited number. So step right up!"

Chapter 9

WELL, COME ON, NOW! STEP RIGHT UP! Lucy, it's your turn. Let's go!" Estelle Williams snapped her clipboard at me. As a volunteer, the large African-American woman who always dressed in bright colors only cooked lunch at the woman's shelter … and a few other things, I guess. But now, now that they've hired her part time, she acts like she runs it. Still, she's always good to me, so … Once I got myself up and moving, she smiled and went back to her knitting.

I hated seeing the nurse at Manna House. But it's not just her. I just don't like seein' *any* nurse. But Fuzz Top was right; I needed to get rid of this cough! She even took me down to the clinic at the county hospital. 'Course didn't do me no good. Knew it wouldn't. And now, here I was back again talking to the Manna House nurse.

She gave me some meds and said, "Avoid gettin' chilled." Ha! Easier said than done in Chicago if you're on the streets, even in summer. But I'll be okay … if Fuzz Top don't drag me back down to the county again. And she's around all the time, now that she finagled gettin' a job here at the shelter as the … whatever they call it, program director, or somethin'.

I came out from behind the privacy divider where the nurse checks you out, and went over to get me a cup of joe. Their coffee ain't all that good, but it's always hot. I sat down there in the dining room, takin' my first sip when I saw a yeller dog. My memories tumbled all the way back to when I was on the lam with that faithful little black-and-white mutt. This dog didn't look a thing like Jigger, but I could tell right off the bat, he had a heart of gold, and that's what counts with dogs … and people … don't know 'bout cats.

Name was Dandy. Belonged to Fuzz Top's mother. Fuzz Top had brought 'em both to work for the day—the dog and Martha Shepherd, as her name turned out to be. First thing I said was, "You don't look like you're from 'round here."

"No, ma'am. I'm from North Dakota, down here visiting my daughter for a while. Well," she cleared her throat and glanced around as though she didn't want others to hear, "guess I'd have to say I'm really here because of my own clumsy feet. I tripped over Dandy, here, and fell and hit my head. Ahh …" She rolled her eyes, reached up, and patted the back of her gray head as though checking to see if it still hurt.

I nodded, knowing what it was to hit your head. "See that lady over there?" I eyed the clipboard snapper. "That's Estelle Williams. She knitted me this here purple hat. She can knit anything. Oughta get her to make you one. Keeps the cold out. Keeps the hair in, and, should you take another dive, it'd provide ya with a good three-quarter-inch a cushion to protect your noggin."

We both had a good laugh at that. But it was true, and I did appreciate my purple knit hat.

"So you stayin' up in that big fancy high-rise with Fuzz Top?"

"Fuzz Top?"

"Ah, beggin' your pardon. Don't mean no disrespect. That's just what I call your Gabby girl … 'cause of her hair and all."

Martha sighed and looked off across the room like it was a wheat field. "Don't know how much longer I can stay. Don't think

78

her husband likes me very much. And he definitely doesn't like Dandy!" She reached down and gave the dog a scratch behind the ears. " 'Course, Dandy growls at him some. Do you know Philip?"

Couldn't say I really *knew* him, but I'd sure seen enough of him to have my opinions. But I held my peace, except for saying, "Dogs know. They just know."

"Yes. Yes. He said I've got to be out in a week, and that was several days ago. Gabby's looking for some kind of a retirement home or something for me, but I'll probably just head on home."

"*Hmm.*" I thought about that. "Sometimes wish I could go home. 'Course there probably ain't nothin' left of it by now."

"Oh? Where's that?"

"Arkansas … though I been 'bout everywhere else one time or another."

"What made you leave your home?"

"Arkansas? Oh, it was the drought—Dust Bowl days, ya know? Whole family had to pick up and hit the road to find work where we could. We were gonna go to California, but Pa didn't think our ol' Dodge could make it."

"Ah, yes, the Dust Bowl. Didn't bother our family too much up in Minot. But I know some farmers had it real tough. That was probably why Noble opened a carpet store." She laughed. "Noble—he was my husband—used to say, 'Carpets don't depend so much on the weather.' What'd you say your name was?" She asked it like I'd told her already and she'd had a senior moment or something. But I hadn't. I'm not one to give out my name to just any ol' Becky Sue.

But Martha Shepherd seemed different. I took a deep breath and coughed once. "I'm Lucinda Tucker." I stuck out my hand to shake. "They just call me Lucy around here, though. Been Lucy ever since I run off with my Romeo."

"Your Romeo? Ooh, you eloped? How exciting!"

"Well, not so much when you're actually runnin' and scramblin' and you're only fifteen years old." I paused, thinking back to those days in Michigan. "Turned out I never saw my family again. That's been the hardest thing, that and losing my Romeo, of course."

"You lost him?"

"Yeah, we was here in Chicago, and …" I couldn't really think how to explain it so she'd understand. "But, hey, he had a little dog named Jigger." I reached my hand out to her yellow dog, and he got right up and came and licked it. "Your Dandy reminds me of Jigger, not how he looks, of course, but … *Hmm*, we loved Jigger."

"Oh, yes. I know what you mean. Now Dandy's … Dandy's about all I got with Noble being gone and the girls scattered to the four winds, or …" She got a puzzled look on her face and then grinned. "… guess it's only three, since I only have three girls."

GABBY BROUGHT HER MOTHER and that Dandy dog to the shelter with her every day that week, so I hung out there, too, until Gabby asked why, seein' how nice the weather was, and all. Well, I didn't consider it any of her beeswax, but I tried to respond civil like. "Why shouldn't I stick around, Fuzz Top? *Somebody* 'round here needs ta spend time with your mother, her bein' a guest an' all. Respect your elders, ya know? Come on, Martha," I said, grabbing the old woman's arm. "We can watch us some TV."

Carolyn and some of the other residents had discovered that "Gramma Shep," as they called Martha, liked Scrabble, but me and words don't go together, never did. "How 'bout some poker?" I offered.

Lucy Come Home

Shoulda seen her face!

"Miz Martha, it's just a game! I wasn't suggestin' we go skinny dippin' in Lake Michigan, or nothin'." The picture of us two old women wading into that icy drink buck-naked nearly set me rolling on the floor. And pretty soon Martha couldn't help laughing either. We had us a high ol' time. I liked that Martha Shepherd! First real friend I'd had in years. But I knew if Gabby Fairbanks found a retirement home for her or sent her back to North Dakota, I might never see her again.

But what could I do?

I DIDN'T HAVE THE STICKABILITY to stay at Manna House over the weekend when Martha Shepherd wouldn't be there. Had to get out and about a bit. But I made it back in time for lunch on Monday, hoping to see her again. Besides, Estelle Williams always makes something good on Mondays.

However, I no sooner got signed in than I caught wind that things weren't right for Miz Martha. She sat at a table by herself, dabbing an embroidered hanky at the corners of her eyes with hands shaking so bad I feared she might hurt herself.

"Martha, what's the matter? Why you so riled up? You didn't fall down again, did ya?"

"No, no! It's Dandy. They put him out, and now he's run off, and I don't know where to find him. I just can't take it!"

"Whaddya mean, *they put him out*? Who put him out?"

"He did. Last night."

I couldn't believe Miz Gabby woulda allowed such a thing.

"I guess it's my fault. I should've taken him out for a walk, because he …" She made a horrible face. "…on the floor, and mister, Gabby's—you know—stepped in it. Then he threw him

81

out." At that point she broke into huge sobs, and all I could do was pat her shoulder a little.

"Now, now, buck up. Dandy's a smart dog. He'll be okay, and we'll find him directly."

"But he says I can't come back either, and I don't know where I'm gonna sleep tonight. I … I … Oh, Lucy, you gotta help me."

"And that I will, Martha Shepherd. We can take care of that right now. You just come with me."

I marched right up to Mabel Turner's office, and by the time we got to the director's door, I had half the residents following me like I was Moses in the wilderness. I didn't even knock but threw the door open, and there sat Mabel behind her desk and Gabby Fairbanks sitting across from her. They looked like they were deep into something, but I couldn't wait.

"So why can't Gramma Shep stay *here*, is what I wanna know? That scumbag Gabby's married to—don't mean no offense to you, Fuzz Top—already kicked Martha's dog out, now he's sayin' Martha's gotta go, too. But she don't wanna go back there anyway, an' she don't have nowhere else to go right now. Don't that make her homeless? Ain't this a shelter for homeless ladies?" I glanced back over my shoulder. "Ain't I right, girls!"

"Yeah, that's right." … "They's a couple beds open upstairs." … "Uh-huh, we want Gramma Shep to stay here."

The Fuzz Top's mouth dropped open like a trap door as she looked back and forth between her mom and Mabel Turner.

"Oh, Mabel, if … if she could," Gabby blurted. "Just for a few days, or maybe a few weeks, or—" With the same look of awe and hope on her face, she turned to her mother. "Mom?"

"I like it here. They're my friends." Martha gripped my hand and lifted it high like she was declaring us the winners in a tag-team wrestling match.

82

Surely that plan would buy Fuzz Top some time if not an outright reprieve from her jerk of a husband. He got what he wanted—the poor woman *and* the dog out of his precious penthouse.

Estelle Williams stepped up to say she could stay a couple of nights to help Martha get settled, but I put my foot down. "Don'tcha think I know my way 'round this place? I can settle her just fine. C'mon Martha." I took her arm. "Let's go get you cozied up!"

Upstairs, I had to throw a hissy-fit to get Tanya and Carolyn to move so we could have a couple of bottom bunks close to one another. No way could Miz Martha climb up to a top one … and I, for sure, wasn't about to even if I could! Finally, we staked our claims and headed back down in time for Martha to say good-bye to Gabby before she left for the day.

Kinda sorrowful, she tugged on her daughter's arm. "Please look for Dandy, won't you, Gabby?" They fell into a big hug, and I knew right then, I had to go find that dog. But I had some ideas.

"DANDY! GET OUTTA THERE! Get out right now!"

How he'd managed to get up into the Dumpster behind that pizza place south of Richmond Towers was beyond me. But there he was! Grinning at me like a five-year-old at a birthday party and wagging his tail so hard he almost lost his balance. Worse still, he seemed afraid to jump down, so I had to lift him out of there, me with my rheumatiz.

So much mud and filth clung to Dandy's coat, you couldn't even tell he was yellow. I made a leash by tying some bandanas together and took him over to the lake for a bath. No way could I take him back to Miz Martha with the mess he was in.

And that's when I saw Fuzz Top sitting on a bench in the park. Couldn't miss that mop of reddish, curly hair. She was sitting

83

sideways with her feet up on the bench and her face buried in her arms on her knees. Could see big sobs shaking her body as Dandy and I got near. Heard her moaning, "Help me, Jesus! I don't know what to do!… I can't lose my boys!… I'm so tired of fighting, trying to keep my life from unraveling … But I can't do it by myself!… I need You, God! *I need You!*"

Well, I guess she mostly did need the Man Upstairs! But right then all I could offer was her mother's mucky dog, so I let Dandy nuzzle up to her until she jumped.

"Dandy!" Her head jerked up, then slowly turned to recognize me as if she were waking up from a deep sleep.

"You an' God havin' yourselves a private *tête-à-tête*," I asked, "or can a body sit down on that there bench too? My dogs're barkin'."

She looked at me completely lost.

"Feet, honey, feet. My feet are tired."

She nodded. "You found Dandy!"

"Yep! Not that you'd recognize him with all that mud." I gave him a brush with my hand then looked up at her. "So what's wrong with you? You look worse'n the day I first found you in this park, wet as a drowned rat and bleedin' like a stuck pig."

She laughed hysterical-like, and then began to sob, big ol' sobs that forced her to gasp for breath between snatches of her story. Slowly they came out. Her jerk husband had kicked *her* out of their penthouse, too, throwing all her stuff and Miz Martha's stuff out in the hall, and he'd changed the lock so she couldn't get back in either.

"And … and the worst part is … he's taken my boys. I don't know where they are! My own boys." She bawled for at least five minutes, and I just let her get it out.

I'd seen this comin' first time I laid eyes on that man up there in their fancy condo that rainy night when Gabby ran into me. But it wouldn't do no good to say so.

"Hey, hey, hey." I patted her shoulder. "It's gonna be all right," I soothed, though to tell the truth, I wasn't so sure. I got my stiff ol' body up. "C'mon, let's go." Instantly, Dandy was ready. "You got enough for cab fare? My feet are killin' me."

"Go?" she said, looking up at me. "Go where?"

"Manna House, of course. Nobody's ever locked outta Manna House."

Dandy tugged on his bandana leash and barked.

"What about my boys? I can't just let Philip take my boys!"

"That's right. But one day at a time, Missy. Them boys are all right. Now, you got cab fare or not?"

Chapter 10

CINDY PULLED ON BO'S ARM as the mass of spectators attempted to flee the rampaging gorilla. "C'mon! We gotta get out of here!" she yelled over the panicky screams.

Bo set his feet and enveloped her loosely in his arms as he spoke into her ear. "Hold on there, babe. It ain't for real! That's just a guy in a monkey suit, and he's not breakin' in here, anyway."

She struggled for a moment and then looked up at the relaxed smile on his face. "Whaddya mean? You got me all befuddled." She glanced at the dimly lit stage where a moment before she'd seen the ferocious woman-turned-gorilla crashing through the cage bars to attack the terrified audience. But now the stage was bare. There was no steel gate hanging off its hinges. In fact, the doorway was completely blank. Nothing there, no broken gate, no raging freak, no stony cell beyond.

Cindy's heart still pounded. "Where'd she go?"

"Take it easy, babe. It was just a trick."

"I don't get it!" She looked again at the blank doorway. "I saw—"

"What you saw was smoke and mirrors, just smoke and mirrors ... I ain't funnin' you."

She let her head relax onto his chest for a moment. "But how?"

He turned her toward the stage. "What you see through that doorway is really just a large mirror on an angle, like a half-open door. But it ain't no mirror you'd comb your hair in"—he touched her curls with tip of his fingers—"'cause you can kinda see through it. It's a halfway mirror. When something straight behind it is brightly lit, you can see it through the mirror, like that woman in her pretend cell. But when it's dark in her cell and something over to the side is brightly lit, you see it reflected in the mirror. Understand?"

"No ... not hardly."

Bo took a deep breath. "Okay. Straight through that doorway, beyond the angled half-mirror is a little room painted to look like a jail cell with a barred gate. That's where the woman was. When the light was on her, you could see right through the mirror, and there she was, moving around, actin' crazy, whatever. Then it got kinda smoky, 'member that? They put a puff of smoke in there and dimmed the light in her cell. At the same time, they began bringing up the light in the cell to the side. It's built to look just the same as hers. But in it, there was a man in a gorilla suit. As he got brighter and the girl got dimmer, you could see more of him reflected in the mirror and less of her through the mirror. Pretty soon, all you saw was him. He roared, grabbed the gate, shook it, and broke it loose—only wood—and by then, everyone was screamin' and running for the exits."

She stared at him in awe. Then she exhaled and let the tension drain from her shoulders. "Well, I'll be switched. Can we go look?"

He grimaced and slowly shook his head. "They don't really like us givin' away secrets." He nodded toward the exit and put his arm around her. "Let's get outta here 'fore the next batch comes in."

"Can we ride the Ferris wheel?" Cindy asked as they pushed through the flap in the canvas doorway.

"I s'pose so." Bo looked around the midway, straining his neck as though he was searching for someone. Then he shrugged. "But it's just an Eli Wheel, ya know ... why not catch the show in the big top instead?"

After the tumbling clowns and the sword swallower acts, a parade of exotic animals were led around the ring: a mangy lion, a zebra—or was that just a white horse with black stripes painted on it? Cindy had her suspicions—three brown bears, and finally a large, gray elephant. The other animals were taken away as the ringmaster introduced the elephant as "Waltzing Matilda," which the five-piece orchestra began to play. The elephant started swaying back and forth, picking up first one front foot and then the other in pretty close time to the music.

When everyone began to clap, the trainer nudged Matilda with the elephant prod and she "waltzed" her way over to the edge of the ring where she climbed onto the solid curb and reared up, balancing on her hind feet while she pawed the air with her front feet and trumpeted her triumph with such volume, it drowned out the music and ended the act.

As Matilda was led away to the applause of the crowd, the orchestra launched into the *oom-pah-pah, oom-pah-pah* of "The Daring Young Man on the Flying Trapeze," and the ringmaster introduced the Amazing Flying Leontini Family. Cindy watched as two men and two women walked into the center of the ring and waved to the audience. The men wore black from head to toe while the women were dressed as ballerinas in pale pink tights under silver tutus.

After a slight bow, the men pulled black masks over their faces, and then all four performers began ascending rope ladders toward the very top of the tent—a man and woman toward one peak and the other two toward the other peak. The house lights dimmed, and the men were lost in the darkness while the women glimmered in the silvery brilliance of arc spotlights.

Cindy stuffed a knuckle of one hand in her mouth. One of the women looked more like a girl no older than herself, and certainly no bigger.

As the orchestra continued playing, both women leaped toward each other through space. Cindy realized there were other shadows moving in the background, but the swinging girls so mesmerized her that she paid the shadows no attention. The swings were also black and visible only occasionally as the girls' arcs grew longer and longer, and then they let go and flew through space …

Cindy gasped and held her breath until they were somehow plucked from the air by invisible hands—the catchers in black—and she allowed herself to breathe again.

With her head tipped back, she watched them doing "ankle hangs," the "inverted crucifix," "gazelles," and "flyaways"—all announced by the ringmaster—passing one another so close it looked as if they would surely collide. And then the girl—the one Cindy had identified as being like herself—swung higher and higher while the other woman paused, perched on her board with her light dimmed.

"Ladies and gentlemen," the announcer bellowed, "can we ask for a moment of silence." The orchestra quieted some, but continued playing. "The young and beautiful Ginger Leontini is now going to attempt the treacherous Triple Cutaway Swan, a maneuver that has ended the careers of every aerialist who has attempted it. But Ginger, who is only sixteen, says she wants to try it tonight. So, please ladies and gentlemen, I beg your silence while she concentrates."

The arcs of the girl's swing extended farther and farther as she hung upside-down by her knees. And then, at the top of her swing, she let go, curled into a ball, and spun ... once, twice, three times. Then she opened and reached, the spotlight showing her flying like a swan and then ... falling ... falling ... falling, without catching her bar.

The light lost her and a terrible thud reverberated from the floor of the arena.

"Lights, please! Lights, please!" called the announcer over the screams and gasps of the audience.

A moment later, the cannon spotlight found her just as the house lights came up. The girl lay on her back, arched over the twelve-inch-high curb of the performance ring, right where Matilda the elephant had stood to trumpet her triumph.

The orchestra whimpered to a ragged stop as silence gripped everyone in the tent. The nearest clown ran over to kneel by the girl but held short of touching her.

And then, as if by a miracle, the young aerialist slowly peeled herself off the curbing like the skin from a potato and sat up ... when that curb surely should have broken her back and probably killed her. She sat there for a moment and shook her head as a hush hung over the audience. Then she got gracefully to her feet. The clown jumped to his feet, and with orange gloves three times the size of his hands began to clap, turning to the audience, inviting the horrified observers to join him. Slowly, they did, one here and one there until the applause was thunderous, and the orchestra began pumping out "Camptown Races" at full volume.

A salty taste told Cindy she'd bitten into her knuckle.

Bo looked at her and frowned. "Oh, wow. What'd you do? Let me go get something for that."

"Nah." She sucked at it once and pressed her thumb over the small wound. "It'll be okay."

The cheering around them stopped. Down in the arena, the beautiful Ginger Leontini walked back to the ladder and began climbing as the house lights shut down again and the spotlight focused on the girl—the girl who should've been dead—as she headed back up to her board. High in the peak of the tent, three people began to clap, the two catchers and the other aerialist. The audience heard them and joined in, tentatively at first, as if it wasn't right to encourage someone who had so nearly died a few minutes before.

Cindy grabbed Bo's arm. "Why is she going back up?"

In the dim reflective glow of the spotlight, he smiled at her. "It's all show business, babe, all show business."

"Whaddya mean?"

He leaned over and spoke into her ear. "She didn't really fall."

"What? I saw her!"

He shook his head as his smile grew. "That was a bullet drop, right into a net. You didn't see her hit the net, because by then, there were no lights on her." He grinned as she tried to digest what he'd said. He continued, "As soon as she hit the net, she bounced off. They pulled the net away, and she laid out over that curb before the lights came up on her again. The big thud?" He shook his head. "Just a noise maker."

With her mouth hanging open, Cindy turned toward the ring again, but it was too dark to see any details. "I didn't see any net."

"Oh, it was there, and it's strung back up by now. But they only put it out in the dark. You see, it's all about focus," Bo whispered hoarsely. "Keep people's attention where you want it, and you can do anything where they're not looking. Even pickpocket 'em."

"What?"

He shrugged and grinned. "That's life!"

Shaking her head, Cindy settled back to watch the rest of the show. After that, each new move, each flight of Ginger Leontini was greeted by louder and louder cheers from the crowd.

A CRESCENT MOON HUNG LOW in the western sky as Bo walked Cindy back to the camp hand-in-hand. She leaned into him. "So, if that was a trick, does she do it every night?"

"Can't. Only once per town. Tonight was our first full house here in Lapeer, so we got to see it. Everybody'll be talkin' about it tomorrow, and they'll all be back … with their friends. We'll have a full house till we jump Thursday night."

"Jump?"

"Yeah. Pack up and move to our next town."

Cindy felt a stab of disappointment. "You're leavin' so soon?" She was beginning to like this handsome carny.

"Yeah, we're on the road, ya know."

They strolled in silence down the small lane that led to the migrant camp until dim lights could be seen from several of the shacks. A small fire glowed near the first shack, and when they got closer, Cindy could see her mother sitting in her ladder-back rocker and heard her softly strumming her little guitar.

She pulled on Bo's hand and stopped under a scraggly cottonwood tree. "That's my ma."

Bo stared. "Maybe I oughta meet her."

"Not just yet." She looked up into his eyes, patches of faint moonlight playing on them as it threaded its way through a low-hanging branch. She'd had such a great evening. Would it happen again? And then she heard Ma begin to sing in a thin, breathy voice. *"Softly and tenderly Jesus is calling …"* Ma paused and fumbled for the next cords. *"Calling for you and for me."* When Ma had worked her way through the verse, she moved more smoothly into the chorus.

Come home, come home,
Ye who are weary, come home;
Earnestly, tenderly, Jesus is calling,
Calling, O sinner, come home!

As the notes drifted into the night, Bo whispered, "Ah, that's beautiful. She sing very often?"

Cindy shrugged. "Not as much as we'd like, I guess."

Just then, Ma stopped, got up, and went back into the shack.

"Guess I better be goin' too." But Cindy didn't move. She could have stood out there all night.

"Think you can come over to the carnival again tomorrow evening?"

Cindy wanted to seize the invitation, tell Bo she'd be there whenever he could get off. And then she remembered ... "Gotta work."

"I mean after you get off."

"I'm on the commissary ... at the boss's house. We passed it back there along the road." She nodded her head in the direction.

"After?"

"Don't get off till seven. Then I gotta come home and eat."

"Need someone to walk you home?"

"No." She laughed lightly. "It's just right there, and it won't even be dark yet." Oh, why had she said that? She'd love to have him walk her home. "Unless ... you're free. Then maybe you can meet my folks."

"Yeah. Yeah, maybe. That big white farmhouse, huh?"

"The commissary's in the barn."

93

Bo nodded. "Can't promise. Might be jockeying some ride. But we'll see." He suddenly leaned forward and planted a quick kiss on the right side of her forehead, just where her hair parted, and then turned and walked away.

Chapter 11

EVEN THOUGH CINDY GOT UP JUST AS EARLY the next morning to help send Pa and her siblings off to the beet fields at 6:30, she didn't feel so pushed. Her new job didn't begin until ten, and, she thought smugly, she wouldn't have to bend over all day in the hot sun. Maybe there were a few perks to being the oldest after all.

After helping Ma clean up their usual breakfast of cornmeal mush cooked with some bacon fat for flavor, she slung one-year-old Johnny up onto her shoulders and took Betty by the hand for a morning walk. She'd no sooner started down the road than the black-and-white dog showed up at her heels, tail wagging, ear cocked. Johnny squealed with delight, though Betty pressed tighter to Cindy's leg. "All right, you can come along," she said. Somehow she felt safer with the dog.

By the time she got back with the little ones, Ma was stoking the campfire. "Whatcha fixin'?"

"You forget your sister's birthday?"

"No." Well … Cindy hadn't actually thought about Maggie's birthday since waking up that morning, but it had crossed her mind at least once in the last week or so. Thirteen now, but still skinny as a stick. Had Ma talked to her about womanly stuff yet?

Maybe she ought to pay more attention to her kid sister—though she could be as annoying as a gnat.

Cindy eyed a bowl of batter and an empty cake pan on the wood stump near the fire. "You makin' a cake ... out here?"

"None of your beeswax, girl." Ma flashed Cindy a sly grin, and Cindy caught a glimpse of the spirit and beauty that must've attracted Pa long before the Dust Bowl hit. "And don't you go sayin' nothin' to Maggie 'bout it either."

"Don't worry 'bout me." Cindy held up both hands, shoulder high. "I won't even see her till tonight." She dipped the tip of her finger in the batter and tasted it.

"Me, me, me." Little Betty jumped up and down, reaching toward the bowl.

"Y'all keep outta that, now!"

Cindy put Johnny down and drew the fussing Betty away. Involuntarily she smacked her lips. Banana! How had Ma squirreled away a couple of bananas while they traveled in that hot old car from the blueberry fields? But she'd done it. Ma always seemed to find a way to add special touches to their family life, even when they had nothing. Her singing and Bible reading and little traditions—like her special banana cake for every birthday—helped keep the family together. And with a family of nine, that meant a lot of cakes during the year!

But Cindy frowned at her mother, hovering over the smoky fire. "Where you gonna bake that cake? That two-plate woodstove inside ain't got no oven."

Ma stabbed her finger toward the fire. "Dutch oven. Right here."

Cindy had to grin. That was Ma, finding a way where there was no way ... or was that God? Ma always said He was the way-maker, making a way out of no way.

As Ma set the Dutch oven down into the coals, Cindy sighed. "Gotta go to work, Ma. Can you take the young'uns?"

Cindy walked around to the backdoor of the big white farmhouse and knocked. She waited a moment, and then knocked again, harder.

A tired voice came from the screened window above. "Who is it?"

"Lucinda Tucker, here to help you out."

"Oh. Come on in, and bring me up a pitcher of cool water, would you?"

Cindy had to search three cupboards in the kitchen before she found a pitcher, but it was a luxury to get water from a faucet instead of having to pump it.

In the second floor bedroom, Lillian Doyle sat in bed, propped up by pillows, wisps of limp dark hair poking out from a scarf wrapped around her head, face pale as a whitewashed fence. Books, magazines, and a newspaper were scattered around on the bed and side table in such a haphazard fashion, Cindy got the impression that the woman was terribly bored and couldn't find anything to interest her for long.

"You're a pretty thing." Her voice sounded wistful. "I thank you for coming over. Can't seem to do much these days … not in this heat." Her voice trailed off. Cindy wasn't sure what to say. She was glad when Mrs. Doyle sent her downstairs to do the dishes and clean up the kitchen. But she'd been down there only about twenty minutes when she heard Mrs. Doyle calling down the stairs. "Deary, could you make me some tea? And make yourself a cup too. Bring them on up and take a little break."

It went that way all day—Mrs. Doyle sending her off on some chore but soon calling her back on some pretext to just sit and chat for a while. It was fine with Cindy, though with every "break" she worried how Mr. Doyle would respond if he walked in on them. She knew he was a hard boss. Would he think she hadn't done enough work at the end of the day? She didn't want him yelling at her.

At half-past four, Lillian Doyle set aside her unfinished cucumber and butter sandwich and gave Cindy a sad look. "Guess you better get out there and open the commissary. I so wanted to make a go of that this year, carry my share of the weight a little. And … and help the workers, of course." She sucked in a deep breath and let it slowly escape. "But maybe you can do that for me."

Cindy went out to the barn and opened the door to the commissary. What was she supposed to do next?… Oh, yes, the moneybox. She entered Mr. Doyle's office, located the stud that hid the key, and glanced at the desk. Only one drawer had a handle. Inserting the key, she pulled it open. But there was no moneybox. Instead, Cindy stared at a leather pouch with a leather loop on the end, not unlike a woman's wristlet wallet. But it was unzipped and filled with bills, more money than she'd ever seen. And then she remembered what Mr. Doyle had said: *"Bottom drawer's for back wages and farm records. Don't be messing in there. Understand?"*

Cindy stared. This must be the money he'd held back trying to force the migrants to return and complete the season. Money Mr. Doyle owed Pa. Money he owed their whole family!

She quickly closed the drawer and locked it. Then she unlocked and opened the upper drawer, lifted out the moneybox, and took it back into the commissary. Her mind was still reeling. There was a lot of money in that pouch! No wonder Pa was so upset, all the time saying, *"Fool me once, shame on you. Fool me twice, shame on me!"*

She tried to put it out of her mind. It wasn't her concern, and she was sure Pa would get what was owed him sooner or later. For now, all she needed to do was keep the commissary purchases straight and record them in the ledger. She wrote the date in the top, left-hand column: 8/24/1942. Like Pa said, she would keep track of every penny. She counted the money: five one-dollar bills and $2.86 in change. She wrote $7.86 on the right across from the date. Then she surveyed the available goods in the commissary. Along with staples like flour, cornmeal, baking powder, and sugar, there was a whole shelf of canned goods: beans, peas, corn, peaches, applesauce, and cherries. She didn't see any cans of lard, which Ma liked to use for cooking—probably because of the war. Instead, the commissary stocked a half-dozen bottles of peanut oil.

Cindy looked over the supplies. Their family sure could use a lot of these things, but Pa didn't want to rack up any debt with the boss man.

She waited, but no customers came to the commissary.

Finally, she stepped back into Mr. Doyle's office because she'd noticed an alarm clock ticking on his desk. It said 6:40. Not much longer, and then she could go home.

Just then, Cindy heard Mr. Doyle's pickup drive up outside. She scurried back into the commissary. The truck door slammed, and in a moment Mr. Doyle loomed in the doorway. "Why ain't the light on?" he barked.

"L-light?"

"It's like a cave in here." The hard-boiled-looking man stepped in and jerked the light chain. "How can the customers see?"

She swallowed. "Didn't have any customers."

"What? Nobody?"

"No sir."

"Well, I'll see to that." He checked each shelf as if he were taking inventory. "Didn't give somethin' away for free, did you?"

"No sir."

"How 'bout yourself? You buy anything for your family?"

"No sir." Cindy was feeling smaller and smaller with each round of grilling, but she tried to speak up. "Ma didn't ask for nothin'."

"*Humph!*" He went over to the moneybox and counted the change. "If I find somethin' missin', you're gonna pay for it, ya know."

Cindy didn't know how to answer.

Closing the moneybox, he gave her one of those down and up looks that lingered too long in the wrong places. "Is Lillian okay? You do what she asked?"

"Yes sir."

"Good." His voice suddenly gentled. "You're a good girl, doin' what you're told." He chewed again on a corner of his mustache. "Well, that's good. Come on into the office and put the moneybox away." He headed for the adjoining room.

Cindy picked up the moneybox and followed. She found him looking out the window toward the house.

"Lillian's gonna be wonderin' where I am pretty soon ... Here, I'll put that box away. You did put the key back, didn't you?" He reached for the stud with the nail in it.

"Yes sir."

Once he'd locked the box in the drawer, Doyle turned back to her and grinned. "Now, that wasn't so bad, was it?"

What was he talking about? Helping Mrs. Doyle and opening the commissary hadn't been bad at all, but for some reason, all the boss man's challenges—especially his insinuations that she would mess up—left a ball of cotton in her throat so dry she couldn't answer even one more question. A tear threatened to creep down her check, and she quickly brushed it away.

Too late.

"Ah there now, no need to cry." The man held out his hands as if inviting her to come closer. Cindy stood rooted to the spot, but Mr. Doyle stepped forward and pulled her head into his chest, running his hand up and down her back. "No tears, now. No tears," he murmured.

Cindy could hardly breathe. Every muscle tensed. What should she do? Break away? Scream? Run? Oh, how different this was than when Bo had put his arm lightly around her. She'd felt safe then. But not this!

The man suddenly released her and she took a step back, but he held onto her shoulders. "You're a big girl now, you know." He looked down at her chest. "You're actually a young woman and a pretty one at that." A humorless smile tipped the corners of his moustache. "You're no fuddy-duddy, are you?"

She shook her head ever so slightly.

"Didn't think so. You know, I could teach you a few things. All you gotta do is trust me."

What things? *Trust him?* She'd never felt so scared in her life. She looked away, lips pressed tightly. Hot tears gathered behind her eyes, but she blinked them back. She didn't want to appear weak. She said nothing. Did nothing.

Abruptly, he let go of her. "You go on home now, girl. But don't you be talkin' to nobody 'bout this."

Talking to them about what? Cindy wondered.

"Just keep it between us." A cloud darkened his face. "You understand? That's part of keepin' a job, ya know, not flappin' your lips 'bout your boss's business."

Cindy nodded, turned, and fled—out the office door, through the barn with its machinery and rusty tools along the sides. Now the tears came and spilled down her cheeks. She gulped air but didn't stop running until she got out to the road and turned toward the migrant camp. She was halfway there before she remembered that Bo had promised to try and meet her when she got off work.

She stopped and looked back the way she'd come, and a quarter mile down the road she saw him running toward her, little puffs of dust swirling up with every footfall.

Relief washed over her. But she couldn't let him see the streaks of tears on her cheeks. Quickly she tried to wipe them away with the short sleeves of her cotton dress ... and then waited as he passed the farmhouse and kept on coming.

And then he was there, crunching to a stop in the dust and gravel. "Hey, babe, told you I'd show if I could." He grinned broadly. "My old man's still mad at me for goin' to look for Jigger yesterday when I was supposed to be runnin' the Ridee-O. So he's got me muckin' out the animal cages. You know the worst smell is those cats—the lion and the bobcat. Oh, man ..." He brushed at the front of his shirt. "Hope it didn't stick to me."

Cindy tried to smile. "You smell just fine."

"So, can I walk you home? Seems like I oughta check in on Jigger, you know, see how those brothers of yours are treatin' him."

"He's okay." A leftover shudder caught her unawares.

He frowned at her. "Are *you* okay?"

She nodded quickly and started walking. "First day, ya know. Got the jitters. Uh ... about Jigger. Best to keep the boss man from seeing him. He don't like dogs."

Bo shrugged. "Yeah well, if he comes 'round causin' problems, just let Jigger go. He can sense when someone don't like him, and he'll hightail it for a hidin' place. He'll be okay. I'm just glad I found him here with your family."

They walked in silence for a while. Cindy wished the walk could last longer, but no sooner had their dilapidated shanty come in view than a black-and-white blur tore toward them and leaped on Bo, nearly knocking him over. "Hey," he laughed, roughhousing with the dog. "Easy now."

Ma came out and insisted that Bo come in and have a piece of banana cake with them. "Forgot to tell you it's Maggie's birthday," Cindy whispered. The boys giggled and poked each other when Bo and Cindy came in, but she ignored them.

Bo nodded at Maggie and grinned. "Happy birthday." The girl flushed and looked down at her lap. "Evening, Mr. Tucker," Bo added, nodding at Cindy's father.

Pa was cool toward Bo, but at least he wasn't rude, and Cindy was surprised a few moments later when Pa commented that working in a carnival and traveling all the time had to be hard. "We never intended to be on the road ourselves, but this is the hand we've been dealt, so we're doin' the best we can."

Bo nodded. "Can't do more." He stuffed the first bite of cake in his mouth and his eyes widened. "*Mm*, this cake's jim-dandy, Mrs. Tucker." The words came out muffled. "You don't know how long it's been since I had *any* kind of home cooking, let alone a piece of cake." In four more mouthfuls, Bo's cake was gone while Cindy was still on her second bite.

Wiping his mouth with the back of his hand, Bo stood up. "Well, thank you very much, Mrs. Tucker." Cindy wondered why he was in such a hurry. Did he feel awkward sitting with her parents? Bo poked a finger at the boys. "I'll be back to check on Jigger again before I pick him up Thursday …" He turned back to Pa. "We have to tear down the carnival Thursday night and pull out for the next town."

Pa grunted and Cindy saw him glance at Ma. He seemed relieved at this news. But Cindy looked at her lap. She didn't even want to think about the carnival leaving town. Not if it took Bo with it.

Bo turned back to the boys. "What if I brought y'all some soda pops next time I come over? What kind you like? Orange? Grape? Coca-Cola?"

The boys jumped to their feet, mobbing Bo and clamoring their choices. He turned to Maggie. "And how 'bout you, birthday lady?"

Maggie blushed again and then smiled shyly. "You got root beer?"

"If they ain't sold out, I'll bring you a bottle."

Chapter 12

BO SLIPPED SEVEN BOTTLES OF COLD SODA into an old gunnysack and took it with him as he slipped away from the carnival the next evening. The cook wasn't likely to notice, not in this heat when the carny crew was grabbing sodas from the barrel of ice faster than they could be replaced. Bo figured he hadn't taken his share anyway the past few days. He had them coming.

He'd been thinking about Cindy all day, and the prospect of seeing her again had made mucking out the animal cages almost bearable. Waiting in the road at the end of the short driveway into the farm where she was working, he watched as five migrant workers came out of the barn, passed him with a nod, and headed toward the camp. A few minutes later, Cindy came out in a rush, looking around anxiously. Was she looking for him?

He waved. "Cindy! Over here!"

Bo's heart leaped when he saw a big smile spread across her face as she hurried straight toward him. But it was already Tuesday, and their last night in Lapeer was Thursday. He *had* to figure out a way to see more of her. The next stop for the Carson Brothers Carnival was Flint, Michigan. That was only twenty or twenty-five miles west. Perhaps he could get away for a day and hitchhike back. But after that came Lansing, that was seventy or eighty miles away, not an easy trip. His dad would have a fit. Well, he'd have to just take one day at a time. See what developed.

He grinned at her as she reached the road. "How'd it go today?"

Instead of answering, Cindy grabbed his arm. "Let's go."

Bo's chest puffed out. He liked the feel of her clinging to his arm—a knight with his damsel. Except … her fingers dug into his flesh, as though she was hanging on for dear life. "Everything okay, Cindy? Don't tell me that lady is givin' you a bad time."

"No." Cindy's voice sounded tight. "She's all right. We get along. I'm … just tired."

Bo shrugged and together they trudged after the cluster of migrant workers on the road ahead of them. The sound of a truck behind them coming over the slight rise in the road from town caused him to glance back. A rusty old pickup was gaining rapidly on them. It skidded to a stop as the driver turned into the farm driveway.

"Hey!" the driver yelled, leaning out the window. "You all done?"

Cindy stopped and turned, but kept a tight grip on Bo's arm. "Yes sir," she called back over the fifty feet that separated them. Bo eyed the man. That big moustache looked familiar … oh yeah, the man coming out of the store in town when he was looking for Jigger.

"Put everything away and lock up?" The man's voice was loud and demanding.

"Yes sir."

For a few moments, the man stared at them and the farm workers farther down the road. "Looks like you had some customers today."

"Yes sir. Had a few."

"Well, they *better* come if they want to keep their jobs." He slammed the truck into gear and spun its tires as he drove into the farmyard.

Bo stared after the truck. "That your boss?"

"Yeah." Cindy clinched his arm as they turned and continued walking. "I don't like him very much."

"Huh. I can see why. You okay?" He hadn't noticed her being so anxious when they met last night, but something was troubling her.

The girl gave a long sigh and looked up at him. "Yeah, now that you're here." He nearly forgot to breathe. Gosh! Those blue eyes of hers were prettier than all the glittering lights under the big top.

"You got a bunch of sodas in there?" She nodded toward the gunnysack clinking against his leg as they walked.

He laughed. "Wouldn't dare show my face without 'em."

When they got to the camp, the rest of the Tucker kids mobbed him for the sodas, and Jigger danced around their feet as if the dog wanted one too. Cindy's mom invited him to stay for something to eat, but Bo could see the remaining beans and rice in the pot was only enough for one more serving. "Uh, thanks anyway, but I need to get back. When I left to … to bring the sodas over, it looked like we were gettin' a pretty big crowd for a Tuesday night."

Bo whistled all the way back to the carnival, already looking forward to seeing Cindy again the next night, but as he was helping the carny crew shut the gates and tie down the tent flaps of the side shows after closing, his father found him. "You're back on the Ridee-O tomorrow," Jeb Bodeen growled. "Just don't go messin' up again, ya hear?"

Back on the Ridee-O! Bo wanted to shout. No more shoveling out stinking straw from the animal cages! And then it hit him … running the Ridee-O meant there was no way he could get away to meet Cindy after she got off work. What would she think when he didn't show up? Would she assume he didn't care? It worried him all night, tossing in his bunk on the crew car of the carnival train. But as he stared into the dark, listening to snores all around him, a plan began to form ...

JOGGING OVER TO THE MIGRANT CAMP early the next morning before he had to report for work, he found Cindy outside, taking care of her littlest sister and baby brother. Jigger was the first one to notice him, and he came racing up with welcoming yaps, his tail wagging so fast it was a blur.

"What you doing here?" Cindy asked, bouncing the baby on her hip. But her smile told him she was pleased.

"Pa put me back on the Ridee-O, so I can't get away tonight. But I wanted ..." Her smile faded. He hated seeing the disappointment in her face, so he hurried on. "Uh, I wanted to ask if you could come on over to the carnival tonight after you get off work. I can get you in again, and there's always hot dogs and lemonade for somethin' to eat. I'll be on the Ridee-O, but I think I can fit you into the doghouse."

"The *doghouse*?" Cindy frowned. "Why would I want to get in a doghouse?"

"To cozy up with me, of course!" Bo said it with a straight face and then grinned. "The doghouse is just the name of the little booth I stand in to operate the ride. You saw it when we rode together."

"Oh, yeah. Well, I don't know." She rolled her eyes at him. "That could be a tight squeeze—ow! Johnny, let go of my hair." She untangled the baby's grip on her straw-colored locks.

"All the better to ..." He was going to say, *"All the better to kiss you with, my dear,"* like the Little Red Riding Hood story, but something warned him not to tease about being a wolf. "All the better to ... to watch the people. Don'tcha think? People-watchin' is the best part of workin' a carnival. There's all kinds."

Cindy set the baby down and wiped Betty's nose with a much-washed handkerchief she pulled out of somewhere. "I don't know. I'd have to ask Ma."

"Let's do it right now. She inside?"

To Bo's delight, Cindy's mother agreed to the plan. "But you be sure to have her back here by ten, okay?"

"Well, I don't have no watch, Mrs. Tucker, but ..." Bo calculated. The only way he could do it would be if he got someone else to shut down the ride and clean up. "But we'll come straightaway." He'd find someone no matter what it took.

Bo fished a dime from his pocket and gave it to Cindy. "This'll get you in the gate. See you tonight!" And he took off jogging back toward town. The migrant camp was barely out of sight when he let out a loud, "Wahoo!"

"So this is the doghouse, huh?"

Bo jumped at Cindy's voice. He'd just thrown the lever to bring the Ridee-O to a stop. Glancing through the window in the side of the operator's booth, his heart beat a bit faster to see her standing there. But the line for the Ridee-O was as long as it had been all evening, and the next bunch of riders was clamoring to get on. "Here, come on in here." He opened the door of the booth. "I'll be back soon as I get this next ride loaded."

"That's okay. I can stand out here."

"Won't be so cozy."

She was still waiting when he stepped back into the booth, moved the big lever forward to start the next ride, and turned the hourglass over to time it. Happy screams told him all was well. Leaning out of the doorway, he held out his hand. "Here, come on in and sit on the bench. There's room for two of us and no need for you to stand up all evening."

Cindy hesitated a brief moment, then took his hand and let him tuck her onto the small bench. "Hey, now, ain't that swell?" he said, squeezing in beside her. But now that she was this close, he realized her eyes looked kind of red and puffy, as if she'd been crying. "Aw, Cindy, what's the matter? Somethin's got you all riled up."

She dropped her head and shook it. "It's nothin', just … work." Turning her face away, she stared out the open window of the booth as the cars of the Ridee-O flashed by, up and down, around and around.

Bo didn't know what to do. She didn't seem to want to talk. And the hourglass was running down. "Uh, you wanna ride again?"

She shook her head, and again he saw the tears at the corners of her eyes.

The hourglass ran out. *Dang.* Bringing the ride to a stop, he jumped out of the booth and unloaded the cars. Once he'd launched the next batch of riders, he squeezed in beside her once more. "C'mon babe, somethin's wrong." Maybe she was as stuck on him as he was on her and just couldn't face the prospect of him leaving the next night. But he had an answer that would cheer her up. He'd hitchhike back to see her, no matter what. "Tell me what's goin' on."

But when she looked up at him, he was startled at the anguished expression on her face. "I … I can't tell nobody. My family needs the money, so I gotta work there whether I like it or not."

Bo's thoughts tumbled. Cindy had said she got along with the woman she was helping take care of. "You mean the commissary?"

She shook her head. "Not the commissary. After ..." Her mouth trembled and she pressed a hand to her face.

"What do you mean, *after*? Is it that Doyle creep?"

She gave a slight nod, but her eyes were frightened.

Heat rose behind Bo's eyes. The image of the man's face yelling at Cindy from the pickup truck rose with it. "That beethead! If he made a pass at you, I'll—"

"Not a pass. He ..." She looked down at her lap, her hands twisting a handful of her dress. Then she blurted, "He's always tryin' to hug me an' touch me in ... in places he has no right."

"He *what*?!" A sudden fury tightened Bo's gut. "Cindy! Did that man—"

"No! No, I push him away, but he's big, and ... oh!" She pointed. The hourglass had run out again.

Swearing under his breath, Bo hurried out of the doghouse to switch out riders for the next customers. Rage boiled within him as unstoppable as a raging river. He was a man, and men had to protect their loved ones. *Yeah, that's right. I love Cindy. And if that sicko touches my girl again, I'll ... I'll ...*

Throwing the lever to send the next riders on their way, Bo sank back onto the bench. "Next time I see that man, I'm gonna—"

"No, no! If he found out that I told someone, I'd lose my job."

"Yeah, but ... that ain't right, Cindy. You should quit. Tell your dad if you need to, but you should get outta there."

"I can't. I just can't!" She sucked in a breath and straightened. "Listen, can we not talk about this? I came over here to have a good time."

Bo frowned. He wasn't ready to let this go. "You get off at seven, and he shows up about then, right?"

She gave a short nod, but suddenly straightened and flipped her hair back. "You said you'd get me a hot dog, and I'm really hungry."

He studied her face. She really *didn't* want to talk about it. He had to respect that. But he wasn't going to forget it. He dug in his pocket. "Here, take these two quarters and go right down there past the carousel, on the right. Get us both a hot dog and something to drink."

She managed a smile and slipped out of the booth.

"Put the works on my dog, babe. I like it all!" he called after her.

ALL DAY THURSDAY BO'S THOUGHTS SWIRLED around Cindy. He wanted to whisk her away, out of the clutches of her slimy boss. He was seventeen and could easily pass for eighteen. Maybe they could get married. Then they could … But every time he got to that point, his mind spun out. What could they do? What could he really do?

As the afternoon dragged on, attendance at the carnival began to slow down. It was the last day, and most of the locals had already come once or twice. As far as Bo and the other carnies were concerned, that was just fine. They were scheduled to jump that night, and teardown was exhausting. It would be nonstop hard physical labor until everything was loaded on the train and they were chugging down the tracks by dawn. If he was lucky, Bo might catch a couple of hours of sleep before it was time to break it all out again and set up in Flint, Michigan, for a Friday night opening.

Somehow, Bo had to pick up Jigger, and he wanted to see Cindy one more time before he left town. But teardown was no time to be away from the carnival. Everyone would be mad at him if he ducked out on that responsibility, and his father would be furious. The only thing he could think of doing was to get someone to cover for him jockeying the Ridee-O during the evening. Then he could meet Cindy as she got off work at seven. Maybe give that filthy boss of hers a talking to, tell him to keep his sticky hands off his girl. *Ha!* Did Cindy know he thought of her as "his girl"? He knew she liked him, could tell by the way she smiled at him. And he definitely liked her. She was a good person—young, innocent, and beautiful. He couldn't let that slob sully her.

"Hey, Cooper!" he called as the older ride jockey walked past. The man who'd filled in when Bo's dad was angry with him ambled over. "You still want this job?"

"Beats buckin' bales for horses and that ornery elephant. Why?"

"I gotta take a break this evening from about six until … until teardown. I'll be back for teardown. Think you could cover for me?"

"Your old man know about this?"

Bo snorted. "Nah. But I can't leave it to him. There's somethin' I gotta do. Somethin' important."

Cooper smiled a toothless grin, deep lines dissecting his weather-beaten face. He took off his soft flat cap and looked off across the midway. "You're keen on a girl, ain'tcha?"

"What if I am? None of your business. I'm just askin' you to cover for me. Whaddaya say?"

"Sure … for a sawbuck."

"*Ten bucks?* You think I'm some kinda hammer-squash? That's robbery!"

"Huh! It ain't robbery. It's a dame, and you're doll dizzy!" Cooper grinned like a sharpie. "And I know you'll ante up."

"Ah, man, give me a break!"

"Just did. I'm willin' to cover for you. Square's square. You get what you want. I get what I want."

Bo blew out a sharp breath. "All right. But you better be here by six. No later."

Cooper put his cap back on and strutted away.

Ten bucks. Nearly a week's pay! Bo shook his head. But … so what? He was gonna see Cindy!

113

Chapter 13

HUGE THUNDERHEADS TOWERED in the southwestern sky as Bo jogged up the road toward the migrant camp. Cooper had been on time, and Bo had three hours. If his dad noticed, he'd be madder'n a bee with its stinger in backward, but at least this time, Bo had turned the Ridee-O over to someone who knew how to operate it.

It was worth the risk. This was too important.

When he got to the farm, he noticed several migrant workers milling around in the entrance to the barn, as if waiting for the commissary to open up. Better not go in yet. He'd go on over to the camp and get Jigger, and then come back. Just so he got here before the boss man did.

Just thinking about that leech putting his paws on Cindy made Bo's blood boil.

Well, nothing was gonna happen tonight. He had plenty of time to get back before seven. Then he could walk Cindy home, maybe stretch it out a bit … like taking a detour to that clearing in the cattails down by the slough. This time of evening, the mosquitoes could be wicked, but it was a secluded place where they could sit and talk for a while. He wondered if she would let him kiss her, not a little peck on the forehead like she was his sister, but a real kiss.

The thought of it quickened his pace as he trotted up the road.

Bo had forty-six dollars in his pocket, money he'd saved over the months. Cooper would get ten. And he'd give each of the Tucker boys a dollar for taking care of Jigger. That was a lot, but they'd done him a big favor looking out for his dog the last few days. Besides, if he wanted a future to develop with Cindy, it'd be good to be appreciated by the whole family. Including her pa.

Thunder rolled somewhere in the distance, but Bo barely noticed, lost in his thoughts.

Mr. Tucker seemed like a hard-edged man. Maybe he ought to tell Cindy's pa what a creep her boss was at work. Surely *he'd* do something about it. But if Bo was hoping to show Mr. Tucker that he cared for his daughter, then he ought to stand up for her too. But how could he do that? He might not even see Doyle this evening, and then he'd be gone with the carnival.

Cindy's Pa didn't seem to be around when Bo got to the camp. Mrs. Tucker was stirring something in a pot over the campfire outside, surrounded by the younger kids. The boys moaned and groaned when he said he'd come to get Jigger, and George, the youngest of the three middle boys, even cried. "Don't want your ol' money. I want our dog! We found him, and we oughta get ta keep him."

"Boys!" Mrs. Tucker shook her spoon at them. "You thank Mr. Bodeen for lettin' you play with his dog."

"Aw, Ma!" Reluctantly the boys backed away, but they tucked their dollars in their pockets.

Mr. Bodeen ... now that had a nice ring to it. Bo's chest expanded. "Uh, ma'am, I'm gonna drop by Cindy's work and see her home, but, uh, would it be okay with you if we took the long way around?"

Mrs. Tucker shot him a look. "*Long way around*? From that farm over yonder? There ain't no long way around."

"I mean … I mean, would you mind if we went for a walk so we can spend some extra time together? I'm leavin' tonight and kinda wanted to say good-bye."

Mrs. Tucker stopped stirring and looked at Bo a long moment. "I s'pose it can't hurt. She ain't had her supper yet, though. And I bet you haven't eaten either." A small smile tipped the corners of her mouth, softening the worn lines in her face. "Sure, sure, why don'tcha. And I'll put somethin' aside for the both of ya. But you watch out you don't get caught in no thunderstorm." She glanced up at the clouds. "Looks to me like it's headin' this way."

"Yes, ma'am!" Bo grinned, backing away. "Thank ya very much, Mrs. Tucker. I'll keep a watch out for that storm."

As he turned and strode down the road, Jigger ran this way and that, nosing into bushes, sniffing at trees. Bo laughed at his antics, happy to have his dog at his side again. But suddenly Jigger took off, streaking after a rabbit he'd scared up. "Jigger! *Jigger!*" Bo yelled. "You get back here!" But bent on chasing the rabbit, the dog soon disappeared from sight.

"Dang it!" If that dog didn't come back soon, he was going to be late picking up Cindy!

By the time Bo rounded up his dog and made it back to the farm, the rusty pickup was already in the barnyard and the sky was growing darker and grumbling with distant thunder. Bo quickened his steps. No one was in sight and the barn doors were shut. Looked as if the commissary was closed. Bo had passed and greeted several of the farm workers on his way from the camp, so hopefully Cindy was finished by now.

And then he heard it … a scream. For a split second, he was confused. Had it come from the house or the barn? Heart in his throat, Bo started off at a run, Jigger at his heels. Only one way to find out.

Pulling open the wide barn doors, Bo darted inside, then stopped, his eyes adjusting to the dim light, searching the piles of hay bales and what he could see of the loft above. Had he imagined it? Where was she?

Then he heard muffled cries behind one of the doors on the right. "No! No! No! Please, no. Please ..." and then another scream, a scream like Bo had never heard before.

Cindy!

His mind exploded! Bo grabbed up a large pipe wrench from a pile of tools and ran to the door. Pulling it open, he saw that beast, Doyle, pinning his Cindy down on a cot. In an instant, Bo saw that he'd pulled up her dress and was trying to hold her flailing arms.

"Get off her!" he screamed. "Get off right now!"

With a flying leap, Jigger sank his teeth into the man's arm. Cursing, Doyle came up and knocked the dog off with a heavy fist. He faced Bo, breathing heavily, fire in his eyes. "You get outta here, boy! This ain't none o' your business. You're trespassin' in here." He raised his fists with the confidence of a John L. Sullivan, and in an instant Bo recognized a trained pugilist. The first blow hit Bo's cheek like a jackhammer, sending him reeling. The second one caught him in the solar plexus.

He doubled over, sucking air, while Jigger barked furiously and leaped at the man again, trying to catch another bite. Then an uppercut smashed into Bo's face, so powerful it picked him off his feet and flipped him backward, crashing into the doorframe. Bo had been in his share of fights, couldn't avoid them as a carny. But this guy was fixing to kill him.

Slumping against the doorframe, Bo saw Cindy sitting up on the cot, her hand clamped over her mouth. He wanted to yell at her to run, but just then a kick caught him in the kidney and he heard a scream from the other side of the room. *Where … what? Screams coming from different places?* He felt disoriented. *I'm losin' it … gonna black out if this guy doesn't lay off.*

Shaking his head, trying to clear his mind, Bo rolled to his knees and realized he still had the wrench in his hand. Another kick was coming for his head when he dodged it, clambered to his feet, and swung a roundhouse.

The smack and crunch of bone stopped everything as the big man reeled, then thudded to the floor like a collapsing pillar. He lay on his face, not moving, as Bo tried to catch his breath, hovering over his assailant with the wrench still in his hand.

An eternity passed.

As if from a distant place, he heard Cindy's voice. "Bo! Bo! Are you all right?" From the corner of his vision he saw her struggle to her feet, pull down her dress, and stare at Doyle. Bo finally stood up as Cindy looked up at him, her face ashen. "Will … will he be okay?"

Bo swallowed. His throat felt dry and thick. This had to be a bad dream … a nightmare! He gaped at the wrench in his hand and dropped it as if it had suddenly turned hot.

"Will … will he be okay?" Cindy asked again, her voice shaking. But the words sounded surreal. Why would she even ask about Doyle's welfare after what he had tried to do to her?

Slowly, his body screaming with the kicks and punches he'd endured, Bo leaned down and saw a small puddle of blood spreading from the wound on Doyle's temple. "I don't know." He straightened. Anger wrestled with the pain in his gut as he looked at Cindy, hair disheveled, her face tear-stained. Her dress was torn at the shoulder. *Torn!*

Trying to keep his voice level he asked, "How about you? Are you hurt? Did he … did he actually … you know?"

"No! No ..." Her lips trembled. "But he was fixin' to." She turned away, using the hem of her dress to mop at her eyes. Jigger whined and went to her, and she squatted down and hugged the dog's neck.

Bo glanced again at the man at his feet and noticed that all his clothes were still on. Relief washed over him. He'd stopped that fornicatin' beethead in time. Still, the man had violated Cindy horribly. He deserved ... Bo remembered helping a carnival vet geld a horse once to make him tamer, more manageable. That's what oughta happen to this guy!

But a sense of urgency rose in his sore gut. They couldn't just stand there. They had to go ... get help ... something! Squatting down, he shook Doyle's shoulder. No response. Putting both hands under the man's side, he heaved and rolled him onto his back. Bo's eyes narrowed. He'd never forget that face for as long as he lived. The big moustache drooped over the man's slack mouth. Blood was coagulating in the wound at his temple.

And then he realized the man wasn't breathing.

Bo's own breath caught. *Oh no! What have I done?*

The room suddenly filled with bright light, then was gone, followed by a loud crack of thunder that seemed to shake the whole barn. For the first time, Bo heard rain smacking at the window. He'd promised Ma Tucker he'd get Cindy home before the storm ...

"Is he dead?" Cindy's voice, barely above a whisper, carved into his thoughts. Jigger sniffed the man on the floor and whined as Bo checked Doyle again, putting his fingers to the man's throat, trying to find a pulse. Nothing. He laid his ear to the barrel chest but heard no thumps.

Panic, real and urgent now, bubbled into Bo's throat. "I think he's gone." He stood up suddenly, his own heart racing. "We gotta get outta here. I gotta get you home. I promised your ma."

She gasped, eyes wide with fright. "Oh, Bo. Shouldn't we tell the police or somebody?"

"No! No. We gotta go!" But where? Where could he go? He looked around wildly, as though an answer might be posted on the bare stud walls of Doyle's office.

"But, Bo—"

"Look! I'm ... I'm just a carny—an outsider. We don't count in this world." He threw up his hands. "Anytime some of the boys get into it with townies—somethin', anything, doesn't have to be serious—the Chief ships 'em out to the next city, 'cause there ain't no justice for carnies."

He stared at Doyle again, his own breath now coming in short gasps. "I'd be charged with murder. No, no ... I gotta go. Gotta get outta here." He reached for Cindy's hand. "But you wouldn't be blamed. I'll take you home, or ..." Another flash of light, another burst of thunder. Rain pounded on the window. " Or better yet, once I'm gone, you should run up to the house. The missus, she'll call for help. Tell 'em you had nothing to do with it. You could say I came in to rob him or something."

"Oh, Bo! I'd never say that! You saved me." Cindy's fingers curled tightly around his. "Besides ..." An edge hardened her voice. "I'm just as much an outsider as you are. Migrants get railroaded all the time for things they didn't do."

He groaned. "Oh, Cindy, I'm so sorry." Taking her into his arms, he held her for a long moment, kissing her hair. This was going to ruin her life, no matter what happened. Then, forcing himself, he let go of her and turned toward the door, Jigger at his heels.

"Wait! I'm comin' with you—but I gotta get something first."

Startled, Bo watched as Cindy took a key off a nail hidden behind one of the studs, opened the bottom drawer of the desk, and pulled out a pouch. She zipped it closed without showing him what was inside and held it up. "This is the money Doyle owes Pa. If I leave it here, my family'll never get it. I'm gonna take it to 'em."

Urgency fired all Bo's nerve endings. "Cindy, if you're coming with me, we can't go see *nobody*. Because somebody's gonna find him, and the police will be investigating. They'll figure out your folks have seen us—seen us *after*—and they'll be in trouble for helping us get away."

"But ..." She stared at the pouch, seeming to weigh what he'd said. "All right." She slipped the loop over her wrist. "I'll give it to 'em later."

Bo could hardly believe his ears ... or his own heart. Was this girl really going to come with him? A spark of hope—joy?—fought with the panic and pain in his gut. If they were together, they'd make it. He'd see to it.

"Come on, then!" He grabbed her hand. "Let's go, Jigger!"

The black-and-white dog dashed out ahead of them into the raging thunderstorm.

Chapter 14

THE THUNDERSTORM NEARLY DROWNED THE YELLOW DOG and me before we got back to Manna House. And as soon as they buzzed us in, Dandy shook himself all over the foyer like a lawn sprinkler going off. Luckily, Sarge, the ex-marine night manager for the shelter, hadn't come on duty yet or she would've kicked us both out for sure. When it came to dogs, she was nearly as lowdown as Gabby's jerk husband.

The double doors swung open, and Gabby Fuzz Top Fairbanks cruised in and over to the reception desk, giving me the once-over as she passed. "So where have you been?"

"Out. Don't it look like it? *Humph.* Gotta get me some dry clothes. Here …" I tossed her a rag. "You can clean up the dog. An' if I was you, I'd put him up in the bunkroom 'fore Sarge shows up."

I don't mind helping out with Miz Martha's dog, but some responsibilities—like cleanup—oughta be done by family.

I got changed and downstairs in time for supper, but Gramma Shep—Why can't they call her Miz Martha?—was too busy taking care of Tanya's little Sammy to talk much. Tanya, a tall, skinny black girl, had left early that morning and pretty much dumped her son on Martha. And she still wasn't back by supper. In fact, she didn't get back till almost curfew.

Sarge, who was on duty by then, jumped all over her. "You're outta here, girl. There's no bed for you gettin' in so late."

"But I got here before curfew, Sarge! Look. It's only 7:57!"

"So? This isn't a babysitting service, Tanya. *Capisce?*" The night manager gave the side of her head a light slap. "What were you thinking, leaving Sammy alone here all day while you were out? Rules are rules, no?"

"I know! I shouldn't a' done that. It—it was j-just ..."

I couldn't believe it. That girl—who was probably as street-tough as I am—began sobbing and whimpering like a heartbroken war bride. Her little boy, Sammy, clung to her like a wet dress, and poor Gramma Shep stood there wringing her hands as if she wanted to rescue the whole bunch of them.

Finally, Gabby stepped in. "Uh, Sarge? Why don't we leave Tanya's case till tomorrow when Mabel can decide what to do? If you want, they can move to our bunk room tonight. I'll take responsibility for the decision."

Oh yeah! I rolled my eyes. Fuzz Top was homeless herself, but because she works at the shelter, she thinks she can give up space in our bunkroom just to make peace. No wonder she'd let that husband of hers run all over her.

"Humph," Sarge grumbled as she walked away, firing a final shot back at Gabby—and me, too, I guess. "Some people sure do feel free to bend the rules. Like a certain *dog* that's not supposed to be here. No?"

Martha and I watched a little TV and then headed up to bed. As we walked into the bunkroom, Tanya whispered, "Shh. Just got Sammy to sleep."

Huh! Tanya, Sammy, Martha, Fuzz Top, me, and Dandy—too many. "Howza body s'posed ta sleep packed up in here like a bunch a' sardines … Too many lungs usin' up all the air … Humph. Dandy an' me gonna go sit inna lounge till you all go ta sleep …"

I fell asleep in that chair and didn't wake up until the morning—and with such a crook in my neck I couldn't even turn it to the right. Next couple of nights I did the bunkroom thing, crowded as it was. Just went to bed so late it made me groggy in the morning. Guess that's why when I woke up early Friday and saw Gabby fixing to take Dandy out for a walk, I growled, "Hey, whatcha doin'?"

"I need to get out. You can sleep in today. Where do you go— the cemetery?"

"Cemetery don't open till eight-thirty. Gotta go someplace else." I rolled over and was nearly back to sleep when I realized Fuzz Top might put two and two together and conclude I knew too much about Graceland Cemetery. Should've kept my mouth shut. My visits there were no one else's beeswax.

But she never said nothing about it, so I was probably okay. In fact, when she got back, her only concern was that Sarge was breathing down our necks. Sarge was dead-set against harboring a dog in the shelter—said it was against the rules. Fuzz Top had negotiated a brief exception, but the deadline for getting Dandy out was tomorrow!

Even that deadline faded in the afternoon when we had a surprise birthday party for Estelle Williams, the Manna House cook. I doubted they'd been able to keep it a surprise from her given how fancy she was dressed in a long, flowing blue thing with silver fringes. Made her look like cool water flowing in and out of any room she entered. But Mister Bentley—the doorman in the building where Gabby used to live—got Estelle real good. I think he's sweet on her. After lunch, he brought in this beautiful cake for her to share with everyone. Only thing, *hee hee*, it wasn't a cake at all. It was a round foam-rubber pillow all decorated with frosting to look like a birthday cake.

When Estelle tried to cut it, her knife wouldn't go in until she stabbed it like she was chipping ice with a pick. We were all laughing and yelling so hard, I barely heard Estelle say, "Harry Bentley! I oughta throw this whole frosted pillow in your face, but I'm too … I'm too—" And then she did it! Splattered it all over his shiny dome.

Finally, when they got the mess all cleaned up, someone brought out a real cake, and we finished up the party in style.

Knowing Sarge was still on the warpath for Dandy, I took him out for a real long walk that afternoon. Even missed supper, and didn't come back until just before curfew. I slipped in, hoping I could get the dog up to our bunkroom without Sarge even noticing, but Dandy blew it for us when he started barking with joy upon seeing Miz Martha in the multipurpose room.

"Oh, Dandy," Martha said, "good boy, good doggy. Are you hungry? You are? Oh, look at your red bandana. Look, Gabby, Lucy dressed him up!… Yes, yes, good doggy. I missed you too."

Sarge was right there as though we'd rung her alarm bell. She crossed her arms and swaggered up to me like a drill instructor. "Rules are rules, Lucy Tucker. No pets at the shelter. *Capisce?*"

"This ain't the army, and you ain't commander in chief."

"And this ain't no pet hotel. The dog goes—tomorrow."

I had a mind to punch her one in the nose. "Dandy's *family*. Miz Martha's family. Her mean ol' son-in-law already kicked the dog *an'* Miz Martha out. Ya gonna do it again? Huh? Huh?"

"'Course not. Miss Martha can stay. But the dog gotta go. *Sabato.*"

"Humph!" What could I do? I may be tough, but I'm too old to take her on like I might've back in the day. Nevertheless, I growled, "Over my dead body," as I pushed past her.

Poor Miz Martha. As I left the room, I heard her say, "What does the night lady mean, the dog has to go? Not Dandy. She's not talking about Dandy, is she?"

I went upstairs to our darkened bunk room, not wanting to let anyone see the tears that broke out of my eyes. It wasn't fair what was happening to my friend. She was losing it a little bit—calling her daughter Gabby by the wrong name and getting confused from time to time—but she still had a good heart, the best friend I'd had in years, and now she was getting mistreated again.

And I knew what it was to have a dog as your best friend …

Well, I wasn't gonna let it happen. I'd find a way. But as I crawled onto my bunk and turned toward the wall, I began to think of all the times in my life when I *hadn't* found a way, at least not like Ma had seemed to be able to do when I was a girl. Of course, she never took credit for it. She always said God was the way-maker, making a way out of no way.

Making a way out of no way! I thought about that for a while. Maybe I owed God another chance. Maybe in a situation like this where it wasn't for my own benefit, He'd listen. The idea played over and over in my mind until in stammering whispers, I tried. "Uh, God? If you're there, I need Ya to do a favor … not for me, mind Ya, but for one of your *good* lambs—well, I guess she ain't a lamb no more. Anyway, she's lost a lot, don't let her lose no more. Don't let them take away her dog. Can Ya do that … for her?"

I had no idea whether God heard me or not, but I did go to sleep. Didn't even hear Tanya come in to put Sammy down.

I awoke from an intense dream. Bo and I and Jigger were running along the tracks in the rain, checking the boxcars of a slow-moving train, looking for one with an open door into which we could climb and escape the pounding rain. Suddenly, Jigger stopped in front of us and began barking, his hackles up ...

But it wasn't Jigger's barking that woke me up. I listened ... and in a moment realized it was Dandy! Angry barks and growls from somewhere downstairs. Was Sarge trying to get rid of him in the middle of the night? The thought bounced me out of bed—well, not quite like a jack-in-the-box, but I did get moving. How dare she! I staggered to the stairs, my rheumatiz causing me to trip over my clumsy old feet as I clung to the banister and hobbled down, step by step in the dim light of the stairwell exit signs. Ahead of me, making the turn at the landing, I glimpsed Fuzz Top descending at top speed.

"Call him off!... Umph!" That wasn't Sarge's voice! It was a man yelling from below! "Get that damn dog off me—Ow! Ow! My hand! You—" A string of curses followed. "Call him off, I tell you, or I'll cut him!"

Dandy yelped in pain.

I tried to hurry, past the door into the multipurpose room and on down to the lower level where the kitchen and dining room was.

Gabby got down there well ahead of me, and I heard her yell, "Dandy!"—followed by another woman yelling, "Watch out! He's got a knife!" The second voice was Sarge.

What in tarnation?

A couple of other residents scurried past me—darn my rheumatiz—and got to the dining room before me while Sarge shouted, "Grab the knife, Fairbanks!... And untie me now!... Call 9-1-1. I've got it!"

I pushed into the room behind the others to see Sarge pinning a man to the floor while Dandy played tug-o'-war with his outstretched arm. "Call off the dog! He's tearing my hand off!"

"Lie still, buster. Then we'll call off the dog." Sarge looked up and spotted us bug-eyed spectators at the door. "Somebody, turn the lights on!"

Guess it was Tina, carrying a plastic baseball bat, who flipped the switch, and then I saw the blood.

"Somebody tie his free hand to that table leg there," Sarge barked. "Tie his feet too. Get those dish towels or an extension cord—anything!" Once the man was securely tied up, she sighed and got up. "Okay, Fairbanks. Call the dog off—and we better wrap something around this sucker's wrist. There's a lot of blood there."

A lot, for sure! As Gabby eased Dandy away, I shuffled forward and knelt beside our dog. Then I realized most of the blood on the floor had come from a wound in Dandy's side, and Dandy was whining with the pain. A knife lay several feet away on the floor, probably where Sarge had kicked it. Still trembling, Dandy rested his head in my lap and looked up at me, his eyes pleading for help.

"Oh, Dandy, Dandy," I moaned, cradling his head. "Help's comin', help's comin'." I didn't know what else to do.

But once the police and paramedics arrived, it was all Gabby and Sarge interrupting each other, telling about the intruder and how Dandy had warned them and sacrificed himself in an attempt to protect us all. Finally, one of the cops scooped up Dandy and headed up the stairs. Took me a minute to get to my feet, but I followed Fuzz Top outside and saw the cop had already put Dandy in the backseat of a squad car parked behind the ambulance. Gabby started to climb into the backseat of the squad car too.

"Hey, where you goin' with my dog?"

Gabby looked back at me. "This kind officer offered to take Dandy to a vet hospital."

"Well, I'm comin' too!"

"Lucy! You can't come dressed like that."

"Been dressed better. Been dressed worse." Even though I only had on my pajamas and my purple knit hat, I pushed her aside. "Officer, unlock that front door so Fuzz Top here can ride shotgun. I'm sittin' back here with my dog!" But I did feel a little funny. Usually sleep in my clothes because you never know when you might get rousted out of a place, but at Manna House they want you to wear pajamas, even give you loaners if you don't have your own. So ... there I was in them baggy flannel things, but I wasn't gonna be left behind.

As we raced through red lights—siren howling—I looked down at Dandy, who again had his head in my lap. His eyes looked up at me, and in the glare of passing streetlights I could see blood still oozing from his side. I sure hoped I wouldn't have to give Miz Martha bad news come morning.

I pulled off my purple knit hat—didn't think Estelle Williams would mind—and began wiping up the blood. After all, some responsibilities—like cleanup—oughta be done by family.

Chapter 15

SOME RESPONSIBILITIES—LIKE CLEANUP—*oughta be done by family.* That's what Ma always said. And she and Pa had always been there to do it, no matter how tough life got. But as Cindy slogged through the rain, hanging on to Bo with one hand and clasping the money pouch in the other, her despair grew deeper. This was one mess even her parents couldn't clean up.

Of course, Cindy knew there'd been a lot of things they hadn't been able to "clean up"—not the Dust Bowl, not the loss of their farm, or the time the car broke down and left them stranded for three days in the middle of a blizzard, and not the way the growers took advantage of the farm workers. Still, they'd always stuck together as a family.

But here she was running … running away from family.

"Where we goin'?" she gasped as they passed the lot where the carnival lights still shone through the rain. "Thought you said you were going to tear down and move on tonight."

"Yeah. It's jump night, but we can't go with 'em." Bo hunched his shoulders against the rain and leaned closer to her ear. "Ain't like I'm some drunk and disorderly rousty the local sheriff would just as soon see hit the road as lock him up. When they find your boss, it'll be a murderer they're looking for, and they'll search everywhere, startin' with the carny train."

"But Bo! Where we goin' then?"

Bo's pace suddenly slowed. "I … I dunno, but we gotta get out of town. Maybe we can catch a ride on the highway."

"Hitchhike?"

He didn't answer.

"Bo, if we're standin' out in the rain with our thumbs up—a guy, a girl, a dog, and no duffle or suitcase—everyone who passes will remember such a peculiar scene. That don't make no sense!"

"Yeah, you're right." He picked up the pace again. "Let's head for the tracks. Maybe we can hop a freight. Jigger! Come on."

Though Cindy followed, she hung back enough so she had to reach forward to keep a hold of Bo's hand. "But you said they'd search the train, first thing."

"The carny train. It's parked on a siding. Maybe we can find another train going east … maybe to Detroit. We can lose ourselves easy in a big city."

Big city? Cindy had never lived in a big city. Pa hated cities. They'd even looped all the way south through Indiana to avoid Chicago when they came to Michigan. Still, Bo's idea made sense, and she knew they had to get out of the rain pretty soon. Summer or not, she was getting chilled to the bone.

They took side streets through Lapeer, hoping to attract less attention. But it might have been a mistake. Every dog on every block set to barking as they passed. Most were tied or fenced in yards, but at one point a dog twice Jigger's size raced out to challenge him. They circled each other, hackles up. Jigger marked a tree, and the other dog marked over it. But finally, Bo succeeded in getting Jigger to follow him as they made their escape. The "king of the block" celebrated his success at repelling intruders by throwing a few halfhearted barks after them.

Just south of town, Cindy saw the circus train sitting on its siding, but Bo steered them clear of it, heading for the station on the mainline of the *Grand Trunk Western.* "When we pulled into Lapeer, one of the yardmen told me three passenger trains stop here every day … from each direction. If we have to, we can take one of those. I've got some money, but I don't like the idea of facing the ticket man and all the other people we'd meet on the train. Hey …" He pulled on her hand. "There's a freight sittin' on the eastbound track."

Its whistle wailed in the distance, and Bo pulled hard on Cindy's hand and began to run. "Come on, babe! This could be our chance."

Rain fell harder, and soon they were out of the yard where the dirt along the tracks had been pounded smooth by foot and truck traffic. Cindy's ankles threatened to turn on the uneven crushed stone ballast, and she nearly stumbled. "Bo, I can't. Slow down."

He kept pulling on her hand. "Gotta find an open boxcar!" But they were only passing hoppers full of coal.

The whistle moaned again, and down the line came the *bam, bam, bam* as the couplers took up the slack between cars and the train inched forward.

"There," urged Bo, panting hard, "car after next. Door's open."

The train's speed was catching up to theirs. Soon they would be falling behind.

"Faster, babe!"

Cindy concentrated on keeping her footing and running faster until Bo was no longer pulling on her hand. And then she was there, alongside the gaping maw of the open boxcar. But how could she keep running and jump that high? The train was matching their speed as Jigger loped along beside them, barking at the train like some dogs chase cars.

"Grab that bar!" Bo pointed to a bar at the front of the door. "And swing yourself ... up in there!"

She grabbed and hung on. The train's pull helped her keep pace, but she couldn't add a jump.

"Here ... here, let me do it ..." Bo pushed her aside and accomplished the move on his second try, rolling into the dark interior of the boxcar as Cindy and Jigger ran alongside. But she'd fallen behind a couple of paces. Was he leaving her? After all this, was he just looking out for himself? And then he was back at the doorway, hanging onto the inside of the door as he reached his other arm out to her.

The train continued to gain speed while Cindy's legs got heavier and her lungs screamed for more air. One final push! If she didn't make it this time, he'd be gone ... out of her life forever. With all her strength, she pounded the stony path, ignoring the pain of wobbling ankles as she tried to keep her balance and reach Bo's outstretched arm.

And then he had her, and in one mighty move pulled her off the ground, dragging her over the rough threshold, and into the boxcar.

They lay in a heap on the straw-strewn floor, gasping for breath for a minute ... two minutes ... until Cindy sat up with a start. Jigger's barks had faded with the *clickety-clack, clickety-clack* of steel on iron rails. "Jigger! What about Jigger?"

Bo jumped to the doorway. "Jigger ... come on, boy! Come on, you can make it! Come, Jigger! Come!"

Cindy leaned out also. She didn't think there was any way that dog could jump that high while running at full speed. She grabbed onto Bo to keep her balance against the rock of the train as it gained speed, but Jigger was still coming, racing along as fast as his legs would carry him. She watched while Bo called encouragement, but the train was winning, and Jigger was falling back ... back to the coal cars ... and then as the train went around a slight bend, the little black-and-white piebald dog was out of sight. Cindy sat back on the floor, the wind from the moving train swirling the rain into the car.

"Ji-i-i-gger!" Bo cried one more time at the top of his lungs. His shoulders sank as he turned to stare at Cindy. Then he looked out again. When he turned back to her, pain etched his face, and she knew he was deciding whether to jump for it and go after his dog or remain with her.

After a moment, he let go of the bar at the edge of the door and plunked down beside her. He crossed his arms over his knees and leaned forward, burying his face. Cindy reached out to rub his back, but it was as though she'd touched a nerve that released all the pain and tension of the evening—the attack on her, his fight with Doyle in which he took some mighty hard licks, the swing with the wrench that killed the man, their run for safety, and now the loss of his beloved dog ... his broad shoulders shook with quiet sobs.

What could she say? He'd abandoned his dog in order to take her to safety. She laid her head on his shoulder as she held him and just stayed that way until his breathing returned to normal. She wanted to say something—thank him or say Jigger was smart and would be okay—but everything she thought of seemed like offering dust to a thirsty man.

They sat in silence for fifteen or twenty minutes until Cindy realized the *clickety-clack* rhythm of the wheels had changed. She raised her head and listened more carefully.

"Bo, we're slowin' down. Get up."

"What for?"

"What if someone sees us in here?"

"I'll check." He got to his feet and slowly rolled the big door closed as if he were shutting the gate on their personal prison. Maybe that was why he left it open a couple of inches and looked soulfully at her in the dim light. "I'm sorry, Cindy. I never shoulda brought you along. You didn't do anything wrong. You'd be okay if you'd gone home. They can't pin anything on you."

He peeked through the crack in the door. "I think we're stoppin', and the rain's lettin' up too. We haven't come more'n a dozen miles or so. Look … you oughta walk back. Go home. Tell your dad what happened. Tell him the whole thing, and let him figure out what to do."

Cindy stared at Bo's back, feeling dust devils of confusion spinning in her gut. Maybe he was right. What had she done? Everything else had happened *to* her, but she'd been the one to run. That one thing had been *her* choice, and she could see that it might change her life forever. Was there still time to turn back? Bo seemed to think so. Go home, let Pa handle it! Should she take his advice? But to do so would be to leave Bo … maybe forever.

She watched as he sat down on the straw facing her. The train coasted slower and slower, and then there was a screech of brakes and a series of jerks. "Hey …" He tried to sound upbeat. "You could probably even find Jigger. Take him back to the boys. Nothin'd make them happier. Right?"

Cindy raised her right arm with the money pouch hanging from her wrist. "And what about this?"

Bo shrugged. "What about it?"

"You know! What if the sheriff's lookin' for it? He'll know I was there!"

"But why would he be lookin' for it?"

"Records. Mr. Doyle kept records. Made me account for every penny. I'm sure he had it written down somewhere."

Bo threw up his hands as the train came to a complete stop. "How should I know what you should do with it? Tell your Pa 'bout that too. He'll know what to do. All I know is, you gotta go!" He said it like a verdict.

Cindy stared at him in shock. Was he trying to get rid of her? She'd run off from her family, a man had been killed, and the guy she thought wanted her to share his life was now telling her to leave. Tears sprang to her eyes. She felt alone. She'd never asked for any of this, but now her whole life—the only one she'd ever known—had blown away. She tried to control the sobs, and at first, as Bo moved closer and slipped his arm around her, she jerked away and didn't want him to touch her.

"Oh, Cindy. I'm sorry. I don't want you to go, but I'm afraid …" He persisted, drawing her closer. Slowly her resistance melted. She lay down on her side on the straw, and even in the dark, she knew that he lay down beside her, his hand lightly touching her back. They stayed that way, Cindy drifting off to sleep from time to time, hoping the train would start again soon. Once it got up to speed, he couldn't ask her to jump, and in thinking that, she knew she'd made her choice.

Cindy awoke to see golden light coming through the cracked door. The train still wasn't moving. Bo's steady breathing assured her he was in a deep sleep. She got up, crept to the door, and peered out. The storm had passed, and it promised to be a bright day.

A loud bark from below made her jump.

"Bo! Bo! It's Jigger! Get up. He found us." She pushed on the door, rolling it aside, and as soon as it was open a foot, Jigger leaped into the boxcar. The pads of his feet left bloody streaks on Bo's shirt as the dog bowled his master over with excitement, licking his face as though it were cotton candy.

Chapter 16

MAGGIE TUCKER WAS TIRED OF TAKING CARE of three-year-old Betty and baby Johnny. Why wasn't Cindy home yet? Ma had been holding supper so late everyone was getting cranky. And now it was raining, and it was all the harder to keep the babies corralled under the awning stretched between the shack and their car. Johnny made a dash for the fire pit, oblivious of the storm. He liked to play in the ashes. They were cold now, of course, but someday he was going to grab a live coal and set off screaming to high heaven.

She retrieved him and took the opportunity to peer across the beet fields toward the white farmhouse where her sister worked in the commissary. She was probably hiding somewhere out of the rain, sparking with that carny guy who kept hanging around.

The door of the shack opened. "Bring the young'uns on in," Ma said. "Can't wait no more on your sister."

Finally!

Maggie herded Betty and Johnny toward the door, glancing once more toward the farm to see if Cindy was yet coming along the road. What she saw through the rain caught her breath. "Pa! Hey Pa! There's a police car turning into the boss man's place."

"Maggie, get on in here like your ma said." Pa called from inside.

She knew he didn't like to get up once he sat down to rest, but what if something had happened to Cindy? "Pa, ya gotta come here."

"I'm not about to come out there. It's time to eat. What makes you think it's a police car, anyway?"

"Got a red cherry light goin' 'round on top. And I saw the man get out. He's wearin' a uniform."

"Well, it ain't none of our business. Now get on in here for supper."

Maggie pushed the two little ones ahead as she came through the door, a big pout on her face.

"Sit down so Ma can pray."

Everyone got settled around the table, and Ma blessed the food and began serving up the soup.

Between spoonfuls, Pa kept looking at Maggie. "Why the sourpuss?"

"It ain't fair me having to take care of the babies after workin' all day in the field. You oughta tell Cindy to come straight home."

"Well, she's s'pose'ta." Ma sighed. "But sometimes when you're workin' for someone else, you gotta do a little extra."

"Yeah, but then why's the police car over there?" Maggie was more inclined to think her sister was with Bo. But why not kick up a little dust? It was Cindy's fault she got stuck with the extra childcare, anyway.

"Police car?" Ma tucked her chin and frowned. Apparently she hadn't heard what Maggie had said to Pa. "Whadda you carryin' on 'bout, girl?"

"I done tol' ya, already."

"Watch your mouth, girl."

"Well, Pa heard me. I said a police car just turned in to the boss man's place."

"What? A police car?"

Pa spread his hands over the table. "Now Harriet, ain't none of our business."

"Whaddya you mean? That's our firstborn workin' over there!" Ma got up and pulled back the raggedy tea towel she had thumbtacked up for a window curtain. "Lester ... Lester!" Her voice became urgent. "There sure enough *is* a police car there, and it looks like an ambulance too. You better get over there and see what's happenin'."

Pa got to his feet and headed for the window. The boys jumped up, too, and pushed their way in for a look. "Don't get all het up, now." Pa craned his neck this way and that as he peeked out. "Probably just that woman havin' her baby. You said she was doin' poorly, didn't ya? Ain't that why Cindy's over there in the first place? Probably why she's late. Everybody sit down, now, and finish your food. I'll run on over there directly and check it out. But right now it's suppertime."

They finished their meal in silence. Then Pa got up and took his hat off the nail on the wall.

Maggie wiped her mouth on the back of her hand. "Can I go with you?"

Pa stared at her a moment as if he was considering the idea, then he shook his head. "Still rainin', girl. 'Sides, too many people wouldn't be welcome. Best stay here and help Ma."

"But I'm tired of doin' all Cindy's work." Maggie turned and stalked away. "She better get back here soon!"

MAGGIE STOLE A LOOK AT THE FARM whenever she could while helping to clean up from supper and get the little ones in bed. In the gray of the storm, she saw two other dark cars turn in and park in the farmyard. They looked like police cars, but they didn't have a red cherry on top. Then the ambulance left, but it didn't turn on its red light or sound its siren. Finally, through the evening's gloom, she saw her father returning, head down, hat pulled low even though the rain had stopped. He turned into the lane for the migrant camp, walking slowly toward their cabin, his shoulders sagging.

"Where's Cindy?" Ma asked as soon as Pa came through the door.

Pa shook his head and clinched his lips in a straight line.

"Well, when's she comin' back?"

Pa looked at Maggie. "Boys down?"

"They're sleepin' in the car. Is Mrs. Doyle all right?"

"Yeah, she's okay. Maggie ..." He turned to her. "You go check on the boys, tell 'em a story or somethin'. I need to talk private with your ma."

Maggie recognized the steely look in her father's eyes and protested only with a pout and a toss of her head as she went out the door. But outside, she turned back and stood with her ear to the door ...

"... didn't just say he died. Said he'd been killed. Hit in the head with a wrench or something, right there in his own barn."

"Lord, have mercy! But why?"

"Who knows?... Reckon there's lots who don't like him, but this ... this is ..."

"What about Cindy? She staying with the missus?"

"Didn't see hide nor hair of her."

"Les-ter! What're you sayin'?"

"Calm down, now. My guess is she mighta seen somethin'—maybe the attacker, or who knows what?—and ran off scared. I s'pect she'll come around once she settles down."

"That ain't good enough! Cindy—"

Maggie couldn't make out the rest of what Ma said because it was garbled by her sobs and crying. She turned away from the cabin door and stuck her head in the back door of the old Dodge. Both Willy on the seat and George on the floor were asleep.

Tom sat up in the front seat. "What's happenin'?"

"*Shh.* Pa's back, but Cindy's still … she's still at work. You lay back down and go to sleep, or I'll tell Ma."

Tom frowned but laid back down, and Maggie tiptoed back to the door of the shack. Pa and Ma were arguing back and forth, talking over one another so she couldn't decipher what they were saying, so she opened the door and went in. That stopped 'em.

Pa frowned at her. "Thought I tol' you to check on your brothers!"

"I did. Willy and George are out, and Tom was almost asleep." Before Pa asked the question that would send her back outside, she added, "Couldn't be tellin' Tom no story without wakin' up the others."

Pa rolled his eyes in surrender and turned back to Ma. Maggie shrank into the corner, hoping to hear as Pa kept his voice low. "As I was sayin', the sheriff figures it was someone from the carnival, maybe a gang of those guys who came to rob the boss, but I don't think so, because the moneybox for the commissary was right there in the drawer, and the ledger Cindy was keepin' showed nothin' was missing."

Ma's eyes widened. "That must mean she finished out her work day if she tallied up everything. Oh Lester, we gotta go lookin' for her. What if she was kidnapped or somethin'? Did you tell the sheriff our daughter was missin'?"

"No, I didn't! Think about it, Harriet! There's been a murder, and our daughter's gone missin'! What's that look like?"

Their voices were getting louder. Maggie looked from one to the other trying to follow the conversation.

"It looks like our daughter might be in trouble! That's what it looks like to me!"

"Oh yeah? Well, what direction do you think the investigation's gonna take if we tell the sheriff our daughter was in that barn? At this point, he figures it was some carnival bums, but even still, he questioned *me*! He wanted to know where I'd been since we came in from the field and who could vouch for me. Then he wanted me to tell him the names of every worker who'd gone over there to the commissary. How was I s'posed to know that? But believe me, those carnival folks aren't the only outsiders around here. We're strangers, too, ya know. And if we tell him our daughter's missing—which we don't know yet—he'll be all over us."

"I don't care! I'm gonna look for my daughter." Ma grabbed a shawl, threw it around her shoulders, and headed for the door, even as another crack of thunder shook the windows.

"Hold on a minute. I don't know where you're gonna look, but was thinkin' 'bout this whole mess as I walked back here, and I think we gotta hit the road again. That carnival is pullin' out tonight, and as soon as it's gone, all the sheriff's attention is gonna be on this migrant camp."

Ma stopped halfway through the door and looked back at him, shaking her head with an incredulous look on her face. "But ... but wouldn't that make us look all the more guilty if we pull up stakes and hightail it outta here?"

"Well ..." Pa seemed arrested by her logic. "Maybe ... But our work here's over anyway. Who's gonna pay us with the boss man gone? He's the one who owns this whole place."

"What about the sugar mill? There's still a lot of beets in the ground that they're gonna want to process."

"Maybe so, but this was a murder, Harriet! Those beets'll rot in the ground before they get things straightened out enough to put a crew back to work. There isn't even a way to collect the money he owes us. How can we prove it? Who would pay us?"

"Well, I'm still gonna go look for Cindy. Wherever she is, she needs me!"

Looping the shawl over her head, Ma slammed the door as she headed out into the rain. Maggie watched Pa as he removed his hat and scratched his head. He hung the hat on its nail and turned to stare at her for a few moments. Finally, his eyes dropped. "Didn't mean for you to be hearin' all that, child. Best if you get to bed now. We'll figure out what to do in the mornin'." He sat down at the table and reached out to turn down the light in the kerosene lamp.

"Pa! But … but if we leave without Cindy, how would she ever catch up with us?"

Pa just shook his head, his shoulders sagging as he stared at the flickering flame in the dim lamp.

Chapter 17

THE SHERIFF WAS MOST LIKELY TO SEARCH close to home first for Buster Doyle's killer, so the farther the boxcar took the young couple away from the carnival and Lapeer, Michigan, the easier Cindy was able to breathe. But what they were going to do when they got to Detroit, she had no idea. By midmorning the train slowed to walking speed, rocking gently from side to side as it proceeded along the track.

Cindy went to the door on the right side of the train and pulled it back far enough to stick her head out and looked ahead. "Bo, are there any mountains around Detroit?"

"Nah, don't think so." He sat up and gave Jigger a scratch under his ear. "Sorry, ol' boy. I ain't got nothin' for you to eat this mornin'."

"If there's no mountains, why are we goin' underground, 'cause there's a big tunnel up ahead, and we're headed right down into it."

"What?" Bo jumped up and pulled Cindy aside so he could lean through the open door. His voice filled with awe. "Well, I'll be tarred and feathered. We're goin' under the St. Clair."

"*St. Clair* what?"

"The St. Clair River. Can't you see? Says so right on the sign above the tunnel: 'St. Clair, 1890.' I read 'bout this once. It's the first train tunnel ever built under a river."

"We're goin' *under a river*? Not me!" Cindy tried to push Bo aside. "I ain't goin' under no river!"

"Hold your horses, now! This is a good thing. We'll come up in Canada."

"That's crazy! What if it caves in on us and we drown?"

"It's not gonna cave in. It's been here fifty years."

"Still …" She wasn't very reassured, but … "What'd you say 'bout Canada? What are we gonna do in a foreign country?"

Bo pulled himself back into the car just as they plunged into the tunnel and spoke to her from the darkness. "Don't you see? There ain't no way they can search for us in Canada. The sheriff can't go over there. We'll be safe!"

"Dagnabit, Bo, I don't want to go to Canada! I can't even speak Canadian."

She heard him laugh. "They speak English … and some French, I guess. But we don't have to stay there. After a few weeks, when the heat dies down, we'll come back to America, and everything'll be hunky-dory."

The iron wheels of the train screeched along the tracks as the train slowed even more, and the dark air became dank and heavy. Jigger whined somewhere in the darkness.

"Bo …" Cindy cried out. "I don't like this!"

"C'mon, sit down. You'll be okay, babe."

She felt his hand on her arm, and let him ease her down to the floor beside him. In a moment she felt the wet nose of Jigger on her hand, and then he put his head in her lap. Absentmindedly, she petted him. "How long will it take?"

"Just a few minutes, I reckon."

But the train cars jerked and screeched, and then came to a stop. Cindy's anxiety hiked up a notch. "What's happening? Why are we stopped?"

"I don't know, but don't worry." His voice didn't sound quite so certain as it had a few moments before.

Cindy sat still, trying to be brave, trying to be patient, trying to not panic. But ... "Bo ... I hear water running. Sounds like the tunnel's leakin'."

After a moment, he said, "I hear it too, but I'm sure it ain't nothin'."

Cindy listened. It was only a trickle or perhaps just a small stream falling from the ceiling into some pool below. Still, swallowing the lump in her throat, she said, "Back in Arkansas, before the drought, we used to irrigate our whole garden with water from the pond in the hollow above us that was filled by our windmill. We'd run it in little trenches from row to row and keep our feet cool in the mud. But Pa used to hate gophers. He always shot them with his .22, said just one of those varmints could destroy the dam and flood us out." She was quiet for a few more moments. "And Bo, there's a whole river above us ... What if that leak gets bigger?" She scrambled to her feet. "I think I want to get out and walk back."

"No, no! Sit down, Cindy!" He grabbed her leg then stood up beside her, putting his arms around her. "We can't walk back, not beside the train. What if it starts moving again? You can't see a thing out there. You could trip over a rock or anything and fall under the wheels. There's only a tiny space on either side." He was breathing hard. "We gotta wait it out, babe. I'm sure everything's okay."

Just then the train jerked and clattered as it began to move forward. She shivered. "How long is this tunnel?"

146

"I dunno." He was quiet a moment. "Actually, that thing I read? I think it said it's about a mile long. But trains move fast. Doesn't take long to go a mile. I reckon we're already going up to the other side."

"Bo, how can you tell? How can you tell at all? There ain't nothin' sayin' whether we're goin' up or down!"

He had no answer.

"Besides, we're not going very fast. We're barely moving. It could be forever before we get outta here!"

Forever was probably not much more than ten minutes, but they were the longest ten minutes Cindy had ever endured. Relief finally flooded her whole body as blinding sunlight knifed into the car again through the partially opened door.

If Bo was right, they were in Canada!

Cindy stood in the doorway with Bo behind her, his arm around her waist, as the train squealed and jerked its way up to level ground. "It don't look like no foreign country," she said.

TORONTO. WHAT WAS SHE DOING IN *CANADA*? Late that afternoon, as Cindy followed Bo and Jigger across the rows of tracks in Toronto's switching yards, she suddenly felt lost. As if she was somebody else. What was she *doing* here? With a boy she'd only known for a week, away from Ma and Pa, running, afraid ...

Buster Doyle on the floor, lying in a pool of blood.

The little purse stuffed with money still strapped to her wrist ... until she could get it to Pa.

That was why!

A sob erupted from somewhere deep inside, and she stumbled.

"Cindy!" Bo's voice shook her back to reality, and she caught herself before she fell. "Look!"

147

They'd come to a fence surrounding the switching yard. She looked in the direction Bo was pointing. A huge billboard across the street boasted: "Sunnyside Amusement Park! Rides! Thrills! Fun for the whole family!" Bo was laughing. "That's us! I bet we can get jobs there, easy!"

Jobs? But what about tonight? Where were they even going to sleep?

What they found was a large cardboard box that they arranged in a niche under an overpass.

Running in the rain. Hiding in a boxcar. Sleeping in a box under a bridge. She was going down, down, down! Cindy had stayed in some unpleasant places with her family since they'd fled Arkansas, but nothing as hardscrabble as this. She began to cry, softly, but unable to stop. She didn't even notice when Bo left until a streetlight came on under the bridge, shining its dim light into their little cave.

She looked around. "He ditched me!" But there was Jigger lying in the corner, head on his paws, looking up at her with his soulful eyes.

A few minutes later, Bo returned with two big hamburgers wrapped in wax paper, and two frosty bottles of Coca-Cola.

"Where'd you get those?" she sniffed, wiping her tears with the backs of her hands.

"At a diner up the street. I would've taken you with me, but I didn't know where I was going or how long it would take. You looked like you needed some rest. Besides ..." he laughed softly, "somebody might have called the police, seein' how you were cryin' and got your dress torn, and all. Here, hold these."

He handed her the food, reached into his pocket, and pulled out what looked to Cindy like two small shiny wires that he held up in the dim light. "Now ain't they just the cat's meow?"

"What? Are those safety pins?" She made a face. "What for?"

148

"Your dress, silly. I had to beg the waitress for them. She was using them to hold her nametag to her dress." He shrugged. "Safety pins aren't usually on the menu, you know."

Cindy laughed ... and then laughed harder as the tension poured out. Bo did care. He cared a lot!

THE NEXT MORNING, CINDY COULDN'T BELIEVE how Bo—like a bee returning to its hive—found the amusement park on the waterfront of Lake Ontario. A wide boulevard separated the rides and concessions and restaurants from a sweeping beach with a bath pavilion that looked to Cindy like a Greek temple.

"Now, the first thing we do," Bo said as they entered the amusement area, "is find the public restrooms and get ourselves cleaned up. No one's gonna hire us lookin' like we slept in a boxcar." He laughed. "Use those pins to fix your dress the best you can and wash up. And here, here's my comb. I'll use it later when I come out. I don't need a mirror."

Cindy knew a comb wasn't anything like a brush, and what her hair really needed was a good washing, but she did feel fresher when she came out of the restroom.

With Jigger at her side, Cindy stood back as Bo approached the foreman for the Flyer Roller Coaster. But she could see that the man was impressed with Bo's knowledge of rides as they talked, and before they were done, he had a job, not as the ride jockey, but as an attendant who helped people get seated in a quick and safe way. "You start tomorrow," the foreman growled.

"What about her?" Bo asked, nodding at Cindy.

The man looked her up and down, then shrugged. "Don't let females run the rides. Check with the concession stands. They do their own hiring." He stalked off, chomping on a cigar.

Bo leaned toward Cindy as they walked away. "Don't worry, babe. We'll find you something too. And I'll be the ride jockey soon enough. That pays more money."

But that wasn't so easy. At every concession or diversion the managers would look at Cindy and shake their heads. "Sorry. Don't need anyone right now." "Come back a little later. We might have something then." "You might try the Fun House."

Cindy felt like quitting. "Bo ... I'm tired and hungry. We didn't have anything to eat this morning, and I feel like I'm about to fall over."

"Ah, I'm sorry. I wasn't even thinkin'. Here, let's grab a couple of hot dogs and some root beer." There were tables and chairs in the Hires Root Beer stand, and Cindy was so glad to sit down. After a while, the rest and food gave her the energy to go on, though she felt pretty discouraged.

"Let's knock off for the day. I got a job. That's enough for now. Let's go find a place to stay."

Not far from the amusement park, they found The McDougal House with a vacancy sign. "I don't allow no cohabiting," sniffed the tight-lipped matron. Her white collar on her dark dress stood so high and tight she couldn't even turn her head. "So don't even try to tell me you're married. I've got men's rooms—three or four beds in each—and women's rooms, and never the twain shall meet ... except around the supper table or right here in the parlor. However, no eating in the parlor. And no cigar smokin' in the house." She frowned and glared at Jigger, who sat on his haunches by the gate. "And no animals in the house. I serve one meal a day, at six-thirty sharp. If you're not here to sit down with your hands and face washed when I ring the bell, don't bother."

She paused, her eyes darting back and forth from Cindy to Bo. Bo took the opportunity to say, "Uh ... I'm workin' at the amusement park and probably won't get in till late."

The woman sniffed and tilted her head up a little. "That so? Well, I'm glad you have a job. I guess … if Jenny is in a good mood you might get some leftovers in the kitchen, but don't count on it." Then she went back to her set spiel like a carnival talker. "Coffee and biscuits will be available by six in the morning. Everything else is on your own."

Cindy looked at Bo and nodded. He smiled and turned to the matron. "How much?"

"A dollar a day, paid in advance by the week."

Bo pulled out the little fold of money from his pocket and peeled off seven bills.

"That's seven dollars a week, *each*! And I don't take Yankee money, only Canadian."

"But this is all I got."

"And I'm not a bank. Come back when you have Queen's money." Mrs. McDougal closed the door in their face, leaving Cindy and Bo standing on the porch.

Bo growled, "That old woman is gonna be hard to live with. Our US dollars are worth a dollar-ten in Canadian, but she still didn't want 'em. She's just makin' it hard on us."

When they finally found a place to exchange their money, they went back and paid the fourteen dollars, Canadian. And Cindy was surprised that Mrs. McDougal quickly made a place for them around the table. At least they had a place to live and a good meal that evening. After they ate, Bo leaned over to Cindy. "I got a roll and a piece of chicken. I'm gonna try and sneak it out for Jigger."

"Where is he?"

"Out back, under the porch. I put out a can of water out there for him and told him to stay."

The next morning when Cindy came back from the washroom, there was a small stack of someone's neatly folded laundry on her bed—two dresses and some underwear. She really didn't have time to deal with it right then. She needed to be ready to go with Bo to the park. Nevertheless, she bundled them up and went down to find Mrs. McDougal at her desk in the foyer.

"Excuse me, ma'am, someone left these on my bed, and I don't know who they belong to."

Without looking up from her writing, the matron said, "Didn't you read the sign?" She pointed toward the wall above her head. "Says, 'You leave 'em, you lose 'em.' People are always leaving stuff behind."

She had to turn her whole body to stare stiffly up at Cindy. "When you came yesterday, I noticed you brought no luggage … nothing but that purse you carry all the time. Figured you could use a few things. What others leave, I'm free to give, so they're yours if you want them." She turned back to her writing. "Oh, by the way, I think there's an old suitcase under your bed. You can put your stuff in that. In fact, you can have it too, if you want."

Cindy stood open-mouthed for a moment before she could think how to respond. "Oh, thank you! Thank you, very much. I can most certainly use these. Thank you."

Running upstairs, she changed into a blue jumper over a white blouse. Funny how clean clothes could make a body feel like something good was going to happen.

Chapter 18

IT STILL TOOK CINDY THREE DAYS of going from one concession to another before she got a job in the Hires Root Beer stand—the same place she and Bo ate hot dogs when they first came to the amusement park—but the job didn't pay much.

And she wasn't sleeping well.

That first night in Dorothy McDougal's rooming house had been a respite after two nights in the rough—sleeping in a boxcar and under a bridge—but then Cindy began experiencing nightmares. Buster Doyle assaulting her with nowhere for her to flee in that little office. Bo hitting the man on the side of his head with the big wrench. The wild run through the rain to catch the train. Separation from her family that felt like being cut off from her very source of life itself. Finding herself in another country.

Tears stained her pillow.

Each morning she got up feeling more tired and stiff than when she'd gone to bed the night before. This was no way to live!

She also worried about the purse with Pa's money that she'd taken from Doyle's desk. She couldn't carry it strapped to her wrist when she went to work, so she left it hidden under her mattress in the rooming house. But then she worried someone might steal it. She barely knew the other two women with whom she shared the room, and new people were coming and going all the time. She had to get it to her folks … but how? If Bo was right that the boss man's death had shut down the beet harvest, her folks would need their back pay even more.

Tuesday evening she got off work early—a couple of hours before Bo—and returned to the rooming house by herself in time to eat at the dining room table with the other roomers. After dinner she took the purse, went outside, and called Jigger. He came bounding around the house ready for anything. But all Cindy wanted was a companion for a walk. In a small park not far away, she sat on a bench while Jigger set off to explore each tree and bush in the park. She sat watching him absentmindedly and then looked down and unzipped the purse for the first time since she'd fled with it. Checking to make sure no one was watching her, she counted the money by walking her fingers through the bills without taking them out, adding as she went. Her eyes widened—$383! She had never held so much money! Surely, that was far more than Doyle owed her father, but her family had been the only migrants who had returned to work the harvest. All the others had gone on to other jobs, forfeiting the pay Doyle had held back. But not Pa, of course. "Fool me once, shame on you. Fool me twice, shame on me!" He'd been determined to collect the money Doyle owed him for the planting, thinning, and weeding they'd done earlier in the season.

She recounted the money … lots of twenties, when she'd imagined the little stack was only ones. Again, it came to $383. She zipped the purse closed. A hot wave burned up her neck and face as she recalled something Pa had said about Doyle: "He'd use any excuse to keep that hundred and fifty bucks he owes us …" A hundred and fifty? Then who did the rest of this money belong to? Cindy felt dizzy, ready to faint. It wasn't hers! It wasn't Pa's! It wasn't money the Tucker family had earned. She had taken money that didn't belong to her family. She'd stolen it! She was a thief!

Again she scanned the park, this time with the dread that someone was about to catch her. Bo had killed a man in self-defense … and in defense of her. But she had stolen money that didn't belong to her.

She had to return it! Right away!

But how could she do that without giving away Bo?

She had to … And then the answer came: She would mail it back to Pa. He'd know what to do.

But the moment she realized she'd have to mail the money, she broke into tears. She wanted to *give* it to him. But the stark truth hit her. She wouldn't be seeing her family … perhaps for a very long time. She'd probably known that as soon as she'd run, but now, sitting in this little park so far away with stolen money in her lap, it seemed so final.

She was alone!

"MRS. MCDOUGAL, I WONDER if you could help me with something?" Cindy stood behind the matron who always seemed to be working at her desk in the foyer.

"What now, child?"

Cindy held a small package—a box wrapped in brown paper and tied carefully with string. "I … I never learned how to read and write, but I need to mail this to Pa in America, so I wonder if you would write the address on it for me?"

The stiff woman turned around with a scowl that could wither a rose. "I hope you realize this whole continent is America. But I suppose you mean *the States*?"

"Yes ma'am. Michigan."

"And why didn't you learn how to read and write? Weren't you paying attention in school?"

"Never got no schoolin'. We were—"

"Never mind." The woman reached out and took the package. "Where's it going?"

"To Mr. Lester Tucker ..." Cindy had been thinking about this, and as much as she hated saying the name of her attacker, the only way she could address it was ... "Doyle Migrant Camp, Lapeer, Michigan."

Mrs. McDougal had been writing as she spoke. "And that would be USA, right?"

"Yes ma'am."

"And for the return address, that would be Cindy Tucker? Or are you actually married to that boy?"

"No, no, no. Just put *your* name on it."

Mrs. McDougal looked up at Cindy, turning her neck in a collar that must have nearly choked her. "And why *not* your name?"

"Because ..." Cindy stood tongue-tied. She couldn't tell Mrs. McDougal she didn't want anyone in Lapeer to know she was in Toronto. "Please. Just your name."

Mrs. McDougal gave her a strange look, then sighed in exasperation. "All right. If you insist." She turned back to the package and finished writing. "Here." She thrust it at Cindy. "You'll have to take it to the post office yourself. I don't do errands, and I doubt they'll take Yankee money."

But the next day, they did.

ONE EVENING, TWO WEEKS LATER, Cindy met Bo as he came off work, but as they walked away, he grabbed her hand and whispered in her ear. "We gotta leave this place."

156

Having been in a foreign country so long, relief flooded over her. She looked up to see if he was serious. "Really? Where we gonna go?"

"*Shh.*" He glanced over his shoulder. "Don't say nothin'! Just keep walkin'."

A few minutes later, as the sounds of the amusement park faded into the distance, Cindy couldn't wait anymore. "Bo, what's goin' on? Why are you looking around like someone is following us?"

"Because ..." He looked behind them again. "They might be."

"What are you talkin' about?"

"Today a guy asked me if I was related to that Bodeen they're looking for in Michigan, the guy who killed a farmer. I nearly did the baby thing in my pants, but I asked what he was talkin' about, and he showed me the latest copy of *The Billboard*. That's the newspaper for carnivals and amusement parks and circuses. Goes all over the country—and Canada, too, I guess—and there was an article about the killing in Lapeer."

"About us?" Cindy's eyes widened.

"Yeah! Said the sheriff claimed the suspects were a carnival worker—it named me—and a migrant worker. But it didn't name you. It said we disappeared right after the killing, and that's why he thinks we did it."

Now it was Cindy who looked over her shoulder, her heart pounding. "Does this guy at the amusement park know you're the one they're lookin' for?"

"Don't think so. He just asked if I was related. I brushed him off and changed the subject. But if he puts it together with when I started work or if he sees you and figures we're together, he's liable to get an idea of who we are."

They walked in silence until they came to the rooming house. Bo put out his hand and stopped before they climbed the steps. "I think we oughta leave tonight."

"Tonight? But tomorrow's Friday, and I get paid every Friday … you too."

"What's a few dollars if we get arrested?" Bo hissed. "Or if someone identifies us and the police start chasing us?"

Cindy's mind churned like a waterfall. She didn't like the fear she heard in Bo's voice. She needed him to be strong. Calm. To keep her from drowning in her own pool of fear. Finally, she said, "Maybe it'd be better to stay. If we run again, won't that cause people to think somethin's strange?"

"Nah. People come and go all the time in the carnival world. We're like nomads." Bo looked up at the rooming house door, warm light coming from several windows, but not those in the dining room. "Doggone it!" He snapped his fingers. "We're too late for dinner again. Let's go to that little café on the corner and get some chili."

Seated across from each other in a booth, both were quiet as they chowed down the spicy chili and crackers. Suddenly Bo said, "We gotta build new identities too."

Cindy's spoon stopped halfway to her mouth. "What?"

Bo leaned forward, his voice low. "I never told my boss I used to work for the Carson Brothers' Carnival, even though it might've gotten me a better job. He just hired me 'cause he could tell I knew what I was talkin' about, that I'd worked somewhere on rides. But I did use my real name. Can't do that no more, and neither can you."

"But … I'm Cindy Tucker. I don't want to change my name."

"Cindy, we gotta. Word's already out about a man gettin' killed in Lapeer and they're lookin' for two missing people—me and you! The carnival world's tight, and not just because of *The Billboard*. People all over know the name 'Bodeen,' 'cause my dad's run rides for a long time. But now that name's been associated with a murder."

"It wasn't murder, Bo! You just—"

"I know! I know … but we can't risk it."

Tears swam in Cindy's eyes. "But you're *Bo*! And to me, you're *my* Bo." The implications of what she said hit her, and tears spilled over. "How could you be anyone else?"

He reached across the table and held her hand for a few moments. "Maybe … well, I know I can't keep usin' the name Bodeen. How 'bout if I become Hansen. That was my mama's maiden name." He stared across the small café at the waitress who was making fresh coffee. "Hey, I knew a guy named Borick once. It was his last name, but so what? I'll be Borick Hansen. That way you can still call me Bo, and no one'll think anything of it."

Cindy grabbed a paper napkin to wipe her eyes and then smiled shyly at him. "Guess that'd be okay, especially if I can still call you Bo."

They ate in silence for a few moments. She'd never imagined things could get this complicated.

"What about me?" she finally said. "Tucker's a pretty common name, ain't it? I don't need to change it."

"Maybe not, but …"

"What if I changed my first name?"

"To what?" Bo shoved a soda cracker into his mouth, a few crumbs escaping to fall to the table.

Cindy shrugged. "Well my real name's Lucinda. How 'bout Lucinda Tucker?"

Bo grimaced and wiped the crumbs off onto the floor. "If the police are lookin' for you, I'm afraid they'd use your given name. How 'bout changin' it to Lucy … Lucy Tucker."

"Lucy?" Cindy snorted. "I'm not a Lucy. Lucy's short for Lucille or Luciann. I knew a girl named Luciann—"

159

"Wait, wait. That's the beauty of it. Think about it: If you always insist your name is Lucy, people won't even think *Cindy* and hopefully not even *Lucinda*. Even if they do, Lucy's short for several names that could match. Don't ya see?"

"I guess ... *Lucy, Lucy, Lucy*." She tried the name over and over. "I'll think about it, but maybe it don't matter. We never had to give our names when we were working in the fields."

"That's probably 'cause they paid you in cash. But these are real jobs and we gotta give our names, like you did at the root beer stand, Right? But now we need to break the trail and start creating new identities. Besides, there're other reasons we might need names, like ... like ..." Bo made a silly face and winked at her.

Cindy's heart tripped.

What was that about? Her mind leapfrogged ahead. Was he hinting at getting married? Nah! Couldn't be. She wasn't even sixteen yet. Still ... She put it out of her mind and took a deep breath. "You still think we need to leave right now?"

"Yeah ... the sooner the better. We got enough money to hold us for a while. I'm thinkin' we could go down to Niagara Falls. There's a lot of tourist stuff down there. We oughta be able to get jobs, easy."

"Is that America?"

"Or Canada. There's two sides, you know. Though I've never been there myself."

When they got back to the rooming house and were climbing the front steps, Bo whispered, "Get your stuff, and I'll meet you 'round back with Jigger."

Inside, Mrs. McDougal called from the parlor. "That you, Cindy? Something came for you today. It's on my desk there."

Cindy stared at the desk as Bo went on up the stairs. It was the package she'd mailed two weeks before, a little scuffed from wear but definitely her package to Pa. She carried it in to Mrs. McDougal, who had her lap full of knitting. "What's this mean?"

"Mean? Means they couldn't deliver it!" She sighed and took it out of Cindy's hands. "Those stamps with a finger pointing to the corner say 'Return to sender.' Guess they couldn't find your father."

"And what's this other writing?"

The older woman held the package at arm's length. "Says, 'Moved. No forwarding address.' Postman probably scribbled it on there when he found no one home at this"—she waved her hand—"this migrant camp or wherever he was supposed to be."

"Does that mean—"

"It means," she turned back to her knitting, "nobody knows where he is, or they would've forwarded it."

Chapter 19

SPIRIT SAGGING, THE GIRL WATCHED yet another set of taillights disappear down the road ahead of them. At this rate, they might have to walk all eighty miles to Niagara Falls. Even the few drivers who'd started to pull over, sped up again as soon as they saw Jigger.

"Next time, stand off to the side a little more," Bo said, "and keep Jigger outta the headlights till we for sure got a ride." But he never once suggested leaving Jigger behind, and Lucy—as she was trying to call herself—wouldn't have agreed to it, anyway. She remembered how Bo had stayed with her on the train when they were fleeing Lapeer rather than hop off to go find Jigger. The fact that he'd chosen her brought tears to her eyes as the three of them trudged along Lake Shore Boulevard, around the bottom of Toronto.

Lucy tugged lightly on Jigger's leash, and the little dog good-naturedly gave up sniffing a bush and trotted along after them. She'd made the leash from an old cotton rope to be sure Jigger would be close by and ready to jump in if anyone offered them a ride.

"We're in the wrong place," growled Bo, shaking his fist at the receding taillights of the fifth car that had stopped and then roared away. "It's gettin' late, and these people are all headin' home from fancy restaurants and nightclubs. We need to be on a road with trucks and farmers and working people."

"At night?"

"Sure. A lot of stuff gets shipped at night."

"In trains, maybe, but … Hey, how about the train? That switching yard ain't far, is it?"

"No, but …" Bo scuffed the toe of his shoe in the gravel as they walked. "I thought about the train, but I'm not sure how we'd find out where it's goin'. We didn't know we were comin' here when we hopped that other train. We just needed to get out of Lapeer. Besides, I've heard ya really gotta watch out for those railroad bulls in a big city like this."

"Bulls? What bulls? Did they escape from some cattle car?"

"No, silly. Railroad policemen. They're mean, and they're always on the lookout for hobos tryin' to hop a train."

"Well, I ain't no hobo!"

"That's 'cause you got a suitcase and look like a tourist. But me …" He held up the denim drawstring bag he'd found to carry a razor, soap, and his few extra clothes.

Lucy laughed and swatted his arm. "Oh, you're a regular 'Hobo Bo', that's for sure!" Though he always took care to look clean-cut … and handsome.

"Yeah, and guess what's in this duffel bag? I picked me up a harmonica, and I'm gonna learn how to play it." Noticing headlights from an approaching car, Bo spun around to walk backward with his thumb out. "Music for the road, you know. I'm gonna get so good people'll be beggin' us to ride with them, just for the music."

But when the car didn't even slow down, Lucy said, "What if we could find a real hobo? Bet he'd tell us what train to get on … and how to keep from gettin' caught too."

After three more cars passed them by, Bo threw up his hands. "All right! All right! Let's go try for a train."

They turned and trudged across some vacant lots toward the switching yard. "Hey, I know where we are. Isn't that the bridge we stayed under the first night?" She pointed to an overpass that crossed a street ahead of them as well as the railroad tracks. "And there's somebody up there in our place too. Maybe it's a hobo."

"Yeah, well we don't need no trouble hornin' in on someone else's camp. I say we keep our distance."

"But what if he can help us?"

They came out onto the cross street and approached the overpass more slowly. A small fire glowed from a bucket in the little cave. "I don't know," Bo said. They stopped under a streetlight, trying to see who was in their old shelter. "Look," he said, "you wait here out in the open where I can see ya, and I'll go check it out. If anything goes wrong, *do not* come up there. Go back to the rooming house and wait for me. You hear?"

Lucy nodded. "But Bo ..." She reached her hand out toward him, but he was already gone.

An hour later, Lucy, Bo, and Jigger sat huddled in a dark Toronto, Hamilton, and Buffalo boxcar half filled with new folding wooden chairs, probably a shipment from some local manufacturer to an outlet in the States.

"Think they're gonna come back and put more stuff in this car?" Lucy shivered in spite of the warm night.

"Hope not, but ..." Bo jumped up. "Let's see if we can move some of these stacks around and create a hollow in the corner where we could hide if they do load more stuff or if the bulls come lookin' for hobos."

Lucy scrambled to her feet and helped Bo wrestle the stacks of chairs around inside the dark car, muttering under her breath.

"What?"

"I'm just sayin', we may not have much …" All she actually had with her was a tattered little suitcase with her meager extra clothes, six hard rolls Jenny had given her from the kitchen, and the little purse of money for her folks. "… but I ain't no hobo!"

"Okay, okay! You're no hobo, but we still don't want to get caught in here."

THE TRAIN DIDN'T MOVE UNTIL early the next morning when thin beams of sunshine knifed through the cracks in the old wooden boxcar. Lucy sat up stiffly and looked down at the still sleeping Bo. Their cramped quarters hadn't made sleeping all that easy, but— uncomfortable or not—she hadn't minded pillowing her head on his shoulder while his arm tucked her in close. She smiled. Had he made their hideout this small just to be sure they'd have to cuddle up?

Bo stirred and looked up at her with deep frown lines creasing his brow, then sat up sharply. "How long we been movin'?"

"Just started. Why?"

"Oh, good! Phew! Guy under the bridge said we gotta get off at Welland. This train's bound for Buffalo, don't go into Niagara. So we gotta walk from the closest stop, and that's Welland."

"How far's that?"

"Didn't say, but we sure don't want to overshoot it, or we'll be walkin' even farther." He stood up and paced around in the boxcar for a few minutes until the train had gained speed. Then he grabbed the door and rolled it open. "Can't stand not seein' where we're goin'." When he came back to sit down beside her, he dug his harmonica out of his bag and began blowing into it.

Lucy wasn't sure she was going to like listening to him learn.

165

A little before noon as they sat in the open doorway with their feet hanging out, Bo pointed to a water tower not far ahead. "There, can you read that?"

Lucy knew he was referring to the word on the side of the tower, but had he figured out that she couldn't read? Was he testing her? "*Hmm,*" she said, "can't quite make it out."

He grinned at her. "Maybe you need glasses. Says, 'Welland.' We're comin' into Welland, just like that hobo said we would. And the train's slowin' too. Get your bag, and let's be ready to drop off before it stops."

NIAGARA FALLS PROVED TO BE A PRIME ATTRACTION for newlyweds. On the second day, by claiming she was eighteen, Lucy got a job as a housekeeper in a large tourist home on the Canadian side frequented by starry-eyed couples on their honeymoon. But there were other guests as well—salesmen, groups of traveling students, even an occasional family that couldn't afford the Red Coach Inn or the Brock Plaza Hotel.

Lucy's pay included a room in the basement where she slept. It had an outside entrance but was too small and damp to rent out. Somehow Jigger had the sense to stay in her room without barking all day while she worked, and go out only when she took him for walks. But Lucy could tell it was a sad life for such an active pooch.

Bo—Borick Hansen, now—sold tickets for the *Maid of the Mist* tour boats that carried people so close to the bottom of the falls they got soaked by the spray. He hawked tickets like a carnival talker and sold more than anyone else. The boss liked him, but the only place Bo could find to stay was a room in the YMCA across the river on the American side. He had to pay a toll every day to cross the newly opened Rainbow Bridge across the Niagara River, but that wasn't as bad as the time it took, given the security during wartime. Until the border guards got to know him, crossing back over to the Canadian side every day took an extra half hour ... each way. "I keep worrying some new recruit is going to insist I show some ID," he told Lucy one day. "But so far all they seem concerned about is that no one smuggles weapons."

They managed to see each other early each morning before they had to go to work, sometimes meeting in a little coffee shop near Lucy's house. But this was Monday, and they had some extra time before the tourists emerged from their hotels and breakfasts to "see the sights." Lucy knew it was a beautiful day, but she was struggling with the blues, so she bought two scones from a bakery and shared one with Bo as they sat together on a stone wall in Queen Victoria Park overlooking the roaring falls while Jigger raced around marking every lamp pole and fire hydrant.

Bo smiled at her as he took his first bite. "How'd you know this was my birthday?"

"Your birthday! Really?"

"That's right. September twenty-first ... comes every year 'bout this time." He grinned and elbowed her in the ribs.

"I didn't know it was your birthday." Lucy giggled and punched him back. "Well, happy birthday, then." It was one of those moments when everything should've felt great, but it didn't quite make it. The fact that she hadn't known it was his birthday made her feel worse. What was wrong with her?

She took a bite of her pastry and chewed slowly, trying to count her blessings, as Ma used to say. The scone wasn't bad, she guessed ... for English food, but it was no match for Ma's biscuits. Even in a Dutch oven over an open fire, Ma could ... No! She couldn't think about home. She took a deep breath, cut short by an involuntary gasp as though she'd been crying and wrestled her thoughts back to the present. She stared across the chasm carved by the great river, searching for something happier to say. "Think that's what heaven looks like?" she finally asked Bo.

"What?"

"That." She pointed toward the mountain of mist rising from the falls to create an impenetrable white glare in the morning sun.

Bo shrugged. "If that's what it looks like, I sure hope that ain't what it sounds like. The roar's gonna deafen me before I'm twenty."

She grinned at him. "What? Cain't hear ya. Falls're too loud."

"Ha, ha!"

His laugh at her little joke sounded hollow. She studied his face as he stared out at the raging cataract. He seemed to have grown older and sadder this past month. Maybe it was getting to him too. Maybe would've been better to stay in Lapeer and face the sheriff's questioning. At least she'd have had her family.

But then Bo would've ended up being the one to face the music.

Dagnabit! She had come out here trying to look on the bright side of things this morning, offering a couple of pastries for them to munch on. The falls had looked beautiful ... near like heaven itself. But she hadn't known it was his birthday, and now she felt bad and couldn't think of a good way to celebrate it. If she could only make him a banana cake like Ma did ... There she was doing it again, moping about what she couldn't change. Or could she?... Could they?

"What are we doin' here, anyway, Bo? We work long hours for ... what? Peanuts! We only see each other for a few minutes in the morning, and we haven't been able to find you a closer place to live. What's it gettin' us?"

He finally turned to her, determination galvanizing his features. "We're trying to stay free, that's what we're tryin' to do, Cindy ... I mean, Lucy."

"I *know*. But we can't live like this forever."

"We won't ..." He paused like he had more to say, but then seemed to change his mind.

Lucy sighed. "Well, I don't like being in a foreign country. At least you get to go home every night."

"Home? I'm stayin' in a flea-bitten room at the YMCA, and at least one of them's a thievin' crook. So what if you're on this side of the river and I'm on that side? Everything's the same—same language, same food, same weather. Just look, that cliff you see across the river is the United States. Same rocks on this side of the gorge. What's the big deal?"

"I don't know, Bo. It's just ... I'm just homesick, I guess."

"Humph." He glared at the roaring waters below them. "What's there to be homesick about? You're a migrant and I'm a carny. We're travelin' people. We don't have no home except what we make for ourselves."

Lucy put the last bite of her scone into her mouth. She hated arguing with Bo, but she couldn't stop herself mumbling just one more thing. "At least I had Ma and Pa and Maggie and the boys and the babies ... all of us. We were a *family*, and we stuck together."

Chapter 20

THIS PLACE AIN'T NO FAMILY! No matter what Mabel Turner says. What kinda family has a "board" or a "director"? And Mabel Turner is the *director* of Manna House! And what kind of family would kick out a member as loyal and brave as Martha Shepherd's dog? That's what I wanted to know.

I pulled my purple knit hat a little lower over my ears and watched as Miz Mabel came into the multi-purpose room. I knew why she'd called this meeting. She was going to tell us about getting rid of Dandy. But we had a surprise for her!

At the front she clapped her hands. "Everybody here? Good. Ladies, quiet down ... hello! Ladies! We need to brief you about what happened last night, and—"

Everybody knew what had happened. How could they not know? I raised my hand. " 'Scuse me, Miz Mabel!"

"We'll have time for questions later, Lucy. First—"

" 'Scuse me, Miz Mabel. We got somethin' ta say first, right, ladies?"

I looked around and knew I had everybody with me.

"All right, Lucy. What is it?"

I poked Carolyn. "You go. They gonna listen to you, 'cause you got all that book learnin'."

Tina rattled off some Spanish words that made several people laugh, but not me. I think she said something about my big mouth. But I can take it in, and I can dish it out too. So I just frowned at everyone.

Actually, Miz Mabel didn't laugh either. "Ladies, please …"

Carolyn stood up. "Sorry, Mabel. We don't mean to joke. We've been talking—all the ladies here—about what happened last night, and we have a proposition to make."

"That's right" … "*Sí*" … "Uh-huh" …

We were together again. Whadda they call that, *solidarity* or somethin'? Anyway, I poked Carolyn to continue.

"Lucy, if you poke me one more time, I'm—!"

Well, maybe not so much solidarity, after all. I rolled my eyes and looked away.

"Anyway," continued Carolyn, "we all know Dandy's been living here on borrowed time. Sarge has been saying he's gotta be out by this weekend."

Sarge, the night manager, threw up her hands. "Well, not *today*. The dog's hurt."

"Exactly. Gramma Shep's dog got injured protecting all of us from an intruder. Hurt bad. So all of us here agree we owe him somethin'. We took a vote—"

"You what?" Mabel's eyes got big as saucers.

"—and we all agree that Dandy should be made a resident of Manna House Women's Shelter as official watchdog."

All right, now we were cookin' with gas! Everybody started cheerin' and clappin' as Carolyn handed Mabel a sheet of paper. "See? We've all signed a petition."

I crossed my arms and leaned back. I reckoned there wasn't nothin' Miz Mabel could say to that. We were all in agreement! All, that is, except Sarge, who had objected to Dandy in the first place.

And then the most amazing thing happened. Miz Mabel handed that paper to Sarge.

I thought she was going to tear it up and throw it back at us like confetti, but instead she frowned at it a few moments and then shrugged. "Humph. I'm overruled, no? City inspector might not like it, but tell you what …" She grabbed a pen, laid the paper down on the table, and signed it.

I couldn't believe my eyes. But everyone was up and cheerin' and slappin' Sarge on the back. I stood back and smiled. I was the one who thought up that petition idea. Though, of course, I only put my X on it. I've tried writin' my name before, but no one can read it, so why bother?

I looked over at my friend, Martha Shepherd. She seems a little frail today, mostly stayin' in her chair with a kinda lost look on her face while everyone else was up and carryin' on like the Cubs had won the pennant. But at least no one was gonna take away her dog for a second time like Fuzz Top's man had done.

So maybe, just maybe, we were more of a family than I gave us credit for.

"Hey, Martha, wanna play some poker?" That always got a rise out of her.

I DELARE, I HAD NO IDEA what was comin' our way after Dandy showed such grit by attacking that intruder. The TV and radio and all those news reporters were callin' him "Hero Dog," and people from all around were sending him dog food an' toys an' chews an' what-have-you. It filled up the foyer and like to overrun the whole Mana House. And people were droppin' stuff at the front door without even botherin' to see if we needed it. Poor Martha had no idea what to make of all the fuss.

And then Fuzz Top tells me that to get away from all the hubbub—especially the media—she's takin' Martha and Dandy to Jodi Baxter's house for a while. Didn't even ask me!

I got right in her face. "Why all a' sudden you think that other lady can take better care o' that dog than me, huh? Didn't you say next to Gramma Shep that I was his fav'rite people?"

She gave me some cock-an'-bull story about it bein' a quieter place and there bein' a yard where Dandy could walk around without attracting lots of attention, but I could see through it all. Didn't even try to convince her that I knew how to keep Dandy away from all those people—if that really bothered him. Not sure it did. But I could take Dandy on a walk to a real quiet place. Made me so mad, I decided to go there myself.

I went upstairs and threw my stuff in my cart. Some of it wasn't worth luggin' around, but you never know. I pulled the knit hat off my head and checked it out. I'd washed it in cold water quick as I could, but some of Dandy's blood had already set, makin' it look a little dingy. But who cared? I put it back on and snuck into the service elevator with my cart. No sense trying to wrestle it down the stairs.

If I had Dandy with me, I'd go up to the Challenger Dog Park between Graceland Cemetery and the El. It was a nice grassy strip where the Wrigleyville people walked their dogs. Nobody had ever bothered me when I brought Dandy there, but it wasn't quiet. The El ran every few minutes nearly overhead, loud as a tornado. In spite of the roar, I had—on occasion—taken shelter in one of the many Dumpsters that serviced the gated apartment buildings along there.

You'd think that would be no place for a person to hide out, but fact is, those liberal folks pride themselves on bein' tolerant. So long as I didn't create a mess, no one seemed to get too upset seein'

173

me come and go. Of course, I got rousted by the cops from time to time if they happened to notice my cart and figured I was hiding out nearby. But that happens everywhere.

Without Dandy, I went west on Irving Park, which cut right through the cemetery, and turned south. Unlike the northern part of the cemetery with its high wall topped off by barbed wire, this section had nothing but an old chain-link fence around it. And I knew where there was a break behind some bushes that I'd used more than once, but it was always risky, so I usually went around and through one of the gates on the west side. When I got to the third gate, I looked both ways and slipped in when I was pretty sure no one who mattered was watching. I knew a couple of the groundskeepers by sight, and they didn't much like me, but I told 'em they couldn't keep a citizen from visiting the dead. And I came often enough they probably figured it was true.

In about the middle of the cemetery, there's one of those little stone houses where rich families put their dearly departed, and if you jimmy the gate lock just right, it opens. I never went inside unless I was sure no one could see me, but it was a place to get outta the rain. And if I stayed the night, I made sure I was long gone before anyone stirred the next mornin' … an' I left no mess.

But that's not where I went this time. I stopped at my little stone bench where I'd sat so often over the years. Most of the markers in that area are newer, the small kind that are level with the ground, for poor folks, ya know. But there are a couple large, upright stones right in front of the bench. I could read the dates on both of 'em, 1885, worn and streaked with moss. Bench looked the same, so I reckon it was put there so kith and kin could mourn in comfort. But they were long gone, leastwise I never saw anyone around.

Dandy was about as obedient as ol' Jigger used to be, and more than once I snuck him into the cemetery. When the groundspeople came around, I told Dandy to lie down and stay put in the lilac bushes that had grown up behind those two ancient stones, and he'd do it.

Those groundsmen usually rode around on lawnmowers or in their pickups, and I had plenty of time to tuck Dandy away, but one day one of them came through on foot, pickin' up trash, I s'pose, and he snuck right up behind us.

"What's that dog doin' in here? Can't you read? Sign at each gate says no dogs allowed outta respect for the dead. Now get him outta here, and don't you come back either."

Dandy and I left … but I came back. They couldn't keep me out, though they was always a-lookin'. It took awhile before I tried to sneak Dandy back in, but I managed to do it more than once.

For the rest of that afternoon, I sat on my bench, not studying at the big stones, mind you. I faced the other direction, looking at the row of ground-level stones from a much later era. I couldn't actually read 'em, but all the same, I knew what one of 'em said.

I STAYED CLEAR OF MANNA HOUSE for the next week. Slept rough for a couple of nights and grabbed a bed in some other shelters, but had to admit, the food wasn't nearly as good as Estelle Williams's. I like her lasagna better'n about anything I ever et. And in some of those places there's just too many ossified residents. It's like the drunk tank in a jail. Can't even have a decent conversation. People flappin' their lips, without makin' one bit of sense.

But when I dropped by Manna House the next Saturday, I met Gabby Fairbanks walkin' out on the sidewalk. She didn't look to be in a very good mood, stompin' along like a clod-bustin' farmer. Figured if I wanted to see Martha, I'd better cheer her up.

"Hey! What time ya got, Fuzz Top? Anybody take that dog out yet since ya been back this mornin'? No, 'course not. Don't know why I bother ta ask. Just wanna know if I got time afore supper."

Gabby's shoulders slouched, and she shook her head, as a smile transformed her frown. "Hey yourself, Lucy. I know somebody inside who'll be mighty glad to see you."

Things was good that night and for the next couple of days. Martha even tried to learn how to play poker with me! And I went so far as to go to church with her and Gabby on Sunday. But I couldn't abide that loud music for very long, so I slipped out afore the preacher got up and headed back to Manna House.

"Why'd you leave?" Martha asked over Sunday dinner. So I told her. To my surprise she said, "Well, I don't blame you, but the preacher wasn't near so loud as those drums and guitars."

Maybe I shoulda stuck it out a little longer.

But that evening, they set up for church right there in Manna House. I'd forgotten that they do that most Sundays. Martha wanted me to sit with her, but I'd had enough church for one day, so I headed upstairs. It wasn't far enough away to escape the music, though. And one of the songs they sang reminded me of Ma.

> 'Tis so sweet to trust in Jesus,
> Just to take Him at His Word;
> Just to rest upon His promise,
> And to know, "Thus saith the Lord!"

Almost made me wanna go back downstairs, but then I started blubberin' a little and didn't want folks to fuss, so I stayed put on my bunk and listened.

Next day, I took Dandy out for a walk. Might've taken Martha, too, but I'd been noticin' she seemed kinda tipsy lately, shaky on her feet. So, it was just Dandy and me. I took it slow, 'cause he was still kinda stiff, but I could tell he loved bein' out.

I was no more'n a couple of blocks from Manna House, when the close-by *Wee-hoop! Wee-hoop!* of a cop siren made me jump. It wasn't a full-blown howl racing to a bank robbery, but it was loud enough, especially when the car screeched to a stop at the curb right beside me. I looked around to see what the problem was, not wantin' to get caught in the middle of them tryin' to nab some shoplifters.

A couple of salt-and-pepper officers jumped out of the car and the white one pointed at me. "Stop right there, ma'am."

I looked behind me, certain he was speakin' to someone else, but there wasn't anybody within half a block.

"That your dog?"

"Yeah …" What in tarnation? You'd think with all the kids shootin' each other and drugs as common as snow in January, Chicago's finest would have something more important to do than enforce the leash law. I rolled my eyes and leaned down to grab the end of the red bandana I'd given Dandy. Martha said it made him look like a cowboy, but right now, it was the closest thing to a leash I could come up with.

"We noticed your dog seemed to be limping."

"Yeah! That's 'cause he got hurt. But … he's better now." What was with these two? While the white one kept talkin' to me, the black officer sidled around us to get on the other side of Dandy. Dandy didn't like that much and started growlin' and pullin' away from me. "Hold on, boy," I muttered. "They ain't gonna do nothin'" … I hoped. Confound it, I wasn't even trying to sneak him into the cemetery. We weren't even headed there, so what was with these two, anyway?

"Ma'am, unless you can provide some proof of ownership, I'm afraid we're going to have to take you down to the station."

Well, I hadn't lived on the streets most of my life without learnin' a thing or two. "On what charge? You can see I got my dog on a leash. You gonna take me in just for droppin' it a moment?" I looked back down the sidewalk. "Look!" I pointed. "He ain't left no mess or nothin'. And if he had, that's what this is for." I pulled a plastic bag out of my sweater pocket. "I always clean up after Dandy."

"You say, *Dandy*?" said the cop behind me.

"That's his name!" I was about ready to launch these guys to the moon!

From behind, the black cop added, "That's the one. That's the name of that Hero Dog on TV. I remember, 'cause my little Shatiqua was glued to the local news for three nights straight, just to get a glimpse of him."

"So what's this about?" I asked. "You want his pawprint to take back for an autograph, or somethin'?"

"Don't get smart, ma'am!" The cop in front of me held up his hand like he was stopping traffic. "We wouldn't want to add resisting arrest to the trouble you're already in."

"*Resisting*? Before I can resist, don't you have to tell me I'm under arrest? And what's the charge, anyway?"

"The charge is dog … dognapping!"

"*Dognappin'*! There ain't no such thing." That was a guess. "And even if there was, how could I be a dognapper for walkin' Miz Martha's Dandy? I think you guys been smokin' the evidence you shoulda been confiscatin' from those drug dealers! Now get outta my way." I gave Dandy a little tug and started down the street.

But in two steps—one on one side and one on the other—the two coppers grabbed my arms and spun me around. Before I knew what was what, they'd tucked me into their cruiser. Good thing I had on my purple knit hat though, 'cause they let my head bump the doorframe. Maybe I'd sue the city for hirin' such idiots.

"Where do you live, ma'am?" asked the white cop from behind the wheel.

"I currently reside at Manna House Shelter for Women, just a couple of blocks over. Why?"

"We'll ask the questions." The driver turned to his partner. "Isn't that where Hero Dog nabbed that perp?"

"That's the place."

I piped up. "And that's where I live. In fact, if you're into fillin' out more paperwork, I was a witness to the whole event, and you can interview me for blow-by-blow."

The black cop eyed me through the grill that kept me from beatin' the both of them over the head. He must've seen the fire in my eyes, because he muttered to his partner, "Maybe we oughta stop by there and check it out before takin' her in."

"Yeah, you do that! And you'll find out you're nothin' but a couple of Keystone Kops!"

Two minutes later, we pulled up to Manna House, and they "escorted" me in, keepin' a tight hold of both arms. I think it was Wanda, that loud-mouthed Jamaican woman, who saw us first, and she wasted no time rallying the troops.

We had us a near riot goin' right there in the foyer. "Leave 'er alone." "What y'all doin' with our Lucy?" "You okay, Lucy?" Those cops probably were glad they had on their bulletproof vests.

Pretty soon Fuzz Top's voice cut through the hullabaloo. "What's going on?"

"You in charge here, lady?" asked the black cop.

"No. But that's my dog. What's the problem?"

The cop glanced down at Dandy. "Is this the Hero Dog we've been hearing about on TV?"

"Some people call him that. Why?"

The two officers glanced at each other. "Depends. We saw this, uh, derelict person here with the dog, and she tried gettin' away from us. We thought maybe she was stealing the dog. We brought them here in the squad car to check it out."

I jerked my arm loose. "I *tol'* these uniforms I'm jus' walkin' the dog, but they treatin' me like some two-bit looter."

"She's right," Gabby said. "Lucy is Dandy's caregiver."

The two officers squirmed. "So why'd she run, then?"

"*Run*? What a crock! I'm almost eighty … case you hadn't noticed." I stood up straight, batted my eyes, and patted my knit hat. That got a laugh from the residents.

Just then, Mabel Turner came into the foyer. "I'm the director of Manna House. Is there a problem, Officers?"

Finally, someone to take charge. "Come on, Dandy. We ain't got time for these shenanigans!" I made a face at the cops as I elbowed our way through the knot of people. "Let's us *run*! Old lady and crippled dog!" We pushed open the double doors and "escaped" into the peace of the multipurpose room.

Chapter 21

LUCY COULD NEVER HAVE GUESSED that it would be the war that finally got them out of Niagara Falls. But as Bo had feared, while heading over Rainbow Bridge one Sunday evening after work, a border guard told him he'd better begin carrying his ID because they were going to start checking everyone.

Lucy didn't hear about it, however, until Tuesday morning when they both had a few hours off and Bo dropped by "just to talk." Sitting on the porch of the tourist home, Lucy gazed at the cotton-white clouds drifting in a crystal blue sky. It was so relaxing to have a little time together, almost as if they were tourists themselves—until Bo told her what the guard had said.

"What?" She sat straight up in her Adirondack chair, her fantasy of being tourists as fleeting as one of the clouds. Tourists were travelers who could go home. "But we don't have any ID. How will I get home without it?"

Bo clinched his mouth into a thin line and turned away from her for a moment. Then he raised both hands in helplessness. "Lucy, we don't have no home! We *can't* go home."

"Yeah, but I still got a *country*. At least I can go back to it!"

Bo shrugged. "I s'pose. But maybe we oughta wait until things settle down. This war can't last too much longer. Tide's turned in the Pacific, and pretty soon our boys'll be burnin' ol' Hitler's britches."

Lucy dropped her head and mumbled, "That's not what I heard." She wished she could read the newspaper for herself, but the guests at the tourist home were always talking about the war, and she often overheard them. "Some people are sayin' it could go on for years," she said.

"Shh ..." Bo looked down the veranda to where two other couples—paying guests—sat in the other Adirondack chairs, the young women sipping Bloody Marys through painted lips while their much older men smoked cigars. Bo leaned toward Lucy. "That kinda talk could get us in trouble." But the couples were too busy impressing each other to notice.

Lucy shook her head. "I just wanna go home, Bo. I don't wanna get stuck in a foreign country."

He reached out and took her hand. "I know, babe. I know."

Jigger bounded up on the porch with a stick in his teeth and gave a muffled bark, begging one of them to toss it. "Not now, Jigger." But Bo reached out and petted the dog absentmindedly, scratching him under his ears. Jigger dropped the stick and sat down on his haunches, looking at his master quizzically, his eyebrows pursed, head tipped to one side.

"Why don't we just go, Bo? If we ain't got no home, then why stay here? I could cross the bridge with you this evening. Then both of us'd be back in America, and we could just keep on goin'."

Bo laughed at her. "*Back in America*, huh? You know what Mrs. McDougal back there in Toronto would say, don't you?"

"Oh yeah. She'd say all this is America, but this ain't *my* America. I'm a Yank—at least, everyone keeps tellin' me that—

and I want to go back to the United States of America, that's what I want!"

Bo nodded. "Okay, okay. You're right. Nothin's holdin' us here but a couple of jobs, and we can always find those. With all the boys goin' off to war, there's plenty of jobs around."

"Really? We can go home?" Lucy threw her arms around him and squeezed. "Oh, Bo! I'll have everything ready to go soon as you get off work tonight."

"How about money? You think your boss'll pay you?"

"Got paid Friday, so it's just two days, but I'll ask him. Either way, I don't care! I just wanna go!" Even as she said it, she remembered how she used to hate moving. Every time her family pulled up stakes and headed for a new migrant camp, it brought back all the old feelings of leaving their farm in Arkansas. But not this time. She couldn't wait to move this time. If not home, she'd at least be getting closer.

"Let's see," Bo said, "the last run for the *Maid of the Mist* is at seven this evening. So I oughta be able to get outta there by half-past. Can you meet me at the bridge by then? And bring Jigger, of course."

"Oh, Bo, I'm so happy!"

But once Bo left for work and Lucy was back downstairs in her little room trying to figure out how she was going to tell her boss, she couldn't think of the words that would show why she had to leave so quickly. The fact was, they had no place to go. There was no future in what they were doing. They were just surviving from day to day, moving on like some rolling stone with no clear plan, no fresh dreams.

Her old dreams—about combing her hair so she could look like Myrna Loy or notions of going out to Hollywood to become a movie star—had withered like the last flowers she'd planted in the front of her Arkansas home. Even the drudgery that had come with caring for her little brothers, washing the blueberry stains out of their clothes and the smears of dirt off their faces before dinner, had become a memory as pleasant as a cool dip in the old reservoir. Even after they'd gone on the road, it didn't matter so much whether they were living cramped into some migrant shack or camping by a creek; they'd always been together. That's what counted.

From under her bed, she pulled out her old cardboard suitcase and began packing her meager clothes into it. The old case was scarred and the latches didn't work. But she had a rope that would hold it closed.

CARS AND PEDESTRIANS WERE BACKED UP for fifty yards on the US side of the Rainbow Bridge. Lucy craned her neck to see what the holdup was. "You have to wait like this every night?"

Bo shook his head, a grim look pinching his face. "Save my place." He handed Lucy the rope that tethered Jigger and ducked out of line, pushing his way forward, even as people protested.

Three minutes later, he was back. "They're checkin' IDs. But when we get near the front, go to the queue on the right even if others are shorter. I know that guard. I think he'll let us through."

"Are they turning people away if they don't have an ID?"

"I don't think everybody, but they're askin' a lot of questions, especially if you don't have ID. But that guy might let us through."

Ten minutes later when the main line divided into four queues, Bo swore under his breath and stamped his foot.

"What's wrong?"

"That guard's gone."

"Gone?" Her throat tightened. "What's that mean?"

"I don't know. I don't know. But let's go right anyway. Maybe he'll be back. Maybe he's just on a smoke break or something."

"Aren't there any others you recognize?"

Bo surveyed everyone he could see who wore a uniform and shook his head.

"Well, you said they were letting some people through even without ID, so we'll just have to answer their questions."

"Yeah." But he didn't seem very confident. "Yeah. Guess we'll have to answer their questions, but keep away from mentioning Lapeer, Michigan. Never can tell when someone might remember somethin'. We're just a couple of Yanks who've been workin' here at the falls and are headin' home now." He started fishing in his pockets until he produced a key with a small tag attached. "Here! This is the key to my room. That'll prove we're from the States."

"I thought you said you were at the YMCA. Is that what that tag says?"

Bo looked it. "Oh, yeah, *Young Men's* ... Guess that wouldn't be much help for you. And you're the one with a suitcase."

"Then you carry it." She thrust it toward him.

Bo took it and looked at it. "Maybe we oughta ditch it. Makes us look like we're movin'."

"Well, we are, Bo. We're movin'. And that's all the clothes I got in the world, and I'm not about to throw them away." She turned her back toward him as their queue crept forward. She knew this situation wasn't Bo's fault, but she felt mad at him anyhow. Lucy wanted him to take care of her, *to fix the things that have no fix.*

The moment that phrase crossed her mind, she recalled the last time she'd heard it. They'd been driving across the desert that had once been Oklahoma on a blistering hot day when their old Dodge began to overheat. They'd poured every cup of water they had with them into its radiator, and it was still boiling over.

"It's the wind," Pa had said. "It's blowing from behind. Radiator won't even work if no air passes through."

"Well, then," said Ma, "we just gotta pray, pray to the One who can *fix the things that have no fix*." And she began to pray. She prayed like Jesus in the Garden, so fervently Cindy had peeked to see if there were streaks of blood in the sweat rolling off her brow.

She prayed on as the car lost speed, the engine overheating to the point of nearly seizing up. And then suddenly, the wind changed its direction and swung around to blow directly toward them as a front nearly fifteen degrees cooler swept over them. Their speed picked up as the remaining dregs of water in the radiator began to cool the engine enough for it to function. Thirty miles later, when they arrived safely at the next gas station, a small squall brought the first rain the people in that part of the country had seen in three months.

"Bo ..." Lucy swung around to face him as fast as if she'd been sitting in a Ridee-O car. "Bo, we gotta pray!"

"What?" He looked at her as if she'd lost her mind.

"Pray! We gotta pray that we'll get in even though we don't have no ID. Pray, that's what Ma did. We hafta pray!"

Bo shrugged. "Okay. Pray if you want, see if that'll help. But ..."

Lucy didn't have time to explain, let alone convince Bo. She just bowed her head, clinched her eyes so tightly closed that little tears squeezed out of the corners, and prayed while Bo gently moved her forward as the line slowly progressed. "Oh, God, fix what ain't got no fix. We gotta get across this border. I can't stay in this foreign country one more day, God. Make those guards not even see us and let us pass right through. You can do it, God. I know You're the one *to fix the things that have no fix*, so—"

"Lucy, Lucy, it's our turn. Come on."

She opened her eyes and saw a boy in an army uniform reaching his hand out toward her. Wisps of hair on his upper lip had been curried with dark wax to resemble a mustache.

He cleared his throat and produced a deep voice. "Your ID, please."

"Uh …" She just stared at him as though she couldn't believe he was speaking to her.

"That'll do, Crump." An older soldier stepped up, a man with a real mustache and three stripes on his sleeve. "I'll take it from here … Crump? You're dismissed, private." As the younger guard frowned and walked away, the larger man held his stomach with both hands and rubbed it gently. "Musta been something I ate. Phew! And that latrine smells as bad as a slit trench."

Then he looked at Bo. "So, how's it goin', Hansen? You off work early tonight?"

"Yeah. They don't run so late on Tuesdays."

"You're lucky. Look at this mess." He waved his hand at the lines of people and cars trying to cross the border. "You with him?" He pointed at Lucy. When she nodded, he motioned with his hand. "Come on through, then. As you can see, I'm gonna be here for a long time."

Lucy walked through the checkpoint beside Bo with her mouth hanging open. The man had glanced at her, but it was as though he hadn't even seen her.

Chapter 22

Once safely on the US side of Niagara Falls, Lucy and Bo hitchhiked down around Lake Erie and into the heart of Ohio without really knowing where they were going. It was nearly sundown when their fifth ride in two days—this one in the back of an old pickup that had last hauled hogs—stopped for gas at an intersection somewhere northwest of Columbus. Lucy roused herself from sleep and looked around, blurry eyed. The day's humidity that had glazed its grit and grime into her skin was settling like smoky haze in the grassy ditches beside the road and drifting in ribbons across low-lying pastures. Cicadas struck up a rasping din in the overhanging oaks.

Lucy stood up and stretched. *Whew!* Somehow she had to wash the stink of travel off her, except … she glanced down at Bo … except, he also smelled like bad fish and vinegar as he practiced his harmonica. Still, she couldn't stand herself. She looked west at the amber sky, and her breath caught. "Bo, Bo, look!" She tapped his shoulder and pointed across the cornfield. "A carnival! Maybe we could get something to eat! My stomach's growlin'."

Bo got up slowly, dusting straw and other debris off his pants. Jigger whined. The corn had been harvested by hand, which left enough of the six-foot-high stocks to create a jagged fence of sorts, concealing much of what lay beyond, especially since everything in that direction was silhouetted against the setting sun.

"Maybe … Tent's about the size of a big top with pennants and all, but I don't see any rides or side shows or concessions or …"

Lucy grabbed his arm. "No, look there … uh …" She was momentarily distracted by the firmness of his bicep. "… uh, there's a second tent, a smaller one on the end. See? Maybe it's just a circus and they don't have rides. Or maybe the rides are on the other side, and there's no big wheel or anything tall enough for us to see it from here? Let's check it out, Bo. Get somethin' to eat, maybe even a job. I'm tired of this hitchhikin'. Aren't you?"

"You're darn tootin' I am." He squinted against the setting sun. "Ugh! Two nights without a bed and havin' to hoof it half the time, I've 'bout had it. Come on." He dropped his harmonica into his duffle bag and hopped out of the back of the pickup, followed by Jigger, and helped Lucy do the same. While she retrieved her small suitcase, Bo again stared across the cornfield. "I don't know, though. Somethin' don't seem right."

They thanked the pickup driver for their ride and, with Jigger marking every post and bush, headed along the shoulder of the road until they'd passed the cornfield. The big tent sat at the back of a twenty-acre pasture filled with cars parked in neat rows. No longer backlit by the sunset, the tent glowed dimly from lights within. The sound of the crowd reached them, not screaming and yelling like folks on thrill rides, but talking and laughing in a pulsating buzz that blended with the cicadas in the surrounding trees. Over it all an electric organ belted out music as buoyant as any circus warm up.

Bo's pace slowed. "It still don't look like no circus I've ever seen, and it sure ain't no carnival."

"How do you know?" Lucy pulled on his hand. "It's somethin', and a lot of people are there. Besides I'm starvin'. We gotta get us somethin' to eat."

Bo relaxed enough for her to pull him through the parking lot. Even some boxy, black buggies were parked among the cars. "Amish," Lucy noted. "And look back there, a couple of little trailers and a big flatbed truck. Couldn't that carry the tent?"

"I s'pose. Maybe you're right. It sure enough is some kinda show."

"There!" Lucy pointed at a banner across the front of the tent.

Bo stopped as though he'd run into a wall and read aloud. "'Gospel Revival. Signs, Miracles, Wonders. Only Believe!'" He stiffened. "Believe what?"

"Believe God, silly! It's a tent meetin'. A revival. Haven't you seen one before? Used to come through Arkansas all the time. Ma woulda gone, but Pa wasn't much for church. Said it was better to read the Word at home. But come on. Cain't hurt nothin'!" She pulled him forward.

They took Jigger around to the side of the tent and told the dog to sit and stay. He'd do so for a while, but Lucy knew if they made him wait too long, his curiosity would get the best of him, and he'd go exploring. But she didn't worry. He was smart and wouldn't venture out of earshot.

As they entered the gaping entrance in the end of the tent, the hubbub of the crowd quieted, and a voice boomed over a squealing PA system. "Turn to number sixteen in your song sheets, and let's begin this evening with 'Blessed Assurance.'" The organ played a short introduction, and the crowd began to sing while a man on the stage waved his arms expansively to direct the singing.

"Welcome! Welcome!" A short man with curly red hair and a black bowtie accosted them from the shadows just inside the tent door. He stepped up to Bo and handed him a piece of paper. "You're just in time. We still have plenty of good seats up front. If you'll come with me."

Lucy started to follow the little man down an aisle thickly strewn with sawdust, presumably to prevent the heavy traffic from churning the damp ground into mud, but Bo hung back and put his hand out to restrain her.

"Bo ... what're ya doin'?"

He leaned down to speak in her ear above the singing. "I ain't no pushover. I need to check this out first."

Realizing no one was following him, the redheaded man stopped and turned back, motioning Lucy and Bo to follow as he smiled warmly at them. But when Bo held up both hands, the man shrugged, raising his shoulders and eyebrows as though the same marionette strings connected both, and walked back toward them, searching the rows on each side until he spied two seats in the next-to-last one. He held up two fingers and pointed down the row, lifting his animated eyebrows again in question.

Bo shook his head, and the man gave up and returned to where they stood in the wide doorway. He gave them a puzzled frown and for the first time seemed to notice Lucy's suitcase. Beckoning with his finger for them to follow, he led them outside and away from the entrance.

He was obviously about to ask what was wrong when Bo took the initiative. "Uh ... we're actually lookin' for work. We're both experienced show people and are kinda on the road. We saw your tent and were wonderin' if ..."

The man looked down at Lucy's suitcase again and shook his head. "People from our local churches volunteer for pretty much everything pertaining to the revival. Now, the Reverend Cecil Barns—he's the evangelist—he does have a staff that travels with him, but you'd have to speak to him about that after the service." He looked up, studying Lucy and Bo through squinted eyes. "However, if you've been on the road, you probably need something to eat, don'tcha? Go 'round to the back." He pointed the direction. "You'll find a smaller tent. Volunteers and staff always come early, and some of the ladies fix a meal for us. They had some pretty good chicken and dumplings tonight. You might see if there's any leftovers. Ask for Esther Cooper, and tell her Joey sent you and that you're new, uh, volunteers ... that's if you're willing to stay after and help clean up and straighten the chairs for tomorrow. But tomorrow's the last night."

Lucy looked up at Bo, who nodded his head as they headed around to the smaller tent. Jigger saw them and came bounding over, his whole rump wiggling.

"You got a place to stay the night?" the man called after them.

"No sir. Just got in."

"Look me up afterward. I'm one of the elders from The River of Life Tabernacle. We'll find you a place." He disappeared back inside the large tent.

"Well, I'll be, if that weren't right nice of him," Lucy said.

"Yeah." Bo trudged through the grass beside her. "But I don't get it."

"Don't get what?"

"Why he'd help us out, that's what."

Lucy shrugged. "Pa always said, 'Don't look a gift horse in the mouth.' So I'm just hopin' they still got some food."

THEY COULD HEAR SINGING from the big tent the whole time they ate their chicken and dumplings. Lucy recognized some of the songs as ones Ma used to sing, but the words were muffled inside the

192

food tent where they sat on benches, one on either side of a table made from sawhorses with boards on top. The dumplings had become a little soggy, but Lucy would have eaten nearly anything by then.

Esther Cooper came up to their table. "Would you two like some shoo-fly pie and a mug of coffee?" She was a stout woman with rosy cheeks and dark hair packaged like a huge sausage around the back of her head in a black net.

After a moment's hesitation, Bo held up both hands. "Just the coffee. Thank you."   Lucy would have loved a piece of pie with coffee, but had that woman actually said it was made with flies? "Uh … yes, ma'am. I'll have some coffee." She couldn't have said *flies*. Lucy took a deep breath. "And I'll try a small piece of the pie too."

Lucy couldn't see any evidence of flies in the scrumptious, sweet pie that seemed to be made with raspberries. "This pie's swell," she said, offering Bo a bite, but he still wouldn't taste it.

Instead he got up and asked Esther Cooper if she had a can he could put some water in for their little dog outside.

"You got a dog? He must be very well behaved not to come nosing in here."

"He only goes where he's invited."

"Well then, here's a pan. There's fresh water in those milk cans along the side. And I've got some scraps I was going to throw out. Might be some chicken bones in it though … would he choke?"

"Haven't known him to, ma'am. Thank you. Thank you very much."

By the time Bo came back from caring for Jigger, the singing in the big tent had ended, and someone was preaching. "Should we go back in?" Lucy tipped her head in the direction.

"Ah, I dunno. Wouldn't want to interrupt."

"We could stand in the back."

Bo studied her a moment. "You wanna go in, don'tcha, babe?"

Lucy shrugged. "Yeah. Kinda."

"All right. Just for you … as long as that eager beaver don't make us sit down front." As they walked back to the big tent, he added, "Who knows, we might learn somethin' new 'bout showbiz."

Lucy never thought of a church meeting as show business, but then she'd seldom been in a church. In fact, she could count on her fingers the number of times her family had attended church, and that included Christmas and Easter. Maybe it was all showbiz.

The *eager beaver*, as Bo called him, just nodded and smiled when they stepped into the tent. He pointed to Lucy's suitcase and a space by his chair that was situated back against the tent wall, but Lucy shook her head and put it down beside her. The man was just being courteous, but that wallet with all the money was in there—along with the only spare clothes she had—and no way was she letting it out of her sight when she was in public.

At first Lucy thought Bo might be right. The preacher onstage sounded pretty much like the Talker who enticed people into the woman-to-gorilla sideshow at Bo's carnival. He was loud—aided by the fist-sized silver microphone on the end of a pole stand he dragged with him as he walked from one side of the stage to the other—he was smooth of speech, and he was animated, gesturing widely with the open Bible he held in the other hand. But the more she listened, the more she felt he was speaking right to her, even though fifty rows of people separated her standing in the dark entrance from his brightly lit stage.

"… and the Bible says"—the preacher lifted high the book, causing its thin pages to roll over—"'Seek ye the Lord while he may be found; call ye upon him while he is near.' He's near to you tonight, dear brother, dear sister." There, was he talking to her? "Do not harden your heart against him. Take this word as if it were spoken personally to you, not to your neighbor, not to someone who is better than you or someone who you think is worse than you, but to you!" *Oh, no!* Lucy's shoulders slumped. He *was* talking to her.

Taking long steps all the way across the stage, dragging his mike with him, the preacher shouted into it. "'If thou seek him, he will be found of thee,' First Chronicles twenty-eight and nine says. 'If thou seek him, he will be found of thee.' It's a promise for *you!*"

Lucy's thoughts drifted back to their crossing of the Rainbow Bridge at Niagara and how she'd prayed to "the One who can *fix the things that have no fix.*" Had she been seeking the Lord when she prayed that little prayer? Is that what the preacher was talking about? Had God answered her by getting them across the border when it had looked like they might be turned back? *He will be found of thee* ... is that what happened? Had she, Lucinda Tucker, found God in that moment?

"Ha!" She clapped her hand over her mouth and glanced at Bo to see if he'd heard her.

He leaned down and muttered. "I'm goin' out to check on Jigger. See ya afterward."

She watched him go, then pondered her question again. Maybe that wasn't God answering her prayer after all. They got across the border because the sergeant had come back and knew Bo ... but then again, he'd come back at the very moment they'd needed him.

The preacher caught her attention again, pointing a finger toward the crowd, but somehow his finger seemed to be pointing right at her. "Many of you think faith is a very mysterious thing, something that applies only to religious people ..." *Yeah, like Ma,* thought Lucy. "... or perhaps you think you'll look into it when you're on your deathbed. But that's not what the Bible says. 'If thou seek him, he will be found of thee.' It's a promise with only one condition ..." He paused, and Lucy thought, *Here it comes. Something I can't do.*

The preacher held his pause and then whispered into the mike, "Sincerity. Did you hear that? I said, sincerity!" he shouted. "You can't play with God. You can't ask His help today but forget Him tomorrow. The psalmist wrote, 'Blessed are they that keep his testimonies, and that seek him with the whole heart.' You can't play with God."

Lucy squirmed. Had she been playing with God, asking for His help and then forgetting about Him once they were across the border? If it *had* been God who'd helped them, she knew it wasn't right to forget about Him. But why would God have responded to her in the first place? She'd only prayed because she was in a panic.

The preacher closed his Bible and dropped it flat on the front edge of the stage with a loud thump. Then he pulled a large handkerchief out of his pocket and wiped the sweat from his face. Lucy recognized the showmanship in his actions, but he still had her attention when he pulled the microphone right up to his lips. "There's just one question for you tonight: Will you seek Him? Now, right now, will you seek Him?

"As the organ plays—every head bowed, every eye closed—will you seek Him tonight? If so, make your way down here to the altar, where we will pray with you and show you from God's Word how Jesus Christ can help you find God.

"Come now! Come as we sing!"

Lucy *did* want to find God. He was the strength that saw Ma through hard times, the strength she needed now when she was so far from home. Her feet started to move … then caught on the suitcase, almost causing her to stumble. She stared down at it. It held the money she'd taken from a dead man. Sure, she thought it belonged to Pa, but she had no right to take it herself. And the wallet had turned out to contain far more than was owed her family.

She was a thief. And try as she might, there seemed no way to make it right.

She looked up at the people from all over the tent, making their way out of their seats and down the sawdust aisles. Tears clouded her sight as she reached down, picked up her suitcase, and walked outside to find Bo.

Chapter 23

JOEY, THE REDHEADED USHER AT THE TENT MEETING, turned out to be the husband of Esther Cooper the cook, and he invited Lucy and Bo to stay with them that night after they helped straighten the folding wooden chairs and picked up the trash.

A half-moon shown across the trampled pasture where the wispy mists of a few hours earlier had settled as heavy dew on the grass, soaking their shoes as they walked to the Coopers' streamlined Hudson, one of the last cars left in the parking lot. Mr. Cooper had to wipe the windows with a towel before he could see to drive. In the backseat, Lucy shivered. This was the first cold snap of the season, and she did not have the clothes for it.

But she was so tired as they rode to the Coopers' house that she fell asleep leaning against the window and awoke only when the car bounced over chuckholes turning into their hosts' lane. The silver moonlight painted the square, two-story house and its wraparound veranda in ghostly shadows, unsoftened by any welcoming lamps from within. A single bulb glaring from a cone reflector high on the corner of the large hip-roofed barn illuminated a pyramid of the rusty red barn, the only color to be seen. Skeletons of two towering cottonwoods behind the house and a large weeping willow out front tied the homestead together like an island in the middle of the surrounding fields.

Pa could've made our place this nice, thought Lucy, *if it hadn't been for the drought and dust stripping everything bare.*

"You can let your dog run loose for the night as far as I'm concerned," said Mr. Cooper as they got out of the car. "Big Red's our rooster, and he can take care of his hens just fine. Saw him chase off a fox the other day."

Bo laughed. "Oh yeah? Well, Jigger won't bother nothin'. He's used to being around all kinds of animals. In fact, back when …" He stopped.

Lucy knew what he'd almost said. She took a loud, deep breath of the night air, damp and smelling of cows and old hay. "We sure appreciate you lettin' us stay the night."

"It's our pleasure," said Mrs. Cooper. "With our kids gone, we have extra space, and I'm sure the good Lord wants us to share it. So come on in and make yourselves at home. I'll fix some tea. Sorry to be taking you in the back way, but we hardly ever go around to the front."

Once inside, the house lost its chilly appearance as soon as the electric lights were turned on, revealing a cheery kitchen and warm rooms with comfortable furniture beyond.

In the living room, Mrs. Cooper pointed to pictures on the mantel. "Our Bill's in the service. He and our son-in-law, Roger— that's Roger and Ann's wedding photo right there—were best friends growin' up, so they signed up together, and now they're both marines somewhere in the Pacific. I pray every day for them. Ann's in Chicago. We keep trying to get her to come home, at least while Roger's gone, but she's got a job she likes and goes to a real good little church up there. We visited a couple of times, but now with the rationing, it'd be hard to make the trip."

While Mr. Cooper pulled on a pair of boots and went out to check on the cows, Mrs. Cooper led them upstairs, stopping a couple of times to catch her breath. "Whew!... This is Ann's old room on the right. You can sleep in here, honey." She switched on the light. "And if there's anything you need, just let me know. The bathroom's at the end of the hall if you want to take a bath. Towels are on the shelf, and the water heater should be working, though it's been giving Joey fits lately."

Lucy suspected she was hinting at her need for a bath, but it sounded too good to take offense.

"And you, young man, you can use Roger's room. We pray he'll be back with us soon, but he's not here now, so make yourselves at home. I'll have that tea ready for you in just a minute."

"Oh, please don't bother," Bo called after her as she headed downstairs. "We'll be fine."

"You sure?" She stopped and looked back as he nodded his head decisively. "Okay then. I'll leave you be." Her sensible shoes clunked on each step as she descended.

Lucy waved Bo into her room and swung the door closed quietly. "She knows we're not married."

Bo shrugged. "I reckon most people can guess that much."

"Yeah, but ... we're travelin' together."

"So?"

"So they're likely to wonder why."

"No doubt, but that ain't none of their business, is it?" He left, and Lucy heard him enter the room across the hall and shut the door.

Maybe he was just tired. She sure was. But she didn't like him being so short with her. She opened her suitcase and got out some clean clothes. A few minutes later she nearly fell asleep in the steaming hot tub. What a luxury!

THE SMELL OF FRESH COFFEE and frying bacon woke Lucy the next morning before Mrs. Cooper called her.

"Good morning, honey. You sleep all right?"

"Yes. Thank you, ma'am."

"Your friend's out helping Joey with the cows. They'll be in directly. In fact, could you step outside and give them a holler?"

The men came in ten minutes later and washed up. After Mr. Cooper prayed over the food and the eggs, bacon, and biscuits were being passed, he said, "I sure appreciate your help with the cows this morning." He eyed Bo while he put some pepper on his eggs. "You grow up on a farm?"

Bo chewed his bite of biscuit and jam much longer than necessary. "Not really."

"But you said your dog was used to being around all kinds of animals."

"Yeah, but, uh … they were more like pets, I guess."

"You know what, Joey?" Mrs. Cooper got up and brought the pot over to freshen everyone's coffee. "I think it's time we got ourselves another dog. We used to have this beautiful German shepherd named Adolph. Of course, I wouldn't name a dog that now for all the tea in China. But he was a good dog. Belonged to Roger, really."

Mr. Cooper poured a dose of cream into his coffee. "So where are you two from, out here travelin' the highways and byways?"

When Bo didn't answer right away, Lucy spoke up. "Back east. You know, New York and them parts."

"Really? The both of you? Your accents sound more like …" He waved his hand toward the southwest.

Bo cleared his throat. "Like you said, we've been travelin' a lot. Probably mixes the accents all up."

Mr. Cooper frowned. "Well, you're both mighty young to be on the road. Your parents approve of you traveling by yourselves?"

"Joey, stop giving these kids the third degree."

"I'm not! But it doesn't hurt to get acquainted. How old are you, son?"

"Almost eighteen. Been on my own for quite a while, though."

"Then you'll probably be signin' up with Uncle Sam or get drafted pretty soon, won't you?"

Lucy stopped eating, fork halfway to her mouth. She looked at Bo.

He avoided her eyes. "I s'pect so."

"*Hmm*, draft age was twenty-one, but now that we've entered the war, your duty begins at eighteen. You be signin' up?"

"Enough of this war talk," cut in Mrs. Cooper as she sat down and reached for the jam. "Where are you two headed after this?"

"Now who's giving them the third degree, Esther?"

"Oh, hush. I'm just trying to be friendly. We know people all over the country—through the church, that is. Might help them out."

"We're going to Chicago." It was the only city Lucy could think of in the moment.

"Chicago! Well, maybe you ought to look up our Ann, then." Mrs. Cooper beamed.

Mr. Cooper slid his chair back and addressed Bo. "Mind helping me buck some bales? I have a wagonload of hay that needs putting in the loft. Don't have one of those newfangled conveyors, so takes two to spear 'em and lift 'em up with the pulley, but you look strong enough for it."

Bo quickly finished his plate and followed the man outside. Lucy helped Mrs. Cooper with the dishes and then peeled apples— and more apples—for five apple pies. "I'm the pie woman," she chuckled. "Easier than cooking huge pots of chili or whatever they're having this evening. Lord, Lord, I love the revival, but I'm glad this is the last day."

Lucy was glad to be done peeling all those apples and had slipped upstairs to her room when Bo came in to wash up for lunch. With hay sticking all over him, he stepped into her room and closed the door softly. "We gotta get outta here," he hissed. "That man's askin' too many questions. He knows I ain't tellin' everything, and that keeps him goin'."

"But … won't it be kind of late to hit the road after the service tonight? I mean, might be hard to get a ride." She was so looking forward to one more night in a comfortable bed before they headed out to who-knew-where.

"I don't mean tonight. I mean now—right after lunch."

Disappointment pinched her breath. "But Bo! I wanted to hear that preacher again. He was saying' some things last night that—"

"Look, you can always go to church if you want, but right now we don't need no one figurin' out who we are. Why did you tell them we're going to Chicago?"

"I don't know. Just seemed like a place one might go."

"Yeah, well … I'd been thinkin' the same thing. There's an amusement park there where I thought we might get work, but now that they know that's where we're headed …"

"It's a huge city, Bo. No one can find us in such a big place. That's what you said about Detroit, wasn't it? And that was in Michigan, close to where …" She didn't finish.

Bo paced back and forth in the little room, running a hand anxiously over his head. "Yeah, I guess. But I don't like dropping clues. That's what Mr. Cooper's gettin' out of me with all his 'innocent' questions—a scrap of information here and a scrap there. Pretty soon he'll be able to put it all together like a jigsaw puzzle."

"But ... but ..." Lucy had been thinking about what the preacher said the night before. She wished now she'd gone forward for prayer. What could it have hurt? He'd said if she would seek God, she would find Him. He didn't say she *couldn't* seek God or find Him if she was a thief. God *had* answered her prayer when they were trying to cross the border, and that was after she'd taken the money. But ... her spirit sagged. Maybe Bo was right.

Still ... "If Mr. Cooper's getting suspicious, we can't just disappear. That'd just raise more suspicion, wouldn't it? We have to come up with a good excuse and say good-bye properly, don'tcha think?"

Bo frowned, then slowly nodded. "I s'pose. Let me noodle on it."

"SURE DO APPRECIATE THIS LUNCH, Mrs. Cooper. But I'm afraid we're gonna have to take a hike this afternoon."

Mr. Cooper chuckled. "Haven't I been giving you enough exercise bucking bales?"

"Oh, yes sir. Didn't mind the work. We really appreciate your hospitality, but we gotta get on the road."

Lucy closed her eyes. That wasn't a very "good excuse" Bo had come up with after all his "noodling."

"So soon? Just what are you going to be doing when you get to—"

"Now Joey, quit interrogating these kids. That's their business." Mrs. Cooper gave Lucy's head a motherly pat. "We've just been pleased to help you out as we could. And you, young man, Joey's got straw and dust all in your clothes. Tell you what, our Roger is about your size, tall and slender. I have a bag of clothes he was planning to put in the missionary barrel. Nice jacket in there too. I don't think he'd have any question about giving some to you. You could even take a bath first."

"That's mighty nice of you, ma'am, but—"

Lucy jumped in. "He's more than happy to accept, ain't you, Bo. Thank you so much, Mrs. Cooper. You've been great." Bo needed a change of clothes, and he sure did need a bath if they were going to hitchhike, or people would be putting them out before they got a mile down the road.

"And you, young lady," Mrs. Cooper said, looking sternly at Lucy. "You need a coat, and I've got just the one." She hustled through the living room and returned a few moments later shaking out a dark peacoat. "Outgrew this one quite some time ago," she laughed.

Excusing himself from the table, Mr. Cooper went back out to the barn and Bo headed upstairs for a bath while Lucy helped clear the dishes.

Mrs. Cooper took the last two pies out of the oven and set them on the table to cool. Then she turned to Lucy with her hands on her wide hips. "Lucy girl, I know you two aren't married, so I don't know what you've been doing when you don't have two bedrooms like we have here, but—"

Lucy's face got hot. "Oh, we haven't been sleepin' together. No, ma'am!"

"*Hmph.* Well, that's good, but … but it's not going to get any easier, young lady. I can see you two like each other, and there's gonna come a time when it just seems natural, when all the reasons to wait fade away." The plump woman motioned for Lucy to sit, then leaned forward earnestly. "Before you get to that point, and I do mean *before*, ask yourself some questions. Is this young man the one you want to marry? Pray—you do pray, don't you?"

Lucy nodded, remembering the border crossing and times with Ma … not very often, actually.

"Good! Pray that God will show you whether this man would make a good husband. And if so, get yourself married. Do it first! Do it God's way, and you'll be blessed."

Lucy nodded, not trusting herself to say anything about the longings that rose in her heart. Bo was a good man, the best friend she'd ever had, and she did want to get married someday. That was her dream, and she often imagined Bo fulfilling that dream. But … she was only fifteen. Did she know enough to make a lifelong decision?

Mrs. Cooper took Lucy's hand in her own. "Listen to me, now. When you get to Chicago, you look up my daughter, Ann. Here, I'll write down her name and address for you." She let go of Lucy's hand, rummaged in a drawer, and came up with a stubby pencil and an old envelope. "Take this and find her. She'll take you to church. It's a good little church, and the pastor there can help the two of you get started on the right foot. That's so important, honey. So important! Joey and I have been married twenty-six years come Christmas, and I wouldn't change him for any other man. He's the right man for me, even though we don't always see eye to eye. So you do it right, and you'll have a better chance of a good life together. Hear me, now?"

Lucy nodded and got up to dry the remaining dishes before Mrs. Cooper could see the tears gathering in her eyes.

Chapter 24

I WAS ON KITCHEN DUTY, drying the breakfast dishes *again,* when Dandy startled me with his wet nose against my leg. My first thought was, *if Estelle Williams catches him in her kitchen, she'll ban him from the whole lower level of Manna House.* But then I realized Dandy was goin' nuts—moanin' and whinin' and nudgin' me to follow him somewhere.

"Okay, okay! I'm a-comin', but you better get your waggedy butt outta here 'fore Estelle sees you." I tossed the towel on the counter, and as soon as Dandy saw I was following, he took off, bounding up the stairs as though he hadn't just gotten his stitches out a few days before. It was good he was feelin' so frisky, but I'd just come down from that multipurpose room not ten minutes before because they were startin' that book club meetin' in there. Not my cup of tea, ya know.

Now Dandy was making me climb the stairs again.

When I came through the door, he was over near my dear friend, Martha Shepherd, still whinin' and carryin' on like he had with me. But he wasn't nudgin' her to go anywhere.

She pulled a book off the shelf and turned to hand it to that bookworm with the brown ponytail. Name's Carolyn, and I think she used to work in a library. But as Martha handed her the book, I realized something wasn't right. She didn't let go, even though Carolyn said, "Thanks, Miss Martha. Uh, I've got it; you can let go." Martha just stood there starin' at her like she'd gone into some kind of a trance or somethin'.

Dandy went from moanin' and whinnin' to outright barkin' and jumpin' around like he was havin' a fit.

"Grab her before she falls!" Carolyn yelled, and Gabby jumped up to help lower her into a chair.

"I think she's having a stroke!" Carolyn cried. "We need help!" She ran for the foyer.

I got over there as Gabby tried to get her mother to smile and raise her arms. For whatever reason, I didn't know. I pushed my way in and grabbed Martha by the shoulders. "Miz Martha! Wake up, honey!" But she just stared straight ahead, her eyes not focusing on anything. "Do somethin' girl!" I said to Gabby. Certainly a daughter oughta know what to do. And she did ... I guess. She opened her cell phone and dialed 9-1-1.

That's when it hit me: Carolyn might be right! Maybe Miz Martha *was* having a stroke. I glanced down at Dandy. He'd settled down and was lookin' as much like a little lost boy as a dog could look. How he knew something was wrong with Martha before anyone else did, I'll never know.

I felt useless. This wasn't diarrhea from eating bad food from a Dumpster or a bloody toe or a summer cold—the kinds of things I dealt with all the time. Something was seriously wrong with Martha. What if Carolyn was right? People died from strokes. Felt as if my insides were turning inside out. I couldn't handle losing my best friend right then.

It took four of us to move Martha and lay her down on a couch. Then I got a damp paper towel from the washroom and put it on her head, hoping that would revive her, but her eyes had gone as dead as burned-out coals. I couldn't get her to look at me, and she didn't even flinch when I snapped my fingers. But she was still breathin'.

I stood up and looked around at all the people starin' at her. "What's the matter with you all? Somebody oughta be prayin', don'tcha think?" I was gettin' so angry I was about to snap my cap. "Don't they say, 'Where there's life, there's hope'? So why ain't some of you good Christians bangin' on heaven's door?" I'd have done it myself, but it'd be about as useless as me tryin' to write God a letter. I stomped off to the washroom to get another damp towel.

When I came out, the paramedics were barging through the front door with their whole kit and kabboodle, including a tank of oxygen, which they immediately hooked up to Martha, so I couldn't even cool her head with my damp towel. It didn't take them long, checkin' her out and talkin' to some doctor on their little radios before they decided to take her to Thorek Memorial Hospital.

Gabby got in the ambulance with her mother, but they wouldn't give any of the rest of us a ride. No matter. It was no more than a hop, skip, and a jump—none of which I did anymore, of course. But Mabel called a cab, and Carolyn and Precious McGill insisted they should go with her. I just drifted out the door and started walking. Probably could have gotten there first, but that wasn't what I was aimin' for. I knew that until they brought Martha around, they weren't gonna let any of us in to see her anyway.

In fact, it was temptin' to go over to the cemetery and sit for a while, but instead I just walked slow, thinkin'. Why was it that every time I had a good thing goin', somethin' happened, and I lost it? Lost our farm to the Dust Bowl. Lost my family in Michigan.

209

Lost … I stopped myself. Even though my heart felt as hollow as an empty egg shell, this wasn't about me. It was about Martha. I picked up my step and hoofed it on over there. Maybe I'd get a chance to see her and encourage her a little.

When I got to the ER—they all look the same—I searched the waiting room. Mabel sat in one of those green plastic-covered chairs staring straight ahead like a schoolgirl on punishment. Carolyn was pacing around as if she were having a nicotine fit. But Precious, bless her heart, was sitting in the corner prayin', out loud sometimes in spite of the other patients and families sittin' around waitin'. Her head was sometimes bowed so that her tiny braids covered her ebony face and sometimes up as if expectin' God to speak from the ceiling.

I nearly went over and joined her, not that I thought I could match her prayin', but to keep anyone else away who might try to interfere. But then I worried that even I might distract her, so I went to a chair on the other side of the room and sat.

Finally, Gabby came out, and we all gathered around for some news, but there wasn't much. She said her mom was still unconscious but breathing normally. The doctors were pretty sure she'd had a stroke and were giving her a CAT scan to determine the degree of damage. And that's all she could say before she broke into quiet sobs.

I'm not much of a hugger, but I knew this was a time for one and slipped my arms around her. She leaned her head against my head—my frizzy gray hair separated from her wild carrot top by nothing more than my purple knit hat.

We stood there like that—the other ladies standin' back a little as if they didn't know what to do—until a doctor came through the double-swinging doors and said, "Mrs. Fairbanks?"

Gabby pulled herself away and nodded at the doctor.

He frowned at me and glanced at Mabel and the others. "Would you like some privacy? We can go to a conference room."

"We can talk here. They're with me." Gabby and Mabel sat down. Precious and Carolyn huddled around as the doctor pulled up another chair to face them. I stood back, not sure whether it was my place. But I wanted to know.

The snatches I heard didn't sound good. "… a massive brain hemorrhage … never seen such a large bleed … weak blood vessels that break … without warning."

Finally, Gabby asked, "What can you do?"

"With a smaller bleed, we might be able to do surgery … the hemorrhage is so massive … she's in a coma … life support … or … let nature take its course."

Let nature take its course? Surely Gabby wouldn't do that! They kept talking, but I stepped away, feeling like I was goin' to pass out myself. This couldn't be happening. Surely Martha would recover. They just needed to give her some time. Yes, time, time is what she needed.

As soon as the doctor went back into the ER, I rushed up to Gabby. "He sayin' jus' let 'er *die*? Ya can't do that!"

"So ya think she oughta play God?" Precious snapped. "Step in an' keep Gramma Shep goin' after her body give out? What about you? If you was in a coma, wouldja want some machine ta be doin' your breathin'? Not knowin' anything?"

"That's diff'rent." Though I hadn't thought of it that way. What would Martha want?

"Why?" Precious challenged. "Why would it be different for you?"

"'Cause—"

"Both of you, shut up!" Carolyn grabbed my arm. "Come on, let's go get some coffee, leave Mabel and Gabby."

I yanked my arm free. Why Mabel and Gabby? What did Mabel have to do with deciding about *my* best friend? But something caused me to go with Carolyn and Precious anyway, and it wasn't that I needed coffee. It was just that … that Gabby hadn't invited me to stay, I guess.

The worse insult came an hour later when Mabel found us in the hospital café, buzzing with more coffee than I usually drink in a whole day. "They've put her in a private room. So now it's just a matter of waiting."

"*Waiting*? Waitin' for what?" I knew what she meant, of course. But it made me mad, and I wanted to force her to say it.

Mabel took a deep breath. "Until she passes," she said in a tired, thin voice.

"Guess we ain't prayed hard enough, then, huh?"

"Lucy …" Mabel dug in the purse she had slung over her shoulder until she found her keys. "Lucy, I'm going to take you back to Manna House so you can look out for Dandy." She turned to Precious and Carolyn. "If you two got the time, why don't you go up and sit with Gabby. It's room four-eighteen."

I couldn't help it. "*Sit with Gabby*? Who's gonna sit with Miz Martha? You're talkin' like she's already gone."

"Come on, Lucy. Let's go."

I trudged after her—after all, Dandy was probably beside himself—but I wasn't about to give up. After I'd walked and fed the dog and talked to him some, I told Mabel I was headin' back to the hospital. She sighed and insisted we have some lunch first. Said she was goin' over herself and wanted to give me a ride. But I reckon it was to keep an eye on me.

When we walked into the room, Gabby was tellin' stories about her mom, sayin' something about snakes, not the kind of thing a sick person needs to hear, so I went right around the bed

212

and planted myself in a chair on the other side. "Hey there, Miz Martha. It's me, Lucy. Just wantcha to know, Dandy's missin' ya real bad, so don't pay these people no mind. Just come on home."

I just held Martha's hand while the others chattered on. I have to admit that Martha's color did not look good, kinda pasty yellow. Her eyes were closed, of course, and her cheeks were saggin'. No one had fixed her hair, so I tried to smooth it down a little on the pillow. What she needed was a knit hat like mine. Maybe I'd get Estelle to make her one.

At first, I thought she was breathing slow because she was relaxed with me bein' there and talkin' to her. But then her breaths got too far apart, and I started to worry. I don't think the others even realized what was happenin' until she completely stopped, and I cried out, "Miz Martha! C'mon, now, breathe!"

She heard me and drew another long slow one.

"That's right. C'mon!" I urged.

I waited and waited, listening for a response. But all I heard was the slight hiss of the oxygen in the little tube to her nose.

My Martha was gone!

Chapter 25

CHICAGO WAS MUCH LARGER than Lucy had ever imagined. She peered out the car window as they rode past steel mills and through neighborhoods with little brick bungalows side by side for miles and miles, and still the tall buildings of the skyline were well north of them.

The man and woman who'd picked them up somewhere in Indiana in the middle of the night had been kind enough to let them sleep for most of the trip.

"You kids said you're heading to Chicago," the driver said, "but I'm afraid this is as close to downtown as we're gonna get." He turned into a Texaco gas station and pulled up to a pump. "Of course, if you want to head on south with us to Springfield, you're welcome. We'll be catchin' Route 66 west of here and then head on down to visit Helen's mom. But right over there," he pointed with his finger, "is the Jackson Park elevated station. Trains run regular from there into the Loop. From there, you can catch a train or a streetcar or a bus that'll take you anywhere, like spokes on a wheel."

The gas station attendant in his olive-drab uniform and peaked cap with its red star and shiny visor showed up at the side of the car. "What'll it be, sir?"

"Fill her up with ethyl, please, and check the water and oil—Havoline 30-weight."

"Can we help with the gas?" Bo held a dollar bill over the back of the seat.

The man started to reach for it, but his wife swatted his hand down. "Oh, no. You kids need your money. We were making the trip anyway. We do it all the time to visit my mother, and that train to the Loop'll cost you a dime each."

"We sure do appreciate that." Lucy opened the door and let the eager Jigger out as she picked up her small suitcase and put on her jacket.

"You folks seem to know a lot about Chicago," Bo said. "I was wondering if you know of any amusement parks?"

The man chuckled knowingly. "Now there's where you can spend a lot of money, take it from me. Best amusement park in the whole country is Riverview. Got every ride you can think of. We both grew up in Chicago, and I'd take Helen there all the time when we were your age. In fact, it was when she was screaming on the Big Dipper roller coaster that she finally agreed to marry me."

The woman swatted his shoulder. "That's not true. I didn't say yes until we got off."

"Yeah, and the next year they renamed it the Zephyr. Dumb name, if you ask me. In fact, I heard they renamed it again, but I can't recall what. But if you want some fun, ask anybody how to get to Riverview. It's up there on Western and Belmont."

"Thank you." Bo stepped out of the car. "Thank you very much. We appreciate the ride."

Lucy followed his lead, and they both went around the side of the filling station, looking for restrooms.

"They're inside!" called the attendant, as he slammed down the hood of the car.

DARK CLOUDS WERE GATHERING to the northwest when Lucy and Bo stepped off the Western Avenue streetcar that afternoon and headed confidently toward Riverview Amusement Park, Jigger trotting at their heels. Lucy grabbed Bo's arm and pointed at a huge billboard. "Is that for the park?"

"Yeah. Wow! Six—count 'em—six roller coasters. Plus all the other rides." But suddenly his pace slowed.

"What's the matter?"

"Not sure, but if that's the main gate ..." Bo pointed to two towers painted in red, white, and blue stripes, big onion domes on top, and what looked like a covered bridge running between them. Fences extended from both sides. "I don't know, looks closed to me. Don't see anybody going in and out. And that parking lot over there's nearly empty. This ain't good."

"But I see people in there."

"Who? Those two guys painting the towers?"

"No, no. I saw a couple of others walking past inside." Lucy didn't like the discouragement she heard in Bo's voice. The park had to be open! They'd come so far ...

She clung to his arm as they walked slowly toward the gate, peering through the fence, trying to see what was happening. When they were nearly under the arched bridge of the main gate, Bo called up to one of the men on a ladder. "Is the park open today?"

The painter looked down and wiped his forehead with the back of his wrist. "Been closed since after Labor Day. It's the off season, ya know."

"Oh ... yeah?" Bo swore under his breath.

"Yep. You must not be from around here. Riverview's open from mid-May through Labor Day. We're just maintenance."

Lucy could feel the strength deflate from Bo's arm. She let go and took a step closer. "Can we just go in and look around?"

"Not s'posed to. Don't want anyone to get hurt." The man turned back to wielding his red paintbrush. "But then, I ain't on the gate. I'm just paintin'."

Lucy grabbed Bo's hand and without saying anything dragged him under the arch, stepping around some sawhorse barriers.

"What are ya doin'?" he said. "We don't need people yellin' at us."

"They won't be yellin'. We're gonna find someone who can give you a job. They still got people workin' here. We should at least check it out." She looked behind them. "Jigger, come on. Get over here."

Once in the park, Bo stopped and looked up, and Lucy saw a big smile spread across his tan face. "Now ain't that the cat's meow, a double Big Eli Wheel! I ever tell you I was the ride jockey on our Big Eli? Did it for a whole season."

"That's swell, Bo. Once they learn that, you'll be in like Flynn."

His smile faded. "Yeah, but that's a problem, ain't it? We gotta be careful how much we tell about our past."

Lucy frowned. What was wrong with him? Bo was usually the one who saw possibilities everywhere. She depended on his confidence to make sense out of this madcap trek they were on— or she'd lose her courage to keep going another day. Well, she wouldn't let him give up now.

She was almost pulling him as they passed one of the roller coasters, the freak show building, and another ride. Finally, Bo shook his hand loose and spun to walk backward in front of her, his arms out to both sides. "I don't know, Lucy. This seems crazy. We don't even know who to talk to."

"Don't matter," she said stubbornly. "We're here on business. We'll just ask directions."

"On business, huh? With a dog, my duffle," he held it up, "and you carrying that little suitcase?"

She grimaced. "Guess we gotta ditch Jigger somewhere. Hey, how about that picnic area over there with those tables. He'll stay there if you tell him, won't he?"

"I guess."

Three men raking leaves in the small park, and Lucy was feeling bold. "Is your boss around here somewhere? We need to talk to someone in charge."

The men looked at one another and shrugged. "Guess you could go to the office," one said. "Go down that road between the Casino and the Caterpillar." He pointed. "See that building on the right?"

"Mind if we leave our stuff on this table for a little while?"

The man shrugged. "We won't bother it."

"See?" Lucy said as they hurried toward the little square building. "It's gonna work out."

But as soon as Bo announced his "business" to the woman at the desk inside, she said, "I'm sorry. We don't have any jobs open right now. But if you come back next spring—"

"But Bo knows about all kinds of different rides. He worked the Big Eli Wheel for a whole season."

"Lucy," Bo hissed quietly through clenched teeth.

But the woman only shrugged. "Then you might have a good chance next spring. But right now if we needed someone, we have a whole list of seasonal employees who'd love to come back."

"You worked an Eli Wheel?" came a loud voice through the door of the office beyond the secretary's desk. A middle-aged man appeared in the doorway, clean-shaven, dark blond hair slicked down. He wore a tie without a jacket, and the sleeves of his white shirt were rolled above his elbows.

Lucy poked Bo in the ribs.

"Yes sir. I've run lots of different rides."

"But we have all those people—" the secretary started.

The man put out his hand to stop her. "Come on back, son, and tell me about it."

Bo glanced at Lucy. His eyebrows went up.

She hid a grin. "I'll wait outside ... with Jigger."

THIRTY MINUTES LATER, Bo came out of the office, striding toward the bench where Lucy sat under a tree with the suitcase and Bo's duffle beside her and Jigger at her feet. He had a big grin on his face.

She jumped up. "You get the job?"

"You're darn tootin' I did, and I didn't even have to mention Bodeen Midway Rides or the Carson Brothers' Carnival." He picked her up and swung her around until she laughed.

"How'd you finagle that?" she asked when he put her down.

Bo snapped his fingers for Jigger to follow as they headed toward the exit. "I started to tell him that I'd worked the carnival circuit—hopin' not to have to mention which one—but he cut me off and said, 'Anybody can make up names about where they've worked. What I want to find out is what you know.' Then he began quizzin' me on all these technical things, like how often you have to grease an Eli, how much tension's supposed to be on the cables, and when you need to replace a pulley. He asked me that kind of stuff about lots of different rides. If I hadn't worked it, I just said so, but for the ones I knew, I answered. And I guess he was satisfied."

Lucy squeezed his arm. "He knew you were the real McCoy."

"Yeah. He said that just today he'd lost two good men to the draft. Apparently, the war's been snatchin' up his men regular as

219

clockwork for the last few months. That's why I got the maintenance job. Starts Monday."

"Oh, Bo. That's super. Now we gotta find us a place to stay."

A PLACE TO STAY ... That was always the big question in a new town. Lucy knew landlords looked at the two of them suspiciously. Too young. Unmarried. Vagrants. Not knowing whether they'd have a roof over their heads made her feel even more anxious now as fall was approaching.

But she tried to keep her chin up as they walked the streets in the neighborhoods around the amusement park until it began to get dark, even though every "For Rent" place they found was too expensive or had just been taken by someone else or wouldn't allow a dog. And finally, the rain clouds that had threatened all afternoon opened up and dumped a chilling deluge on the city, and they had to run, taking cover under the Western Avenue Bridge over the Chicago River.

Bo tried to keep Lucy dry and warm with his coat, but they spent a miserable night under the bridge, and Lucy's courage was slowly ebbing. The only thing they had to eat were some carrots that another homeless person shared with them. Unable to sleep, she couldn't help thinking about Ma and Pa and her brothers and sisters. Where were they? Would she ever be able to find them again?

By the time she finally drifted off to sleep, the rain had stopped and the sky was beginning to lighten. But when they emerged from their "cave" later that Sunday morning the skies were still heavy and gray. They pounded the streets with determination, but it wasn't until late in the afternoon that they found a building on Seeley Avenue with a "For Rent" sign in the window.

Lucy was surprised when the woman who answered the door turned out to be black with short-cropped gray hair. Almost everyone in the neighborhood seemed to be Polish or German and often didn't even speak English. And the only black people Lucy had ever known were migrants, but apparently this woman owned a house. She frowned as she eyed Jigger, who sat on the porch near Lucy and Bo. "That y'all's dog?"

"Yes, ma'am. But he's well behaved. Doesn't bark or bother anyone."

"Uh-huh, that's what they all say." She looked up at Bo. "You need to know, if he messes in my yard or wakes up anyone in my building, you're outta here. Understand?"

"Yes, ma'am."

"Still interested?" When Bo nodded, she took a deep breath and nodded her head like she'd just decided to dive into a cold pond. "Well, come on, then. Follow me."

She turned and led them in through a small entryway to the stairs. "My name's Betsy Mason. Last people I had in here didn't stay but two months. Hope you last longer than that." She was a very heavy woman with a severe limp that forced her to take one step at a time as they climbed to the third floor. The furnished one-room apartment was the only one on that floor, creatively carved out of the dormers and former attic space. It had a kitchen alcove and a Murphy bed and was clean and cheery. It even had a little bathroom, which they wouldn't have to share with anyone. Everything about it seemed perfect to Lucy ... except the landlady required first and last month's rent upfront.

Between them, Lucy and Bo only had fifty-eight dollars.

Lucy's shoulders slumped and she thought they were leaving, but once outside on the porch by themselves, Bo said, "Whaddaya think? I know it's kinda small, but there's the bathroom for dressing, and I … I'll sleep on the couch … if that's worryin' ya."

Lucy frowned. The woman hadn't even asked if they were married, and though she'd talked kinda harsh, she was at least willing to give Jigger a chance. But that wasn't the biggest problem. "We don't have the money, Bo! Your job might cover the rent once you get paid, but we don't have it right now, especially not since she wants a deposit too. And there were no pots and pans or dishes, and we gotta buy food. What would we do about all that?"

"But this place would fit us and is more affordable than some we've looked at. Besides, you got all that money in that little purse you—"

"Bo!" Lucy could hardly believe what he was saying. "That ain't *my* money! We can't use it."

"Why not? We'd just be borrowin'. And you said it belonged to your family."

"Some of it, Bo. Only some of it. The rest belongs to other people. It'd … it'd be like stealin'."

"Yeah." His voice deepened as he looked down the street. "Well, seems to me like that already happened."

His comment felt like a slap in the face, and tears came just as quickly.

"Ah, come on now, babe. Didn't mean nothin' by that. But think about it. Every day we don't have a place to live—even if we keep sleepin' under a bridge—we end up using what little money we have. By the time I get paid, we still wouldn't have enough to cover first and last month's rent and have enough to eat on. But I promise, we'd just be borrowing. We can pay it back. We just have to spread it out a little. But we can do it. *I'll* pay it back. I promise."

Lucy wiped her eyes with the back of her hand and turned away from him. But how long would that take? If she ever found out where her folks had gone, she'd want to send them the money right away.

Bo touched her shoulder. "Really, I didn't mean nothin' by my comment. But don't you think your pa and ma would want you to have a roof over your head? Don't you think they would loan it to you if they knew how much you need the money?"

She nodded slowly. "Yeah. They'd do anything they could, but … it's not all theirs."

"But we don't need the other people's money, just some of your folks' money. Just enough to get us started."

Lucy stared at the ground. What he said made sense. She couldn't deny it. And though the secretary in the park office hadn't been about to give Bo a chance, it did seem like God had helped him get that job. Maybe … maybe God wouldn't be too mad if they borrowed her family's money. But not the other money!

The trouble was, she had no idea how much belonged to Pa.

Chapter 26

IF I ONLY KNEW HOW MUCH OF THAT MONEY belonged to Pa, I might have had the courage to use a little bit of it to honor Miz Martha. After all, when your best friend dies, you oughta do something to remember her by. I was almost eighty, so Pa had surely passed on and wouldn't have any more use for the money. And that gave me a powerful desire to use a little of it for Martha. But I'd only touched it once and wasn't about to do it again without knowin' how much belonged to other people.

After Miz Martha breathed her last in the hospital the other night, everyone stood around her bed, holdin' hands as they prayed the Lord's Prayer. That wasn't so bad, but when they began singing "Amazing Grace," I didn't see no grace in all that hoopla, so I lit a shuck outta there.

Went back to Manna House and got my cart and Dandy. Fuzz Top would be too busy to look after him anyway. We walked all night, I reckon, but I couldn't tell you where we went. Next mornin' I sat down on a bench in the park not far from the high-rise where Fuzz Top's man still lived and dumped a load of sand outta my shoes, so I guess we'd been down on the beach for a spell at some point. That was when I began thinking about the money in the purse at the bottom of my cart. Hadn't checked it for months. But it was all I had, and I needed somethin' for Martha.

I dug through my cart, piling everything on the bench beside me until I found that purse. It was scratched and the leather had gotten old and stiff, but I could still feel the stack of money within. I looked all around. The only other people in the whole park were a couple of joggers at the north end, so I opened the zipper, stiff as it was with corrosion, and walked my fingers through the bills, counting them as I went. Still $383. Good … no one had robbed me when I wasn't lookin'.

I packed everything back in my cart and took Dandy down to the McDonald's on the corner of Foster and Sheridan, thinkin' all the way about using that money for Martha. I found a couple of half-eaten Egg McMuffins in a remote trash can and shared them with Dandy before one of the employees came out and chased us away. We hung out like that all day. I just couldn't bring myself to go back to Manna House that night and sleep in a bunk so close to where Martha had been, so I slept rough again.

The next afternoon I was sitting on the rock wall, lookin' out over the lake and thinkin' some more about Martha. Dandy was beside me, as patient as if Martha's spirit was there with us. Don't know why Martha had meant so much to me, maybe it was because she was from the country and reminded me of home and family. But why would things from so far back in my past come bubblin' up now, makin' me homesick? So much had happened in my years on the streets. I'd come to think that was the life that defined me. Everyone called me a bag lady. Didn't mind. In fact, I was proud of it, proud that I'd learned how to take care of myself in all sorts of situations, proud that I'd grown toughened to the streets and all they could dish out, proud that I was free. I'd seen a lot of folks come and go, droppin' into one shelter or another when we was sick or the weather got too bad. Some died on the streets, some went back on the grid with a nine-to-five and an apartment and bills. But I'd stayed on, outlastin' most all of 'em.

Proud, that is, until I'd met Miz Martha. She was so down-to-earth and yet a real lady that she'd grown a hankerin' in me, a hankerin' to be something other than a bag lady, somethin' I couldn't explain or even name. But now she was gone, and my heart felt like someone had scraped out its core like an empty coconut shell. I gasped for breath. "Dagnab you, Martha Shepherd. I loved ya, but ya left me worse off than you found me."

The tears came drippin' down my cheeks, and my body shook with slow, silent sobs that would not stop.

Dandy whined and nosed me hard, tryin' to get me to stop, I reckon. I flopped my arm over him and patted his side, not too hard 'cause of his injury that was still healin'. He understood … the way only a dog can.

Don't know how long we sat like that when I sensed the presence of someone who sat down beside us. Dandy pulled away from my arm, and I turned to see him lickin' the face of Fuzz Top.

"Hey, Dandy," she said, scratching his rump. "Easy now. How you doing, boy?… All right, all right, that's enough. Sit … sit! That's a good dog."

Gotta give her credit. She let the three of us just sit there in a row for the longest time without askin' me where I'd been or whether I'd been tryin' to steal Dandy.

Finally, I figured I owed her some kind of notice. "I was goin' ta bring him back."

I saw her nod out of the corner of my eye, and we continued sittin' there, watchin' a couple of seagulls scrappin' over a dead fish in the shallows of the lake. But I wasn't sure what she was thinkin' 'cause she still hadn't said boo to me.

"We jus' needed some time," I offered, "the two of us, what with Miz Martha dyin' off so sudden like. Couldn't get no peace back there! Ever'body yappin' an' cryin' …"

"I know," she finally said. "I got worried, though."

"Worried? You shoulda known I'd bring him back."

"I was worried about *you*, Lucy."

"Me?" I couldn't believe she was actually worried about me. Maybe she just said that to hide the fact she was really concerned about Dandy. "S'pose ya gotta take him back with you."

"Yeah. My boys are coming for their grandmother's funeral tomorrow, and I know they'll want to see Dandy. Paul, especially. He took care of Dandy for my mom when she was staying with us … kinda like you."

"Funeral? What funeral?" I turned and gaped at her. Of course there'd be a funeral. Guess I'd gotten so used to street people passin' without any ceremonies that it hadn't even crossed my mind. But if they were gonna have a funeral for Miz Martha, I certainly couldn't miss that!

Gabby smiled at me like she was announcin' a party. "We're going to have a service at Manna House tomorrow morning because she had so many good friends there. And then we'll have another one in North Dakota, probably on Sunday."

"North Dakota? Back where she came from?"

"That's right. My dad is buried there. We want to bury my mother beside him, so we're taking her home."

Ah, so she'd be takin' her home, huh? Figured! At least Martha had a home to go to.

I slid down off the rock wall and turned away, thoughts comin' at me like a freight train. We'd only known each other at Manna House. But of course they wouldn't bury her in Graceland Cemetery where *I* could visit her whenever I wanted.

227

Suddenly, I felt like I was losing her all over again. I couldn't even imagine her gettin' planted in the ground way up there in North Dakota. I had to at least be able to think of where she was ... what her home was like. I'd forget her otherwise, like all my other family whose faces I could hardly conjure up anymore.

That's when I knew what I had to do. To honor my best friend, I had to see her all the way to her final restin' place. But buyin' a bus ticket to North Dakota was gonna take me a chunk of change. Still, I had to do it, even if it meant breakin' into that purse for a second time. How I'd pay it back, I had no idea.

"How much'll it cost to go up there?"

"I'm not sure ..."

"Well, how you gettin' from here ta there? You flyin' in one of those airplanes?" I'd have to talk her outta that, 'cause I certainly figured to keep my feet on good ol' terra firma.

"Uh ... driving."

"Drivin', huh? Hmm." Good. My mind was spinnin'. If I got a bus ticket, I might get there in time.

I looked over at Dandy and recalled how worried she was about him bein' missin' ... or maybe thinkin' I might have *dognapped* him, like how those fool cops once accused me.

"You takin' Dandy?"

Fuzz Top didn't answer. So! My suspicions were right on the money! She was afraid to leave him with me. She was takin' Miz Martha home. She was takin' Dandy home.

Made me mad!

"Well?" I put my hands on my hips and got right up in her face. "I *said*, are ya takin' Dandy back to Dakota ta bury your ma?"

"Yes!" she shot back.

"Okay then."

That settled it! I climbed back up over the rocks and pulled my cart out from under the bushes where I'd parked it. Then I turned and stared the Fuzz Top right in the eye. "I'm goin' too!"

"Ah, Lucy, you don't have to do that. We're going to have a nice service right here for all of Mom's friends. It's a long way to North Dakota, and—"

"Doesn't matter. I'm still goin'." I turned and walked away, dragging my cart behind me.

Fuzz Top and Dandy followed me, tryin' to talk me out of it, but I was not in the mood for communicatin'. There's a time to speak and a time to be silent … think that's in the Bible somewhere … and this was a time to stay out of conversatin'.

When I got back to Manna House—had to make my mark on the sign-in sheet again—I went straight to the laundry room behind the kitchen and loaded all four washing machines with my clothes. I needed them clean for my trip, and it was a lot cheaper to wash them at the shelter than at Ramon's Double-Bubble Laundromat.

I was nearly done, when the Fuzz Top burst in, still followin' me like a fox on a rabbit trail.

"Lucy! What are you doing? Are all these yours?" She pointed at my washers.

"Yep! What of it? Decided to dump it all in, wash everything. Don't know what it's like in North Dakota. Might need my winter coat an' stuff."

"Oh, Lucy," she moaned.

I gave her a snarly look and sent her on her way. She really didn't want me to go. But I was goin' anyway!

I WAS OUTSIDE GIVIN' DANDY one last walk when a big black hearse drove up to the curb like a ship comin' into dock. Men in their black suits rolled out Martha's light blue casket and took it into Manna House. I followed a little ways back, not knowin' quite what to do with Dandy, but once inside, I just let him go.

Haven't been to that many funerals, but this one sure was purdy—if you can say that about a funeral. Lots of flowers, soft music playin', and everyone dressed up nice. I had on my white blouse under my best blue sweater. Thought it tied in real swell with some of the blue flowers on my skirt. Everything bran'-spankin' clean too.

Martha's casket was up front by this time with its top up. I could just see the tip of her nose and a little of her gray hair from where I stood in the back. I wanted to go up and have one more look, kinda to say good-bye to her, but I wasn't sure if that'd be proper. Then Fuzz Top went up with her boys, and some other people followed. So I got up my nerve and walked around the edge of the room past all the rows of chairs with folks sittin' in them and talking softly.

Martha didn't look like herself. In fact, at first I thought they had the wrong body in that fancy box. Her skin wasn't right, and her cheeks sagged down, and her mouth was closed too tight. She always slept with her mouth open, said it kept her from snorin'—guess what she didn't hear, she didn't know. Still, those were her glasses on her face, and I recognized the dress. And the more I studied the body, the more I realized why it didn't look like her. Her sweet spirit was gone.

When no one else was lookin', I pulled my purple crocheted hat—the one Estelle made me—out from under my sweater and slipped it down inside the casket. Figured it gets cold up there in the north country, and though she wouldn't actually need it, it was a comfortin' feelin' to know I'd given her a little somethin' of mine.

They closed the lid on the casket, and I found a seat in the back. Edesa Baxter read the obituary tellin' about Martha's life. Guess there were a lot of things I didn't know about Miz Martha, and I'd forgotten she had two other daughters 'sides Fuzz Top. Why weren't they at the funeral? Oh well.

Then Avis Douglass—she was runnin' the service—invited people to say nice things about Martha. That got me thinkin', and after several others spoke, I made my way to the front and took a turn. I didn't really have much to say to anyone else, so I turned my back on them and put my hand on the casket.

"Miz Martha, this is Lucy," I said, just loud enough for her to hear if she'd been there. "Me an' you, we was kinda unlikely to be friends, but that's what you was—my friend. Don't have too many friends. Got one less now that you're gone. But you an' Dandy here …" The dog was right there beside me, so I reached down and gave him a pat before I went on. "You was some of the best friends I ever had. An' I really don' know what I'm gonna do now that you gone, Miz Martha … but if you're in that happy place they talk about 'round here, I'm thinkin' I'd like to find out how to get there, too, so we could …" I'd been thinkin' about a song Ma used to sing when I was a girl, somethin' about 'Will the Circle Be Unbroken?' "Jus' wantchu ta know, Miz Martha, you trusted me ta take care of Hero Dog, here, an' that's what I wanna do"—I looked around at Fuzz Top, hopin' she was listenin'—"though ain't nobody tol' me yet who he's gonna live with. But if Dandy needs a guardian angel down here, that's me."

I stood there a moment more, wonderin' if Martha could hear me. Then I went on back to my seat. But I didn't stay there for long. As far as I was concerned, the service was over, and I needed a breath of fresh air. And then I had to get downtown and catch a Greyhound Bus to Minot, North Dakota.

But once I was outside, I couldn't believe my eyes. The long black hearse that had brought Martha's casket to Manna House was gone. Maybe the driver had gone off for coffee before startin' his long trip. But in its place sat Moby Van, Manna House's fifteen-passenger bus to haul residents around the city to various events. Josh Baxter and Harry Bentley were pullin' the seats outta the back. I walked right up to them. "Y'all better move this van before that hearse comes back. I think the service is 'bout over, and they'll be wantin' to put Miz Martha's body in it."

Mister Harry straightened up, ran his hand over his shiny baldhead, and smiled at me. "I believe she's gonna be ridin' in this, Lucy. At least, that's what Gabby told me."

"In that thing? That'd be like puttin' Jonah back in the whale."

Harry and Josh both laughed. "Well, that's the plan," said Josh. "My mom's goin' with 'em."

"You sayin' they're gonna put Miz Martha in the back of that van and drive all the way to North Dakota? Is that even legal?"

"Yes, ma'am. They even have the papers for it."

"How ...? Well, now I've seen it all!" I turned away all befuddled and glad to be shut of these crazy people. At the top of the steps, as I was opening the Manna House door, Jodi Baxter came hurrying out.

"Oh, there you are, Lucy. Gabby asked me to find you and tell you we'll be leaving in about fifteen minutes. She wants to get out of town before the traffic builds. Can you get your stuff down here by then?"

Such meddlesome people! "I'll catch the Greyhound in my own good time. Thank ya, just the same."

Jodi looked confused. "But ... but aren't you goin' with us?"

"Not unless you're plannin' to detour down through the Loop to drop me at the bus station."

"But Gabby said you're ridin' to Minot with us."

I stared at her. "You joshin' me?"

"No. She said you wanted to go. That's why they're leavin' one of those seats in there … a place for her and me and you … and Dandy, of course. And there'll still be room for the casket."

I looked away before Josh's mama saw the big ol' tear that came outta nowhere. "Well, I'll be …"

Chapter 27

O<small>N MONDAY MORNING, YOUNG LUCY</small> walked Bo down the stairs and to the corner, letting Jigger do his business under the bushes of a vacant lot along the way. She gave Bo a quick peck on the cheek as she sent him off to work at Riverview Amusement Park. When he looked back, she waved once and then turned back with a shiver. Fall was definitely in the wind and furnaces all across the city were firing up, irritating her nose with the sulfuric scent of coal smoke whenever she took a deep breath.

Back in the third-floor apartment of the old Victorian house, she made up the Murphy bed and folded it away. Bo had certainly been the gentleman he'd promised to be and hadn't even hinted at crawling in bed with her. She almost wished he'd tried. The thought fluttered in her stomach as she folded the blankets he'd used on the couch. It was kind of fun playing house, especially with him. Would they ever become a real family? She pushed the thought away. Today she had to focus on finding a job of her own.

The sting of borrowing money from the purse to pay their rent was already subsiding, but the quicker she got a job, the faster they could repay it.

Her search that morning took her south, and she ended up near the Chicago River. An old woman coming out from under the same bridge where she and Bo had spent the night so recently caught her attention. Her brown stockings were falling down and bunching around her swollen ankles. A dirty overcoat, missing a couple of buttons, was stretched like a sausage skin over her expanding girth. Her stringy hair was of no nameable color, and as she came close, Lucy smelled the sour scent of urine.

"Can you spare a dime, honey? All I need's bus fare to get to my daughter's."

Lucy hesitated. She didn't have much change herself.

"Daughter needs me to take care of her chil'ren so she can go to work." When Lucy still didn't respond, the woman added, "Baby's sick and can't be left alone."

That did it. Lucy dug into her jacket pocket and pulled out a quarter and eight pennies. She stared at them. In spite of often being broke, her family's table had always been open. Ma would say, "Eight were invited"—meaning the family—"and twenty have come. Put water in the soup and bid them all welcome." Sometimes it was more water than soup, but they made it.

Lucy handed the woman the quarter and went on her way. Perhaps God would notice her generosity and bless her with a job.

But by midafternoon, discouragement drove Lucy back to her apartment. A block away she met the landlady, Miz Mason, coming down the street pulling a shopping cart filled with clean laundry with a bag of groceries on top.

"Well, how'd ya sleep, chil'?"

"Oh just fine, thank you," she said, trying to sound more cheerful than she felt.

As they approached to the house, Lucy again noted how seriously the woman limped, rocking from side to side just to give her bum leg a chance to swing forward. "Here, can I help you take those things up the steps?"

"Oh, thank you, dear. I'd appreciate that so much. And by the way, I forgot to tell you, I wash the sheets every other week. Just bring 'em down on Friday and get a clean set. That's when I take everything over to the Chinese laundry on Damen. And there's an A&P food store next door."

"Yeah. We found that last night. Picked up a few things. But whadda we do for ice?"

"Oh, I'm gettin' so forgetful. Iceman comes by Tuesdays and Fridays. If you're out front here by six, you oughta be able to catch him and set up regular deliveries. There's three tin boxes on the porch. Yours is the one on the end."

Once they were inside, Miss Mason asked, "You been out explorin' the neighborhood today?"

"Lookin' for a job." Lucy grimaced. "Not much luck so far."

"Well, you just wait here, girl. I'll lend you the *Daily News*. You might find somethin' in the want ads."

When she returned, Lucy took the newspaper, and then without knowing why she did so, she confessed, "Actually, I can't read much," and started to hand the paper back.

"Oh, chil', that's a shame." She frowned and shook her head. "I taught school for thirty-two years, and I guess I could teach one more to read, if you want some help."

Lucy felt her face blush. "That's mighty nice of you, but I wouldn't want to put you out none. Besides, I gotta put all my attentions on gettin' a job. Bo ain't earnin' that much, ya know, so I need to help for us to get by."

The woman stared at her with a steady gaze as though she were evaluating what Lucy had said. "I understand, but ..." she nodded slowly, "we can find a way to fit in a few readin' lessons on the side, if you want." She turned, holding on to the doorframe to keep her balance. "In the meantime, bring that paper on in here, and let me go through it with you. Bet we can find somethin', even if you can't read ... *yet*." She emphasized it like she was confident the situation would change. It gave Lucy a chill of expectation.

Miss Mason waddled in ahead of Lucy. The room was neat and clean but smelled of dust and rosewater and cooking from the day before. Miss Mason sat down heavily at the large oak dining table and folded back a crocheted tablecloth to create a desk. "Now what are you good at?"

The question made Lucy feel like her insides were melting. What could she say? Picking blueberries? Taking care of her brothers and sisters? Working in a commissary? No, no, she'd never do that again! "I dunno. I guess ..." Her voice drifted off like a wisp of smoke.

"You've had a job before, haven't you?"

"Oh, yes ma'am. But ..."

"Well, what were you doin'?"

"Workin' in a tourist home as a housekeeper."

"Well ..." Miss Mason shook her head in determination. "That's a place to begin, at least. Let's see what we can find." She flipped through the paper. "Here we go. Help wanted." She scanned her finger down the columns. "Lots of factory jobs on the south side if you want to be Rosy the Riveter. *Hmm* ... Here we go. The Blackhawk Hotel is advertising for a maid. Thirty cents an hour, six days a week. Wouldn't take more than fifteen minutes to get there by streetcar."

She looked up at Lucy, her eyebrows raised, her eyes wide.

Lucy was tired of changing beds and cleaning up after people, but what else could she do? "Guess I could go see if they'd have me."

WHEN BO GOT HOME THAT EVENING, Lucy flung her arms around his neck. "Guess what?"

"We're gonna have a baby!"

"Bo! What's got into you? We haven't even ..." She stood back, feeling her neck and face flush as a sly grin spread across his. "Bo, that wasn't funny." Though it was, and she knew it. She took a deep breath and folded her arms across her chest. "I have *real* news. And now you have to guess ... serious like."

He shrugged and threw his jacket on the couch. "All I know is I'm plum tuckered out. I've been loadin' sandbags onto the Big Dipper all day so they can make test runs with that roller coaster tomorrow." He flopped down on the couch beside his coat.

"You gotta guess, Bo. It's somethin' good. Somethin' for both of us."

"You found a dollar bill."

"Better'n that. I got a job! I got a job, Bo!" She was standing before him bouncing up and down with excitement.

"Really?" A grin spread across his face, lighting him up with a joy Lucy hadn't seen since the tragedy in Lapeer, Michigan. "Hey, that's swell, babe. We're gonna make it!" He jumped up as though all his tiredness had evaporated. "Whaddaya say, we take in a flick tonight?"

"A picture show? You think we can afford it? I ... I gave away my last quarter this afternoon."

"Gave it away?"

"Yeah, there was this old lady, down on her luck, and I—"

"Ah, forget it. Just so she wasn't a grifter. But we got the cabbage now ... or we will soon enough. All the guys were talkin' about a new movie, *Desperate Journey*. This British bomber that gets shot down near Poland, and the crew has to make it home through Nazi territory."

A war movie? Lucy wasn't so sure. "Aren't there any new movies with Myrna Loy? I think she's the cat's meow."

Bo frowned. "I dunno. Guess *Crazy Love* came out not too long ago, but I have no idea where it's showing … or even if it's still in theaters. But the guys told me where *Desperate Journey* is. We can even walk to it."

Lucy hadn't seen that many movies. But it was fun sitting in the dark next to Bo, and this one was plenty exciting. There was a little romance in it, too, involving a nurse who helped the men escape, but it wasn't a real love story.

They walked home through the chilly night air, Lucy hanging on Bo's arm. She looked up at him. "Penny for your thoughts."

"Ah, nothin'."

"Come on, now. Still thinkin' about the movie?"

"Kinda. But mostly it was that newsreel that came before it. The movie was great and all—especially with Ronald Reagan and Errol Flynn playin' those wise-crackin' heroes. But the real scenes in that newsreel of those marines scrappin' and scrapin' their way across Guadalcanal, that was somethin' else." He was quiet for a few moments. "Makes me feel like I oughta be over there with 'em."

"Oh, no, Bo. You don't have to do that. I mean, we gotta have boys back here at home to keep things runnin'."

He sneered at her. "Yeah, like a roller coaster." They walked on a way. "Roller coasters and amusement parks and carnivals are keen enough for peacetime. But the world's at war, and I'm eighteen."

"Not even a month ago," she snapped back.

He frowned at her as though she'd uttered some inexcusable insult. "I am eighteen," he growled.

"Well, okay then. So you're eighteen." Lucy pulled away as if he weren't still walking beside her.

Upstairs, their apartment felt cold and dark, nothing like the cheerful honeymoon nest she'd fantasized that morning. The smell of collard greens, garlic, and smoked neck bones—probably from Miss Mason's kitchen—had wafted upstairs and lingered beneath the gables of their room. It made Lucy both hungry and slightly nauseated. The strangeness of it all settled over her like a suffocating blanket. She didn't want to be there. How could things have changed so quickly? Even a migrant camp shack seemed more like home than this.

Chapter 28

LUCY FELT NERVOUS THE NEXT MORNING as she waited for the trolley to take her down to her new job at the Blackhawk Hotel. Would she catch the right trolley? Would she arrive in time? What would her boss be like? How hard would the work be?

"Hey, brother, can you spare a dime?"

She turned at the familiar gravelly voice behind her, and there was the same old woman in a dirty overcoat who had accosted her the day before. Lucy listened for a moment as the woman told a man about needing bus fare to go take care of her sick grandbabies.

"Hey." Lucy stepped between the two. "That's the same thing you told me yesterday when I gave you a quarter, a whole quarter!"

The woman glared at her as the man took the opportunity to hurry on. "What if it was? Baby's still sick, and I gotta go help out."

The answer took Lucy aback. For a moment, she'd been sure the woman was running a flimflam, but maybe her story was true. What if she did have a sick grandbaby and needed bus fare just to get to her daughter's? Or even if it was a line, so what? Maybe it was her only way to survive. Times weren't easy.

The ding of the trolley pulled her attention away, and she caught her ride. But the encounter troubled her all the way to the hotel.

The Blackhawk was a beautiful four-story building, nearly a hundred years old, with a restaurant, meeting rooms, a spacious lobby, and an elevator ... "But for the guests, only," her boss, Leon Kowalski, quickly informed her. On her first day at work, he told Lucy to dust and polish the dark ornate woodwork in the common areas. She suspected he wanted to keep her working where he could keep an eye on her and make sure she earned her pay. Which she most certainly did! By late afternoon, she was exhausted, and her hands were stained from the tung oil.

"Tuesday, it's the slow day after the weekend, you know," Mr. Kowalski said when it was quitting time. "Good day for orientation, yeah?" Some orientation. All he'd done was hand her a pile of rags and a bottle of tung oil and set her to cleaning. "But from now on, Tuesday will be your day off." He smiled as though proud to give her such a big gift. "See you tomorrow."

Lucy got home a half hour later to find Bo asleep on the couch. Obviously, he'd worked hard too. But since it was off-season, he got two days off each week while she was only going to get one. And today—her first day—she'd come home totally worn out. So who was going to fix something to eat? She looked at Bo for a moment, debating whether to just fix something for herself or cook for them both. Finally, she shuffled over to the little sink and began peeling a couple of potatoes to boil. She opened a can of green beans and a can of Spam. Bo woke up while she was frying the slices of Spam.

"Hey, sleepyhead," she said, trying to mask her irritation. "Better wake up or you'll miss supper. By the way, since I'm cookin', you're on cleanup."

He sat up blinking and gave her a sour look as he ran his hands through his hair. "I'm whipped. Bags of sand again, all day. But … I did get to ride the Bobs. Pretty good ride."

Apparently, he wasn't too upset at being expected to share the chores.

"What are the Bobs?"

"One of the roller coasters." He stood and stretched, his hands touching the low ceiling of the third-floor apartment.

Lucy juggled the three pans on the two-burner stove so everything could be served hot at the same time. She doubted whether Bo could even cook, let alone manage on a two-burner. But that's all there'd been in many of the migrant shacks her family had lived in for the last couple of years.

The thought of family set her to wondering where they were now and whether they'd forgotten her. She was sure Ma hadn't forgotten her, but what about her brothers and sisters, especially baby Johnny? He was only a year old. And was Pa angry at her for taking off and causing the whole family so much trouble, forcing them to move? How were they doing without the money she had in the purse … or the money they might have earned if their time in Lapeer hadn't been cut short?

Oh no! The Spam was burning. She snatched the pan off the heat and flipped over the slices of meat to their not-so-done sides.

"If you'll set out the plates, we can eat. Everything's done." Bo needed to learn to do his share. After all, this wasn't a carnival mess tent. Out of the corner of her eye, she saw him frown at her, but he dug the mismatched plates and tin forks out of the box on the floor and put them on the little table.

Bo ALWAYS SEEMED TO ARRIVE HOME from work first, probably because he only had to walk a few blocks from Riverview Amusement Park while Lucy had a thirty-minute trolley ride plus a walk. But when Lucy climbed the stairs on Friday evening, the apartment was dark. At first, that didn't bother her, but an hour passed and the pot of soup she'd made was ready and he still wasn't home. She began to worry. When she finally heard him coming up the stairs, his steps were slow and heavy as though he wasn't all that eager to come home. She knew things had been a little tense between them, but she didn't think it was that bad. Or maybe it was his job.

He came through the door, threw a newspaper down on the couch, and went straight into the bathroom without even speaking to her. Had he lost his job?

"You okay?" she called. There was no answer. Maybe he was sick. "You want supper? It's ready."

He finally mumbled through the door, his voice low and deflated. "Yeah. Be out in a minute." When he emerged, he plopped down in his chair and held his head in his hands, elbows on the table.

"Bo … what's the matter? Your job?"

"No … not exactly." He leaned back and looked up at her as she put a steaming bowl of chicken noodle soup before him—more noodles than chicken but still tasty, she hoped. But the sheen in his eyes troubled her. "It's that." He thumbed at the newspaper on the couch.

Lucy glanced over at it. "What? That carny newspaper?" And then she remembered. "Is that the one with the article about Lapeer?"

"No … but it's nearly as bad."

"What do you mean?"

Reaching to grab it off the couch, he flipped through the tick tabloid until he got to the pages near the back. "Right here!

The Billboard runs a service for all us carnies traveling around the country. They collect our mail in their offices in four cities: Cincinnati, New York, St. Louis, and right here in Chicago. We can use those offices as our permanent addresses. If we get mail, they print our names on this list, and we can send a postcard telling them where to forward it." He gave her an *are-you-getting-it?* look.

"So ... sounds like a pretty keen plan."

"Yeah, but look at this right here." In the middle of a page with ten columns of names, he pointed to a box. "See this? Says, 'Notice, Selective Service Men! The names of men in this list who have Selective Service mail at *The Billboard* offices are set in capital letters.' And there, right there ..." He stabbed his finger on the page. "Under the Cincinnati office is my name in capital letters: JAMES EARL BODEEN. And that ain't for my old man, either. Selective Service don't have no reason to send him any mail."

Lucy was trying to grasp why this was so upsetting. "But if it's at the Cincinnati office, then that means no one even knows we're in Chicago. Seems like good news to me."

"No, what it means is my number's up. That's my draft notice! I gotta go!"

"Gotta ... you gotta go to war?" Lucy's insides froze.

"Well, if my country's callin', I ain't gonna be no draft dodger. That's for sure."

"But ..." The implications avalanched through her mind. "But what about us?"

Bo let his head fall forward, shaking it slowly from side to side. After a moment a deep sob convulsed his body. "I don't know, babe. I just don't know. I'm so sorry. I got you into this, and now I don't know how to get you out."

Lucy put her arm around his shoulder and stood beside him, pulling his head to her stomach. "It wasn't you, Bo. You saved me from that beast, and I'll love you forever for that." Her words shocked her, but she *did* love him. She loved James Earl Bodeen. He was her Bo. She knew it now more clearly than ever. "But you don't have to go right now, do you? I mean, you haven't received your notice … at least not yet."

"Only 'cause they don't know where I am." He pulled away and stood up, his chair scraping on the floor. "And I can't tell 'em where I am, 'cause then they'd find you too. And we still got that killin' hangin' over us."

A long silence hung between them. Then Lucy whispered, "What're we gonna do?"

"I don't know …" Bo shook his head, then looked her in the eye and put his hands on her shoulders. "One thing I do know is, I'm not gonna lead 'em to you."

She fell against him, and he held her tight. Somehow they moved across the small room and collapsed onto the couch, still locked in a clinch. He was stroking her hair and kissing her forehead. She reached up, grabbed his face in both hands, and brought her mouth to his lips. She kissed him again and again and didn't stop until they were lying prone on the couch.

Lucy pulled back to catch her breath.

Oh, how she loved him, and she knew he loved her, but this wasn't the way she wanted it to be. She looked hopefully into his eyes. *Please, please, ask me to marry you*, she willed.

Instead, he sat up and disengaged himself from her.

"You don't have to send them a card, Bo. Just stay here with me. It'll all work out. Everyone says the war'll be over pretty soon, and then there won't be a draft. Then we can …"

Bo was staring across the room at nothing, slowly nodding his head. Maybe he was agreeing. Finally, he let out a long sigh. "Soup's gettin' cold. Better eat."

246

THEY SAID NO MORE ABOUT THE DRAFT or the war or whether someone would find them, and with each passing day, Lucy's hope grew that everything would work out. Their days fell into a comfortable routine of walking Jigger, going to work, having dinner together, walking Jigger again, and in the evenings while Bo read, Lucy went down and got a reading lesson from Miss Mason. It was like a fairy-tale life, living with the man she loved, except for one thing: their days off didn't coincide. Bo had his weekends, and she was home alone on Tuesdays.

The only time they could do stuff together was in the evenings.

But this year, her birthday—November third—fell on a Tuesday. She would be sixteen. That's how old Ma had been when she got married, and it made Lucy feel she could do the same.

In the morning she went downstairs and asked Miss Mason if she could use her kitchen and oven to make a cake—a banana cake, just like Ma always did. It would be a total surprise to Bo. If she'd ever mentioned her birthday to him, he'd surely forgotten. She worked all day, cleaning the apartment, shopping, cooking, setting the table with candle stubs they'd found. And if Bo did ask her to marry him, she might even … no, it would still be better to wait. But it was so hard to wait! But maybe if he asked her, if they were going to get married for sure, they could just enjoy a little preview of "coming attractions," like they always said about the movies. The idea made the heat rise up her neck and face.

Just after five-thirty, she heard Bo's determined tread on the stairs, stomping like he was marching off to … Well, he was right on time, and not too worn out. She switched off the electric lights. The candles would be enough.

He flung open the door and stopped, startled. "What's this?"

"Surprise!"

"Surprise, what?" Bo threw his jacket on the couch and ran a hand through his hair. "Today was a surprise, all right. Two men in dark suits came by the park lookin' for a James Bodeen. Wouldn't say what for, just wanted to talk to him—"

"How do you know?" she shot back. "They ask you?"

"No." He sauntered over to the table, flicking the silverware at his place with his finger as if it was dawning on him that the tablecloth and candles meant something special. "They stopped by the office and talked to the boss. I wouldn't even have heard about it except the boss was laughing about the suits at break. Called 'em G-men, actin' like they were after Al Capone."

Lucy licked her dry lips. "But he had no idea they were lookin' for you, did he? I mean you said your name was Borick Hansen, right?"

"Yeah, yeah. That's the only name he's got. But that was too close! They're onto me, Lucy. Whether it's the draft or that thing in Michigan, I gotta disappear!" Bo sat down at the table and looked it over, spreading his hands. "What's all this about?"

Lucy hardly knew what to say. But finally she murmured, "It's my birthday. It's a birthday dinner."

"Birthday?" A bewildered look spread over Bo's face as though he had just woken up to find himself in a strange country. "How old are you?"

"Sixteen."

"But I thought you were …" He waved his hand. "Doesn't matter. Happy birthday, babe. What'd you fix?"

"Uh …" She felt disoriented, as though their little apartment was sitting on a tower of sticks that were about to crumble. "Pot roast." She went over to the stove and brought back Miss Mason's black cast iron Dutch oven, and began serving up generous helpings of vegetables … and small pieces of meat, since she'd only been able to afford a little roast.

"Pot roast. This is great." But Bo's appreciation sounded rote, as if his mind was a thousand miles away.

Lucy sat down, hands in her lap. "So … what're you gonna do?"

He took a bite of the roast, then laid down his fork and met her eyes. "I'm leavin' tomorrow—"

"What?" Lucy couldn't believe what she'd heard.

But Bo held up his hands. "I've made up my mind. I can't put you in danger, but I'm at risk from two sides, the law and the draft. The only way around it is to sign up with the army under a different name. Then, if the law comes lookin', you can say I'm gone. It'll be the truth."

Lucy's world was crashing down around her. "But … but you can't do that! You can't leave me here, Bo." She started to cry, the fancy meal and the romantic evening completely forgotten.

Bo reached for her hand, but she yanked it away. "Hey, hey," he said, "Now don't cry. It won't be that bad. Everyone says the war'll soon be over. No more draft to worry about, and by then the Michigan thing'll be so cold, no one will be looking for me. We can start over."

Lucy shook her head, and her tears came faster. "If they're on to us," she hiccoughed, "we can *both* run. We've done it before. But you can't—"

"Lucy, I've told you! I ain't no draft dodger. I gotta face that right now, even if those guys weren't askin' for me because of the draft. C'mon, buck up, babe. Lots of guys have to leave their girls. It's what's happenin'. Don't make it harder for me. You know this is somethin' I've gotta do." He got up and came around to her, kneeling down and putting his arms around her as she cried. "Hey, when I get back, we'll get married. How 'bout that?"

Lucy caught her breath in a shuddering sob. Had he said the word? Had he said they would get married? She stared at him, wiping her tears with the back of her hand.

Bo grinned. "How 'bout that? You want to get married? I'd planned to ask you, but I was lookin' for a better time. I had no idea this was comin'."

He moved back from her a few inches but remained kneeling on the floor. "Lucinda—no, Lucy Tucker—will you marry me ... as soon as I get home?"

Chapter 29

S OON AS WE GOT BACK TO CHICAGO from burying Miz Martha in North Dakota, I traded in that old suitcase Mabel Turner had loaned me and repacked my wire cart. After bein' cooped up in that van with two other live women, a dead one, and a dog for so long, I needed some space. But before I was done repackin', Mabel invited everyone to gather in the multipurpose room for coffee and some of Estelle's brownies so they could hear a travelogue of our trip—like the last thing I wanted to do. Then she topped it off by wanting to pass on a hug from Estelle.

I pushed her away. "Aw, c'mon, none o' that mushy stuff. But them brownies sound good." I said it just to be sociable and ended up hangin' around all afternoon and sleepin' in my old bunk that night with Dandy's bed on the floor beside me.

Things moved quicker than greased lightning during the next few days. Fuzz Top decided to use the money she inherited from Miz Martha to buy an apartment building. Said she was gettin' it so women with kids could have more permanent places to live … beginnin' with her and her two boys. I got a laugh outta that 'cause nothin' seemed better to put that lowlife mister of hers in his place. He'd kicked her out, kidnapped the boys, and froze all her money and credit cards. Left her destitute in a homeless shelter, but now she was buying a building, and there wasn't nothin' he could do about it 'cept whine when she refused to pay his gambling debts … at least, I hope she wasn't givin' him any of that money. He'd just burn it!

Hee, hee, hee! Harry Bentley even let her into her old penthouse apartment to clean out her stuff right from under her ol' man while he was gone that weekend. Served him right!

But the most amazing thing to me was, Fuzz Top let me keep Dandy!

Yes siree Bob! She sat down on the end of my bunk before I even got up and said, "Lucy, I know you've been taking real good care of Dandy, and I think Mom would want you to have him."

"Who me? With a dog?"

"Well you've been taking care of him all along for some time now."

"Yeah, but …"

"There's just one thing you need to promise me if you're gonna take him."

"And what's that?"

"That you'll take shelter with him in the winter. I don't want him out there freezing to death in a Chicago winter."

I nodded, but I had this sneakin' suspicion that it was her way of gettin' me in off the streets. Confound it, I know how to take care of myself, but I made her the promise, nonetheless.

"And if you can't care for him, I want you to give him back. In the meantime, there's plenty of dog food here at Manna House to last six months or more, and it's all for Dandy, so make use of it."

That's because he was the Hero Dog for savin' us from that burglar. With all the TV cameras and reporters, we had fans dropping off bags of dog food and other stuff for days. I usually carried a little bag of it around in my cart all the time. Dandy likes snacks, and I figgered if things ever got real bad, we could share. He wouldn't mind.

Anyway, I said thank you to Fuzz Top and told her Dandy and I needed to stretch our legs a little—I was still feelin' cooped up from the trip.

We lit outta there that very evening.

EVEN THOUGH I DESPISED THAT SCALAWAG of a man who treated Miz Martha and Fuzz Top like dirt by kickin' them out, he was still the father of her boys. So Dandy and I moseyed on over to the park that runs along between the lake and those pricey high-rises where he was livin'. When we was taking Miz Martha's body up to North Dakota, I was ridin' in the backseat near the casket, and Fuzz Top thought I was asleep. But I was just restin' my eyes when I heard her say that Philip had started gamblin' serious-like, most every weekend.

Gamblin' can get you into a world of hurt, so thought I'd just check to see if he were home safe from his weekend jaunt. I saw lights on in his top-floor penthouse, and a figure passed by the big wraparound windows, so I figgered he was okay. "C'mon, Dandy." I decided to take a load off my feet on one of those benches across the park.

I was just catchin' my breath when Dandy started to growl. He set his feet, head low and hair up, facin' back the way we'd come.

"Hey, you! You with the dog!" called a man running across the grass toward us. Wonkers, it was Philip Fairbanks! Musta parachuted from the thirty-second floor to get down so fast.

"Bandit, eleven o'clock," I muttered as Dandy moved stiff-legged to plant himself between me and any attack. But when Philip skidded—and almost lost his balance—to a stop at Dandy's growl, I could hardly keep from chuckling.

"Is that Dandy? Martha Shepherd's dog?"

"Was." I couldn't figure what it mattered to him, but still …

After catching his breath, he put both hands on his hips. "Okay, so you know Mrs. Shepherd died a week ago. But that dog belongs to my wife now. Our son Paul is crazy about that dog. You—whatever your name is—you stole him. Give him back—*now*." He thrust a hand out as if he thought I was gonna hand him Dandy's leash.

Who did he think he was? I stood up. "Well! Don't that just rot my socks. You sayin' you want the dog?" I gave 'im the eye, and Dandy backed me up with another growl and a show of his teeth. That set 'im back. He retrieved his hand like he'd touched a hot stove. I looked him up and down. What a sorry sight. "*You?* Mister high-an'-mighty Philip Fairbanks? Who don't even have the decency to give food an' shelter to that *wife* you mentioned two breaths ago? You kicked her out on the street, left her no place to go. Now you want a *dog?*"

The look on his face was worth a chicken dinner. I stabbed my finger in his chest. "And if'n I got my facts straight, you don't even have time ta take care o' them two boys o' yours. Just packed 'em off to they grandfolks. Guess you thinkin' this dog can take their place."

He stood there like I'd scalded him with a pot of coffee.

"Oh yeah. Almost fergot. You kicked poor Miz Martha outta your fancy digs too. But, hey." I shrugged. "Guess you figgered if ol' Lucy here could live out in the street, must be good enough for your wife and her ol' lady too. Why, I'm kinda flattered—for about half a second."

Whoopee! I poked him again, and he stumbled back a step or two. "But I *feel* for ya, Mister Fairbanks. Now that you don' got no wife, no kids, no mother-in-law ta take care of, must get kinda lonely up there in the sky. Guess you be needin' a *dog* to take care of. Ain't so hard. Just gotta take him for a walk mornin' an' evenin', and pick up his poops—they got a law, see, says ya hafta clean up after ya dog. Sign's right over there."

I thumbed toward the sign, and held out the leash to him. "So … here. Guess he's yours. Go on. Take him."

He stood there weighin' the odds, like I suppose he did when he was playin' poker down there at the casino in Gary, Indiana. Finally, he folded. "Look. I can't take the dog now. I have to go to work. But you …" He took a deep breath, tryin' to save face as he shook a finger at me. "You have no business with that dog. An old lady like you can't take care of a dog living out on the streets. Just take the dog back to Gabrielle, wherever she is. If I see you around here again with Dandy, I'll … I'll call the police."

That was it!

He spun on his heels and headed back toward his ivory tower without one look back.

"*Hee, hee, hee.* How 'bout them apples, Dandy. I think we came outta that dogfight pretty good. Don't you?" We turned and ambled under the overpass toward the lake. "But don't you worry none. I'd never let him take you. I had my B-plan if'n he woulda reached for your leash. But it's just you an' me now, buster. Just you an' me."

STILL, I SWUNG BY RICHMOND TOWERS ever' so often. Was kinda watchin' out for Fairbanks, but halfta admit, I was also darin' him to catch me hangin' around and make good on all his threats. I figgered Dandy an' me came out good enough in the first bout that we had nothin' to fear from a rematch. Steered clear of Manna House those first couple of weeks of August, 'cept to pick up more dog food for Dandy from time to time. Actually, it ain't so bad sleepin' rough when the weather's good and the cops leave you alone.

But it was on one of those drop-ins at Manna House for dog food that I learned Fuzz Top's boys were back. Earlier, Fairbanks had shipped 'em east to spend the summer with their grandparents in Virginia, but I heard his pa sided with Fuzz Top an' brought the boys back to their mom in time to get registered for school. *Hee, hee!* The man just lost round two.

But on the last Monday of the month, it was rainin' so hard I threw in the towel and went to the shelter. No one I knew was around, so I headed for the multipurpose room. There was a big sign on the door. I worked on the letters for a few moments but couldn't make no sense of 'em. No matter, I dragged my cart in, stretched out on the couch, and took a snooze. Dandy curled up on the floor beside me, both of us contented as cats in a flowerbed.

Contented, that is, until a high-pitched voice sceeched, "Mom! It's Dandy and Lucy!" My eyes flew open, and there was Fuzz Top's youngest on his knees, his face getting' a total tongue bath from Dandy. The kid looked back at the door just long enough to say, "Look, Mom! You can hardly see where the stitches are anymore."

As I sat up, Fuzz Top detoured around the boy-and-dog circus act in the middle of the floor to come over and sit down beside me. "You dropping in for your weekly spa treatment, Lucy?"

I touched my head. My hair was wet and still plastered down. Probably did look a sight. Well, that's what I get for puttin' my purple knit hat in Miz Martha's casket. But I don't regret it. It was my way to honor her.

"Hey, Paul," Fuzz Top said, "why don't you give Dandy a bath and a blow-dry this morning? Is that okay with you, Lucy?"

I shrugged. "Guess so. Though he jus' gonna get dirty again on a day like this, mud everywhere."

"Then why don't you stay a few days until the weather dries out? Weather guy said rain today and tomorrow. Want me to see if there's a bed available?"

Didn't feel like commitin' myself yet, so I just shrugged and pointed to the double doors to change the subject. "What's that sign on the door out there?"

She glanced that way as though she could see through the door. "The 'Shepherd's Fold' sign? That's the new name for the multipurpose room. You know, Shepherd was my mom's last name, and a shepherd's fold is where the shepherd keeps his sheep safe and secure."

The meaning exploded in my mind like the lakefront fireworks. Why hadn't I been able to sound out those words and figger what they meant? I shoulda worked harder to learn to read when Betsy Mason had tried to teach me so many years ago. Always so embarrassin'.

"Whatchu think I am, stupid? I *know* what it means an' I know it's named after Miz Martha. What I wanna know is, where's the bronze plaque? That stupid paper sign gotta go. It's an insult to her memory. We gotta put that name up on a nice, big bronze plaque that says, 'In memory of Miz Martha Shepherd' or somethin' decent. Maybe frame her picture too."

Fuzz Top stared at me with a puzzled look on her face. "Yeah … yeah, that's a good idea. I'll mention your suggestion at the next staff meeting."

She got up and went back to work, but I think she was gettin' suspicious 'bout me not readin' and writin'. Maybe I should try one more time to learn … if I could get someone around Manna House to teach me on the QT. Wouldn't want the whole world to know.

Chapter 30

IT WAS NEARLY THREE MONTHS after Bo joined the army before Lucy heard one word from him. And then it came in an envelope with Pvt. B. J. Moon, 16328466, and a return address on the outside. At first, she didn't recognize the name, though she thought B. J. might stand for Bo. But since it had her name on it, she opened it and found a note wrapped around three twenty-dollar bills and a small snapshot of Bo with an army buddy. Lucy counted the money twice—as though there was any way to miscount three bills—and then studied the picture. Bo looked so good! He and his friend were dressed in fatigues, wearing their helmets, and holding their rifles at an angle as they stood in front of army barracks, sober expressions on their faces.

She scanned the note with so many meaningless words on the paper that she couldn't even guess what it said. After Bo left, Lucy had taken a part-time job in the evenings waitressing at a little streetcar diner, which left her no time for reading lessons with Miss Mason. Both jobs barely earned Lucy enough to live on, but she was determined not to borrow any more money from "The Purse." Now—staring at the letter from Bo—she shook her head. Shouldn't have given up those lessons. But Miss Mason had taught

258

her enough that Lucy lingered over the "Love, Bo" at the end the note. Did he really love her? She sure thought so on that last night when he said they would get married as soon as he came home. And she believed it later, as they clung hungrily to each other in the Murphy bed.

The experience hadn't been what Lucy had imagined it'd be. Bo had been gentle enough and caring, but the soft candlelight couldn't transform the frantic mood created by their impending separation. Afterward, she'd felt empty and cried quietly into her pillow once Bo fell asleep. She'd wanted to tell him, "You can't leave me now!" when his leaving was the very reason they had sealed their relationship and given each other a memory they hoped would sustain them through their time apart ... and the terrifying possibility that Bo might never return from the war.

But after Bo left, Lucy could almost hear the little talk her mother had given her: "Don't give away your virginity, honey. Marriage comes before ... before the bed. That's how God recognizes family." But what difference did it make since they *planned* to get married?

She'd noodled on it for days. Something was missing. It wasn't the possibility that Bo might not keep his promise ... or even the fear he wouldn't come back from the war. But they'd "sealed" something that hadn't yet happened—a secret bonding between the two of them, but not a marriage others or even they could recognize and celebrate. She had to admit it: they really weren't a family, and she felt incomplete. Was Bo feeling the same?

At least she'd heard from him and he'd still signed his letter, "Love, Bo." She shivered with excitement. Maybe it would all work out okay after all. She got The Purse out of her tattered old suitcase and slid the money into it, promising herself to make do on what she could earn until it was all paid back.

259

For the rest of the evening, Lucy wrestled with the other words in the note, but couldn't make any sense of them. She took it to work with her the next day and unfolded it at least a dozen times during the day half imagining that the words would suddenly leap off the page in coherent phrases and sentences, spoken in Bo's mellow voice. It was, after all, a message for her from him.

But each time she studied the paper—getting caught once and scolded by her boss for not working—the letters coalesced into nothing more than a few words scattered here and there: "Dear Lucy," "the," "but," "can," "and," concluding with "Love, Bo." She could almost hear him say it.

That night when she got home from the diner, Miss Mason's light still shone from her window. Inside the entryway, Lucy knocked tentatively on her door.

"Who is it?"

"It's Lucy. Are you still up? I have a favor to ask you." She heard shuffling, and in a moment the door opened to reveal Miss Mason in a lime-green housecoat.

Lucy held up a hand. "Oh, sorry. Thought you might still be up."

"Well, so happens I am, child. What do you need?"

"I can come back later—"

"Not tonight, I hope." She grinned broadly. "Come on in, come in. You look troubled. How about some tea? Water's still hot."

She hobbled away on her bum leg, leaving the door open. Lucy hesitated a moment, but followed the old woman into the room with its familiar scent of roses and dust and sat down at the old oak table.

"Now, what is it?" Miss Mason said when she returned with a cup of tea, a few leaves swirling in the bottom, staining the steaming water a golden brown. "Want some honey?"

Lucy nodded and busied herself stirring a spoonful into the tea. Finally, she pulled the letter from her apron pocket. "I got this in yesterday's mail, but"—she began to cry—"I can't read it." She pushed it across the table to her landlady.

The woman held it at arm's length and scanned it for a moment. "So you're wanting another reading lesson?"

"No ... well, yes, if I had time ... but right now I just need to know what it says."

"*Hmm.*" Miss Mason frowned at her as she nodded her head slowly. "What better reason could you have for learning to read? But don't worry ..." She held up a hand to deter any response. "I'll read it for you."

Dear Lucy,

Here's a picture of me outside our barracks at Fort Benning, Georgia, with my buddy Bruce. We're shipping out tomorrow to somewhere in the Pacific, an island, probably. But they won't tell us which one. I'm in good shape and haven't been sick.

We got a great company commander, though a couple of the lieutenants are nothing but 90-day wonders. Still, us enlisted guys look out for each other, and the NCOs are okay too.

I hope you're doing all right. Maybe this money will help. I'll try to send more each month, but the government doesn't pay buck privates very much, and I couldn't list you as a dependent without giving us away.

You can write to me using the name and address on the outside of the envelope. The letter will catch up to us sooner or later.

I miss you so much! Once the war's over, we'll tie the knot!

Love, Bo

261

Tears in Lucy's eyes made everything in the room glisten as Miss Mason sat in respectful silence. Finally, she pointed tentatively to the letter that she'd laid on the table. "What's this about him not claiming you as a dependent? You both deserve that money, you know."

Lucy put her hands over her face and fought to hold back a sob.

"*Hmm*, I see. I had assumed ..." She patted Lucy's hand. "All right, all right, now. It isn't my business to pry, but if you want to talk ..."

Talk? What was there to talk about? Bo would be coming home, and they were going to get married. He'd promised. No one could blame them if the war had gotten things out of order. But the fact was ... she still felt that hole in her heart, as though she had lost something that had not been replaced. In a moment, she straightened up and took a deep breath. Couldn't do anything about it now. She wiped her eyes. "Thank you," she whispered as she reached for the letter. "Thank you so much."

"Well, if you want me to help you to write something back ... it would be good practice."

Miss Mason was always the teacher, but Lucy shook her head slowly. "Not right now. I don't quite know what I'd say, but maybe in a day or so." She stood up and backed toward the door. "Thanks again. You don't know how much this means to me."

Upstairs, Lucy stepped around the Murphy bed—which she seldom folded up anymore, even though it made the apartment feel cramped—and leaned close to the wood-framed mirror hung on the wall. She brushed her hair off her forehead with her fingers and studied her image. She *was* pretty. She knew that ... at least she thought so. But could Bo still remember what she looked like? She wedged the snapshot of him into the corner of the frame. At least now, she had a picture to help keep his memory alive.

But her memories were all she had, and she cried herself to sleep that night and for the next three nights. Her days were spent trying to think what she would say in a letter to Bo. But the more she delayed, the more urgent she felt to say something, anything, just to let him know she'd received his letter.

"Miss Mason," she said, meeting her landlady on the porch one freezing Thursday morning in February, "could we do that letter this evening?"

"Sure, honey. Just come on down whenever you're ready."

On the way home, as flakes swirled around from the lake-effect snow, she stopped at a Walgreens drugstore and used the photo booth to print out eight small snapshots of herself for twenty-five cents. They made her look kind of silly—not nearly as pretty as she knew she was—but it was the best she could do. And that night Lucy dictated all the news she could think of for Miss Mason to write—that she got Bo's letter, had found a second job, how much Jigger missed him, and that it was fiercely cold and windy in Chicago now with nearly a foot of snow on the ground.

But at the end she frowned. "All that seems like such silly things to put in a letter, when what I really want is to ..." But she didn't know what that was. What do you say to a man who might be facing death every day?

Miss Mason patted her hand. "Don't worry about it, honey. He's over there fighting for his country, probably in a miserable situation. Who knows? But it'll mean a lot to him just to hear about ordinary things, that everyday life is continuing for you. After all, that's what he's fighting for. It's those little things that will keep him in touch with home."

"But ..." Lucy watched Miss Mason in silence, tears swimming in her eyes. She wiped them away with the back of her hand.

"I know, what you really want to do is tell him how much you love him and miss him, and he needs to hear that too. Am I right?"

Lucy nodded.

"I'm writing it all down, just like you said it." She worked with her pen, scratching across the page for a few moments. "Here, what do you think of this?"

You're in my thoughts and dreams every night. I can hardly wait for you to come home. I pray for your safety every day. I love you.

Lucy was crying openly by the time her landlady finished reading. She rose from her chair and gave Miss Mason a hug. "Thank you." Then she took the letter, determined to sign her own name.

Miss Mason watched, elbow on the table and chin in her hand as Lucy carefully wrote, "Love, Lucy" on the bottom of the letter.

"You are praying for him, aren't you, dear?"

Lucy started to nod ... but it wasn't true. She'd been "fighting this war" entirely on her own, God all but forgotten. Slowly she shook her head and looked down at her lap as the tears came again.

"Then maybe it's time to start. If fact, if you don't have anyplace else to go, I'd be glad to take you to my little church. We take time every week to pray for the boys overseas, and there are a lot of them from our families." The woman sat quietly until Lucy had composed herself and wiped her eyes. Then she said, "If you want to come with me, be down here about eight-thirty Sunday morning, and we can catch the trolley together. Okay?"

"I ... I usually have to work on Sundays, but I'll see if I can get off this Sunday."

Upstairs, Lucy found a pen, an envelope, and Bo's original letter. She sat down at the table, tucked the letter and snapshots into the envelope, and carefully copied the name and address from Bo's envelope. She studied the name: *Pvt. B. J. Moon, 16328466.* "M-o-o-n" … Lucy sounded out the name. So "Moon" was the name he'd chosen to enlist under in order to protect their identity. Her Bo was now Private Moon, and those numbers must be his ID.

Miss Mason's church was not that far away, though for such a crippled woman, getting there through the snow was a real trek. When they transferred to a bus going west on Madison Avenue into the East Garfield Park, Lucy watched out the windows as the neighborhood changed and turned to Miss Mason. "I didn't know so many black people lived around here—" She clapped her hand over her mouth. Had what she said offended?

Miss Mason patted her knee. "We're everywhere, dearie." Then she winked. "Just joshing you. It's true that most Chicago Negroes live down on the south side—a lot of them just moved up here from Mississippi, Alabama, and Louisiana to get war jobs—but there's a narrow strip of nicer homes along here where we've lived for ages. Thought of moving over here myself for a while, but then the war came and prices …" She wobbled her hand like an unstable boat then turned suddenly to look out the window. "My, my, we're already here! Yank that cord." She grabbed a pole and pulled herself up as the bus came to a halt.

At first, Lucy did not see a church because she was looking for a white building with a pointed steeple and gothic windows, like every country church she had known. But Miss Mason led her along a half-shoveled sidewalk until they reached a small brick structure with nothing more than a rugged wooden cross on the peak of the roof. One might have mistaken it for a slightly larger-than-usual Chicago bungalow except for the cross and double doors that opened onto a small stoop.

"Now, isn't that nice?" Miss Mason stopped and pointed to a freshly painted sign in the tiny front yard. "'Mount Olive Tabernacle Church.' Deacon Edwards finally finished putting up our sign. I'll have to thank him." Lucy could see fresh footprints and dirty snow around the base of the two supporting posts.

If only she could have read the sign for herself ... she flushed at the reminder. But the more she studied the building, the more she could see that it looked like a little chapel. On either side of the doorway were matching windows of amber crinkle glass, and a stream of people were arriving in heavy coats over their Sunday finest. Given all the black people in this neighborhood, Lucy relaxed when she saw a white woman herding two little girls bundled in snow pants and jackets up the walk.

Inside, people greeted one another and chatted as Miss Mason guided Lucy down to the third row on the right. The service began with hearty singing—mostly songs Lucy had never heard—and then the pastor said he wanted to welcome any visitors.

"Sister Mason, would you like to introduce your guest?"

Miss Mason used the back of the pew in front of her to pull herself up and gestured for Lucy to stand. "This is my upstairs neighbor, Lucy. Her ... her man, Bo, is overseas in the army, and she came for some prayer for him."

Lucy sat down quickly, feeling her neck and face flush, but everyone acted as though this was as common as sunrise, with murmurs of, "Welcome, sister." "Lord have mercy." "All right, now." "We'll all be prayin', sister."

And they did, right then. Pastor Winfred mentioned half a dozen other men who were in the service, and everyone began praying out loud at the same time. Lucy didn't know what to think or do, but she heard various people mentioning the names the pastor had said, and she could hear Bo named here and there as well.

If all these people were praying for him, she figured she ought to be praying, too, but she couldn't bring herself to speak in anything louder than a whisper. "Dear God, I haven't talked to You much lately, but I know You answered Ma's prayers from time to time, and I think You answered my prayer when we were crossin' the border at Niagara, so ... so maybe You'll listen to me one more time. Please keep Bo safe and bring him back to me soon. Amen."

She couldn't think of anything else to say, but while others were speaking out a loud cacophony of appeals to the Almighty, she wondered how He could possibly sort out everyone's requests.

That night, after she'd walked Jigger and come inside with her cheeks so frozen she feared they might crack, she got into bed and curled up under the blankets, thinking about the day. How could God have heard her that morning in all that clamor? Maybe she should try again, now that it was quiet and He wouldn't have to choose whom to listen to.

Crawling out of bed, she knelt on the cold floor in her dark apartment and shivered as she prayed.

Chapter 31

Y OU DOWN THERE PRAYIN' FOR SOMETHIN', Lucy?"

"Now why would I be a prayin'? I'm just tryin' to reach my shoes. Dandy musta knocked 'em under my bunk last night. Couldn't get hisself comfortable. Kept rotatin' like a merry-go-round 'fore he'd lay down and go to sleep. Durn dog!" I leaned back, knowing my face was probably red and puffy from bendin' over, and looked up at Estelle Williams standing in the doorway. "You got young bones. Why don't you get down here and reach 'em fer me?"

"*Young bones*? Ha!" Estelle looked back down the hallway and called to an eight-year-old. "Sammy, quit your runnin' and come in here to help Miss Lucy with something."

Once the rascal got my shoes, I sat on my bunk puttin' 'em on and glanced up at Estelle. "You still here? Hey, if you came up here recrutin' for the kitchen, you came to the wrong place."

"That's exactly why I'm here. I need—"

I held up a hand as I shoved my left foot into its shoe. "Cain't help. I'm headin' out."

"Out? Out to where?"

I stood up. "A berry farm, of course." I held my hands out to my sides to show off my coveralls. "Cain't ya see what I'm wearin'?

Oh, and by the way, could you ask Fuzz Top to take care of Dandy for a couple of days?"

"Yeah, well …" She shook her head. "… you're somethin' else, Lucy Tucker." Estelle turned and stomped away. I knew she was fumin', but she'd get over it.

An hour later, I'd stashed my cart in Fuzz Top's office and was on the El down to the Loop, fixin' to catch the train to Michigan. The last few days, a strange hankerin' had come over me that I couldn't even put my finger on until I found a half-full box of blueberry yogurt cups behind the 7-Eleven over on Montrose. They were still good, but they didn't taste nothin' like fresh blueberries … not the way I remembered 'em from when we picked 'em as a kid.

Anyway, right then and there, I decided I was goin' berry pickin'! Thought I might have to hitch, but on a hunch I called the Amtrak, and they were runnin' a half-price special: twelve bucks from Chicago to Bangor, Michigan. I counted my laundry quarters and everything else I could find—not The Purse, of course—and came up with $14.35, plenty to get me there and buy a Coke to boot. And I figured I could pick enough berries to get myself home.

Maybe it was that road trip to North Dakota to bury Miz Martha, but whatever, I had a wanderlust about me and had to follow it.

MICHIGAN WAS AS BEAUTIFUL AS EVER, and the blueberries were in the height of their season, but it took me the rest of the day after I got up there to find a farm where I could work. I holed up in Bangor overnight and made it back out to the farm early Thursday morning to begin pickin' berries at forty-four cents a pound. The hours passed slowly, as I filled my pail again and again and took it to be weighed. Almost everyone around me spoke Spanish, so it was like I was alone out there in the hot sun.

So much time had passed since I did this with Ma and Pa and my brothers and sisters. Those were the happy days. We might've been poor, but we were together. 'Course, all that ended in Lapeer when Bo killed Doyle. There've been times over the years when I almost wished Bo hadn't come into the barn that day. I can't fully imagine the horror of what that boss man tried to do to me, but maybe I could've fought him off myself. Even if I hadn't, would my life have been all that much worse? The thought of it caused me almost to faint ... or maybe the heat was gettin' to me.

I went for some water.

Where had the years gone? No Bo, no family, now no Miz Martha. I was alone and closin' in on eighty. Wouldn't be long, and there'd be no more me.

What then? Where would I go? Couldn't say as I'd ever been very religious. Still dropped by Mount Olive Tabernacle Church once in a while. Name's changed now. They call it Missionary Baptist somethin'-or-other, and no one remembers me. Still ...

I remember that preacher way back in the old days in the tent meetin' Bo and I stopped at sayin' if I'd seek God with my whole heart, he would find me and bring me home ... or was that the black preacher at Mount Olive Tabernacle? Anyway, can't say as I've ever been very serious 'bout seekin' Him.

Ma used to sing ... how'd it go? *"Softly and tenderly Jesus is calling ..."* Ha, don't got much of a voice left anymore. But Ma did. She sounded beautiful ...

> *Come home, come home,*
> *Ye who are weary, come home;*
> *Earnestly, tenderly, Jesus is calling,*
> *Calling, O sinner, come home!*

Well, I sure am weary and never pretended I wasn't a sinner, but I'm not sure I know how to get home.

By the end of Friday, I'd had about enough workin' in the fields for someone my age and planned to head on home the next day. They kept track of how much we'd picked on little computer cards—nothin' like the old days—and mine added up to 46.73. Seemed about right for two days' work as I'd calculated in my head. I asked them to deduct a couple of pounds of berries for me to take home, and then took my voucher over to the pay table to get my money. But when they paid me, the lady handed me a check.

"Hey, where'm I gonna cash this?"

She shrugged. "Anywhere … bank, currency exchange. Any of those payday loan places will do it for you."

"Yeah, and skim off half my earnin' while they're at it. Can't you just pay me in cash? How'm I gonna get home with a piece of paper?"

"Sorry, ma'am. We don't keep any cash on the premises. You'll have to go into town."

I finally hitched a ride in the back of a migrant worker's pickup. Wasn't so easy me climin' up in there, but by the time we got into Bangor the currency exchange was closed, and no store would cash my check without a photo ID.

I didn't know what to do. Sat on the edge of a big flower box on the curb of downtown Bangor thinkin'. I could find me someplace to hole up for the night and try the currency exchange tomorrow … if they were even open on Saturday in such a little burg. Why wouldn't that berry farmer pay in cash? He should know migrants might have problems cashing checks.

271

Next day the currency exchange and the bank both said they needed an ID, too, especially since I was from out of state. Made me so mad, I started walkin' as though someone my age could hoof it all the way to Chicago. By the time I cooled down, I was outside of town walkin' along this two-lane road where I saw somethin' nearly popped my eyes. There was a little church on the side with 'bout fifteen motorcycles sittin' in the gravel parkin' lot. I don't mean just any ol' bikes, I'm talkin' real hogs and choppers with all these outlaws sittin' around in their leathers and vests with bandannas tied around their bald heads. Tats all over their hairy arms. They were a raw-lookin' crew.

But each of 'em had a big white cross on the back of their vests, and there they sat in a church parkin' lot, of all places, engines rumblin' and rappin' like they were 'bout to hit the road. Contradictions never sat very well with me, so I wandered over to nose around.

"Where you boys headed?"

A great big dude in leather pants and sportin' a beard with at least three different colors—red, fadin' to blond and finally gray—grinned at me. "This your church, sister?"

"No siree Bob. I don't got no church, but it just seemed a little peculiar to see fellers like you in a church parkin' lot. So …?" I stared him in the eye, letting my question hang.

He laughed till his big belly shook. "We're the God Squad on our way to a Christian Biker Rally north of Chi-Town."

"Christian Biker Rally? Well, I'll be a cross-eyed possum if I ain't heard it all now. Are y'all fer real?"

"Yes, ma'am. Real as God can make us. 'Course He ain't finished with most of us yet."

"I should hope not." I gave him the eye. Then an idea struck me. "Hey, you say you're goin' to Chicago?"

"No, we're goin' *through* Chi-Town. Rally's at a park almost up to the Wisconsin border."

"Same thing, far as I'm concerned. Any chance I could hitch a ride with y'all? I live in Chicago and need to get home."

"An old lady like you? Who do you think you are?" He laughed again and started to turn away.

"Name's Lucy Tucker, and I'm good to go. Never been on one of these contraptions before, but I've always wanted to. I see you got an extra seat behind you there, so how 'bout it?"

"You're serious, ain't ya?"

"You bet."

"Well ..." He looked around at the other riders. "Whaddya say, boys? Should we be good Samaritans?" Most of them turned away with a grin on their faces as though they thought it was a joke they'd rather not answer. Then the big boy turned back to me. "But you gotta wear head protection. Hey, Bob, toss me that steel pot of yours." He raised his eyebrows at me. "It's an old army helmet, but you can use it."

"I already got my protection." I put my hand to my head, but my knit hat wasn't there. "Oops, plum forgot, I put it in Miz Martha's ... Ah, you wouldn't know 'bout that. But my head's hard."

"No doubt, but still ..." He handed me the helmet. "It's one of our laws."

I WAS SO SORE AND TIRED by the time those bikers dropped me off out west of the city so I could make it back to Manna House, that I flopped on my bunk without a bite of food and slept straight through till Sunday mornin'. Probably woulda slept till noon if there hadn't been such a ruckus among the residents wakin' me up.

273

"What in tarnation's goin' on?" I growled, sitting up.

"Picnic." Precious rummaged deeper into her duffle bag on the end of her bunk.

"Whadda you talkin' 'bout, girl? What picnic? What's today, anyway?"

She stopped and looked at me. "What's with you, Miz Rip Van Twinkle? You been asleep for twenty years? It's our Labor Day picnic, and we're goin' out to the forest preserve. You better get a move on if you're comin'." She headed for the door with the Sox hat she'd dug out of her stuff.

"Who's cookin'?"

"How should I know?" she called back. "Estelle, probably."

In that case, I figured I'd better get with the program.

Ten minutes later, I hobbled down the steps just in time to pound on the window of the old Moby Van as it started to pull away. "Hey! Hey, wait for me, dagnabit!" Fuzz Top heard me and slammed on the brakes. I squeezed myself into the back and enjoyed a wet-tongued welcome from Dandy. But I could see Gabby's boy wasn't all that thrilled about my wide hips crampin' his space. And then I remembered ... I dug around in my cart. "Got somethin' for ya, Paul," I said. "Little thank-ya present for takin' such good care of Dandy. Share 'em with your ma."

The bag of blueberries made enough peace for us to get goin', and in no time, I'd dozed off again.

When I woke up, people were piling out of the van to join a cluster of other Manna House folks who'd arrived at the forest preserve ahead of us in other vehicles, and all of 'em talkin' to a group of strangers near the picnic shelter. Uh-oh! Looked like someone else got there before us. I scanned the meadow for some other place where we could set up when I saw a pack of motorcycles parked on the other side of the lot.

Seemed like everyone outside the city was ridin' bikes these days.

And then I realized that some of those bikes looked familiar.

Harry Bentley's voice rose above the hubbub. "I told these fellows you have a permit for this picnic grove, Gabby." Well, if anybody could get things straightened out about who had first dibs on that location, it was Harry Bentley, him being an ex-cop and all.

But it wasn't just the bikes that looked familiar. The next voice I heard had been yelling in the wind at me all the way from Michigan the day before. I pushed my way through the crowd. "Hey, wait a minnit!" And sure enough, it was my biker dude in his leather pants and colorful beard. "Ain't you the guy gave me a lift on that big bike t'other day in Michigan? What're you doin' back down here? I thought you would be up at your rally."

On seein' me, he broke into a wide grin and pointed a rough finger at me. "Lucy Tucker, right? Yeah! You was hoofin' it along that two-land road, tryin' ta find the bus station. I see ya made it back to Chi-Town okay." He laughed his jolly laugh. "We're done rallyin' and are on our way back home."

I turned to Mr. Bentley and Fuzz Top. "*Hee, hee, hee.* You guys don't hafta worry. These dudes are all right. They just a bunch of Jesus freaks on wheels."

"Show 'em, fellas!" The big boy turned around, and there on the back of everyone's vest was that cross with the words stitched in red above and below.

"God Squad," Fuzz Top read. "Christian Motorcycle Club."

"Hey! That's fantastic!" Josh Baxter said. Leave it to a young guy like him to ooh and ahh over a gang of bikers. He stepped forward with his hand out, and within moments, the leather-clad wild men were shaking hands and greeting the women from

275

Manna House. *Hee, hee, hee!* Some of 'em looked like they thought they were greetin' aliens from another planet.

So Fuzz Top invited the bikers to join the picnic. They contributed enough grilled chicken, chips, and soft drinks to feed all us vultures, and everyone ended up playin' softball together … everyone, that is, 'cept me. I was stuffed and ready to head back to the shelter and fall back into my bunk. But down inside I felt a chuckle a-stirrin' at havin' brought together such unlikely picnickers who ended up havin' a great time together. Come to think of it, though, I didn't really have much to do with us meetin' up like that. Guess it was Estelle I overheard when we were cleanin' up. "Look at God!" But she wasn't lookin' up. She was lookin' around at the rowdy bikers pickin' up trash while those trepidatin' street girls put away the leftover food, all workin' together like long-lost kinfolk. "We make our plans," Estelle chuckled, "but God comes up with an even better idea."

Humph! I had to walk away from that. It might seem like God had a better idea for today—friendly picnic and all—but I couldn't see anything "better" about His ideas for my life.

Chapter 32

Mail from Bo came fairly regularly during 1943, often with a little money, which Lucy tucked faithfully back into The Purse to repay the "loan." Miss Mason read each of Bo's notes to Lucy and helped her write brief replies. "But you've got to learn to read and write for yourself, child," she always emphasized. "It'll stand you in good stead the rest of your life."

Lucy wanted to. She longed to read those notes over and over to herself. But for some reason, the letters in the words resisted fitting together to sound the way they had the last time she saw them, and even when she memorized short words, she couldn't seem to break apart the longer ones into recognizable syllables. And then there was her work schedule. By the time she got home and took Jigger for a walk, she fell into bed without fixing anything to eat and only woke up the next morning in time to walk Jigger again and hurry off to the hotel. Fortunately, there were always a few leftovers at the diner that she gobbled on the run.

Tuesdays were her days off, and she knew Jigger needed more attention. He was going bonkers being shut up all day. When Riverview Amusement Park opened up the next spring, she often took him over there and walked around. The brightly colored lights, whirling rides, and delighted screams reminded her of what it was like when she and Bo were together. When the weather turned cold again, she went to the movies on Tuesdays—a real splurge—but it was more to see the newsreels about the war than the feature films. The war reports often left her chilled, trying to imagine what Bo was going through. And the rest of each Tuesday always seemed filled with washing and ironing and shopping, and by evening, there was no time left for learning to read.

Shortly before Christmas—it'd been over a year since Bo left—she got a letter from him delivered in an envelope that looked as if it'd been stepped on with muddy boots. Inside the envelope there was a brown smudge across the bottom corner. Was it … blood? She ran quickly to Miss Mason. "Please … Sorry to bother you, but you gotta read this to me! Is he hurt?"

"Calm down, child. Let's see …"

Dear Lucy,

As soon as we secured the last island (can't tell you which one), they packed us onboard this ship to head for another assault. I haven't slept in two days, and we haven't eaten anything but K-rations for weeks, but hopefully before we hit the next beach we'll get a hot meal.

Got my hand cut open, but otherwise I'm OK. Thirteen guys in our platoon have either been killed or wounded and aren't with us anymore.

They say they're going to reorganize us with some green troops just out of basic training. Hope they don't get us all killed by doing something stupid.

How are you doing? How is Jigger? Did you have Thanksgiving?

I love your letters. You have such nice handwriting. Keep them coming. I read each one a hundred times.

Love, Bo

Nice handwriting …? What would Bo think of her when he discovered it wasn't hers but Miss Mason's writing?

Her landlady sat silently while Lucy digested the rest of Bo's news. It didn't sound good. She studied Miss Mason's round face. "He said his hand was cut. How bad would he have to get hurt before they'd send him home?"

Miss Mason shrugged. "If it's something he can get over, they would probably hold him onboard ship or in some field hospital until he recuperated and then send him back into the fight. I hear they're running out of new recruits, so they're not going to waste anyone with experience." She reached out and put her hand on Lucy's. "So you wouldn't want him wounded bad enough to get him sent home."

"Better'n him gettin' killed."

"Maybe … maybe not. There are worse things than dyin', you know."

Lucy couldn't imagine what. She'd nurse Bo even if he came back like some of those men she'd seen from the Great War without their legs or blind or burned by mustard gas. It made her shudder, but she'd nurse him the rest of her life, if need be.

She took her letter upstairs, held it tight against her chest as she crawled into bed, and then cried herself to sleep.

But the next day she made a decision. Working up her courage, she begged her boss at the hotel to let her have Sundays off. "I'm glad to work Tuesdays or any other day, but … but I need to go to church on Sunday. I need to pray for my … for Bo. He's fightin' the Japanese, and they're havin' it rough."

Leon Kowalski raised his hands in a shrug. "We all got people needs praying for, yeah? Tuesdays I gave you because weekends are busy, ya know. If you're gonna work here, you work. The guests, on weekends, they always calling for service, an' 'dats you."

Lucy stood in front of him, her chapped hands clasped behind her back. She studied the floor. She needed this job to pay her bills, but if prayer helped, Bo needed her prayers even more than she needed the money. Finally, she looked up at the man with his dark, bushy eyebrows that met in the center of his brow. She gritted her teeth. "I'm sorry, Mr. Kowalski, but … I just gotta go to church on Sundays."

The man slammed down some papers on his desk and stood up. "We all got a part to do, and your part's right here!" He stabbed his index finger down on the papers and glared at her as if he could beat her down with his eyes. "If not you, I can always get someone else, you know!"

So it had come to that! Lucy looked down at the floor again and decided to make one more desperate attempt. "You're Polish, right?" She didn't wait for him to answer. "This is a *world* war, Mr. Kowalski, and from what I've heard, Hitler kicked up a lotta dust over in your old country. So, like they say in the newsreels, 'This is your war!' 'We're all in it all the way.' Right?" She watched his face. Would those slogans matter to him?

Slowly, his hard expression began to melt. "Oh, all right!" He threw up his hands. "I'll have Esther come in early, and you can start at two in the afternoon and work till ten at night. But you better be on time! If I'm doing this for the war effort, you better work twice as hard while you're here!"

"I always do my best!"

"Yeah, yeah, yeah! Just do more!"

Going to church with Miss Mason brought a measure of comfort to Lucy at first. But months passed without any more letters from Bo, and worry ate deeper and deeper into her insides. Each Sunday after they got home from church, Miss Mason helped her write another letter to Bo, after which she always offered a reading lesson, but Lucy had to hurry off to work. And though she tried not to show it, she was always so upset, she wouldn't have been able to concentrate on the words, anyway.

The months dragged on. "Why doesn't he write back?" she wailed one Sunday as she sat at Miss Mason's oak table.

Miss Mason only shook her head. "Lord only knows, dear. Lord only knows."

July arrived, hot and muggy, and with it came one of Lucy's letters to Bo … returned unopened, with nothing but the purple stamp of a hand on it with a finger pointing to her address in the top left hand corner. Heart breaking, hands trembling, she stared at the envelope. She knew the stamp said, "Return to sender." But why? Her mind jumped to the obvious conclusion: *He'd been killed!*

No, no, no! She wouldn't accept it. But she had to find out!

Skipping work the next morning, Lucy hurried to the post office where she'd seen all those posters encouraging young men to join the army. When she got up to the window, the clerk looked at Lucy as if she'd already answered the same question a dozen times that morning. "Army recruiters can't help you. They bring 'em in. Red Cross helps you get 'em out." She craned her neck to look past Lucy. "Next!"

"Where's the Red Cross?"

"Downtown." The clerk ran her finger down a list of addresses pinned to the wall beside her window, then wrote the address on a slip of paper and handed it Lucy.

When Lucy finally found the Red Cross office, a waiting line stretched all the way down the hall. Oh, no. She had to know. *O God, O God, please don't take my Bo away from me!* But it was another hour before she met with someone who could help her.

"I'm looking for my, my—" She hadn't even thought what to call Bo. "My fiancé. He's in the army, on some island in the Pacific, fighting the Japanese. But I think he's missing." She handed the returned letter to the woman and pointed to the address she'd carefully copied onto the front. "That's him, uh, Private B. J. Moon, number 16328466."

The woman took the envelope and looked at it. "Local boy, huh?"

"How can you tell?"

"His I.D. number. But listen, missy, right now, things are so crazy in the Pacific, there are tens of thousands of boys we can't put our finger on. He might be wounded, a POW, or AWOL. Most likely, this letter just missed him and got sent back by mistake."

But by this time, Lucy was sitting on the edge of her chair, gasping for breath. "He writes regular, but … but it's been months since I got a—"

"Calm down, girl. Just because you haven't heard from him for a while, doesn't necessarily mean he's been killed. But here …" She thrust a form across the desk to Lucy. "Fill this out, and I'll submit it to the military and get you the best answer we can. Okay?"

"How long will that take?"

"Hard to say. Within a few weeks, hopefully."

Lucy took a deep breath and picked up the paper, then handed it back. "I … I can't read and write. Could you …?"

The woman rolled her eyes. "You see that line behind you? Maybe you could get a friend to help you fill it out."

"Please? I need to know as soon as possible."

"Oh, all right." She smacked the form down on her desk and began asking questions while she filled in the necessary lines.

A LETTER WITH THE RED CROSS INSIGNIA on the outside of the envelope arrived two weeks later. She ripped it open and then ran to pound on Miss Mason's door. Without a word, she handed it to the motherly black woman.

Miss Mason scanned the letter, and her eyes begin to glisten. "Oh, babe." She said it just like Bo used to say it then grabbed Lucy in a bear hug. "It says B. J. Moon was killed in action in the attempt to take the Solomon Islands in the Southwest Pacific."

Chapter 33

I DON'T MUCH LIKE PEOPLE HUGGIN' ME, so when the rain drove me inside Manna House one Sunday evening, I kinda hung back at the edge of the group that had gathered in the multipurpose room for one of their church services. You never could be certain what they might do if the Spirit got a'hold of 'em, 'specially with those SouledOut church people leadin' it. Like as not, folks'd end up runnin' around huggin' everyone within reach.

But after it was over and everyone seemed to be in their right minds, I made my way over to the coffee and juice cart and helped myself. Fuzz Top was there, along with her youngest on the floor, wrestlin' with Dandy. "Thanks for dryin' my dog off," I said. "Guess he was kind of muddy."

Paul looked up and gave me a snarly stare. Yeah, yeah, yeah. He thinks Dandy should be his dog, but I'm the one who cares for him, so I didn't pay him no mind.

I munched another cookie and looked around the room, the room they'd named the Shepherd's Fold. "So where is it?" I said to no one in particular.

"Where's what?" Precious piped back, as feisty as usual. She reached for another cookie and almost tripped over Paul and Dandy.

"Martha's plaque! A big mural on the wall! The name in lights ... *some*thin'!" I planted my fists on my hips and did another survey. "This room got a new name, ain't it? But I don't see *nothin'* yet sayin' ya named it after Martha Shepherd." Seemed downright disrespectful.

Fuzz Top stepped in to make peace. "Oh, Lucy," she broke in. "It's only been a few weeks since we chose the name. We haven't had time—"

"Somebody say somethin' about needin' a mural on the wall?" It was Florida, that other yappy African-American woman, about ten years older than Precious. But she wasn't a resident of Manna House. She'd come with the SouledOut people.

"Well," Fuzz Top offered, "Lucy was just wanting something in this room to let people know why we named it Shepherd's Fold."

They talked on, with Florida pointing. "Hm. Plaque would be nice with the lady's name an' all ... That wall there. As people come in, it'd be real nice to have a mural of the Good Shepherd, don'tcha think?"

They was all goin' at it, makin' plans and decidin' what oughta be. *I think this, and I think that!* "That's the trouble 'round here." I jerked my cart and turned away. "People do too much thinkin' an' not enough doin' ... Where's Dandy?"

I found him over with Paul, who was brushin' him with someone's old hairbrush. "Hey, now, that looks real good." Figured I owed him a little encouragement.

But he looked up at me kinda suspicious like. "I saw you, you know."

"Did ya now?"

"Yeah. Saw you last week, saw you again yesterday in the park outside Richmond Towers where my dad lives. Like you're spying on us or something."

Oh, so that was it, was it? I turned to see a surprised Fuzz Top, who had followed me over and held up my hand to let her know everything was okay. "You got a real smart kid there, Miss Gabby. Real smart ... C'mon, Dandy. Time fer us ta be goin'."

Hopin' I hadn't said too much, I lit a shuck outta there, glad when I went through the front door a few moments later to find that the rain had stopped.

Truth be told, I had been spyin' a little on the boys' father up there in that penthouse of his, and he'd caught me that one time—though I got the best of him. But somethin' didn't seem right about that man, so I was lookin' out for Fuzz Top and her boys. I mean, that man was more than just rude to me ... kickin' out Fuzz Top and Martha and Dandy. Maybe it had to do with his gamblin', but whatever, I aimed to find out!

I swung by the park and watched Fairbanks's windows for a spell that very evening, but the lights never came on, so I figured he wasn't home.

Weather was warm and nice for the next several days, but I musta been gettin' soft stayin' at Manna House so much 'cause I didn't feel like sleepin' out in the open every night. So I spent the nights in that little stone house in Graceland Cemetery. It kept the dew off, at least, and in the mornings, before I went over to check on Fairbanks, I usually sat a spell on that little bench lettin' the sun warm the kinks out of my old bones. I'd just sit and think on the old days with Jigger and Bo and meetin' him at that circus and the times we had together. I never appreciated those times much when we were runnin' from place to place. Guess we were just too young.

The lights came on and off in the penthouse the next few evenings, so I guessed Fairbanks was okay, but I started noticing a couple of peculiar characters hangin' about, lookin' up at the apartment same as me. I could see one was an undercover cop—

they're never *undercover* if you know the streets—and the other wore a suit. Now why would they be interested in Fairbanks?

I got bold. "You gentlemen into real estate? Lookin' to buy this place or somethin'?"

They looked at me like I was Moses' burnin' bush speakin' to 'em. "Uh ... no, no ... we were just takin' a walk in the park."

"Uh-hm. But ya ain't from around here, are ya? Even though I have seen ya before. Whatcha lookin' for?"

The undercover looked around as though someone else might be watchin' us. "We're actually looking for a Philip Fairbanks. Supposed to live in this building. You know him?"

"Why would I know him? Do I look like I'm one of the residents?"

"Ha! Not hardly. But here's my card and five bucks. There's five more for you if you happen to come across him."

Dandy growled as the man extended his hand toward me. I ignored it and gave a tug on Dandy's leash as we wandered off ... slow like, lookin' back whenever I pleased. Pretty soon they left the park.

THOUGHT MAYBE I OUGHTA TELL FUZZ TOP, but when I got to Manna House, a couple of surprises were waitin' for me.

Estelle Williams had knitted me another purple hat and left it at the front desk with strict instructions to Angela the receptionist to give it to me soon as I walked in the door. I put it on and—warm as the day was—it felt good. Made me feel close again to my dear friend, Martha Shepherd, my old one being buried with her in her casket an' all.

Better still, when I pushed open the double doors to drag my cart and Dandy into the multipurpose room, I halted ... flabbergasted.

Directly across the room a large, colorful mural had been painted on the wall. Right away, I recognized Jesus, the Good Shepherd, surrounded by a flock of raggedy sheep that He was bringin' into a sturdy enclosure. Some were a dirty white, some black, some brown, but none were neat and fat. The shepherd had a long walkin' stick in one hand, and a tiny lamb was tucked into the crook of His other arm. Over the top of the mural flew a long open scroll with some bright blue lettering.

"Wonkers!" I mumbled. "Now *that's* more like it!"

Angela had come up beside me and swept her hand across as if she were painting it herself. "'The Shepherd's Fold,'" she read, "in letters so big no one can miss it. What do you think of that, Lucy?"

"I ... I ... How could anyone do this so fast?"

By then Mabel had joined us and told me Florida Hickman's son had painted it. He'd been a tagger, and quick, too, 'fore the cops put a stop to him decoratin' underpasses and buildings. But now, she said, he was an art major at Columbia University.

"It ... it kinda blows my mind."

"And look over here, Lucy." Mabel pointed to a little brass plaque on the side. "Says, 'In memory of Martha Shepherd, fondly known as Gramma Shep. A resident of Manna House from June 19 to July 10, 2006.' Pretty nice, wouldn't you say?"

I didn't have any words. Just stood there, tears streamin' down my cheeks and fallin' on Dandy like rain. Before they could say anything, I hustled on downstairs and loaded up a lunch plate with Estelle's Caribbean rice and beans and Mexican sausage and sat down at one of the tables by myself. But in a matter of minutes Mabel and Estelle and Fuzz Top and a couple of others joined me. Estelle looked at me with her head cocked to the side and one eyebrow raised. I just touched my new hat. She knew how

288

I felt and smiled. Then Mabel launched into tellin' the whole story about how the wall got painted all over again.

When she was finally done and I reckoned I had the valves turned off on my waterworks, I said what was on my mind. "Well, maybe we oughta have some kinda dedication or somethin' for Shepherd's Fold, now that ya got a decent plaque an' ever'thing."

"Good idea, Lucy," said Fuzz Top. "A *really* good idea." She stood up and collected her dishes. "Time to get back to work."

"Hey, don't run off," I said. "You the one me an' Dandy come here to see. Just got sidetracked by that mural thing upstairs. You an' me gotta talk. But somewhere private like."

Once we bused our dishes and squeezed into her tiny office, I told her about seeing those strange guys hangin' around Richmond Towers.

"You *are* spying on them!" Her eyes squinted so I couldn't tell whether she was glad or mad.

"Now hold on there, Fuzz Top. I was just makin' sure they was all right when not with you. Can't seem to forget how I found you that night when that mister of yours kicked you out, cryin' your eyes out on that park bench ... an' don't forget who found Dandy here, wanderin' 'round the park after bein' lost all night an' all day. So you got a problem with me keepin' an eye on your boys? Huh?"

She said she was grateful, but said it was freakin' out her boys. I don't understand some people, but maybe she didn't get the drift of what I'd told her. "Look, that ain't all. Those guys were askin' 'bout your mister. Now what do you think 'bout that?"

She frowned and slowly sat back down, lookin' as puzzled as if her skull was as thick as my new hat. "I suppose it could be one of Philip's creditors trying to find him. He's, uh, run up some big debts. But I appreciate you keeping an eye on my boys."

"Yeah, well …" She sure didn't seem very pleased about it. I got up and sighed. "Mostly wanted to know the boys was okay since I didn't see 'em this weekend up at the Tower."

"That's because they stayed with me this weekend. They're okay, Lucy."

She didn't say it, but I kinda felt like she was tellin' me to butt out of her business. Then she scribbled a note on a scrap of paper from her pocket and handed it to me. "But here are my phone numbers—both home and cell phones. Call me if you're concerned about anything, okay?"

"Now, Fuzz Top, whatcha think I'm gonna do with that? You know I ain't got no cell phone."

She stood up. "Just take it, Lucy. If you need to call me, you'll find a way."

Five days later, I found a way.

Chapter 34

AFTER THE TRAGIC NOTICE FROM THE RED CROSS that Private B. J. Moon had been killed in action, Lucy walked through the days as if in a fog. She hardly took notice of how one day began or another ended. What did it matter? What did anything matter? Her whole life had become a nightmare from which she could not awake. She went to work, not because she was being industrious or recognized that she needed the money, but simply because her cheap little alarm clock rang every morning, and that was what she was supposed to do.

Coming home after work one night, Miss Mason's door opened. "Lucy? Lucy, come in here, girl. I need to talk to you." Miss Mason held her faded pink robe closed at the neck with one hand. "I know it's late, but I made tea and I've got cookies." The older woman swung the door wide as Lucy backed down off the first step on the stairs and reluctantly followed the landlady into her apartment. "Now you sit there at the table like we used to do, and I'll get the tea."

Lucy watched the old woman hobble into her kitchen and stared blankly after her until she emerged with the teapot and a plate of cookies.

Miss Mason eased herself into a chair and poured. "You know, they've been asking about you at church for the last few weeks. I told them it wasn't your man who needs prayer now. I trust he's with Jesus. But it's *you* who's standin' in the need of prayer. And so we've been praying for you. But you need to come back. You need to hear the Word. You need encouragement, dear. How about day after tomorrow? Will you come with me?"

Lucy stared at her and calculated. Was this Friday? Was Sunday the day after tomorrow? "I don't know. I'll have to think 'bout it."

"Well ..." Miss Mason leaned back and crossed her arms. "Well, you do that, but don't think on it too long. It may be Friday, when everything looks dark—like Jesus hanging on the cross— but Sunday's coming. Sunday's a-comin', chil'. Sunday's always coming for them that love God. Know what I'm saying?"

They both sat in silence for ... Lucy had no idea how long, and she had no idea what the old woman meant. It was as if her mind was in a fog.

Finally, Miss Mason clapped her hands and then raised both of them to her face as though she were praying. "Lucy, dear, there's one more thing I need to speak to you about. I'm sorry to say it's a Friday-type thing that I hate to bring to you at a time like this." She hesitated.

Lucy tried to clear the fog and concentrate, but all she could do was nod and hope Miss Mason's meaning would become clearer.

"My hip's been gettin' worse and worse, and I can't handle these Chicago winters anymore. I'm not safe on the ice. So my granddaughter has talked me into coming down to Mississippi to live with her before the cold sets in. She has two little ones and wants to go back to work. She has a good job offer, and I could help take care of the babies now that they don't need lifting all the time."

Lucy found herself nodding again. Somehow this wasn't good news, but her landlady was a kind woman, so of course she'd want to help out her family.

Miss Mason cleared her throat. "The thing is, I've had to sell this house. Just received word today that the new owner wants to remodel it back into a single-family dwelling. He thinks there'll be a market for those soon as the war's over and the boys start coming home and building fam—" She caught her breath. "Oh, forgive me, dear. I didn't need to bring that up."

Lucy didn't move. Bo wouldn't be coming home, and they wouldn't be starting a family. That fact was with her every moment. It was more real than anything around her. It made no difference whether Miss Mason mentioned it or not.

"Anyway, they've given us thirty days to clear out, which is all right for me, because I've been planning this for a while and I know where I'm going. But I never imagined the new owner would close down the other two apartments and kick you out. I'm real sorry."

Lucy stared at her, the fog clearing. So that was the "Friday" part of Miss Mason's news.

As Lucy left in the morning for work three weeks later, a large moving truck pulled up in front of the house. It had the image of a green sailing ship painted on its yellow side along with a company name. Lucy was late and paid no further attention. But when she got home that evening, two men were putting the last of Miss Mason's things in the back of the same truck. A taxicab was waiting behind the van, and Miss Mason was struggling to come down the front steps. She had finally yielded to using a cane, which, along with the railing, helped her keep her balance.

"Oh, Lucy, there you are. I was so worried I'd be gone before you got home. Now, like I told you, the new owner takes possession on the first of the month, December one. Got that? You need to be out by then. Do you know where you're going yet?"

Lucy shook her head.

"I feel so bad. Here …" She put a small note in Lucy's hand. "I wrote down the address for Jessie and Emma Brown … from the church, you know. You might not remember them, but I introduced you. They said they could put you up for a while, but that's not permanent. You've got to find yourself another apartment."

"Yes ma'am. I'll be sure and do that. Don't you worry about me. You have a safe trip, now." It seemed like the right thing to say.

Snow was spitting through the night air as Miss Mason made her way to the cab. Just before she got in, she turned back. "And you work on your reading, you hear?"

"Yes ma'am." Lucy watched the truck grind its way down the block with the cab following. The cab, she supposed, would take Miss Mason to the train station, and her things would probably catch up with her in Mississippi in a week or so.

The two vehicles turned at the corner and were gone. Lucy's teeth chattered, but whether it was from the biting wind or the realization that she was alone—truly alone now—was hard to tell.

Tears blurred her eyes as she climbed the steps to the empty house. The second-floor tenant had left a week earlier, and she was the only person left in the house. She went inside but didn't even lock the door behind her. Why bother? She had nothing worth stealing. Besides, Jigger would protect her.

Jigger … she still needed to walk him before she could go to bed. It was so cold she was tempted to just let him out without going with him. With Miss Mason gone, there was no one to care about the bushes in the yard. No … Jigger was her last contact with

Bo. Taking care of Jigger made her feel as if she was still able to do something for Bo.

A LOUD BANGING AND SCRAPING WOKE LUCY on Tuesday, just two days before the end of November. Why had she stopped locking the downstairs door? Someone was in the house … tearing it up by the sound of things.

Lucy slipped into a dress and sweater and told Jigger to stay before slowly creeping down the stairs. A blond-haired, red-cheeked man in coveralls was trying to knock the pins out of the hinges that held the door to Miss Mason's unit. Lucy descended a couple of more steps. "What do you think you're doing?"

The man jumped. "Oh, I'm … I'm just removing this door so we can begin work on this dump." He frowned at Lucy. "What are *you* doing here? I bought this place, and it's supposed to be empty."

"What's today?"

"Tuesday—"

"I know that. What day of the month?"

"Uh, November twenty-eight, as I recall."

"Then, I don't have to be out yet. Miss Mason said so."

"Ah, you're the one who lives upstairs." He pointed up.

"Third floor."

"Yah, well … Friday's the deadline. I got a crew comin' in to gut the place."

Lucy pressed her lips together. It was actually happening. She went back upstairs. *O God, O God, what am I gonna do?* When she got to her apartment, she scrambled through her things looking for the address of the church family Miss Mason had mentioned … the Browns. But she couldn't find it.

She sat down, elbows on her knees, and held her head in her hands, trying to calm herself. People at the church would know where the Browns lived, but still, that was just a temporary solution. Jigger pushed his way between her arms with his wet nose and whined. She petted him, but those people probably wouldn't want a dog in their house anyway.

"What are we gonna do, Jigger? What are we gonna do?" The dog jumped back and gave a sharp yap as his tail wiggled his whole body. He didn't understand that they needed a place to live. All he wanted to do was ... "Okay, ol' boy. Okay, okay. I'll take you out."

They walked aimlessly for the next hour, through the neighborhood around Greeley Avenue and over across Western to the Riverview Amusement Park gate. This was where Bo had worked. There might be people inside on the winter maintenance crew who remembered him. The allure was strong, and she found herself stepping around the barricades that told potential visitors the park was closed, even if they saw activity inside.

Someone yelled at her and told her to get out and take the dog with her, but she ignored him and walked on. There ... the Bobs roller coaster. Bo had worked on that ride. Two men who didn't seem upset at seeing her and Jigger were putting up a new sign.

She stopped near their ladders. "Excuse me ... either of you guys remember Borick Hansen, worked here a couple winters ago?"

"Bo? Oh, yeah! Great kid! Went off to war, didn't he?" One of the men climbed down the ladder and pulled his coat collar tighter around his neck. "Hey, George." He looked back up at the other man. "You remember Bo, don't ya?"

"Come on, Nate, you know that was before my time."

The man on the ground turned to Lucy. "Hey, you must be his girl, aren't ya? Always talked 'bout how beautiful you were."

Lucy looked at the ground, afraid that she would burst into tears. "Yeah. I … I …"

"I hope that war's over soon. If not, they're gonna start draftin' ol' geezers like me. So, how's Bo gettin' along, anyway?"

She swallowed hard and shook her head slowly. "He … didn't make it."

"Ah, gee, sister." Nate reached out as if to embrace her, but Lucy gave Jigger a jerk and turned away.

"I'm real sorry about Bo," the man called after her. "If there's anything I can do, just …"

FRIDAY—THE DEADLINE—CAME, and Lucy still didn't know where to go, so she just went to work. What else could she do? When she got home, more demolition had been done on the first floor, but nothing seemed to have been disturbed upstairs. It was the same for the next three days, but on Tuesday, her day off, the new owner saw her around the house again. "You better move out! I'm warnin' you!" She halfheartedly walked the streets of her neighborhood for the next couple of hours looking for a house with a "For Rent" sign in the window. No luck.

But when she got home Wednesday night, all her stuff was stacked helter-skelter out on the curb, and a new lock had been installed on the door. She sat down on the steps, hugging her coat around her and let the pent-up dam of tears spill over, feeling as if her guts were turning inside out. She had no idea how long she'd been siting there, when Jigger suddenly nosed her so hard she almost lost her balance.

Grabbing him in a fierce hug, she buried her face in his fur. "Hey, boy, they kick you out too?"

But somehow, Jigger's eager presence and wagging tail gave her the courage to wipe her tears and try to think. The dog was a survivor! And if she stuck with him, he might pull her through. Blowing on her stiff fingers, she went out to the curb and began digging through her stuff. The streetlight across the street hardly provided enough light for her to see, but … there. She found it! The Purse she'd tucked in her old suitcase. Without thinking what she was saying, she muttered, "Thank You … thank You, God!" In all the chaos she'd almost forgotten about it. For a moment she wondered whether God had kept the new owner from pawing through her things until he found it. He probably would've kept it. But … if God cared that much, why didn't He care just a little more and keep her from getting thrown out on the street? In fact, if God cared at all, why hadn't He protected Bo's life? *That's* what she and several saints far better than herself had prayed for all those weeks when she'd attended Mount Olive Tabernacle.

No, it didn't seem like God had anything to do with any of it.

It was just luck … good and bad!

Chapter 35

NIGHTS WERE TAKIN' ON A NIP, but as long as the clouds weren't weepin' too much, I preferred to be out and about. I like the fall, 'spite of the cold. Reminds me of when Bo and I were together, comin' to Chicago and getting our little apartment. Thinkin' 'bout him had me hangin' out more and more in Graceland Cemetery, where I could be alone, me sittin' on that little bench while Dandy nosed around … nearby, of course, so the groundspeople wouldn't catch us.

There'd been a drizzle in the middle of the night that sent a chill to my bones I couldn't shake, so Saturday mornin', I figured I needed to get 'em movin'. Took Dandy and hoofed it over to the lakefront, then turned north along the jogging path to Richmond Towers. Probably three miles, so I was all warmed up and ready for anything.

I'd turned into the pedestrian tunnel, thinkin' I'd go under the Outer Drive and get a closer look at the penthouse to see if Fairbanks was home with the boys or off gamblin' again, when Dandy suddenly started whinin' and pullin' on his leash and carryin' on like he was after a pound of hamburger. And there, crumpled on the ground at the other end of the tunnel, I could see a body. Thought it was just a passed-out wino at first, but then I saw the guy was in some fancy jogging clothes. Dandy stopped, stood stiff-legged, and growled. The light wasn't too good in the tunnel—those electric ones turn themselves off at dawn—but when I got close I got a start. Fairbanks!

"Whadd're you doin' down there on the ground? Pull yourself up and act like a man ... if you can!"

But he didn't move, and Dandy was startin' to sniff at him. Got me worried. Was he dead? I looked real close and could see some blood. 'Shamed to say I was thinkin' he deserved whatever had happened to him. But Fuzz Top and the boys didn't. I reached down an' touched his hand. He still seemed warm, and even though my eyesight ain't too good in the dark, I could see he was still breathin'. *O Lord, I sure need some help now.* No way could I move that big lunk, and they always say you ain't s'posed to move an injured person, anyway.

I looked around ... no one. But then I heard the *pat, pat, pat* of a jogger. I nearly ran myself back to the other end of the tunnel to catch him before he passed. "Help! Help!"

Once he saw who was callin', he looked on up the path like he was decidin' whether or not to stop, but finally he did.

"You got a cell phone?" I was diggin' in my pocket for that scrap of paper Fuzz Top had given me.

"What for?"

"In there, dummy! A man's been beat up, and I need to call 9-1-1 ... and his wife."

The guy eyed me like he thought it was a trick to get him into the tunnel where someone could rob him, but finally he dug the phone out of his jacket pocket and handed it to me.

"How do you work one of these things?"

He punched in 9-1-1 and handed the phone back to me to make the report. I've never been very conversational with cops, so it took me a bit to convince them that someone was hurt and where we were.

As soon as I was done, the man reached for his phone.

I pulled it back. "Lady says I gotta stay on the line. What's your hurry? You didn't do this, did you?"

That set him back a step. "Of course not. But I'm on a tight schedule today and—"

"You'll wait till the cops get here." I put the phone back up to my ear. "You still there? How long's it gonna take? Seems like the cops are everywhere these days 'cept when you need one."

They actually got there pretty quick, followed by an ambulance that drove right out into the park and met us at the end of the tunnel. The cops grilled me some, though it wasn't too bad. Guess they could see by lookin' that I wasn't the one who did the damage unless I had a baseball bat hidden in my cart. But somewhere along the line, I mentioned Fairbanks' name, and that set 'em off again.

"How do you know this man?" "When did you last see him?" "What are you doing out here in the park at this time of the morning?" It went on and on while the paramedics were checkin' Fairbanks and loadin' him into the ambulance, and then they lost interest.

I'd seen how the jogger had worked his phone, so as soon as the cops and ambulance left me alone, I punched in Fuzz Top's number. "Gabby!" I didn't have much patience by this time. "Get over here and pick up your boys."

"Wha—? Lucy?" came a panicked voice in my ear. "Is that you? What's going on?"

"Dandy an' I found your mister beat up in the walkin' tunnel under Lake Shore Drive—"

"The boys! Lucy, where are they?"

"Up in that penthouse sleepin', far as I know. Your man was out joggin' early is my guess—"

"Did you say beat up? How bad is he? Did you call 9-1-1?"

The jogger reached for his phone. "Come on, lady. I'm not providing a free calling service here."

"Dagnabit! I'll give it back to ya. Just a minnit!" Then I answered Gabby. "Yeah, I called 9-1-1. Now this jogger guy wants his phone back."

After a few moments of silence, she asked, "How bad, Lucy?"

"Pretty bad, Fuzz Top. He's unconscious. Lotta blood, but still breathin' ..."

"Stay there, Lucy. I'm coming. Just find out where they're going to take him."

I already knew. "Weiss Memorial. Everyone around here gets taken there."

"Just wait for me." The call ended. I handed the phone back to the impatient jogger and headed on over to Richmond Towers with Dandy and my cart.

Fuzz Top musta been drivin' like a bat outta hell, 'cause I'd barely been sittin' on that bench across from the Towers a few minutes when she screeched her little red wagon to a halt in the parking lot and ran over to me.

"How long ago did the ambulance leave?"

I shrugged. "Not that long."

"Was it bad?"

"Weren't good."

"Do the boys know their dad's hurt?"

I shook my head. "Don't think so. He was wearing them fancy jogging clothes—ya know, them silky shorts an' matchin' jacket—like he'd gone out early for a run while they was still sleepin'."

302

"Don't disappear, Lucy. I want to know what happened—but right now I've got to get my boys. I'll be back as soon as I can," she said as she ran for the door into Richmond Towers.

"Hey, is your car open?" I yelled after her.

"Yep."

Once she was gone, I opened the hatch on the back of her little Subaru and wrestled my cart into the luggage space. Dandy would just have to share the seat with the boys.

As soon as Fuzz Top and the boys came down, both of 'em lookin' pretty scared, she insisted I go over every detail as we rode to the hospital.

"Did the paramedics tell you *anything* about how badly Philip was hurt?"

"Nope. But then I was busy tellin' the cops how I found him and all. Then I called you. So if they said anything, I didn't hear it."

Once we got to the hospital waitin' room, a couple more cops began interrogatin' Gabby about whether she had any idea what might've happened.

"Nothing! We're ... separated. Someone ..." She glanced my way. "Someone called me, told me he'd been found beaten unconscious while he was out jogging. I ... well, our boys were with him this weekend. So I picked them up from their dad's place and came here."

I had my ideas about what had happened to Fuzz Top's mister, but the cops weren't askin' me, so I kept my mouth shut.

Jodi and Denny Baxter—Gabby's friends from her church—came rushin' in and got the whole story ... or as much as there was to tell, and in a little while, a doctor came out and took Fuzz Top and her boys and the Baxters into a conference room.

I sat there, feeling like chopped liver. I was the one who'd found her fancy man. If it wasn't for me, he might've laid there a whole lot longer … maybe too long. But no one invited me into the conference room.

After a while, a female security guard came strolling through the waiting room and nodded at me. Still feelin' miffed, I just turned away, and somehow she took that as a clue to check me out. "You waiting to see a doctor?"

"Not this time, thank goodness."

"Then you need to move along. This isn't a warming shelter."

I snarled. "I'm waitin' for a friend in the ER. Besides, it ain't cold outside."

"And who would your friend be?"

"Mr. Fairbanks. He was attacked this morning, and I found him. I came down here with his wife." When she didn't move on, I pointed. "You can ask at the desk."

She nodded and strolled on, lookin' for someone else to kick out.

Ticked me off being hassled like that, so I moseyed outside to check on Dandy. He'd been in that car too long anyway.

I waited a long time, but finally the Baxters came out and found me. They offered to take me and Dandy back to Manna House. Said every hand was needed to help with the move to relocate some of the residents into that House of Hope Fuzz Top was startin' up.

I didn't volunteer, but I got in their van.

"So what's the word?" I said after we'd ridden a couple of blocks.

Denny looked at me through the mirror. "You mean Philip?"

"He's the one in the hospital, ain't he?"

"The doctor said he has several broken ribs, a broken arm, possible internal injuries, probably a concussion, and a broken nose. But they're still doing more tests."

"Huh. Sounds like a world of hurt to me. Did Fuzz Top get to talk to him?"

"He hadn't woken up yet when we left."

I was quiet for a while, then leaned forward. "They gonna have anything to eat at this move thing?"

"Oh, Lucy." Jodi turned in her seat to look at me. "I'm so sorry. We should've had you come in and eat with us in the cafeteria."

"Cafeteria? Nah, that's okay. Don't much go for cafeteria food." But under my breath I mumbled, "But at least it's food." Even though my stomach was growlin', I kept tryin' to tell myself it was *okay*. A man had been beaten up, could have died, everyone had far bigger things to worry about than me ... Like who beat up Fairbanks and why?

Except, I was the one who'd been lookin' out for him. I was the one who'd seen the two hooligans sneakin' around. And I'd even talked to them. But no one was askin' me. No one figured that an ol' bag lady might know a thing or two.

Chapter 36

SHIVERING IN THE SHARP NIGHT AIR, Lucy found her little suitcase and packed it with The Purse, Bo's letters, and as many of her clothes as would fit, stuffed a few cans and other food items into a pillowcase and a couple of blankets into her laundry bag. There was still a big pile of stuff on the curb: pots, pans, dishes, a secondhand picture they'd found to hang on the wall, old *Billboard* newspapers. She squeezed one into her pillowcase to remember Bo by. But how had they collected so much junk? Maybe she could come back tomorrow and retrieve the rest ... if it hadn't been stolen. She poured the last half of a bottle of milk into a pan and let Jigger lap it up.

"Sorry, boy. That's all you get tonight."

When she had collected as much as she could carry, Lucy trudged off through the cold night. Perhaps her boss would let her use a room at the hotel for a day or two and take it out of her pay. But that didn't answer what she would do with Jigger. She couldn't just abandon him.

With the bags over her shoulder and the suitcase in the other hand, she walked halfheartedly over to Western Avenue and headed south, watching for the next trolley, but they didn't run very often at this time of night, and she was soon at the bridge over the Chicago River. She and Bo had taken shelter beneath it when they first came to the city. More out of curiosity than a clear plan, she made her way down to the water's edge and worked her way along a narrow path through leafless bushes until she was under the bridge. Tucked up in the armpit of the bridge, where the barren riverbank rose to meet the abutment, she could see a small hobo's fire with three people sitting around it.

She approached slowly, grateful that Jigger was at her side.

"Yo, the camp!"

"Whatchu want?"

Lucy perked up. A woman's gravelly voice. She'd heard it before, but where? "Comin' in. Got a loaf of bread and a couple of tins of sardines. Can of Spam too."

"Got a bottle?" A man with a thick tongue and slurred speech eyed her as Lucy climbed the bank.

"No."

"We done et. All I need now's a drink and a warm woman. This ol' hag don't put out no more, so come on in, darlin'."

"Ha!" scoffed the woman. "You drink so much, Marcus, you ain't got nothin' to give."

Lucy nearly ran from the crude talk, but as she started to turn away, she realized the "ol' hag" sitting around the fire also looked familiar, like the woman she'd often seen panhandling for money near the trolley line. She stooped to squeeze under the overhanging bridge beams. "Hey, I gave you a quarter once!"

"What if you did?"

As Lucy closed in, she eyed the two men. The half-drunk, talkative one was a no-count. The other one—perhaps Mexican—hadn't said a word, but he didn't appear threatening. She pointed at the old woman. "Well, I think you owe me a night's lodging."

"Hey …" The woman raised her hands and looked up as though she were surveying her palace. "It's a free bridge. But I'm still hungry. I could use some of those sardines."

"That dog bite?" mumbled the thick-tongued man.

"Yeah! He'll tear your leg off you even think about touchin' me. All I gotta do is snap my fingers, so keep your distance."

"Didn't mean nothin'."

The old woman waved her hand dismissively. "Ah … they're harmless. Come on. Sit down and take a load off."

As Lucy arranged her belongings in a pile a few feet away from the trio and pointed Jigger to sit with them, she eyed the old woman by the fire. As rough as she appeared—dusty coat, stringy hair, and dirt clogging the pores of her skin—Lucy felt a certain respect for her. She was a survivor in a world where everything seemed against her, a world like the one where Lucy now found herself. Would she be able to survive? Did she even want to? She gritted her teeth and sucked in a deep breath of cold air.

The trio made a place for her around the small fire, and Lucy sat with them staring into the flames while the others complained about how the world was going to heck and people were getting more and more stingy and how Roosevelt's New Deal fell apart as soon as the war started.

After a while, Lucy withdrew and moved with her stuff up against the bridge abutment. She pulled her coat tighter and lay down on one blanket, spread on the dirt. A snap of her fingers brought Jigger to curl up in the crook made by her body so they could keep each other warm as she tucked the other two blankets over them. Such an amazing dog. He always seemed to know what was wanted.

As her eyes grew heavy, her last image was of the trio, still chattering around the glowing embers of the dying fire. They were makin' it. And she'd even stood up to the rude man. Maybe she wasn't as helpless as she felt. Nothing had really changed, but perhaps she had … just a little.

TELLING JIGGER TO GUARD HER STUFF, Lucy went to work the next day and returned to stay with the bridge people for four nights, bringing some food she'd salvaged from the diner. She took The Purse to work and hid it behind a beam in the ceiling of a utility closet at the hotel. Still, she knew bridge living wouldn't work in the long run. It was too hard to keep clean, even though she snuck a bath at the hotel. And as faithful as Jigger was, she couldn't expect him to watch her stuff indefinitely. So Sunday morning she made her way to Mount Olive Tabernacle, Miss Mason's church, doing her best to brush the dust and smudges from her clothes.

Lucy arrived early and asked the usher if she knew the Browns.

The woman wrung her white-gloved hands and scanned the small sanctuary. "Don't look like they's here yet, but Jessie and Emma and the kids all sit in the third pew. Not Mother Brown, though. She'll be the first one on this end of the Mothers' Bench." The usher pointed to a pew up front that sat perpendicular to the other rows over on the right side of the platform. Three older women, looking like nurses dressed in white, were already sitting there, gently rocking back and forth with their eyes closed as if in prayer.

Lucy remained standing at the side near the back of the church, and the usher waved at her when the Brown family came in, but it just didn't seem proper to approach them right then. And she was glad she hadn't, because in a few moments two deacons got up and began leading the congregation in devotions before the main service began.

Lucy took a seat in the back and tried to concentrate, but her mind kept drifting to Ma, who had read the Bible with the family nearly every night and tried to lead a little church service with them on Sundays … especially since Pa didn't cotton much to formal church. "All they do is fight over who's goin' to heaven and who's goin' to hell—Baptists or Methodists or Presbyterians, and who knows how many others."

It wasn't until Pastor Winfred was halfway through his sermon, repeating every point two or three times and getting more and more into the rhythm of it that Lucy began to really listen. The congregation egged him on with, "Amen, brother!" "Preach it, pastor, preach it!" "Well …" "Praise Jesus!" Lucy leaned forward.

> Don'tcha know—*uh,*
> That if you draw nigh to God—*uh,*
> He will draw nigh to you?—*uh,*
> As it says in the Word—*uh,*
> Cleanse your hands, ye sinners—*uh,*
> And purify your hearts, ye double minded!—*uh,*
> Don'tcha know—*uh,*
> That's how we draw nigh to God?—*uh,*
> If you draw nigh to God—*uh,*
> He will draw nigh to you!—*uh.*

Lucy shook as if a jolt of electricity had gone through her. The man was preaching from a different text, but the message was the same as the one the tent preacher had given back there in Ohio: "If thou seek him, he will be found of thee!" She had never forgotten it. And now Pastor Winfred was saying basically the same thing.

This isn't about your ultimate salvation—*uh*.
That was accomplished by Jesus on the cross, don'tcha know?
But like it says in Ecclesiastes three and one—*uh*,
To every thing there is a season!—*uh*,
And the apostle James is tellin' us here—*uh*,
That there is season—*uh*,
To be afflicted, and to mourn—*uh*.
And there is a season to weep—*uh*,
Let your laughter be turned to mourning—*uh*,
And your joy to heaviness …
O Lord, have mercy! Lord have mercy!

The man paused and wiped his sweating brow with a white towel, then continued in a quieter, more conversational tone. The organ began to play softly as he wiped his glistening head and neck again.

Yes, yes, brothers and sisters, this war has brought many of us to our knees in sorrow and mourning. There's no denying it, no denying it. But here's the good news. James says, "Humble yourselves in the sight of the Lord … and He shall lift you up."

He shall lift you up!
Did you hear me, church?
I said, He *shall* lift you up!

That's the good news, brothers and sisters. That's the great news for days like these! He shall lift you up! It's His promise. Our part is to draw nigh to God, and then He will draw nigh to us and lift us up!

With a final shout of, "Glory!" the pastor returned to his seat behind the pulpit as the choir picked up the melody from the organ and sang. Soon the congregation joined in, repeating again and again …

> *I will trust in the Lord,*
> *I will trust in the Lord,*
> *I will trust in the Lord,*
> *Until I die.*

When the service was over, Lucy was tempted to slip out and walk back to the bridge so she could have time to think about what the preacher had said. It was almost as if … as if God had spoken to her personally, like He knew her loss and pain and was asking her to seek Him, draw near to Him, trust Him. But as she was trying to make up her mind, the Browns came up the aisle toward where she was standing.

As soon as Emma Brown saw her, she rushed up with a broad smile on her face. "You're the girl who lived with Sister Betsy, aren't you? We prayed for your man, you know. I was so sorry to hear he didn't make it back. You doin' all right, honey?"

Lucy gulped. This was not the place for the tears to come. "Thank you, Mrs. Brown. Thanks for prayin'." She halted, not knowing how to go on.

"Well, we all so sorry, but I'm glad you came today. You should come back, make this your church home, you know. The church doors are always open." She gave Lucy a quick hug and then held her at arm's length, looking her up and down with a frown on her face. "Where you stayin', dear, now that sister Betsy's moved and all?"

Lucy laughed nervously, but knew it sounded more like a mumbled cough. "That's kinda what I wanted to talk to you about.

Miss Mason, uh, she said it might be possible to stay with you for a while. It wouldn't be long. I got a good job and could pay till I find another situation."

"Oh, girl ..." Emma Brown waved her hand across her face. "That's not the point, is it, Jessie?" She tugged on the sleeve of her husband's jacket, who was talking to someone else.

"What?" He turned, a questioning look on his face.

Emma Brown explained who Lucy was, that she'd lost her apartment when Miss Mason moved and needed a place to stay.

"Oh, yeah, yeah." He nodded as his wife explained. "Sister Betsy said you might be lookin' us up. We'd be pleased to have you. Now the room ain't much. It's in the back of the house off the porch and don't have no direct heat. But it don't freeze, and the bed's real soft. I slept out there myself a time or two." He waggled his eyebrows in a humorous fashion. His wife swatted his arm.

"Uh, there's just one thing ..." Lucy looked down at the oiled wood floor, sure that what she said next would the kibosh on the whole plan. "I have a dog, He's a very good dog and don't bother nobody. I always clean up after him. Is there any place under the porch or somewhere he could stay?"

"Oh, he'd freeze outside come winter." Mrs. Brown turned to her husband for confirmation.

"Well ..." Mr. Brown scratched his chin. "We could probably fix up somethin'. I been meanin' to stack bales of straw around the foundation of our place for the winter, and here it's almost Christmas. Supposed to be good insulation for the whole building. We could make sure to create a little cubby for your dog, if you think that'd be okay."

Relief brought a smile to Lucy's face. "That'd be perfect, Mr. Brown. I'm sure Jigger would be happy with that."

A harsh frown descended over the man's face. "What'd you say his name was?"

"Jigger. That's what Bo always called him."

"Oh, *Jigger*, with a *J*. I thought you mighta said—"

"Jessie!" His wife swatted his arm. "Of course, she wouldn't say *that*. It'll be fine, dear. He works in a noisy steel mill on the Southside, and his hearin' goin'. Don't pay him no mind."

Chapter 37

I WAS S'POSED TA BE AT MANNA HOUSE for the dedication of the Shepherd's Fold room with its colorful mural. Really meant to be there, too, it bein' in memory of my friend, Miz Martha Shepherd, and I bein' the one who'd suggested the celebration. But I got waylaid, wouldn'cha know it. I was comin' through the park by Richmond Towers again, just keepin' my eyes out, when I noticed lights on up in the penthouse.

Apparently, Fuzz Top's man was finally home from the hospital. Well, good … or not, dependin' on whether he'd learned anything from his run-in with Chicago's not-so-Finest.

I shook my head and headed across the park, planning to go around the tower and head on down to Manna House. But as soon as I got to that little frontage road where Richmond Towers has some parking spaces for guests, I spied an unmarked cop car sittin' there. Wasn't so unusual. You can catch 'em parked most anywhere, engines runnin' for the air conditioning in summer or heat in the winter while the detectives catch up on all their important business, like plannin' a bust or eatin' donuts.

But in this case, I recognized the occupants as the same two goons who I'd tuned up before Fairbanks got mugged. Speakin' of gamblin'—like Fairbanks' been doin'—I'd lay odds that those two lunks were the ones who did it. They just looked suspicious to me, and I'm a pretty good judge of character.

Talkin' to Dandy like I hadn't noticed 'em, I turned back toward the park. "Oh, that's okay, boy. If you didn't finish your business, we can go back." That dog's always happy for a little more time in the park—more squirrels, more smells, more trees to mark. But I guess my ruse didn't fool those cops. After I'd walked back and forth a few times keepin' an eye on them, they started up their Crown Vic and roared out of there, squealing their tires as they went around the corner.

I hung around till afternoon just to make sure they didn't come back, then headed over to Manna House, hopin' to catch at least the tail end of the festivities. But by the time I got there, things were breakin' up and they were calling for volunteers to help with cleanup. Not havin' contributed to the damage, I didn't feel obligated. But I did head on down to the kitchen.

But Dandy beat me down there, and by the time I got there, Estelle was yelling for him to get out.

"Oh, don't go gettin' your panties in a knot, Estelle. Hey, got any food left?"

"Lucy!" Harry Bentley said as he tossed a rag he'd been using to wipe down a counter at the sink. "Where you been? Gabby was expecting you at the dedication. She was lookin' for you."

"Yeah, well, I been lookin' for her too. Where she at?" I pulled off my purple crocheted hat and scratched my head before jamming it back on.

Estelle washed out the rag Harry had tossed in the sink and continued wiping up. "Gabby told me she had to leave early to go down and visit her husband at Weiss Memorial Hospital."

"Well, he ain't there, but I got some intel on him that you"—I pointed at Harry—"Mr. Former Police Officer, need to know. Hey, Estelle, that coffee still hot?"

In a few minutes, I had a hot cup of joe and a plate of leftovers and was sitting across from Harry while Dandy wandered over to the back door of the shelter trying to nose the lid off a garbage can containing enough chicken bones to choke a hog.

"So, what's up, Lucy?"

"You know those two guys who beat up the Fuzz Top's husband?"

"Uh ... didn't know anyone was able to make a positive ID."

"Well, that's who I think did it. Anyway, they was hangin' around Richmond Towers before the attack, and they're back there again today ... and the lights are on up there in Miss Gabby's old apartment. That's how I know her man's already home from the hospital. But s'pect those scumbags are fixin' to work him over again the moment he steps outta the building. So there, Mr. Cop. That's what I seen."

"You're sure it was them?"

"No question. Don'cha think we oughta tell Fuzz Top? She at least needs to know what's up."

"Wouldn't hurt, I guess."

"Of course not! Estelle, you got her number, don'cha? Give her a call and tell her to get herself back over here. Tell her it's an emergen—well, maybe not an emergency, but urgent. I gotta talk to her."

Estelle got on her phone and tracked Gabby down. When she closed it, she pointed at me. "She's comin', said for you to wait."

"How long? I got places to go, things to do."

"Fifteen minutes, plenty of time for Dandy to get real sick from stealin' those chicken bones from the trash if you don't get him outta here!"

I dragged Dandy upstairs to the Shepherd's Fold and sat down in one of those comfortable chairs. By the time Fuzz Top finally came swirlin' through the double swingin' doors like a tornado, a half-dozen people had gathered there, just chattin' about what a nice dedication they'd had. There was Harry and Estelle, me, Precious McGill, and Jodi and Denny Baxter, a couple that did a lot of volunteerin' at the shelter. I called out from where I was sittin', "So what took ya so long?"

"Could ask you the same thing." She came over with a huff and bent down to give Dandy's rump a scratch. "You missed the dedication of the mural, and if I remember right, it was your idea … okay, okay, Dandy, I love you too." She pushed Dandy away. He never did get enough lovin'.

"Sorry 'bout that," I said, "but I was takin' care of business—*your* business, Fuzz Top. I think your ma'll forgive me fer that." I turned to Harry Bentley. "Tell her, Mr. Harry."

Before he got into the story, he told his ten-year-old grandson to take Dandy downstairs and play ball or something. Guess he didn't want to upset the kid telling about the goons I'd seen earlier that day, though he didn't call 'em goons.

"An'," I added, "lights came on up in your penthouse, makin' me think your man is outta the hospital an' back home. But I'm tellin' ya, Fuzz Top, it ain't safe for him ta be there—not if he don't want another muggin' first time he steps outta the building."

She got a real worried look on her face, and spoke in a faraway voice like she was figurin' somethin' out. "Well, that makes the second time I've heard about suspicious characters hanging around Richmond Towers today. And you're right, Lucy, Philip did get discharged today."

"Who else told ya 'bout 'em?"

"Oh, a young man who helped Philip get home from the hospital."

"*Humph*! He shouldn't be lettin' any strangers up in that there apartment with him. Never can tell ..."

"I wouldn't worry about Will. All he cares about is architecture and finding his long-lost great aunt. He met Philip in the hospital. His grandmother's there for a few days."

"Likely story. He's still a stranger, ain't he?"

Fuzz Top shrugged. "Seemed like a nice kid. He picked up Philip's meds and some groceries on the way home, and even saw that Philip got safely up to the penthouse." She turned back to Harry Bentley. "What do you think, Mr. B? Is Philip in danger?"

The ex-cop shrugged. "Depends. The building itself is pretty secure, and the street out front is busy most of the day. But I wouldn't recommend any more jogs in the park or late-night strolls around the neighborhood, at least not until Philip can get Fagan's boys off his back by paying off his loan, or until they slap Fagan in jail for extortion. Though even that's no guarantee his thugs won't stay on Philip's tail till he pays up."

Fagan! So Mr. Harry and Fuzz Top knew more about who might've beat up her man than they had let on. Well, I also knew a thing or two.

Denny Baxter leaned forward, elbows on his knees. "If Philip's gambling debts have piled up like you say, Gabby, he'd be smart to give up the penthouse and rent something cheaper. But if Harry and Lucy are right about this rogue cop—or loan shark, whatever this Fagan is—using violence to put the squeeze on Philip, that might be another reason he should relocate somewhere else."

"Hey!" Precious interrupted. "Ain't any of you just a tiny bit suspicious of a total stranger showin' up to take Philip home from the hospital? Gettin' himself into the parking garage for residents only? Ends up inside Philip's penthouse? Huh? Maybe that Fagan guy is using the kid to get to Philip. Ever think o' that?"

"Harry? Denny?" Fuzz Top responded, "Could she be right?"

Duh! Ain't that what *I* was tryin' to say? But does anyone listen to a street-smart old lady? No, they gotta come to it all by their lonesome!

Harry scratched his beard. "Not Fagan's usual style. Too subtle. But you might want to check out the kid's story. He said he's living with his grandmother? A student at Circle Campus? Ought to be able to check that out."

"As for your man movin' someplace else," added Precious, "just be a matter of time till those goons find him again. Then it's the same story as if he's livin' all by himself. He should be around *people* who're lookin' out for him."

Harry snorted. "Huh. You can't put the Secret Service on him to guard him day and night. No man wants a bunch of babysitters taggin' after him."

"Men!" Estelle muttered, wagging her silver-streaked mane. "What's wrong with people lookin' out for each other?"

Oh, good grief! I stood up. "I'm just tellin' y'all, those no-good characters mean some business." But when I scanned the others, I could see they still weren't listening, so I skedaddled outta there. Let them worry about how to protect Fairbanks. He deserved their harebrained ideas, anyway.

AND THEY SHOULDA LISTENED TO ME TOO. Sunday mornin' late, I was taking Dandy over to the park that's on the other side of the penthouse, still just keepin' an eye out—though I don't know what for—when two cop cars went racing down Sheridan Road so fast they nearly blew me off the sidewalk. Looked down the street and saw a couple more comin' north. Figured there musta been a robbery at the Dominick's Finer Foods. So Dandy and I headed down that way for a little entertainment. Most people watch their cop shows on TV, but if you're out and about, you can sometimes get it live action.

But instead of convergin' on the Dominick's, though, they skidded to a stop just north of there at the bus stop only a block from me and Dandy. All four blue-and-whites nosed into the little alley there like spokes on a wheel, and in two shakes of a lamb's tail, they had a couple suspects spread-eagle over the hoods of their cars, cuffin' 'em.

Along with several other bystanders, I edged closer until I recognized Fuzz Top's man bein' quizzed over to the side by a plainclothes detective. Fairbanks was still all bandaged up, arm stickin' out to the side like a broken chicken wing. He looked real shook. Just by lookin', I could tell he'd been the victim … again. Why hadn't they listened to me?

When the uniforms peeled the perps off the hoods of their squad cars, one of them was definitely a goon I'd been watchin' for the last couple of weeks. The other had the chapped, sunburned-look of an overweight redhead, though his buzz-cut flattop had mostly gone gray. If you'd've asked me, he was a cop, too, but the uniforms weren't treatin' him any too gentle.

That's when the detective turned away from Fairbanks and addressed the chap-faced perp. "Matty Fagan, you're under arrest. You have the right to remain silent. Anything you say—"

"I know, I know! You Mirandized me, now get me outta here!"

In a matter of moments the perps were in the back of a couple of squad cars, and one of the uniforms was sayin' to the little crowd of us who'd gathered along the sidewalk, "Show's over folks. Let's move along. Bus'll be comin' soon and it'll need a place to stop."

321

I shook my head as I gave Dandy a little tug on his leash. So that was Matty Fagan, the rogue cop who supposedly held the note on Fairbanks for his gambling debt ... which he couldn't pay.

Sounded to me like business as usual on the streets of Chicago.

Chapter 38

L UCY MANAGED TO RETRIEVE JIGGER and her things from under the bridge and deliver them to the Browns' before she went to work that afternoon. After meeting the dog, who cocked his head in a winsome fashion, Mr. Brown said he could stay in the back room until he insulated the crawl space under the house and made a cubby for Jigger. Hattie, age four, and Abel, three, were bug-eyed with excitement at having a real dog for a houseguest. They watched, solemnly, as Lucy unpacked her few things.

But "moving in" took so long, Lucy was late to work, which earned her a harsh scolding from her boss, who accused her of falling down on the job lately.

Lucy knew it was true, not just because she'd arrived late that day, but because December was the anniversary of the last letter she'd received from Bo, which meant it was nearly a year ago that he'd been killed and less than six months since she'd received the confirmation from the Red Cross. It was all she could do to force herself to go to work each day, yet she realized her routine was the only thing that kept her from going nuts.

All that day, she pushed herself harder to please her boss, if only so she could keep her job, her thin thread to sanity.

It was so late when she got back to the Browns' that night that she snuck in the back door hoping not to disturb anyone, but Mrs. Brown heard Jigger yap his welcome and came to see how she was doing.

As Lucy took off her coat, Mrs. Brown sat down on the end of Lucy's bed as though she was the one who was exhausted. She shivered. "I'm worried 'bout how cold it is out here. You gonna be okay, Lucy?"

"I've slept where it's lots colder." Like under the bridge for the last few nights, she was thinking. "We'll be fine."

"I saved supper for you. Will you be gettin' in this late every night?"

"'Cept for Tuesday. That's my day off."

"Humph! Hardly seems fair for a young girl like you to have to work so hard."

Lucy explained how she reported to the hotel early, then went to her second job at the diner once she got off from the hotel. "Sundays my boss lets me come in late and work late. I don't go to the diner on Sunday nights. But you don't need to hold supper for me. I usually grab a bite at the diner before I come home."

Mrs. Brown shook her head slowly. "You really need that second job?"

"Pretty much, if I want an apartment."

"*Hmm* ..." Mrs. Brown sat there considering it for a moment. "Well, let's talk about that in a few days."

On Tuesday, Lucy washed up the dishes without being asked and watched "the babies," as Mrs. Brown called them, so she could do some shopping. It was the least Lucy could do to repay the Browns for their kindness.

A week later, when Lucy announced she was going to spend part of her day off looking for an apartment but would be back to help around the house, Mrs. Brown sat her down again and said, "Jessie and I been talkin'. You're so helpful around here, even with what little time you have, we'd like to offer you a chance to stay with us as long as you want. Hattie and Abel both seem to love you, and ... don't know if you've noticed, but I'm expectin' and'll need some help, 'cause my mama can't come this time. If you could ... maybe ... quit your evening job and help out with the chil'ren and such, we'd consider it a fair exchange for your board and room. Would that be agreeable?"

Lucy stared dumbfounded. "You mean I wouldn't have to pay rent?"

Mrs. Brown nodded.

It was almost too good to be true! But if later she moved into an apartment of her own, Lucy realized she'd still need two jobs to pay for it, so it was risky to quit one now. On the other hand, she could pay back The Purse in the meantime and save most of her earnings from the hotel until she had enough to rent a place with a cushion to keep her going while she looked for a second job.

"Oh, yes! Thank you so much, Mrs. Brown!"

CHRISTMAS CAME AND WENT. Lucy loved the family times the Browns included her in—they even gave her a pair of gloves to keep her hands warm as she rode the trolley on those freezing mornings and a little metal tag to clip to Jigger's collar with his name one side and their address on the other. "So he don't get lost," giggled Hattie.

"Yeah," said Abel, who was on the floor near the Christmas tree. He grabbed Jigger around the neck and squeezed. "It's like we adopted him."

"Abel, he's still Lucy's dog." Mrs. Brown shook her head. "Sorry 'bout that. Had to give an address to order the tag."

The Browns were so gracious, but every moment of laughter, every song around the tree, every dish at the table, every hug Lucy observed between Jessie and Emma Brown also drove her deeper into her own well of sorrow. She was drowning. Bo was gone … and with him all her dreams for love and marriage and family. She couldn't even spend the holidays with her own family. In fact, she didn't even know where they were or what they were doing. Ma had always managed to wrap up some little thing to give each child. And each year Pa found a way to get a ham or a turkey for the table.

What had happened to her life? It all seemed so unfair.

Lucy dutifully attended church with the Browns on Sunday—it was the most she'd ever been to church—but whenever she felt that urge in her heart to "draw nigh" to God, it got pinched off. After all, seemed like God owed her big time for letting her life crash and burn!

Draw nigh to God and He will draw nigh to you? Ha! Seemed backward. God oughta fix the mess He'd allowed first. Then she'd draw near to Him. But now it was too late. Bo was gone … her family was gone … the boss man was dead … Wasn't no way to change the past and the heartaches lived on into the present. Didn't seem like God could ever do anything about that.

Mr. Brown never got around to putting bales of hay around the house, but it wasn't long before Jigger had wormed his way into the hearts of the Brown children, and the Browns allowed him into the house at least some of the time and didn't seem to mind letting him sleep in the backroom with Lucy on a regular basis.

The routine of steady work, the milestone of repaying The Purse, and having a place to live—even if it was a little cold at night—were the only things that maintained life, thin as it had become to Lucy. Days turned into weeks, then months, and Mrs.

Brown's baby was born, a little chubby-cheeked dumpling named Martha. As the eldest of seven children herself, Lucy drew on her experience to provide constant help to the Brown household.

Everywhere—at the hotel, at the diner, even around the Brown's table—there was talk of the war. After D-Day, there'd been high hopes that the Germans would be defeated by the end of the year. But it hadn't happened. There were victories, but the war dragged on in Europe, and it was not going well in the Pacific. There was talk that it was all a matter of attrition. Hitler was being driven back, but could the Allies maintain the pressure? The Japanese were being driven from island after island, but the territory they held was so vast, especially in mainland Asia, that it seemed the war could go on for years. Who could fight that long?

Then, after continuing defeats and the obvious evidence that he was losing, Hitler committed suicide on April 30, 1945, and when Lucy went to the movies, she watched the newsreel of Winston Churchill declaring May 8 to be "Victory in Europe Day" in which "we may allow ourselves a brief period of rejoicing." But Lucy didn't feel like rejoicing.

The Japanese continued to fight on until the United States— unwilling to sacrifice a seemingly endless bloody river of soldiers—dropped its new experimental weapons, two atomic bombs, on Japanese cities. Six days later, on August 14, 1945, Japan surrendered.

Lucy followed these events as though they were cars passing on a street, some going the same direction she was going, some going the opposite direction, but none of them having any real impact on her ... except when she heard news of the Japanese prisoner of war camps. After Japan surrendered and those camps were liberated, she sometimes fantasized that perhaps Bo had not been killed in action. Maybe he'd been captured and had been held for the last eighteen months by the Japanese. But her fantasy always turned into a nightmare when she heard reports of how gruesome those camps were and how few men survived.

Still, the possibility haunted her, and she visited the Red Cross again and convinced an aid to help her fill out papers to search for him. But again, the word came back—this time with an exact date—that Private B. J. Moon, I.D. number 16328466, had been killed in action while attempting to secure a beachhead in the Solomon Islands on December 15, 1943.

Lucy set aside her fantasies and cried herself to sleep every night for the next week. Slowly, her tears dried up and she simply felt hollow inside. All over the city there were parades and celebrations for the returning soldiers. Wherever they walked the streets in uniform, people shook their hands and girls would hang all over them. It was tempting to join in and try to celebrate. The war was over! The allies had won! Everyone's grueling sacrifices had paid off! And Lucy ought to be proud of the sacrifice her Bo had made.

But it was just a giddy high that never lasted more than a few moments. Bo was still gone, and her world was in shambles. The joy of people around her turned her stomach. She knew why they were happy and was glad for them, but she just couldn't be a part of that world.

More and more, she lived in the past, in that little window of time between when she'd met Bo and when he went off to war. But it was such a brief few months into which to compress her whole life. A thousand times she reviewed their train ride, the days at Niagara Falls, the trip across the corn fields to Chicago, and ... and finally to that last night before Bo enlisted. She could almost feel the closeness of his warm body. But then ... he wasn't there.

Reviewing her memories may have been the reason that, when the air got nippy again like it had been in early

October when she and Bo first came to Chicago, Lucy took Jigger on a Tuesday and went up to her old neighborhood. Miss Mason's house had been repainted a chalky white with forest-green trim. It looked nice, with new bushes in the yard and no tin boxes on the porch for the iceman. Maybe the remodeled house used a refrigerator now. No one seemed to be home, so Lucy stood across the street, leaning against a tree, staring. If only she and Bo were still living in that third-floor apartment.

"Hey, lady," called a boy, cruising toward her on a bicycle, "that tree can stand up by itself, case you didn't know." Then he passed, giggling at his own joke.

Lucy pushed herself away from the tree and strolled toward the corner, looking back a couple of times just to set the house more firmly in her mind. She walked west, across Western Avenue and into Riverview Amusement Park, closed again for the season. She wanted to find that workman who'd known Bo, just to speak with him one more time and hear someone else say his name and what a good worker he'd been. She needed contact with someone who'd known him.

What was the man's name, anyway? Dick ... Zack, something short. No, it was Nate!

"You know a Nate, an older guy who works on roller coasters?" she asked the first person she met. He was a sullen man, raking leaves, and all he did was point deeper into the park. After three more inquiries, Lucy found Nate working in a garage, replacing wheels on rollercoaster cars. His hands were covered in black grease, but Lucy recognized his white hair.

"Nate, I don't know if you remember me," she said to the back of the workman kneeling on the concrete floor, "but I talked to you nearly a year ago."

He glanced back at her. "Oh yeah. I remember you and that dog of yours. You're Bo's girl, right?"

"Yes sir." Lucy watched as he stood up, wiping his hands on a rag and twisting the kinks out of his aching back.

"How's he doin'?"

The man's question jarred her. "I ... I thought I told you. He didn't make it. He was killed in action on an island in the Pacific."

A deep frown creased the man's brow, and he wiped his nose on his sleeve. "Yeah ... yeah, I know you said that, but ... didn't he end up in a VA hospital in Indianapolis?"

"No ... no, he's—what?"

"Well, I didn't see him myself, but my kid brother, Jerry, did. He's still in that hospital, and this guy was in the bed next to him, so they got ta talkin' like guys do, ya know, 'What'd ya do before the war?' stuff like that. And he tells him he used to work here at Riverview. 'Course, Jerry tells him about me, that I work here too. And the guy said he remembered me, that we worked together." Nate shrugged, palms up with a *who-knows?* gesture. "Anyway, that's why I thought he was your man."

"Aw, coulda been anyone."

"Yeah, I s'pose, but my brother said his name was Bo, and I don't know no other Bo. Figured he had ta be your Bo."

"No, can't ..." Lucy's mind was swirling. "Why would you say such a thing? Bo's dead!" She clamped her hands over her ears and clinched her eyes closed.

"Now hold on there. I didn't mean to upset you. Maybe ..." The man touched Lucy's shoulder, but she jerked away. "I'm sorry. Look, I'll admit Jerry got blown up pretty bad by one of those Nazi potato mashers, but I don't know how he coulda come up with a story like that if he hadn't met Bo. It was like—"

Lucy pulled her hands away from her ears, and her eyes got big. "They musta been in the same unit in the Pacific. He met Bo there, right?"

"Don't think so. My brother was only in Europe. He met this guy when he came back, while they were in the hospital together in Indianapolis. Jerry's still there. I just saw him three weeks ago, and in no time, he was telling me about his hospital buddy who'd worked with me here at Riverview—"

For one instant hope rose. "So, he's still there?"

"No, he got discharged a while back. Jerry's supposed to get out this weekend too. 'Course his wife is there in Indy, so he'll be goin' home to her, but we was plannin' to surprise her …"

Nate kept on talking, but a roar was growing in Lucy's ears, and she didn't hear a word he said.

Could it be that Bo was still alive? How? Twice the Red Cross had confirmed he'd been killed in action. And if for some reason the man in Indianapolis was *her* Bo, why had he ended up down there? Why hadn't he come home to her? Why hadn't she heard a thing?

None of it made any sense, but her heart was pounding so hard she thought she was going to pass out.

Chapter 39

IDIDN'T HEAR THE DETAILS OF HOW THE COPS busted that Matty Fagan guy until I showed up at a party Fuzz Top was throwin' to celebrate her new digs. With the money she'd inherited from Miz Martha, she bought an apartment building so she and her boys could live in one unit while she rented out the other units to women with kids who needed somethin' more home-like than a shelter. Might like somethin' like that myself, someday.

Guess some of the board members at Manna House helped her work things out with the city and HUD, or whatever that rent subsidy program was. Anyway, sounded like a good thing to me so I went to her party. Figured they'd have some good eats there, too.

I was a little late and got there just as a clean-cut young man came bustin' out of the door and down the steps.

"Hey!" I gave Dandy a tug—he was visiting every tree and bush—and hustled up the walk. "Hold that door!"

Surprisin'ly, the guy bounced right back up the steps and held it open.

"Thank ya." I gave him a nod. "Don't think I've had the privilege."

"Privilege? Oh, I'm Will Nissan, friend of Mr. Fairbanks."

"Philip Fairbanks? You the one who brought him home from the hospital?"

"Yeah … seems everybody's heard about that."

"Probably not everybody, but …" I stuck out my hand. "I'm Lucy." You can tell a lot about how a person shakes hands, and as he continued on his way, I had a better feelin' 'bout him. Don't think he had anything to do with muggin' Fairbanks.

Inside, Fuzz Top came right up to me. "Hey there, Lucy. I see you got wind of my invitation!"

"Yep." I reached down and unhooked Dandy to let him go find the boys. "Came by to make sure you were doin' this place right. Might want to live here myself someday."

"Ha! Well, you'd have to have some kids first. The House of Hope's for families."

"Humph, and I don't got no family, right?"

"Didn't mean it that way, Lucy. You're like family to all of us, but—"

I waved my hand to dismiss her and wandered down the hall to the food table where I filled a plate with hot wings and mac-an'-cheese and was just reachin' for a brownie when Estelle caught me and chased me away sayin' they were for later. I kinda milled around seein' who was there until I came across Fairbanks, sittin' on the window seat, telling a couple of guests the story about his latest escape from Matty Fagan.

"That's right." He raised his good arm and made a gun with his fingers. "Fagan was threatening to shoot my knees right out from under me when—according to Gabrielle—Bentley heard what was going on through my cell phone and called 9-1-1. Told the cops right where I was. Don't know how he did it. It was like he had a sixth sense, a second sight, or something —"

Just then, Fuzz Top came up. "Excuse me, Philip. Will wanted me to tell you he had to leave early."

Fairbanks shrugged. "He's probably off on another rabbit trail looking for his Great-Aunt Cindy."

"No, no. Something about picking up things for his grandmother so she can go home from the hospital, but Denny Baxter said he can give you a lift."

"Thanks," Fairbanks said, and went back to tellin' the other people how all these cop cars came racing up from different directions, no sirens or lights.

I knew the rest of the story, so I wandered away. In my opinion, the man was still too full of himself.

"GUESS WE'RE ALL HERE," said a fine-lookin' black man, who I recognized as Peter Douglass, chairman of the board for the shelter. "It's time for the house blessing, but first I'm going to ask Gabby Fairbanks to tell us how this new House of Hope came to be."

But Fuzz Top got all weepy and handed the story off to Mabel Turner, her boss at Manna House. After the history thing, there had to be some Bible readin' by Avis Douglass. If you ask me, she'd make a good preacher, but nobody asks my opinion. Finally, she ended by saying, "Each mother and child who will live in the House of Hope may be a stranger before they walk in the door, but some may be God's angels disguised as the homeless to bless this house."

Reminded me of Ma, who always welcomed strangers to our table, even in the migrant camps. She said we could never know when we might be welcomin' an angel.

Peter Douglass cleared his throat. "Well said. Why don't we pray a blessing over this apartment, and then do the same in the other apartments—"

Without thinkin', I blurted out, "I gotta prayer." Musta been me thinkin' 'bout Ma that brought it to mind, but it just seemed right ... right, that is, until I realized everyone was starin' at me like I'd just turned purple.

Ah well, I'd show 'em. I clasped my hands, bowed my head, an' spoke right up.

> *God bless the corners of this house*
> *An' all the lintel blessed,*
> *An' bless the hearth an' bless the board*
> *An' bless each place of rest.*
>
> *An' bless each door that opens wide*
> *To strangers as to kin,*
> *An' bless each crystal windowpane*
> *That lets the starlight in.*
>
> *An' bless the rooftree overhead*
> *An' every sturdy wall.*
> *The peace of man, the peace of God,*
> *With peace an' love for all.*

I opened my eyes and declared, "Amen. The end!"

Everyone was kinda starin' at me. "Where'd you get that prayer, Lucy?" Estelle asked.

I shrugged. "Dunno. Learned it as a kid. My mama used to pray it ever' time we moved to new digs—which was ever' couple months, seems like. Followin' the crops, ya know. Seemed like it fit this here new House of Hope."

"*Sí, mi amiga,*" Edesa chimed in. "And I want you to pray it again when we get up to our apartment, okay? Shall we go?"

"Our apartment first!" Tanya said. "Sammy, go open the door."

There I was, like some homeless priestess who got brought in to bless other people's apartments when I had no place to call my own. But then ... oh well, what can a body expect who's been on the streets long as I have?

FALL SET IN FOR REAL OVER THE NEXT COUPLE WEEKS, not the crisp fresh-air kind with flamin' tree colors, but the soggy, drizzly kind that chills ya to the bone. The old cough started comin' back on me, and I began to worry 'bout how Dandy would fare over the winter. Maybe I oughta let him live with Fuzz Top and her boys and pick him up again in the spring. Manna House didn't mind him comin' and goin'—he'd earned the right, bein' their Hero Dog, and all—but some of the other places I dropped in on wouldn't allow no pets. I never really thought of Dandy as a *pet*, but I guess that's the way other people saw him.

One day when I stopped by Manna House to pick up some more dog food for Dandy, thinkin' the least I could do was fatten him up before winter, I found out Fuzz Top was takin' the residents for a trip up to Devil's Lake State Park in Wisconsin. Sounded like fun to me, so I told her I wanted to sign up. She looked at me like, Why would you want to do that?

"Well, you know, kinda liked that trip you an' me took out west to bury your ma, but it was real long, ya know? A weekend sounds more ta my likin'. Be good to get off these streets a few days. Where ya goin' again?" 'Course I already knew.

"Really?" she said, her eyes gettin' bigger. "Well, that's great. We're going up to Devil's Lake State Park in Wisconsin to see the fall colors. But this place we're renting doesn't allow pets. What about Dandy?"

"Been thinkin' 'bout that. Thought maybe that boy of yours might want a four-legged visitor over the weekend. Whatcha think?"

She stared straight ahead like I'd sent her off to dreamland. Finally, I had to snap my fingers in front of her face. "You still in there, Fuzz Top? When ya done thinkin', let me know. I'm gonna get somethin' ta eat 'fore mold grows on it. C'mon, Dandy."

I wasn't sure she was gonna let me come, but I figured I had an ace in the hole that might turn the day. Earlier, I'd found out it was Fuzz Top's birthday, and I told Estelle to make her a banana cake. She made the cake, all right, but insisted on chocolate.

When Estelle brought it out after lunch and set it down in the middle of all of us, I pointed to the writing on the top. "Says, 'Happy Birthday, Gabby! Our Favorite Fuzz Top!' I tol' 'em to put that on there. *Hee, hee!* And I told Estelle it *had* to be banana."

Once a piece had been cut for everyone, Fuzz Top savored her first bite with her eyes closed. "Oh-h-h, I love chocolate!" Then she kinda woke up and turned to me. "Don't think I ever had banana cake. Why'd you say it had to be banana?"

"'Cause banana's *my* favorite, so I figgered you might like it too. My ma used ta make it ..." My mind drifted back to Ma bakin' it for everyone's birthday. "But that was a long time ago. So whaddya think, you gonna let me come on that there trip?" I figured since I was the one who remembered her birthday and had Estelle make her a cake, she owed me.

"What?"

"You know, up there to Wisconsin. You gonna let me come?"

It worked. Somehow they found one more seat in that big white van of theirs, but Fuzz Top refused to let me bring my cart. When are they gonna learn that street folks gotta have some things around them that's personal? It's like losin' control of your whole life when you get separated. But I wanted to go bad enough, I agreed to leave it in Fuzz Top's office if she'd promise to lock it up. It still had The Purse in it, ya know.

Chapter 40

LUCY BACKED AWAY FROM NATE IN SHOCK, then turned and ran out of the roller-coaster repair shop. Jigger loped along at her heels all the way to the Riverview gate where Lucy slowed and finally stopped as she came up to the sawhorse barricades indicating the park was closed.

Could Nate have been telling the truth? Or had he been tormenting her with a cruel joke? No, no … It seemed unlikely he'd do such a thing, but it seemed even more impossible for Bo to be alive. And yet … there was something, a clue in the conversation. What was it? Lucy rubbed her temples with her fingertips and closed her eyes as she recalled exactly what had been said. It had to do with when Nate said the two soldiers met. Yes, yes, that was it. She'd said, *"They musta been in the same unit in the Pacific."* But Nate had said no, his brother was only in Europe. If he had been spinning a lie, he'd probably have agreed. It was the most logical connection.

On the one hand, saying his brother had only been in Europe supported his story that the two met in the hospital, but would he have been that quick to insist on that detail when he could have agreed that they had both been in the Pacific?

It wasn't proof, but …

Slowly, Lucy turned and walked back into the park, past the carousel, winterized with gray tarps, past the arcade and the boarded up concession booths, down the central street to the repair garage. She opened the squeaky door tentatively and slipped in. Nate was down on his knees again, working on the car.

"Uh … hey, I'm sorry I ran out on you, but were you pullin' my leg a few minutes ago?"

"Nope."

"But you said that guy's not in the hospital anymore?"

"That's what I said."

"You have any idea where he went?"

Nate finally turned and looked back at her. "Why would I? All my brother said was that Bo got discharged. That's all I know." With that, Nate went back to greasing the wheels.

Lucy's mind was spinning. If Bo had been discharged, where would he have gone? Why hadn't he come to Chicago to be with her? How could she find him?

"You think he might still be in Indianapolis?"

"Haven't the foggiest."

"Any idea who might know?"

Nate shrugged. "Look, if he was hurt bad enough to be in the hospital for several months, like my brother said, then my guess is he'd need some ongoing care—you know, have to see the doctor for follow-up."

"You mean he'd go back to the hospital?"

"Maybe that one or another one. But the VA probably knows."

Lucy felt like she was on a Tilt-a-Whirl, spinning till she was dizzy. "But the Red Cross said he's *dead*. I checked twice."

"Well, maybe he is an' we're talkin' 'bout different people, or maybe the government got its wires crossed. All I know is, the guy my brother talked to sounded like the kid I worked with and everything."

"Gotta find him … gotta …" Lucy's voice drifted off.

Nate shrugged. "Might be worth a try. Like I said, I'm goin' down this weekend 'cause my brother's supposed to get discharged. You can ride along if you want."

A ride? Yes! Yes! She had to try. Had to find out of Bo was alive after all.

Quickly making arrangements for where Nate could pick her up, Lucy headed back to the Browns, trying all the way to control her mind. Like crumbs of a cake too sweet to eat, she allowed herself only the tiniest morsels of the dream that was growing in her mind.

But by the time she got off the trolley, oblivious of the biting Chicago wind, she had imagined a whole new life for them. She would bring Bo back here and find an apartment where she could nurse him back to health. And when he was well enough, they'd get married and maybe have children. She'd have to keep working, of course, but weren't there veterans' pensions for men who'd been injured?

Tomorrow she'd tell her boss she needed the weekend off for a family emergency. He wouldn't understand, but she would insist … politely as possible, of course, because she didn't want to lose her job. But going to Indianapolis and finding Bo was even more important. Even though Nate was willing to give her a ride, the trip would cost something, but she had a little money saved up. Nothing could stop her.

Once she got to Indianapolis, surely someone would know where he was, perhaps in a VA nursing home or something. She tried to imagine the shock and joy on his face when they met … but she couldn't flush the nagging question at the back of her mind: Why hadn't *he* made this reunion happen earlier? Why hadn't he contacted her in Chicago? Why hadn't she heard a thing from him?

A chill washed over her. What if he'd found another girl? What if he didn't *want* to be with her? Lucy's mind groped for a solution. She'd take Jigger. Surely, Bo would want to see Jigger. And once they were together, she'd win him back. She'd never wanted anything so badly in her life. She'd do whatever it took. Then everything would be right again!

"I'M TRYING TO FIND A PRIVATE B. J. MOON. He was a patient here a few weeks ago." Lucy stood at the front desk of the VA hospital after Nate had wished her good luck and headed down the corridor to collect his brother, Jerry.

"You say he's not here now?" The clerk stopped typing.

"No. He was discharged a few weeks ago."

The woman got up from her desk and went to a row of filing cabinets along the wall behind her and began searching in one of the drawers. After a few moments, she turned. "What did you say that name was?"

"Private B. J. Moon." A queasy feeling churned in Lucy's stomach as she saw the woman slowly shake her head, close the filing cabinet drawer, and return to her desk.

"I'm sorry, ma'am, but we haven't had anyone here by that name. Our older records are in the archives, but these files go all the way back to December 1941, right after the attack on Pearl Harbor, and we haven't had anyone named Moon in here as a patient. Now I know a Hester Moon, a colored girl who works in Food Services, but no patient by that name."

Lucy licked her dry lips. "You're sure?"

341

The woman shook her head. "I'm sorry." She sat down at her desk and went back to typing the form in her typewriter.

Lucy stumbled away and collapsed in a heap on the oak bench along the wall in the lobby. Why did her dreams always seem to crash? Was God punishing her for ... for what? For taking The Purse? She'd repaid all the money and planned to give it back as soon as she could. But she never should have taken it. She knew that now, but ... *Please God!*

A half hour must have passed—maybe more—before she looked up in a daze to see Nate coming down the hall pushing a young soldier in a wheelchair, with an olive-drab army blanket draped over his shoulders and a white bandage wrapped around his head and over one eye.

"You find him?" Nate asked as they rolled closer.

Lucy slowly shook her head.

"Humph! Too bad. Jerry, this is the girl I told you about. Tryin' to find your old ward-mate. Lucy, this is Jerry. So what'd they say?"

"Ain't got no record of a B. J. Moon."

The wounded soldier turned his head stiffly toward Lucy. "Who's Moon?"

"He was my ... my man. We was gonna get married soon as he got home, but the Red Cross said he was killed in action. Guess they were right."

Jerry turned to look up at Nate. "Thought you said this was Bo's girl."

"Well, I did. Aren't you trying to find Bo Hansen? That's who I thought you were lookin' for."

"I am! But when he joined the army, he used the name of Moon ... long story."

"Moon?" The soldier frowned. "Come to think of it, Bo talked a lot about a guy named Moon. Got blown up right next to him when he got injured. They were best buddies, accordin' to him. So you're Moon's girl?"

"I … I, no …" What was Jerry sayin'? "No, I'm Bo Hansen's girl, but …" The room began to swirl, and Lucy felt like she was going to faint, even though she was still sitting on the bench.

"Sounds to me like there's a big snafu here needs untanglin'." Nate stepped across the waiting room and retrieved a straight-back chair, which he positioned backward in front of Lucy so all three could sit and confer. "Now let me get this straight," he said as he swung his leg over the chair and sat down, resting his arms on the back. "Your boyfriend's Bo Hansen, who used to work with me at Riverview before he joined the army, right?" Then he turned to his brother. "And the guy who was in the bed next to you was Bo Hansen, who used to work with me at Riverview." Then he looked back at Lucy. "But you're tellin' us you've been looking for B. J. Moon, who Jerry, here, says was killed. And the Red Cross, also told you was KIA?"

"But that was the name on all Bo's letters, 'Private B. J. Moon.' That's who I wrote to. Bo was usin' that name so no one would be able to connect him to me … and somethin' that happened a long time ago."

Nate started nodding his head. "Maybe he didn't join up as B. J. Moon, then. Maybe he just had you send your letters to his buddy who passed them on. Maybe Moon's dead, but Bo—"

Lucy jumped up before Nate could finish and ran across the lobby, throwing herself against the counter above the clerk's desk. "Could you … could you check another name, please? Could you see if you've had a Borick Hansen in here recently? Please!"

"Hold on. Let me just finish typin' in this code." The clerk's fingers clicked the keys for a few more moments. "Okay. What was that name again?"

"Hansen, Borick Hansen. Was he a patient here just a few weeks ago?"

The clerk got up from her desk and went to the filing cabinets again. After a moment, she pulled out a card and turned to Lucy. "Yes. Mr. Hansen was here for … several months last year. Then he was discharged about Christmas …" She continued reading. "But he came back with complications in April and just went home again a month ago." She looked up at Lucy with a big smile on her face. "I remember him now. Nice boy. I think his wife picked him up."

Wife? No, no! That couldn't be. The woman was mistaken. Lucy couldn't quit now. She was so close … "Uh, do you have an address or something?"

The nurse flipped the card over. "Yeah. Here it is, 1928 Howard Street. Uh … I think that's just across the river and a couple of miles south of here."

"Want me to drop ya?" Nate had come up to stand by Lucy at the counter.

Lucy's heart was pounding. She didn't want Nate there for whatever might happen when she arrived at the address. "That's okay. I'll take a cab."

"Cab might not want to take your dog."

"Then … then I'll walk. Sounds like it's not that far, and …" As excited as Lucy was, a fear churned in her stomach. She had waited and prayed for so long, but somehow she didn't feel ready. But she followed Nate out to the parking lot to get Jigger and waited while Nate loaded Jerry and his wheelchair into the car.

"So, how about the trip back to Chicago?" Nate asked as Lucy stood by with Jigger on a leash.

Back? She didn't want to go back without Bo. But she shrugged. "When are you gonna go back?"

"Tomorrow. Gotta be at work Monday. Here, let me write down Jerry's phone number and *you* phone me in the morning. Okay?"

Lucy nodded and waved as they drove away.

Lucy walked past 1928 Howard Street once without even slowing or turning in at the gate of the unpainted picket fence. The house was a small white frame bungalow with a low porch across the front and a window above with a curtain, suggesting the attic had been turned into a second-floor bedroom. Shades were pulled on the two front windows off the porch, but the window in the door looked unobstructed if she had the courage to go up and peek in … not that there was any doubt about Bo being there. Jigger made that perfectly clear, sniffing the air and whining while he pranced and pulled at the end of his leash.

"No, Jigger. Come on, boy. You be quiet! *Shh.* Come on, now!"

She walked on, past a couple of other modest houses in this working-class neighborhood, some yards well cared for, others neglected with broken-down cars parked at the curb. She stopped at the corner by a bus-stop bench just as a city bus slowed to pick her up, but she waved it on. Once the cloud of foul exhaust had cleared, Lucy sat down and looked back at Bo's place, studying it intently as she breathed hard, unsure of what to do next. What if he didn't want to see her? What if …? The questions tumbled through her mind like water over Niagara.

Fifteen minutes or more passed, and then the front door of the bungalow opened and a very pregnant woman wheeled a man out onto the porch in a wheelchair. It was Bo! Thinner, his face haggard and drawn with pain. But still … Bo! But who was that woman? The clerk had thought Bo's wife had picked him up, and she'd said

Bo had been readmitted to the hospital last April. Lucy counted the months absently with her fingers. If he'd been here before that—during the period when he'd been out of the hospital—it would certainly have given this woman time enough to get pregnant and be as far along as she appeared. Despair gripped Lucy as she watched the woman turn the wheelchair and push it to the end of the porch, where she helped guide it down a makeshift ramp Lucy hadn't noticed.

Once in the yard, the woman bent down and gave Bo a warm hug, then turned and waddled back into the house.

At any moment, Lucy expected Bo to look up and see her sitting on the bus bench no more than sixty yards away. But he was intent on maneuvering his chair across the rough grass and onto the front walk. He locked the wheels, got shakily to his feet, and then unlocking the wheels, worked his way around behind the chair and began pushing it ahead of himself. Lucy held her breath, ready to run to his rescue at any moment if he needed help. But once through the gate, Bo turned the other direction and, with the support of the wheelchair, was obviously managing quite well as he shuffled down the sidewalk.

Jigger was going nuts, pulling on his leash and whining and jumping from side to side as another bus pulled up. Lucy stood, and in that moment, Jigger made a great lunge, pulling the leash out of Lucy's hand and raced down the street in pursuit of Bo.

"You gettin' on, lady?" the driver called as he held the door open.

Lucy looked back down the street and saw that Jigger was safely across and closing fast on the retreating Bo.

With tears streaming down her face, she turned back to the driver, nodded, and climbed aboard.

Chapter 41

THE PINE TREE RETREAT HOUSE up in Wisconsin was only a few hours away from Chicago, but ridin' in that big ol' van with fourteen yakety-yak women made the trip a whole lot longer than going all the way to North Dakota with a very quiet Martha Shepherd tucked away in her coffin while her daughter and Jody Baxter took turns drivin'.

One of the worst chatterboxes was a new girl, Monique. Kept spoutin' drivel. "Girl, I'm too blessed to be stressed ... Didn't say being homeless was a blessin'. This just a test. No test, no *test*imony!... God ain't through with me yet. I *know* I'm blessed and highly favored, oh glory!..."

Huh! Reckon she'll learn in the school of hard knocks if one of us don't pop her first.

But we finally made it.

The retreat house was real nice, a rustic two-story log place, nearly hidden under some tall trees at the end of a winding road. It had a big ol' smokey fireplace with some overstuffed chairs and a couch around it. But it was dark outside before Fuzz Top got the damp firewood burnin'. Coulda showed her how, but she probably needed to learn for herself, so I kicked back and put my tired old dogs up on a stool to take a little snooze 'fore we ate.

We hadn't been there that long when some of those city girls started gettin' the heebie-jeebies 'bout bein' out there "in the woods," as they called it. "No way!" Hannah croaked when Fuzz Top suggested they go out for a look at the night sky. "There's bugs and wild animals and stuff out there."

Guess they probably never seen a raccoon or a possum, but they surely stared down a rat or two. So what's the diff'rence?

Not quite sure how it worked out—perhaps 'cause no one wanted to listen to me snore—but I got a room of my own, which suited me just fine, and I was lucky, too, 'cause next mornin' I heard those city girls'd been up half the night scared of branches scratchin' the windows when the wind blew and the 'coons tippin' over the garbage can outside. I slept through it all, but Lord have mercy!

Next mornin', Edesa wanted us to all sit around after we'd had bagels and juice and do a church thing, readin' from the Bible. Have to admit, it was kinda interesting, about this homeless pregnant woman named Hagar who'd been kicked out of her place and was just about ready to pack it in when God sent an angel to ask her, "What's up, girl?"

Accordin' to Edesa, even though God already knew all about her—name an' all—He wanted to give her a chance to tell her story. So we started goin' 'round the circle of women right there in the retreat house, everyone tellin' their story. And believe you me, there were some tales to be told! But I took a pass when it came to me. They wouldn't understand.

After that, we got in the van and spent the rest of the day sightseeing around Devil's Lake State Park and in the town of Baraboo ... where they now have that Circus World Museum. But long before there was a museum, Baraboo used to be the winter quarters for the Ringling Brothers Circus. 'Course, the museum was closed for the winter months when we turned into the parking lot. Nevertheless, just seein' the signs and the red-and-white striped tents stirred up a lota ol' feelin's in me. I tried to not think on 'em much. Wasn't nothin' could be done 'bout 'em now anyway.

When we got out of the van to stretch our legs in the little picnic area beside the museum's parking lot, some of the younger ones started doin' tricks. "Who needs a circus?" Tawny James called. "I can stand on my hands." Then Shawanda did a flip. Everyone was laughin' and clappin' while I was feelin' more and more antsy.

I got no idea why, but suddenly I climbed up on a picnic bench. "Well, watch *me*. I know how to walk a tightrope." Everyone cheered as I held my hands out to my sides and teetered from one end of the bench to the other. Then I stepped—

"No, Lucy!" screamed Fuzz Top at the top of her voice.

But it was too late! When my left foot hit the ground, it twisted in a little hole, and I went down into a world of hurt! Pain shot up my leg like fire. And wouldn't ya know it, Monique just had to say, "'Pride goeth before a fall.'"

Probably was a good thing I couldn't get up right then, or I'd've smacked her upside the head. But as it was, I couldn't move until a couple of the more Jesus-types helped me hop back to the van on my good leg. Fuzz Top wanted to take me to a hospital right then, but no way was I gonna let 'em leave me there. "Jus' a few scratches, that's all. Don't be such a fussbudget."

By the time we got back to the retreat house, my ankle had swelled up like a melon and was hurtin' like a dozen scorpion stings. Everyone had somethin' to say 'bout what I oughta do: get an X-ray, wrap it up, ice it down, keep it elevated, take some aspirin.

"Just shut up! Would y'all? Don'tcha think I know somethin' 'bout sprains? That's all it is. Now, jus' get one o' them elastic things and wrap it 'round."

"You need to just praise your way through it, sister Lucy!" Monique just had to add. Boy, does that girl have a loose mouth, or what?

At least they brought my dinner on a tray while the rest of them sat at the table. Afterward we played some bingo—somethin' I could do from the couch—and I showed 'em I was still good enough to beat 'em all.

Later, Fuzz Top musta thought I'd fallen asleep. She put a couple of blankets over me before she turned out the lights and left me there on the couch in the dim glow of the last embers in the fireplace. But I was just restin' my eyes and didn't sleep for a long while yet. Why'd I been so stupid to jump off the end of that bench? At my age, I didn't need to be showin' off like no kid! And besides, I didn't even care what these city girls thought of me, whether I could walk a tightrope or not ... or even a bench. But somehow, just seein' all that circus stuff, thinkin' 'bout what had happened a lifetime ago ... it was like bein' back there all over again, all giddy and full of the future. Suddenly, I was actin' like the joy-filled girl I'd been. But that was long gone, and I'd just received a painful lesson 'bout leavin' the past in the past.

Tears burned my eyes, and I squeezed them out and wiped 'em away with the back of my hand.

NEXT MORNIN' AFTER BREAKFAST, Fuzz Top wanted to see my ankle. It'd turned black-an'-blue enough that she excused me from havin' to do cleanup. So I hung out on the couch until they gathered for another of those churchy things.

"Hey, can you hold off on that singin' a bit and help me get into the bathroom? I gotta pee!"

They did, and I did ... and hung out in the bathroom until the singin' ended. Then I called for someone to come help me hobble back into the main room. Thought they were all done, but they were just gettin' started. Edesa opened her Bible and picked up from where she'd left off the day before about God knowin' each of us by name, and then she read several Bible stories about people's names and what they mean.

I didn't really get her point until she began goin' 'round the room readin' from a card she'd made for each woman that told the meanin' of her name. Then she prayed a blessin' over each person about their name. Seemed kinda neat, until she told Monique her name meant "Adviser."

Monique grabbed her card. "Amen! Amen! I receive that!" But I was afraid it'd just egg her on to keep preachin' at people all the way home.

And then suddenly, Edesa was standin' in front of me. "Lucy, your name means 'Light' and you do light up a room whenever you enter!" Everyone chuckled, and I'm sure my tired old face turned red as I looked around at these women who were homeless but seemed so different from me. Then Edesa added, "Let God shine His light into every dark corner of your life, so that you are free to be who He created you to be."

Dark corners? What dark corners? Oh ... maybe she was talkin' ... no, she couldn't know anything 'bout The Purse.

Edesa moved on to the next woman while I watched her out of the corner of my eye.

And another thing, wasn't I free? Didn't I come and go whenever I pleased? No one held me down or could tell me what to do ... and, and if God had created me for something more, well, it was too late now! I was near the end, and I knew it. Come to think of it, He'd probably given up on me because of The Purse thing. Never should've taken it. Guess, it'd been my undoin' from that day on.

WE WERE ON OUR WAY HOME IN THE VAN, crossin' the border into Illinois, when it hit me: With my ankle so bad, how could I take care of Dandy? I knew this day would come at some point, but I hadn't expected it so soon. Fuzz Top often hinted that I wouldn't be able to do right by the poor dog once the snow flew, but I had my ways. Now it looked like I might be more of a problem than the snow itself.

First thing I did when they got me settled on the couch in Manna House was to tell 'em I needed to see Dandy.

"Not tonight, Lucy," Fuzz Top said. "Not till we figure out what we're going to do with you."

What they're gonna do with me! "Dagnabit! When did you get so bossy?"

But she wouldn't budge, and the next mornin' she insisted on taking me down to the clinic at Cook County. "You either let me take you down, or I'm callin' an ambulance." There was a no-negotiation frown on her face.

What could I say? She was probably right, so I decided to let Fuzz Top take me to the doctor to get my ankle checked out. If there was somethin' the doctor could do to speed up the healin'— for Dandy's sake, of course—I oughta do it. In the meantime, her boy, Paul, could help out. I always felt kinda bad takin' Dandy away from him, anyway. But of course, it was for Miz Martha.

Cook County was Cook County ... wait, wait, wait. Then forms to fill out. At least Fuzz Top stuck with me while the woman at the desk grilled me like some cop sweatin' a perp.

"What is your full name, ma'am?"

"It's 'miss,' not 'ma'am.' I ain't married."

"All right. Your full name?"

"Lucinda Tucker."

"Age?"

"Kinda lost track."

"Well, your birthdate then."

I had to think a minute. "November three, nineteen hunnerd an' twenty-something ... um, slips my mind right now. Twenty-six, I think." I frowned, *November three*, that was this comin' Friday ... and I'd be eighty years old, then. My, how the years fly by.

"Ma,am, ma'am, are you tracking with me here? Are you on any medications?"

"No."

"Why do you need to see a doctor today?"

"I don't. But she forced me to come in 'cause of this." I stuck my leg out, and the purple balloon that was supposed to be my foot spoke for itself.

When they finished with the X-rays, I finally saw a doctor. "It's a severe sprain."

Ha! Maybe I shoulda been a doctor. I could have told him that myself.

"We'll wrap it up to give it some support. Ice it three or four times a day. You'll be on crutches for a week, six weeks with an Aircast, and maybe six months before the ankle fully heals."

"It ain't gonna take that long. Anything I can do to speed it up? I got things to do and places to go."

He shook his head. "Too bad you didn't break it. Might've healed faster."

Oh, yeah! Real cute! Real cute! "Come on, Fuzz Top, get me outta here."

Chapter 42

THE RIDE BACK TO CHICAGO WITH NATE passed in a blur. Her family was gone. Bo was gone. And now Jigger was gone.

She might as well be gone too. Lucy forced herself to go to work on Monday simply because that seemed easier than figuring out how to end her life, though she couldn't see any reason to continue it. But even though she expected her boss to yell at her, that seemed preferable to the voices in her head repeating how worthless life had become.

Leon Kowalski did not disappoint her. From the moment he saw her, her boss at the hotel began complaining about her taking time off. "Never should you have gone away! Yesterday, we need you. Rotary Club spill wine all over big luncheon table. But the extra tablecloths," he threw his hands up in the air, "where did you hide them?"

"I don't do the laundry."

"But you not tell me where they are before you run off."

"Probably the linen closet."

"Ha! So you say. But there we not find them. You be working here every day, or I fire you! Understand?"

It went on that way nonstop until the man wore himself out and Lucy finally slipped away to the fourth floor where she began cleaning the guest rooms.

But as she had feared, once she was alone, all Lucy could think about was Bo. Why hadn't he written to her? Why hadn't he come home to her? What had happened to all their dreams? She thought he loved her. But who was this other woman, and when did they meet? Had he known her before he went away to war? Before she and Bo began living together? Before they had even met? Bo had never mentioned another woman.

The questions swirled in her head throughout the afternoon and during her shift at the diner and as she walked slowly from the trolley stop to the Browns'.

Because they'd become almost like family, she'd taken to coming in the front door where she greeted the kids as they scurried off to bed in their cute little pajamas. Mrs. Brown often urged her to sit down and have a cup of tea so they could talk a while before Lucy retired to her room and went to bed.

All Lucy had told Mrs. Brown when she got back from Indianapolis was that things hadn't worked out. But tonight, Lucy didn't think she could face giving the "fuller report" her new friend would probably expect. Slipping around to the back of the house, she snuck in as quietly as possible. The door into the kitchen was ajar, and as she reached to pull it closed, there was a sharp bark from the living room. It startled Lucy so much she jumped. If she hadn't left him in Indianapolis, she could've sworn it was Jigger's bark. And within seconds, toenails clicked across the kitchen floor, and a nose poked into the crack in the door.

Lucy gasped. "Jigger? How'd you get here?"

Yap! Yap! The dog forced his nose through the gap in the door wagging his whole behind, his tail a happy blur. He jumped up on

Lucy, knocking her back onto her bed. Then Jigger leaped onto the bed beside her, licking her face.

A *squeak, squeak, squeak* rolled through the kitchen, and the door swung wide. Lucy pushed Jigger down and sat up. For a moment she thought her heart was going to stop.

"What ...? Bo? How did you ...?" There in the doorway, grinning at her from his wheelchair, sat Bo in his full army uniform, ribbons and all.

Lucy was too stunned to move. Then she dove across the room and flung her arms around him. But she pulled back nearly as quickly as though he was nothing more than a red-hot iron statue. There were too many questions. She couldn't let her hopes soar again.

"What ... what are you doing here?"

He shrugged. "Jigger brought me back."

"Jigger? But ... how?"

"That nametag on his collar. That was a real brainchild, babe. But what I don't get is why you just dropped him off and then skedaddled back up here. Why'd you just disappear? Ah," he waved his hand dismissively, "don't matter, now. I'm here, and you're here, and ... and these nice people ... come back over here and—"

"Bo, just slow down." Lucy held her hands out in front of her. "I don't know what's happenin' here. I thought you were dead. Red Cross said you were dead twice, and then ... and then that guy from Riverview said his brother saw you—"

"So that's how you found me. Well, that's great! Now come on over here."

"No. I can't. I need ... I need to know some things, like why you never wrote me after ... after ..."

"I'm so sorry 'bout that, babe. After I took the hit, they barely got me to a hospital ship. Then they had me so doped up I didn't even know my own name. Ha! Started tellin' them my *real* name. Can you believe that? Anyway, when I was finally able to write, I did write, but my letters kept comin' back. Thought you'd given up on me—"

"So you took up with that other girl, just like that?"

"What other girl?"

"The one you knocked up." Lucy gritted her teeth. "Don't you be waggin' your head at me like you don't know what I'm talkin' 'bout. I seen you and her just 'fore I let Jigger go after you. Her pregnant as a blimp, livin' in that little house with a picket fence. I seen you both."

"Who, Kelsey? She's my sister. She and her husband been lettin' me live with 'em until I can get back on my feet. They got two other kids. She's just my sister. I had nowhere else to go when I couldn't find you. So I told the VA to send me to Indianapolis. She checked on me almost every day and then let me stay at their place, both when I got out the first time and then again since a couple of weeks ago." He shook his head and rolled his eyes. "But I really got to get out before that baby comes. They'll be needin' the space."

Lucy glanced through the door and saw Mrs. Brown standing on the other side of the kitchen, looking at her with a worried look on her face as if to ask whether everything was okay. Lucy nodded and sat down on the edge of her bed, feeling so lightheaded the room was swirling. "You never told me you had a sister."

Bo frowned like he couldn't imagine that. "Of course I did. Don't you remember? Surely I told you my folks separated when I was twelve. Kelsey was sixteen, so she and Mom moved to Indianapolis and ... Didn't I ...?" He put his hand to his head. "Maybe I never told you 'bout that, but—"

"So that was your *sister*? Bo, I'm warnin' you! If you're givin' me a bunch of poppycock, I'll—"

"No. I swear. Kelsey's married to Bob. I can take you down there, and you can meet 'em both."

They both sat there—Lucy on the edge of her bed and Bo in his wheelchair—and stared at each other in silence. Out of the corner of her eye, Lucy saw Mrs. Brown raise her index finger and tiptoe away like people did at church when they had to go out to the bathroom. Lucy took a deep breath. She still had more questions, but if Mrs. Brown thought things were okay, maybe she could relax, too. She got up from the bed and took a couple of steps toward him, her left hand outstretched. "Bo ... Bo, you can't imagine how hard it's been for me. I thought you were dead. They said you were dead, that Private Moon was ... was killed in action while you were tryin' to take some island in the Pacific."

"Yeah, he was, when we were trying to secure a beachhead on the Solomons. The Japanese were lobbin' mortars down on us like rain in June. He and I got blown up by the same shell. But he didn't make it."

Lucy felt her eyes going large. "You mean ... you mean B. J. Moon wasn't you?"

"Of course not. What made you think—"

"He's someone else?"

"Yeah. We became buddies in basic. Best friends. That's why I had you send my letters to him. He passed them on every time."

"But why?"

"Well, you know." He turned to check behind him, then continued in a lower voice. "Because of what happened in Lapeer. If the army ever figured out I was James Bodeen, I didn't want it to come back on you. But they never did. As far as the army and the VA's concerned, I'm still Borick Hansen."

"Yeah," Lucy said, her voice trailing off. "That's what they said at the VA hospital. They didn't know any Moon."

"Of course not. Moon was never there."

"But ... but Bo! Why didn't you come home to me, right here in Chicago?"

Bo reached out and took her hand. "'Cause I couldn't find you! After they brought me back to the States, they put me in that brand-new hospital in Fort Ord, California. Best doctors, but they couldn't get the shrapnel outta my gut. I nearly died. But they sewed me back up, and when I was strong enough they wanted to send me to a VA hospital where I had family for my rehab. I wrote to you, but when my letters kept coming back. I thought I was gonna go crazy. They finally sent me to Indianapolis to be near my sister. But ... why didn't you answer *my* letters?"

Bo rolled his chair close to her as Lucy sat on the edge of her bed and told him about Miss Mason selling her house and moving down to Mississippi. "I doubt that man who bought it paid any attention to unclaimed mail. Even if he had, he didn't know I'd moved in here with the Browns."

They were quiet for a few moments as she squeezed his warm hand. "Oh, Bo, I can't believe you're here. But ... how are you now? You gonna heal?"

"Gettin' there. Still got that hunk of metal in me, sittin' right there by my liver like a time bomb, the doc says, but so far it's stayin' put. This is my first trip out. And"—he flicked the Purple Heart ribbon on his chest—"this got me first-class treatment all the way. I jus' tol' the train conductor Jigger was my guide dog, and they let him come too. Even the cabbie here in Chicago wouldn't let me pay to drive me here. I just gave him the address on Jigger's tag. Huh ... guess that's why they call 'em dog tags. I still got mine too." He pulled out a small chain around his neck with two metal tags on it. "See? Says Borick Hansen, not Moon."

Lucy just shook her head slowly. "Oh, Bo, I can hardly believe all this." Tears of happiness welled up in her eyes. Leaning forward, she wrapped him in her arms and planted a long warm kiss on his lips.

Her Bo had come home.

Chapter 43

T HEIR EMBRACE WAS INTERRUPTED by Emma Brown clearing her throat in the adjoining kitchen. "Excuse me, I just wanted to say that if you'd like to stay over, Mr. Hansen, you'd be welcome to sleep on the sofa. I've put a couple of blankets and a pillow on it, and you know where the bathroom is."

Bo spun his chair around. "Thank you, Mrs. Brown. That's really swell of you, but don't go to any trouble on my acc—"

"No trouble. We're happy to have you, and I'll try to see that the kids don't wake you too early in the morning."

"Thank you," Lucy added. "Can't say how much this means to us."

"Well ... goodnight, now." She stood there a moment as if she didn't know whether to leave them on their own or not, then turned and went back through the kitchen as she called, "See you in the morning."

Bo turned back around and Lucy stared into his eyes for a long time as if viewing a newsreel of the past three years. It felt like an eternity, but now that it was over and they were together, it seemed like they were picking up right where they'd left off. Everything the same. But was it?

Before, they'd gone through some deep waters together—Bo killing the field boss to protect her and them both running. It had turned their worlds upside down, but at least they'd experienced it together. But since then, their lives had seemed far worse and very *different* from one another's. So how could they be the same? Was Bo the same? Was she the same?

Once, sitting in the Adirondack chairs on the porch of the tourist home in Niagara, Bo had said he wanted to grow old together with her and someday sit in their own chairs on their own porch. She'd gotten goose bumps imagining he was almost asking her to marry him. But now, as she thought about it, "growing old together" took on greater significance. Only by sharing the challenges and joys of life *together* was there any hope of changing in similar ways. Life changes you, and if you don't experience it together, it's likely to drive you apart. The war had torn them apart, there was no question about that, weaving separate nightmares into the fabric of their separate histories. Could they ever be knit together again? Could they ever really be one?

"What're we gonna do, Bo?" she whispered.

He rolled his chair closer. "I ... I want us to get a place of our own ... like we had before."

Was it a question? She stared at him, unable to say anything.

"I've saved considerable from the monthly disability checks I get, and I aim to get a job soon as I can." He paused, leaning so close she could see his eyes focusing back and forth between hers as though he were trying to figure out what she was thinking. "But if you can keep workin'—at least for a while—I figure we can make it. Whaddya say?"

Was that a proposal? A proposal for what? As much as she'd loved living with him, especially for that brief time in Miss Mason's third-floor apartment—she had relived those days a thousand times—she knew she couldn't do it again, not like that. Was it the fact that they'd made love before they were married? Yes, that ... but their intimacy had meant far more than she'd realized. They had become one, yet they weren't really one. They hadn't committed themselves to being one forever. Their families hadn't recognized them as one. Their community hadn't recognized them as one. The army hadn't recognized them as one. The church hadn't recognized them as one.

Did that mean God hadn't recognized them as one?

Lucy didn't know the answers, but she knew one thing: she wasn't going to do that again.

"Bo ... we can't live together unless we get married first."

"Oh, I want to get married as soon as we can, but—"

"*First.*"

He leaned back in his wheelchair. "Okay." He nodded his head slowly. "Yeah, yeah, first. First thing. That's what I want, too, Lucy. I'm sorry. It's really what I meant, I just hadn't thought it through. I want us to be a real family. I want to commit myself to you for the rest of my life. I'm not tryin' to leave the back door open or nothin'. I love you, so let's do this right. But let's not put it off, okay?"

She lunged forward and flung her arms around him, causing him to yelp in pain. She pulled back. "Oh, Bo, I'm sorry. Are you okay?"

He forced the grimace from his pale face, and in a moment the healthy color returned. "Yeah ... I'll be all right." He took a deep breath with his eyes closed. "It's just that sometimes when I move too fast, that shrapnel in my gut gives me a jab."

After a moment, his eyes popped open wide. "Speakin' of gettin' things right, I almost forgot." He reached into a little pouch hanging on the side of his wheelchair and pulled out a piece of paper that he unfolded. "Here, have a look at this!"

She pushed his hand away and felt her face flush. He still didn't know she couldn't read. "Just tell me, Bo. What is it?"

"Well, when all my letters came back from our old Seeley address here in Chicago and I couldn't find you, I started thinkin' maybe you'd gone back to live with your folks. But I had no idea where they were. However, bein' stuck in that VA hospital with nothin' else to do, I got to thinkin': libraries usually collect newspapers from all over, maybe even from Michigan. So I asked this USO girl to help me. She came around every couple days bringin' books to the fellows from the public library. She agreed to check it out, and sure as shootin', the Indianapolis Public Library kept copies of *The Flint Journal* from Flint, Michigan, not that far from Lapeer. I asked her to bring me a few issues every visit, beginnin' with the ones datin' back to when we first met. Every issue had a little column of news from Lapeer. It told about the arrival of the Carson Brothers Carnival. Then I found one about Doyle gettin' killed and another one sayin' the sheriff considered a carnival guy and a migrant girl the prime suspects. But what I was lookin' for was any mention of whether your parents left town and where they might've gone—"

"Oh, Bo, did you find 'em?"

He shook his head. "Sorry, babe, not really … but I found something else. Two weeks after Doyle's death, there was an inquest when the sheriff was going to formally charge us with murder, makin' us fugitives. But at the inquest, Doyle's wife—Lillian, I think the paper said her name was—showed up and said it wasn't murder."

"What?" Lucy reached out and grabbed Bo's arm.

"Okay, now. Just listen! This here's a Photostat of the article. It says she heard screamin' comin' from the barn that evening and came out to see what was goin' on. Apparently, there's a window in that office room—don't even remember it, myself—but Mrs. Doyle was outside lookin' in and saw enough to know what was goin' on. She testified that 'the boy'—that'd be me—was merely defendin' himself from Doyle's brutal attack. When the judge asked her why Doyle was beatin' on me, she admitted all I was doin' was tryin' to protect 'the girl, Cindy'—that was you—from her husband, that he'd been trying to 'force himself' on you."

Lucy released her grip on Bo's arm, trying to wrap her mind around the news. Had they been running all this time for no reason? No, no, she wasn't gonna keep lookin' back. This was great news! It was time to move on. She and Bo were going to get married. This was a relief, a gift of freedom. Finally, the truth had come out.

"That is the truth, Bo. You were only tryin' to protect me … and then tryin' to keep from getting' killed yourself. It was self-defense." Lucy closed her eyes, trying to recall the details of the event, nodding her head slowly. "I recollect the screamin' while Doyle was climbin' all over me … screaming, 'No, Buster! No! No! No!' But I was so scared, whenever the memory came to me, it was just the horror that flooded over me, and I thought it'd been me screamin'—but … I never would've called him 'Buster.' So she's right, it musta been her."

"Oh, babe." Bo leaned forward and put his arm around her. "See what I'm sayin'? All the charges were dismissed! Ain't no one's lookin' for us no more. We can go back to usin' our real names! We're free!"

Lucy blinked back sudden tears. So much had happened in the last few hours. Bo coming back, saying he wanted to marry her, and now this. It was like rewriting history—rewriting it by the truth, not leaving it the way she feared everyone thought. "But … but, why'd Mrs. Doyle wait so long to say anything?"

"Huh! Judge asked her that too. She said she'd been in the hospital havin' a baby. Had a rough time of it, I guess, and was in there extra long."

Lucy could believe that easily enough. Mrs. Doyle had been havin' a hard pregnancy, which was why Lucy had been hired to help her in the first place. But what an unbelievable string of events—devastating events Lucy had come to believe had destroyed both their lives. What had happened was horrible, no denying that—but somehow the damage seemed to be melting away … no, more than that, their results of those events were being filled with hope. How could that be? She'd almost been raped, then accused of murder. They'd been running for their lives, and then a war had nearly taken Bo's life. She'd lost her family and had a terrible secret she still carried with her …

"Bo! Those articles say anything else 'bout the missin' money?"

"Not a word. I doubt anyone knows about it. It wasn't Doyle's money, anyway. He was the thief. Probably pocketed every penny he could get away with."

Lucy knew that was right. Her father had said more than once that Doyle tried to get the workers to forfeit their held-back wages. But … that didn't make it *her* money, and she still had it—all of it. And someone still might come looking for it. "Um, Bo? Maybe we should keep on using our … our road names. Know what I mean?"

"No way. Why would we do that? 'Course I'll always be Borick Hansen to the army and the VA, but I like my real name. And some day I'm gonna find your folks, Lucy. And we'll get the whole family back together again. That's a promise, babe!"

Lucy tucked that promise into her heart. But right now, she just wanted to feast on the happiness in front of her. Bo had found her. He was home! They were going to get married. She was going to have a real home at last.

THE NEXT DAY WAS TUESDAY, Lucy's day off. And the first thing they did was take a cab to talk to Pastor Winfred at Mount Olive Tabernacle Church.

"You sure we're goin' the right way?" Bo asked as they got close. "This still looks like a black neighborhood."

"It is, mostly. It's Miss Mason's old church, where I met the Browns."

"Yeah, but, uh, do you think they'll marry a white couple?"

"Don't see why not. They's as close to God as anyone I know—'cept maybe Ma. They prayed for you every Sunday ... when we thought you were still alive."

"Really? Huh. Guess I owe 'em, then, 'cause there were times ..."

Pastor Winfred seemed real glad to see Bo. Said Mrs. Brown had called to tell him the soldier they thought was dead had only been wounded and had come home. He talked to them for almost two hours in his small office in the back of the church, asking why they were getting married and whether they understood it was a lifelong, exclusive commitment. "Now, don't be offended ..." He held up both hands. "... but I gotta ask whether you're both free from any other 'entanglements'? Married to anyone else? Engaged? Any children by anyone else?"

To each question, Lucy and Bo shook their heads with confidence.

"Ya know," said the pastor, "entanglements can also include parents. Are you free from your parents? Bible says we're to leave father and mother and be joined to one another as one flesh. Can you both do that freely?" Bo nodded, and Lucy did, too, though an old sadness welled up in her heart. She'd left father and mother all right, but not by choice. Bo was all the family she had.

"Now Bo," the pastor focused on him, "as the head of this family, you need to accept responsibility for the family's welfare.

That begins with providin' and protectin' and children. But do it like Christ, as a servant, not lording it over them. And remember this: If you ignore the wisdom of your wife, it'll be to your peril and your family's misery. So share everything with her and consider her input, and you'll be a happy man with a happy family. All that's in the Bible, but—" he chuckled, "I had to learn it the hard way! Know what I mean?"

Bo nodded. "But, uh, 'bout that providin', I intend to get a job soon as I can, but—"

"No, that's not what I mean," the pastor said. "Circumstances may mean one or the other of you brings home the bacon. I'm talkin' 'bout takin' on the responsibility for seein' to it that the family's provided for ... whatever way you work it out. Understand?"

Pastor Winfred seemed satisfied with their answers and finally shifted gears. "So, do you have a date in mind?"

Lucy and Bo looked at each other and said as soon as possible. The pastor set the date for Saturday, November third, just two and a half weeks away.

So excited she could hardly sit still, Lucy said, "And I'm gonna ask Mrs. Brown if she'll make us a banana cake."

"Banana?" Bo snorted. "Never heard of a banana wedding cake."

Lucy giggled. "Me neither, but ..." She flushed. "That's also my birthday, and Ma always made banana cake for our birthdays, so ...!"

Everyone laughed. After Pastor Winfred prayed with them, he called a cab so they could go down to the Loop and apply for a marriage license at the courthouse.

Bo had his discharge papers from the army with him, but the fact that both Lucy and he wanted to use their real names for which they didn't have any identification almost sabotaged their plans. If it hadn't been for a clerk whose son had died in the war and was eager to help any veteran, they might not have received a license. But she agreed to send a telegram to the counties where they each had been born, asking for copies of their birth certificates. She winked at them. "I still got a little pull around here. Don't you worry none. You'll get your license in time."

Chapter 44

I PRETTY MUCH HAD TO HANG OUT AT MANNA HOUSE while my ankle healed. In fact, for the first couple nights they put me up on one of the couches in the Shepherd's Fold 'cause there weren't no beds open upstairs. At least Fuzz Top was good enough to bring Dandy to work with her during the days so I could give him a little attention. I know those boys love him—'specially the young one—but kids get distracted, and Dandy has a powerful hankerin' to be petted and scratched. He'll sit there all day, lookin' up at ya out of the corner of his eyes with that silly grin on his face, beggin' for more. He near knocked me over when I tried to stand up.

By Friday I was managin' to hobble around on my own a fair bit. No way was I down for a six-month count. I'd be out on the streets 'fore the snow flew ... though, guess there'd been a few flakes a couple of weeks ago. The thought of winter gave me a shiver. Maybe I was getting too old for this life. Had to admit it was kinda nice, folks bringin' meals up to me in the Shepherd's Fold, though most times—like this mornin'—I ended up eatin' by myself. I sipped the last of my lukewarm coffee and thought about droppin' a hint to Fuzz Top that this was my birthday, and maybe—her bein' the program director, and all—she oughta organize a Bingo game or somethin' so I'd have a little company.

But when she came in, she sicced Dandy on me and went straight to her office.

In fact, it musta been a busy day, 'cause everyone seemed to just buzz through with hardly even a howdy-do. I sat there all day twiddling my thumbs till I wasn't even good company for Dandy, and he wandered off, probably downstairs to see what he could steal from Estelle's kitchen.

Guess that's why I wasn't in a very good mood when Sarge came in late in the afternoon. She pulled a foldin' chair over in front of my couch, turned it backward, and threw her leg over it as she sat down. From the stern look on her face, I knew she was fixin' to grill me 'bout somethin'.

"Don't say it!" I put my hand out and turned away. "Whatever it is, I ain't in the mood."

"What? Lucy, you're unbelievable, unbelievable! Whaddaya think I'm here for? I'm gonna take-a you to Gabby's house tonight. You're goin' with me at seven o'clock. No questions asked. *Capiche?*"

"Ha! You ain't big enough to take me." She might've been tough, but she was only five-foot-four.

Sarge stared at me, her black hair pulled back into a knot. "You think I'm '*stupido?* I'm just tellin' you: be ready!"

"Well, who died and left you da boss?"

She stood up and gave a kick to the seat of her chair to fold it up. "I ain't playin' wich you, Lucy. You be ready at seven." And she marched toward the door.

"I thought that was nineteen-hundred hours to an ol' marine like you," I called after her.

Since I had nothin' else to do—and everyone seemed too busy to play Bingo—I let Hannah practice her beauty salon skills on me, braidin' my hair and paintin' my nails. Don't think I'd done that since I was a kid and my sister, Maggie, and I used to fix each other up.

But shortly before seven, I made sure I had my purple hat on and my big old coat in hand when Sarge came into the Shepherd's Fold. She seemed in a much better mood and helped me down the front steps of the shelter and into her car. I had to admit, it was good to get out in the fresh air, even if I wasn't on my own.

I kept wantin' to ask Sarge what this trip was all about as we drove over to the House of Hope, but it didn't seem wise to get into it with her again, so I rode along in silence. Maybe Fuzz Top had figured a way to put me in one of those apartments … but I doubted it.

Climbin' the steps to Fuzz Top's place, even though it was only to the first floor, wasn't the easiest thing I've ever done, given my bum ankle and those awkward crutches. But when I felt Sarge steadyin' my backside, I sung out, "Hey, lay off! What if someone were to see you? It ain't like you're pushin' me up a mountain, ya know. I can do it myself."

Dandy musta heard my voice, 'cause he started barkin' and came chargin' out into the foyer as soon as Fuzz Top opened the door.

"Happy birthday!" shouted a crowd starin' through the open door. Musta been two dozen of 'em or more, pushin' and cranin' their necks to see out. All of them were wavin' and yellin'. I couldn't believe it. But when I pulled my hat off, all the racket stopped like some orchestra conductor brought his hands down.

"Whatchu starin' at?" After a moment, I clapped my hand on my head and knew. Those braids were stickin' straight up all over. "Hannah said she needed some practice doin' whatever she do up at that beauty salon she work at. I was just helpin' the girl out."

I swung myself into the apartment on my crutches. "So, whose party we at?" I turned and frowned at Sarge. "Why didn't ya tell me we was comin' to a party? I woulda wore a party dress or somethin'."

"It's *your* party, Lucy!" Fuzz Top grinned. "Come on now, everybody!"

"Happy birthday, dear Lucy ..." A few were a little off key, but it was the sweetest music I'd heard since the cardinals were matin'. How had they found out it was my birthday? I eyed Fuzz Top. Was she campaignin' to take her ma's place as my best friend? It'd be just like her to come up with the fact by hook or by crook. I dug out my ol' red bandana handkerchief and blew my nose afore someone saw my eyes wet.

They took me on in, and Edesa and Precious set me up in the living room in a comfy ol' rockin' chair with my foot up on a stool and a paper crown on my head. "*Mi amiga,*" said Edesa, "you are now Queen for a Day!" Then her hubby had everyone start playing games in that little apartment. The one that got me laughin' was Pin the Tie on the Mayor. Josh taped up a big poster of Mayor Daley on the brick fireplace and everybody tried to pin a paper bowtie on him. Woulda played it myself, but couldn't very well with crutches. Hard enough walkin' around without a blindfold.

Harry Bentley won the prize—a bag of Garrett Gourmet Caramel and Cheese Popcorn, a Chicago specialty. "Who told you my weakness?" he laughed.

"Don't worry," I said, "I can hep ya out with that!" I'd had some of that stuff before, and it's good!

Truth or Dare was the next game. "Awright, awright," I said, "guess I gotta do Truth, 'cause ain't likely I can do one o' your Dares with this bum ankle."

They all huddled around tryin' to come up with somethin' they could lay on me, and pretty soon Precious said, "Okay, Lucy, Truth. How old are you?"

I looked up as if the answer was written on the ceiling and stroked my chin. "*Hmm*, don't know if I can rightly say. I was born in 1926. How many is that?"

"Wow!" Fuzz Top's youngest looked at me with eyes as big as saucers. "That makes you eighty years old, Miss Lucy!" He gave Dandy a pat. "Whaddya think of that, ol' boy? That's practically as old as you in dog years."

Everyone laughed until Estelle held up her hands for quiet. "Well, then, this is a mighty special birthday, the big 8-0 for Miss Lucy. That means it's time for cake and ice cream."

Suddenly, I forgave Sarge all her bossiness in gettin' me over there. They set up a card table for me and told me to close my eyes. I may have been ready for cake and ice cream, but I wasn't ready for the blazin' inferno Estelle put down in front of me. It topped a huge crescent-shaped cake with yellow frosting.

"What's this?" I couldn't believe it. "A banana cake? For me?" I started to laugh until tears started to run down my cheeks. "My mama always made me a banana cake back in the day, but never one that *looked* like a giant banana!"

Who had been behind this? Then I remembered: in tryin' to get Estelle to make Fuzz Top a banana cake for *her* birthday, I had told them it was *my* favorite.

But it didn't end there. They gave me all sorts of gifts: a new sweater, warm socks, hand cream, earmuffs, gloves—all things that could fit into my wire cart. It had been over sixty years since I'd celebrated my birthday.

Afore Sarge whisked me out the door, I got Gabby off to myself and took her face in both my hands. "Ain't never gonna forget this

birthday, Fuzz Top. Takes me back, it does. Sometimes I wish ..."
But I couldn't finish tellin' her about my last birthday party, the
one combined with my wedding reception.

MONDAY, FUZZ TOP TOOK ME BACK to the clinic for a checkup on my
ankle. Didn't think I needed to go, but after her being so nice and
all, I couldn't refuse when she insisted.

We talked all the way down there, and she seemed real
interested in how I was doin'. Asked me if I'd ever twisted or
broken my ankle before.

"Oh, sure. Lotsa times," I said. "Sprained, that is. Never broke
anything. But I was always climbin' trees an' jumpin' creeks an'
stuff. Ma said I was a bad influence on the other kids, 'cause I was
the oldest an' the younger ones always wanted ta do what I did."

"You have brothers and sisters?"

"Ha. Too many, if ya ask me. But that's the way it was with
migrant families—we needed all the hep we could get pickin', so
had to grow 'em ourselves. Leastwise, that's what Pa used ta say."

She kept on. "So tell me their names."

"Well, lessee. Maggie was next ta me, then came Tom an' Willy
an' George, one after t'other ..." I stopped. Thinkin' 'bout 'em took
me back, that's for sure.

"So there were five of you?"

"Nah. Ma got sick an' lost a few—two I think. But then came
the babies. Betty an' Johnny. I left home when they was real small
... Been a long time now."

We were almost there, and I thought Fuzz Top was done
messin' in my personal history, but she went on. "Have you
been in touch with any of your family? Your, um, next closest
sister, for instance?"

"Who, Maggie? Nah. I knew she'd be mad at me fer leavin', 'cause she'd hafta to pick up all the chores an' stuff families put on the oldest kid. Can't blame her. But I had to leave. Had my reasons."

"Thought you told my mother you ran off with a boy."

"Yeah, well, I did. But let's just say it was complicated." I was itchin' under all these personal questions, but like a little terrier, Fuzz Top won't let go. "Besides, when them two babies came, it was jus' too many mouths ta feed. None o' the rest of them was old enough ta fend for themselves. Had to be me."

I was glad when we got to the clinic, and even happier when the doc said my ankle was comin' along okay.

In fact, I was feelin' so good that when the sun came out and the temperature got up to sixty a few days later, I decided to test my ambulatin' abilities. Carolyn had taught me how to sign my name so people could read it, so I checked out of Manna House all proper like and took off.

I had to go slow, and Dandy seemed to understand, but it was great. Made it down to the Double-Bubble Laundromat and gave Ramon the dickens for takin' out the pay phones. "Pretty soon I s'pose you'll be switchin' out the washers and dryers for credit card models. What're we gonna do without coin returns where a body can pick up a little change?"

"Well, it wasn't your change! Besides, AT&T took the phones out. Everyone's got cells now, ya know. And get that dog outta here!"

"*Hee, hee, hee!*"

But that night it started to drizzle, and Friday a real storm hammered the city with a chilling rain. I began to think I'd made a big mistake as I headed over to the lakefront to take shelter in that pavilion on the beach opposite Richmond Towers. This time of year, the concessions would be closed and only an occasional jogger would venture down on the beach, but I knew the breezeway through the pavilion offered pretty good shelter.

Rain didn't seem to dampen Dandy's spirits none, though. He took off after the seagulls. Should've let him go—he'd come back in a few—but I tried to hang on and run after him. Wouldn'tcha know it, I twisted my ankle again, steppin' in a little hole. Down I went while Dandy scampered off, leapin' through the waves, gettin' soaked.

Had to crawl to the pavilion, draggin' my cart along behind me. Everything seemed wet by the time I got there, and even when we cuddled up out of the wind, I got concerned 'bout hypothermia. Ya gotta know 'bout that kinda thing livin' on the street, 'cause if you get too cold, there ain't no comin' back.

Dandy and me huddled down in my blankets and towels, damp as they were, and I began thinking, maybe I oughta pray, see if God might hear me and get us outta this mess. Fuzz Top always says prayin's just talkin' to God, but since He and I aren't on such familiar terms, I thought maybe I oughta say somethin' more formal, and the only prayer I could think of was that house blessing. And as I looked around, it kinda fit, this shelter bein' 'bout as drafty as those hovels Ma prayed over.

> *God bless the corners of this house*
> *An' all the lintel blessed,*
> *An' bless the hearth an' bless the board*
> *An' bless each place of rest.*

I hugged Dandy close to me. "See, Dandy? We gonna be fine. Someone'll come. Don't worry."

An' bless each door that opens wide
To strangers as to kin …

Dandy lunged up and stiffened.

"Lucy!" Huh? Was that my name or just the wind. Then from closer, "Lucy? Lucy, it's me, Gabby! And a friend."

I threw back my blankets and towels like a crocus comin' up through the last snow. "That you, Fuzz Top? *Hee hee*, see there, Dandy? What'd I tell ya. Told ya somebody would come sooner or later." Thing was, I was the amazed one. Had God heard me? Or was this just a coincidence? I tried to rock my body forward. "*Oof* … Gimme a hand here, will ya?"

"Will!" Fuzz Top said to the guy with her. "Can you help Lucy stand up? Calm down, Dandy. Easy, boy …" Dandy was actin' like he'd expected Fuzz Top all along.

She asked how Dandy and I'd gotten so wet, so I told her and had to confess that I'd sprained my ankle again. But I didn't think it was as bad as before.

The young man kept trying to interrupt. "But Gabby, Gabby, did you hear what she was saying? That … that prayer. That's my grandmother's prayer!"

"Yeah, that and the banana cake and her name and …" She gave a *who-knows* shrug.

What were they talkin' 'bout?

"Hey! Hey you, ain't you gonna help me up?" I frowned at the young man. "Who'd ya say this here kid is?" I actually knew who he was, though I couldn't recollect his name off hand. He was the one who'd been hanging around Fuzz Top's man, and I'd met him briefly at her house blessin' party that day when he held the door open for me.

He answered for himself. "My name's Will Nissan. I'm a friend of the Fairbanks. And you're Lucy, right? Can you walk, Lucy? It's a ways to the car."

"Well, I can if ya give me a hand. Stupid ankle … was doin' fine till ever'thing got all wet an' slippery—hey! Can't leave my cart. Need all them towels an' stuff too."

Chapter 45

B O FELT HIMSELF GETTING STRONGER BY THE DAY, able to spend more time out of his wheelchair using just a cane. He traveled back to Indianapolis to pick up his few possessions and give his sister and brother-in-law the good news that he'd found Lucy and they were getting married. Unfortunately, his sister couldn't come to the wedding because her baby was due any day.

When he told Lucy the news, she seemed genuinely sad. "Ah, I sure hope we can go visit someday. You said she had two other kids? I'll be an instant auntie."

A few days later, Bo located an apartment in one of the newer thirty-unit apartment buildings on Chicago's north side. "It's a jim-dandy place," he bragged. "They even allow pets. But you can't see it till after we get married."

"What? Bo, you didn't rent it on your own, did you? Didn't you hear what the pastor said about considerin' me?"

"But I *did* consider you!" The feeling he'd made a big mistake crawled over Bo like a spider. He fought it off. "You'll love the place."

"But Pastor Winfred said you're supposed to share everything and consider my input. How can you consider my input if you didn't let me see it first?"

"But I ..." He simply hadn't thought about it. "Look, Lucy, you don't understand. I needed a place to stay, and—"

She held up her hand as though she didn't want to hear it, but she said, "It's okay, Bo. I'm sure it's a nice place." Or maybe she just didn't want this to become their first "married" fight.

Bo sighed. He'd blown it when he had no intention of hurting her. They were silent while he privately ate crow. "Sorry, babe. Guess I shoulda taken you to see it first." He paused, knowing he had to say more. "Uh, is it okay if I still keep it a secret for now? Since I ain't workin' yet, I been usin' my time to fix it up real nice before you move in ... Wanted to surprise you, ya know, but if you don't like it, I won't mind if you change things. Honest ..."

She gave him a hug. "We'll see. Maybe I'll like the way you've done it."

Two and a half weeks seemed to fly, during which Bo began to see he wasn't always the one who had to adjust. He had very few expectations for the wedding. But in little comments and brief winces of disappointment, he realized Lucy had a lot of expectations, little dreams that didn't work out the way she would have liked.

Saturday of the wedding blew in blustery and cold, not bright and warm like a June afternoon. And only a handful of people attended: Pastor Winfred and family, the Browns, and a few church members, making the small sanctuary echo with emptiness.

There was no lacy wedding gown with a long train like Lucy said she'd imagined as a girl. Instead, Mrs. Brown had helped her sew a simple white dress. "You'll want something you can wear to church in the summer," Bo overheard her say. "Don't make no sense buyin' a dress to wear just once. You don't want to keep gettin' married just to make use of a dress." But as far as Bo was concerned, Lucy couldn't have been more beautiful coming down the aisle in that handmade dress with a little wreath of flowers on her head and carrying a small posy, a gift from the Brown family.

In a tired moment before the wedding, Lucy had said, "I'd always hoped Maggie could be my maid of honor. And I wanted Ma to sit on the front row and maybe cry just a little with joy over seein' me get hitched all proper like. And Pa won't be here to walk me down the aisle and give me away like he's s'posed to."

Bo only hoped he wouldn't disappoint her, standing up there in the front, waiting for her with no support other than his cane and Pastor Winfred by his side.

But when the piano began playing, "Here Comes the Bride," and Mrs. Brown beamed with joy as she rose to her feet from her seat in the front row, there was no regret in Lucy's beaming smile as Mr. Brown escorted her down the aisle, without missing a step.

Bo took a deep breath and tried to relax. He managed to remember what he was supposed to do and say, and before he knew it, Pastor Winfred was telling the guests, "And now, may I present to you … Mr. and Mrs. James Bodeen!"

After a noisy reception with banana cake, punch, and lots of laughter, Bo and Lucy rode off in a yellow-and-green Checker Cab, to which someone had managed to tie a long string of rattling tin cans.

When they got to their apartment, Bo wasn't able to carry Lucy across the threshold, but he had managed to climb the stairs to their second-floor unit on his own without stopping to rest.

"Welcome home, Mrs. Bodeen," he whispered in her ear as he unlocked the door.

Over the winter, the muscle and weight Bo had lost from his war wound returned and he had less trouble keeping his pants up. He took Jigger for long walks at least twice a day, using his cane only when the ground was icy. In fact, the only time he noticed the shrapnel any more was when he slipped or jerked his body unexpectedly.

He tried to reassure himself that since the jabs were less frequent and severe, they didn't mean anything, but he couldn't get his old VA doctor's speech out of his mind. "You have a time bomb in there, son," the doctor had explained after viewing the X-rays. "It may never give you a problem—and I hope it doesn't—but I can't give you any guarantees. That jagged shell fragment sits right next to the hepatic artery going into your liver. We could operate, but I'm afraid that would be more dangerous than leaving it alone." The doctor had gone on to explain that the occasional jabs of pain probably weren't dangerous in themselves. "If something really goes wrong, you won't even feel it when you bleed out. So my advice is to get strong and live your life as normally as possible."

But it was hard to ignore the reminders.

As usual, "the Hawk," Chicago's infamous icy wind, was often out during the early months of 1946, its talons attacking any exposed skin, but when the first hints of milder weather arrived with April, Bo decided it was time to end his period of recuperation.

A week later, after scouting out the idea he had in mind, he asked Lucy if she thought her boss would let her cut back to forty hours a week. "Even the federal government don't expect more'n that, now that the war's over."

"Are you kidding? Most of us work at least fifty. And then old Kowalski yells if anyone needs time off for anything—sick, emergency, you name it. For weeks he yelled at me for gettin' married."

"He what? He yelled at you for gettin' married? That rotten ..." Bo gritted his teeth, biting off the names he wanted to call the man. "Then it's time for a talk."

"Ha! Mr. Kowalski don't talk. He yells."

"We'll see about that. Tomorrow I'm goin' in to talk to *him*. If he don't like it, he can let you go—"

"Bo!"

"Don't worry, babe. We got money. My checks come regular, and even if you lost your job, guess what … I'm startin' work at Riverview, first of May!"

"You what? Bo, how can you? You can't—"

"Yes I can. The boss remembers me from before, and he's givin' me light duty to start. Then, when the park opens in mid-May and they're goin' full steam, I'll probably just be a ride jockey. But at least it'll be a job."

She gave him a crushing hug that caused the shrapnel to jab him a little, but he hung tough. It would feel good doin' his part, not leanin' on Lucy so much. He broke away and took a breath. "And when I go talk to your boss tomorrow, I got a plan. I'm gonna wear my ol' uniform."

Bo knew it was a risk. Some people were tired of hearing about the war and wanted the country to put it all behind them. But Bo guessed an eastern European like Leon Kowalski might have relatives who suffered under Hitler and could be encouraged to give a little respect to the wife of a man who'd put his life on the line for freedom.

His plan worked … after a fashion. Kowalski grumbled and complained and suggested it wasn't fair and would cause all the other workers to want the same, but he finally agreed. Lucy could have all day Sunday and Monday off (switching from Tuesday). And she'd only have to work eight hours a day on the other days.

WITH THE TIME BEFORE HE STARTED HIS JOB at Riverview, Bo decided he was going to do his best to find Lucy's family. If they were still migrants, there was almost no chance of tracking them down. But following the crops was a hard life, and Bo hoped they might have found something more permanent.

Arkansas was recovering from the Dust Bowl. In fact, the rains had even begun in the fall of 1939. But it had been too late for the Tuckers. They'd already pulled up stakes and hit the migrant circuit. Nevertheless, one evening Bo casually asked Lucy, "Your folks have any savings? A stash of money they might have used to go back to farming?"

"Savings? When you're livin' hand to mouth, there ain't no such thing, though ..." A dark frown plowed her forehead as she looked down at the sock she was mending, "Guess you might say The Purse was that, the largest stash of money they'd saved as long as I can recollect. But ..." She shook her head. "I stole it right out from under 'em."

"Don't say that, Lucy. Even if you hadn't taken the money, your pa never would've seen a penny of it. Doyle was fixin' to keep it all."

"Yeah, maybe ... but still ..."

"Hey, other than farmin', what was your pa good at doin'?"

"I dunno, keepin' our old jalopy runnin', I guess. Seemed like he fixed it with baling wire and chewin' gum more times than I can count."

"So, he was a mechanic?"

"Of a sort."

Bo let it rest. That might be a clue. During the war, thousands of people moved north to the manufacturing cities where jobs were plentiful. If Lucy's pa was good at mechanical things, he might have picked up one of those jobs.

It took Bo two days in the main Chicago Public Library to go through the phone books for the major Midwest cities, writing down the numbers of every Lester Tucker he could find: Milwaukee, Chicago, Fort Wayne, Indianapolis, Cincinnati, Louisville, Columbus, Pittsburg, Youngstown, Akron, Cleveland, Toledo, Detroit.

Next day, he went to a bank and got a bag of nickels—five rolls for ten dollars—and took them to Union Train Station where he laid claim to a phone booth with a stool and a door he could close for an office and began calling.

"Hello, I'm James Bodeen. I'm looking for a Lester Tucker married to Harriet. They once lived in Arkansas. Would you happen to know them?"

Some people wanted to know why he was calling, and when he told them he was trying to find his wife's family, they started naming all their Tucker kin up and down the family tree from shore to shore. Bo wished they'd just say yes or no so he could end the call and save a nickel.

Two people hung up on him, and one woman burst into tears. Her Lester had died last Thanksgiving Day. That had been five months previous, but still Bo's call set off her grief, so he felt obliged to try to comfort her over the phone.

He was down to the Detroit names, of which there were only three, when on the second call, a young voice said, "Well, Ma's name is Harriet, and when I was knee-high to a grasshopper we live in Arkansas—that was before the Dust Bowl, so you must be wantin' Pa. But he's on swing shift at Ford and just left for the plant."

Bo's heart leaped. "Maggie? Is that you?" He knew it was! "This is Bo. You remember me? I ran off with your sister, Lu—I mean, Cindy—up there in Michigan."

385

There was a gasp, then a squeal on the other end of the line that came through the phone so loud Bo had to hold the receiver away from his ear. "Bo, is that really you? Wait till Ma hears about this! Oh, Bo! Oh, Bo! But … where's Cindy? Is she okay?"

"Yeah, yeah. She's just fine. We're down here here in Chicago. Uh … we just got married."

"Married! Really? When? Why didn't you invite us?"

"Wedding was last November, on Lucy's—I mean, Cindy's birthday, and we would've invited you, but we didn't know where you lived."

"Oh, yeah." There was a long moment of silence. "Well, we didn't know where you were either. Ma was all tore up 'bout Cindy and you for the longest time. 'Specially when we heard that them murder charges got dropped an' the police weren't out lookin' for you anymore. Why didn't you bring Cindy home back then? Ma cried nearly ever' day."

Bo felt miserable. But he didn't have time to explain. "I … we didn't know the charges had been dropped till after the war. And, of course, we didn't know where you lived. I'll explain everything when we see you. If you think your ma—"

"Oh, yeah! I know she'd love to see you both. Can you come visit? Pa'll be itchin' to talk to you too."

Bo could imagine what Lucy's pa might have to say to him and was none too eager to hear it. But he took a deep breath. "I was hopin' we could see ya. Actually, Lu—Cindy doesn't even know I've been lookin' for y'all, so this would be a big surprise for her."

"Ooo! That's swell. You wouldn't even have to tell her where you're goin' till you got here. I think that's peachy."

"So, you think it'd be okay if we came?"

"Oh, yeah. You can stay in the boys' room. They won't mind bein' kicked out, and we can fix up a bed up for ya. Hey, you still got that black-and-white dog?"

"Jigger? Oh yeah. He's fine. But we wouldn't be able to bring him." Bo looked through the window of the phone booth at the cavernous waiting room of Union Station. "We'd probably take the train." He figured the Browns wouldn't mind keeping Jigger for a few days.

The long-distance operator interrupted. "Thirty cents for three more minutes, please."

Bo put in his nickels and waited for the operator's thank you.

"I gotta go pretty soon, Maggie. Is your mom there? I should probably make arrangements with her for when we can come."

"No, no. Let's make it a surprise. You just come on any time. Besides, I do everything 'round here these days anyway. Ma ... well," Maggie's voice quieted to a near whisper, "doctor thinks she might be a lunger. That's where she is right now, seein' the TB doc."

Bo's heart sank. Lucy would be beside herself with worry if she knew. "I'm real sorry to hear that. Maybe this isn't such a good time after all."

"Oh, but it is! It is! You should come as soon as possible. They might have to put Ma in a sanatorium for a while, but she still has her good days."

"*Soon as possible*, huh?"

"Yeah. How 'bout next weekend? Think you could come then?"

"Well ..." Bo's mind raced, thinking about starting his new job. "I s'pose we could, if that ain't too soon for you. Lucy—I mean, Cindy—needs a couple of days vacation anyway." And he'd insist Kowalski give her the time without yelling at her.

On the other end of the line, Maggie giggled like ... like the sixteen-year-old she was. "This is so keen! So swell! I can't believe you're comin', and we'll surprise everyone! Keep it a secret, okay? That'll be super!"

Maggie gave Bo the Tuckers' address, and Bo said he'd phone back when he knew what time the train would get in.

Bo hung up and sat there for a moment, satisfied that he would be able to do this for Lucy. Suddenly, he slammed his fist into the palm of his other hand. He'd forgotten to give Maggie *his* address. Well, he'd do it when he phoned back with their arrival time. That made him think as he walked to the ticket counter: He and Lucy really ought to get a phone of their own. Maybe once they saved a little extra from his new job.

Bo purchased two train tickets for the following Friday. When the agent handed them to him, Bo stuffed the scrap of paper on which he'd written the Tuckers' address into the ticket envelope, sealed it, and slipped it into his pocket.

It was quite a hike from Union Station to the El, but Bo was feeling good and decided to walk. He pushed himself hard as he crossed the Chicago River Bridge and was gaining on an antiquated horse-drawn *Chicago Tribune* delivery wagon. A young boy, almost too small for the job, stood at the open back door, tossing bales of the evening edition to newspaper venders on the street corners.

Bo was almost even with the wagon, when the impatient driver of a shiny new Cadillac convertible came from behind and began honking his horn. The horse spooked and suddenly bolted ahead, toppling the boy out of the back of the wagon. To Bo's horror, the boy's foot caught in the door, dragging him along the street as he screamed.

Without thinking whether he could do it or not, Bo ran after the wagon. But when he caught up, there was no stopping it from behind. All he could do was lift the boy and carry him while he continued to run. He went a block like that before he was able to dislodge the boy's leg. They both fell to the street in a pile of tumbling arms and legs.

Burning elbows and skinned knees were almost unfelt, but the jab in his stomach was unlike anything he'd experienced since the exploding shell had ripped him open. He rolled onto his back and lay as still as the cobble stones beneath him, knowing the doctor had been wrong.

It wasn't painless.

Chapter 46

IT TOOK ME ALL NIGHT, HUDDLED under a mountain of blankets at Manna House, 'fore I got warm. Guess I was chilled to the bone more'n I realized, gettin' laid up all wet in that beach house where Fuzz Top found me. I needed to be more careful.

She woke me up from a snooze after Saturday lunch and had Dandy with her, though I could hardly recognize him. "Say, now, don't you look fancy." I gave Dandy a good head rub. "That Paul, he sure does know how to purty you up."

There were a few other guests hangin' around in the Shepherd's Fold, and after Fuzz Top said hi to 'em, she sat down on the end of my couch. "Something I want to talk to you about, Lucy. About you and Dandy—"

"I know, I *know*! Been thinkin' 'bout it all night. Dandy just couldn't stop shiverin' after he took a dunk in th' lake. Tell you the truth, Fuzz Top, I was skeered—skeered he was gonna get pneumony if somebody didn't come along an' find us purty soon. Woulda walked him back here myself if I hadn't twisted my ankle again." I reached out to pet Dandy. "Guess I been an old fool, Dandy, thinkin' you an' me could make it out on the streets this winter." I paused, thinkin' 'bout all the places we'd gone that no one knew about. "But he's good company, ya know? Gets mighty lonely sometimes."

But I knew what she was gonna say. She wanted to me to give Dandy up to her boy, Paul. And I had to admit that might be best ... "at least over the winter."

"But it's not just Dandy I'm worried about," she added. "You're eighty years old. It's not safe for you to still be out on the street in this kind of weather, Lucy—especially not with your ankle still weak. And it's only going to get worse, you know that. But I have good news." She stopped and took a deep breath. "Someone's been looking for you—and I think he's found you. Someone who doesn't want you to have to live on the streets anymore."

I jacked myself up on my elbows and looked her in the eye. "What in tarnation you talkin' 'bout? You not makin' any sense a'tall, Gabby Fairbanks."

She didn't balk for a moment. "You remember that nice young man who was with me when we found you yesterday?"

"Yeah. So?"

"His name's Will Nissan. He's Maggie Simple's grandson—"

"Maggie *who*?" Somethin' funny was goin' on here, and I wasn't sure I cottoned to it. "Don't know nobody named Simple. What kinda name is that?"

"Simple's her married name. But growing up her name was Maggie Tucker."

Now I was sure we were in quicksand.

"Lucy?" Fuzz Top said, like she was tryin' to get my attention. "I'm talking about Maggie Tucker, your *sister*. She's been looking for you for a long time—she and her grandson, Will. They're coming here to see you in about—" She looked at her watch. "Well, any time now."

I heard the buzzer sound out in the foyer, and Fuzz Top's eyes got big like the timing was a surprise. "That might be them now. I'll go let them in."

As she got up and left, I felt like I was gettin' bushwhacked. They were pullin' somethin' on me. Couldn't think what to do. With my bum ankle, there was no way to jump up and duck out the back door, so I decided I'd just have to see it through. But I was gonna watch my step real careful.

The double doors into the Shepherd's Fold swung open and Fuzz Top returned, followed by that young man with an old lady hangin' on his arm, wearin' a brown coat an' a brown-and-tan knit hat. They pulled up some chairs and all sat down facin' me. Then the old woman said in a shaky voice, "Cindy? Is that you?"

I stared hard at her, but I didn't want to let on that it was a little like lookin' in a mirror. "Name's Lucy. Don't nobody call me Cindy."

The young man spoke up. "Lucy, you remember me from last night, right? My name's Will Nissan, and this is my grandmother, Maggie Simple. She's been looking for her sister, Lucinda Tucker, for a long, long time. We think we've found her."

"Oh yeah? Where might that be?" The room was closin' in, and I couldn't get no air.

"But it's me—Maggie! Your sister!" the old woman said, tears leakin' outta the corners of her eyes. "You've got a lot of family! Brothers and sisters, nieces and nephews. Ma and Pa, they've been gone now, oh, twenty years. But most of us children got married, had a passel of kids and grandkids—like Will here." She smiled up at the young man.

I couldn't watch no more. This was like a dream and a nightmare all tumbled together—what you want and what you fear. Finally, I just muttered, "Don't got no family."

392

"Things were bad back then, Cindy," said the woman. "I know that. But all that's past. We know you wasn't guilty of nothin'."

Oh, but I was. She might not know 'bout The Purse, but I was guilty enough, guilty enough.

"Tucker family's doin' well now," continued the old woman, "'Cept for one thing—our missing sister. Everybody thinks you're dead. But not me. I knew one day we'd find you. Will and me, we come to Chicago to look for you, and here you are."

When no one spoke, Fuzz Top got up and went to each of the other people in the room and whispered something to them. Were they in on this shenanigan too?

"I don't know what y'all tryin' to pull," I said when she returned and sat down, "but it's been a long time. Too long. Can't nothin' be different now."

"But—"

The young man interrupted. "I think maybe we should leave now. Maybe we can come back soon." He helped the old woman to her feet, then he bent down and lifted Dandy's chin, causin' me to nearly jump to the rescue before he said, "Thanks for looking after my Great-Aunt Cindy, Dandy. Tell her it's a big job for a dog, though. Tell her we'd like to help you out, look after her now. Tell her we want to bring her home. Can you do that, fella?"

Home? What's he talkin' 'bout? Had they all gone back to Arkansas?

Without another word, he stood and walked the old woman out into the foyer. Fuzz Top followed them. Once the doors swung closed, I sat there, piecing together what they'd said. The old woman thinks she's my sister, Maggie, and the young man thinks that makes him my great nephew. They want me to ... to what? Accept all that malarkey? And what? Go live with them?

Huh. Maybe they were kin, and maybe they weren't, but ... how could I go live with 'em? I wouldn't fit. Don't know nothin' 'bout livin' in a reg'lar home … Eh, they were prob'ly imposters, tryin' to scam me, tryin' to get … The Purse. I looked around to make sure no one was watchin' and dug my hand down into my cart, deep down till I could feel the outline of The Purse. It was safe.

"Well, Lucy." Fuzz Top sounded chipper as a squirrel when she returned. "Whadda 'bout them apples?"

"Oh, *Whadda 'bout them apples?* You tryin' to talk country or somethin'?" I held my hand out to stop her. "I ain't got nothin' to say."

FUZZ TOP TRIED TO CORNER ME a couple more times, tickin' off her list of clues showin' I was kin to that Will and the old woman he brought with him, but it wasn't till they came back again on Monday that I let myself even think about the possibility. Maggie, as she called herself, started right in talkin' 'bout things that we supposedly did when we was girls.

Times was hard back then, and she coulda been talkin 'bout any two girls, but then she dropped the bomb: "When you and Bo ran off—"

"Wait! What'd you just say?" As far as I could recollect, I hadn't mentioned Bo's name to anyone in years, certainly not anyone at Manna House.

"I was just sayin', Ma was fit to be tied when you and Bo ran off. She was determined to stay right there in Lapeer until you came back, but with all that folderol over the boss man gettin' killed, Pa said we'd better light a shuck outta there or we'd get pinched too. None of us wanted to go, but then we had no work in the beets either."

Well, that did it! I couldn't deny the obvious. I was lookin' at my kid sister for real. Guess, deep down, I knew it the moment I'd laid eyes on her. But now what was I supposed to do?

They kinda answered it for me by insistin' I go with them to visit Maggie at her place. Ever so often they'd brought up the idea of me livin' with Maggie, so I wasn't about to go with 'em till I learned she only had a two-bedroom condo and this young Will was already stayin' in one of 'em while he went to school. So I didn't think there was any harm in a visit.

But once we got there—real nice place on the second floor of an eight-unit building—Will started talkin' about how he'd been wanting to move into campus housing where it'd be easier for him to study. "So this can be your room, Aunt Cindy."

"*Lucy*, my name's Lucy. Been Lucy for over sixty years. Not gonna go back now."

"Okay, sorry. It's just that we're all used to referring to you as—"

"Means 'Light.'"

"What?"

"Lucy. My name means 'Light,' and I ain't 'bout to give that up."

"But Ma and Pa named you Cindy," Maggie added.

"No, they named me Lucinda. Everyone just called me Cindy like we all called you Maggie when your real name's Margaret. Bet you don't even know what it mean. But Bo and I chose Lucy, comes from Lucinda, same as Cindy does. But we chose it, an' it means 'Light.' Learned that when I sprained my ankle."

Will and Maggie looked at each other like I'd explained one of the mysteries of the universe. Then Will took a deep breath and said, "Whatever! What I was trying to say is that this'll be your room, Aunt … Lucy. Got a great view. Take a look out the window."

Glad for the freedom of the new Aircast on my foot, I took a quick spin around the room and peeked out the window. It was nice—big trees, quiet street.

We went into the kitchen and sat down at the little table—hardly big enough for three of us—and ate Chinese carry-out Will had picked up on our way over there. They chattered on 'bout how conveniently located Maggie's place was—the bus stopped at the corner and a Jewel Food Store was only three blocks away with an Osco Pharmacy in it. "And I've found the best little church," Maggie said, her eyes all aglow. "You'll just love it, Cindy."

"Lucy."

"I'm sorry. I should remember that, because Bo kept callin' you that."

I stared at her. "*Bo*? When did you ever hear him call me Lucy? We didn't decide that till we was on the road."

Maggie put her hand to her neck as if to be sure her blouse wasn't open. "Well, I think that's what he called you when we spoke that time on the phone. He kept sayin'—"

"He called you on the *telephone*? When?"

"Oh, for land's sake, I don't remember what the date was. It was when he was tryin' to find us. He said he'd been callin' all over the country. That's how I knew you were in Chicago. He called from Chicago and said you two had gotten married."

My head was swirlin'! When had this happened? Why hadn't Bo said anything about it to me? Suddenly, I remembered the rest of what Fuzz Top had said about my name on that retreat, could almost hear her voice plain as day: *Let God shine His light into every dark corner of your life, so that you are free to be who He created you to be.*

I'd thought I was always free—didn't let no one tie me down, tell me what to do or where to go—but I was beginnin' to see that darkness had hidden things from me my whole life long, and those hidden things had shaped my life. I hadn't known the charges against Bo had been dismissed. I was in the dark 'bout him bein' alive when I thought he was dead. I hadn't known where my family was or that Bo had found them.

And then there were all the things I'd kept in the dark from everyone else. If Fuzz Top hadn't been shinin' her ol' light around in my private life the other day with all them personal questions, I wouldn't even be here in my sister's condo.

I looked around at Maggie's modest furnishings. They wasn't fancy, but this home was cozy and clean, and she wasn't fightin' the cold and rain tryin' to find a dumpster to sleep in. An' now she was askin' me to move in and share it all with her …

But I couldn't. I didn't deserve it. Maggie'd said she found "the best little church," meanin' she was prob'ly on sweet terms with the Almighty. Huh. If I had a chance to *really* talk to the Almighty, it wouldn't be sweet. If she knew how often I had screamed at God for robbin' me of my family, robbin' me of Bo—not just once, but *three times*, an' then takin' Miz Martha Shepherd, too, just when I thought I'd finally found a friend …well, Maggie wouldn't want me livin' with her if she knew.

An' if she ever found out about The Purse …

No, no. Couldn't risk lettin' the light shine into those dark corners.

"I think it's time for me to go. Mr. Will, I'd be obliged if you could you give me a lift back to Manna House."

"Oh, sure, Aunt … Lucy, but," he winked at his grandmother and grinned like a ten-year-old, "we want you to come back next Thursday and have Thanksgiving dinner with us. That'll give me enough time to make alternative living arrangements, and it'll give you enough time to consider Nana's invitation to move in with her. Okay?"

I tried to give him a big smile. "Where's my coat?"

As we were leavin' the condo, I turned back and gazed for a long moment at my kid sister. "Bye, Maggie. Thanks for lookin' for me for so long."

But she had no idea who she'd found.

Chapter 47

In Room 426 of the Blackhawk Hotel, Lucy smoothed the spread after making her last bed of the day. She was tired—but at least she'd be going home to Bo in a few minutes. Just then, Mr. Kowalski slammed through the door and stood there red-faced and gasping as though he'd run up all four flights of stairs.

He bent over, steading himself with one hand on a knee to avoid collapsing as he clutched his chest with his other. "You! Your husband have bad accident ... very bad!" He gulped air. "He's hurt, in hospital ... You go now to him!"

"What!" Lucy clapped both hands to her face to stifle her cry, and then ran past her boss, almost knocking him down. She turned back just as she entered the hall. "Which hospital?"

"Cook County. Down Western, over on Harrison. My wife had baby there. Can't miss it."

Outside the Blackhawk, Lucy waited five or six minutes for a streetcar, then gave up and hailed a cab. This was no time to save money. Bo needed her!

What could have happened? Mr. Kowalski said it was an accident and he was hurt bad, but what could have happened? And what was Bo doing down in the city this time of day?

"Faster!" she urged the cabbie. "It's my husband. Faster!"

She ran in the front door and asked where James Bodeen was.

The woman at the front desk looked at her logbook, frowned, then shook her head.

Lucy remembered the confusion of trying to find Bo at the VA hospital. "How about ... how 'bout Borick Hansen? Do you have a patient named Borick Hansen?"

The woman flipped several pages on her clipboard. "I'm sorry, miss. I don't see anyone by either name. When was he admitted?"

"Just a little while ago, I think. He was in a bad accident."

"Oh, well, we probably don't have the paperwork on him yet. Go through those doors and down the hall to the end. Ask at the nurse station there."

Ten minutes later, Lucy found Bo—or rather, found where he was—on the second floor in an operating room where the doctors were trying to save his life from a "severe internal injury after he saved a young boy from an accident with a horse-drawn wagon," the nurse said. Lucy would just have to wait until he came out of surgery.

Lucy sat in a chair in the hall. *An accident saving a young boy from a horse wagon?* What was he doing around a horse wagon in the middle of the city? She leaned forward, elbows on knees, chin in hands, and rocked. "O God! O God, don't let him die! Please, God! Please!"

Time ticked on, and Lucy had no idea how long she'd been sitting there when she was startled by someone saying, "Are you Mrs. Bodeen?"

Lucy looked up to see a man in a blood-spattered white lab coat. She swallowed. "Is he okay, doctor?" Obviously, Bo wasn't okay or the doctor wouldn't look like a butcher.

"He's still alive, and that's something. We removed the shrapnel, and he's very lucky it didn't sever the artery, or he would've been gone in a minute. But it did pierce the liver, and he's lost a lot of blood. I'm sorry to say it's too early to tell whether he'll make it, but we're doing everything we can for him."

"Can ... can I see him?"

"*Hmm* ..." He turned and looked down the hall. "They'll be moving him into the recovery ward in a few minutes. I think there are only a couple of other patients in there tonight." The doctor gestured over his shoulder. "It's through those double doors. Tell the head nurse I sent you, and maybe she'll let you stay."

Lucy nodded, and once the doctor walked away, she headed for the doors at the end of the hall. She slipped into the ward as quietly as possible. It was a large room with ten beds, five down each side of a wide central aisle. Two had curtains pulled partially around them, and Lucy assumed those were for the patients the doctor had mentioned.

"I'm sorry." A heavyset nurse in a white uniform had slipped up behind Lucy, startling her. The nurse continued in a stern whisper. "Visitors are not permitted in the recovery room."

"I'm ..." Unconsciously, Lucy put her hands together in front of her face as if in prayer. "I'm Mrs. Bodeen. The doctor said I could wait in here for my husband, Bo."

"Oh, yes, the boy from the accident. We'll be wheeling him in momentarily, but ... Dr. Eisemann told you to come in?" The frown on her face suggested she doubted Lucy's claim.

"I didn't get his name, but yes, he ..." Lucy waved her hands indicating that the mess on the doctor's lab coat. "He was ... operating on my husband."

The nurse's eyebrows arched, and then she shrugged. "Nevertheless," she took Lucy's elbow to guide her back through the double doors, "why don't you wait out here until we have him situated? I'll come out and get you in a few minutes."

The *few minutes* seemed to last an hour, while Lucy paced back and forth, guarding the doors from ... from whom? The angel of death? "Oh, God, don't let him die. Please!" Finally the nurse peeked out, held her finger to her lips for quiet, and whispered, "You can come in now. He's in the last bed on the right."

Lucy walked the gauntlet between the other beds, glancing into the bays for the other two patients as though they might jump out and grab her. And then she saw the bed at the end. They hadn't yet pulled out the curtain to create a bay for it, and she could see Bo—dark hair, high cheekbones, chiseled face, but he was as pale as a penny postcard. His closed eyes and half-open mouth did not look like peaceful sleep. "Oh, Bo." She stopped, wanting to rush to him, but afraid of what she'd find. She crept forward, hand over her mouth. A bottle hung in the space above him with a tube down to his arm, dripping something into him. At least there were no bandages around his head, no cuts on his face. Maybe he was going to be all right after all.

The nurse snuck up behind Lucy again. "Here, I brought a chair for you."

"How is he?"

"Hard to tell, dear." She had lost her brusque manner. "He's lost a lot of blood. Frankly, tonight's the critical night. If he makes it through, there's a good chance he may recover."

Lucy pushed the chair close to the bed and sat down. "Can I hold his hand?"

"Of course. Just no weight on his abdomen."

While Lucy stroked Bo's hand, the nurse fussed with things, sucking fluid from his mouth with a bulb, elevating his head with a pillow, checking another jar that hung below the bed with a tube in it. Lucy glanced at it. An ugly, bloody fluid was draining into it.

When she'd taken his blood pressure, she stepped back. "We've done all we can do for now. I'll check back regularly, but if he needs me, I'll be in the little cubby by the doors. Oh, and just so you'll know, all his clothes and things are in this laundry bag tied to the foot of his bed."

"Thank you." Lucy didn't take her eyes of Bo's face. Strange, it didn't look like he'd shaved that morning.

"Are you going to be okay?" When Lucy nodded, she continued. "You could still get something to eat from the cafeteria downstairs." After a moment, she added, "Is there anyone I could phone for you?"

Lucy shook her head, and the nurse started to turn away. "Oh, wait. Yes, could you call Pastor Winfred? Oh, but I can't recollect his number. Um … try calling DEArborn-3962, and ask for Mrs. Brown. Please tell her what's happened. She'll get the pastor."

THE LIGHTS IN THE WARD HAD BEEN DIMMED and it was well after midnight. Lucy still watched the slow rise and fall of Bo's chest, willing him to take breath after breath when someone touched her shoulder.

She turned to see Pastor Winfred and Emma Brown. Mrs. Brown bent over and gave Lucy a hug. "Nurse only let us in because of Pastor Winfred, so we gotta be real quiet." She nodded toward Bo. "How's he doin'?"

Lucy shook her head. "Not too well. Nurse says his blood pressure keeps dropping, says he might still be bleeding internally."

The pastor stepped around to the other side of the bed, hands clasping his Bible at his waist, while he prayed quietly with bowed head. Lucy heard the name, "Jesus," mentioned frequently, but she couldn't catch any other words. It was like he was praying in a foreign language.

Finally, he raised his head and looked across at Lucy. "This is a terrible time of trial for you, young lady. Seek the Lord. Seek the Lord. Call upon His name in your time of trouble."

Hadn't she been calling on God all night? How many times had she said, *"O God, please don't let Bo die! Please! Please! Please!"*? Hundreds of times! She'd repeated it as if she were saying a rosary or something. Why was the pastor talking to her as though *she* were the one in crisis?

Mrs. Brown began to hum some old hymns, swaying from side to side as Pastor Winfred went back to praying, his head bowed and eyes closed. As they kept vigil, Lucy leaned over and laid her head on the bed beside Bo and drifted off to sleep.

AT FIRST, LUCY THOUGHT SHE MUST BE DREAMING when Bo's voice woke her, but then came the squeeze of his hand that she still held. She lifted her head to stare at him. His eyes were open, and he smiled thinly at her. Lucy glanced around to see if anyone else was witnessing his rally, but the pastor and Mrs. Brown were gone, and the earliest of predawn light was coloring the windows.

"Oh, Bo. I thought I was going to lose you!" She gripped his hand harder, tears of happiness springing to her eyes.

He looked at her for a long moment and then smiled again.

"Can I get something for you? Are ya hurtin'? Should I get the nurse?" His face looked so drawn, she was sure he must be in pain.

He licked his dry lips and in a raspy whisper said, "My pants ... where are my pants?"

"Your pants! But you can't get—"

"Please, find my pants for me."

Reluctantly, Lucy got up and went to the end of the bed where she dug through the laundry bag until she pulled out his pants and held them up. "These?"

He nodded. "In the pocket ... right front pocket."

Lucy pulled out an envelope. "This is all that's in there."

Again he nodded. "It's for you …"

Lucy opened it to find two tickets and a scrap of paper with an address on it. Tickets? "These look like they're for more than a Riverview ride. What's up?" She slipped them back into the envelope and looked at Bo. He coughed, and the pain that etched his face caused Lucy to toss the pants and envelope to the side and run to him.

His eyes widened, too wide. He raised his head slightly and stared at her as if he couldn't actually see her. "For our honeymoon … sorry it's so late." He coughed again and let his head fall back on the pillow. "I love you, babe." And then his eyes slowly closed.

Lucy gripped his hand, her face only inches from his and waited. No sound.

"Bo … Bo … breathe! Take another breath, Bo!" She waited what seemed like minutes. "You gotta breathe. Ya know you do. Breathe, Bo! Breathe!"

Jumping up, she yelled, "Nurse! Nurse!" Then she ran to the edge of the curtain and looked around it. "Nurse!" she screamed. "Come quick! He's not breathin'! Hurry!"

The moment she saw the white cap and uniform emerge from the cubby, Lucy dashed back to Bo and grabbed his hand. "Bo, Bo, Bo! Wake up! You gotta breathe!"

And then the nurse was pushing her aside, checking Bo's pulse, and leaning close to detect his breathing. Lucy stifled the cries erupting from within her so the nurse could hear and do whatever was needed to bring her man back to her. Finally, she couldn't restrain herself. "Do something!"

The nurse held up her hand. "Can't push on him, honey. He's all torn up inside." She listened for a while longer, then stepped back, shaking his head. "He's gone, dear. I'm so sorry, but he's gone."

"Nooo!" It all came out in one great howl, and the nurse hugged Lucy to her bosom, trying to quiet her for the sake of the other patients.

"He can't be gone!" sobbed Lucy. "Get the doctor! Do something. He was just talking to me. He was awake. He was gettin' better. Do something!"

"Shh! Shh! Shush now!" The nurse pulled her tighter. "There's nothing that can be done. He's gone."

Lucy shook her off. *She* didn't need the nurse's help. Bo did! "But you said …you said if he made it through the night, and …" She turned and gestured toward the lightening windows. "It's morning. See? It's getting' light out. He made it … so he can't die!"

The nurse wouldn't give up. She hugged Lucy again. "I know, I know, dear. He fought hard, but he didn't make it. Here …" she walked Lucy to her chair, "sit with him for a while. I'll let the doctor know, and he'll be in in a few minutes."

As she went out, the nurse picked up Bo's trousers and hung them back in the closet.

Lucy sat beside the bed, holding Bo's hand with one hand and stroking his brow with the other. Slowly, the last few minutes settled on her like a mountain, pressing all the air from her lungs, ending life for her as well. What was life without Bo? She'd thought he was dead, killed in the war. But he'd come back to her—alive! So how could this be? He couldn't be gone! Why hadn't God answered her prayers? Didn't He care?

When the doctor finally came, he took only a moment checking Bo before he said, "I'm sorry, miss. That much damage to the liver's not like a cut on the skin that can be easily sewn up. It was like …" He stopped himself as though he realized nothing good could come from a fuller description. "We did all we could."

Lucy said nothing. It was as if her tears had frozen and sat in the pit of her stomach like stones.

Some time later the nurse returned, carrying a tray with some tea and hot cereal. Lucy didn't feel like eating, but she tried to sip the tea. "I called your friend again," the nurse said. "She and the pastor will be by before long to take you home—"

"Oh, nooo!"

"I know, I know, honey, but your husband can't stay here in the room. There'll be new patients coming in, so we need to take his body down to the ... you know."

The morgue. She might as well have said it.

PASTOR WINFRED TOOK CARE of all the arrangements for a funeral and Bo's burial while Lucy stayed at the Browns'. She couldn't face going back to their apartment. It turned out that Lucy's old landlady, Betsy Mason, had owned a burial plot in a nearby cemetery where she once thought she'd be buried, but when she moved down south, she'd deeded it to Mount Olive Tabernacle. The pastor had phoned her, and Miss Mason agreed wholeheartedly with using it for Bo.

The days went by like a fog. Lucy sat numbly through the funeral and later stood beside the grave while the simple wooden casket was lowered into the ground. Afterwards, back to the Browns', she clipped the leash to Jigger's collar.

"You goin' for a walk?" Mrs. Brown asked, her brow furrowed with concern. "Want me or one of the kids to come with you?"

Lucy shook her head. "Jigger'll do."

She walked for blocks until she got to their apartment building. Jigger whined and wanted to go up, probably thinking Bo would be there. *Maybe ... maybe he is up there. Maybe I didn't just watch his body be put in the ground.* But she couldn't bring herself to go up and see.

Pulling on Jigger's leash, she walked on, barely aware of where she was going, until she was in a neighborhood she didn't recognize and realized she was lost. The early summer night was warm and mild. Exhausted, she curled up in the alcove of the back door of an Ace Hardware Store, hugging Jigger until she fell asleep.

He woke her up by licking her face when it got to be light, and she got up stiffly and wandered down the alley until she found a loaf of bread in a garbage can behind a nearby bakery. At first she retrieved it for Jigger, but as she walked, she ate a few bites as well. The bread seemed to revive them both, and she kept walking, letting Jigger lead the way until she saw a street sign, Central Park Avenue, and knew where she was.

She arrived at the Browns' about noon.

"Oh, honey, we were worried about you! Did you go back to your apartment?" Emma Brown asked.

Lucy nodded. "Yes, ma'am. I went by, but …"

"I understand, dear. You don't need to tell me. You just take it as you can. Just remember, you've always got a bed here when you need one."

Lucy did not go back to work the next morning or the next day, but she didn't tell Mrs. Brown. She just left in the morning and came back at night. She felt dead. Why go to work to make money?

A few days later, she took Jigger and told the Browns she was going back to the apartment, but when she got there, she again couldn't force herself to go up. She knew it wasn't true, but the image of Bo still living there was too precious to shatter.

This time, she stayed away from the Browns for three days … and then it was a week. She didn't have to think. She didn't have to talk. Just forage for herself and Jigger. They got by.

But the next time she showed up, Mrs. Brown said, "You know, honey, you need to take better care of yourself, look a little more professional. Know what I'm sayin'? And another thing, with Bo being a veteran and all, you should be entitled to a widow's pension, especially since he actually died of his war wound."

Lucy shrugged.

"I'll tell you what, this is Sunday, and tomorrow's your day off, right? Sometimes a body needs a little shove in the right direction. Come Monday, I'm going with you to the VA, and we'll get all that paperwork straightened out so you can get your check."

But when Mrs. Brown and Lucy got to the VA, they discovered that the agency had never heard of James Bodeen. Borick Hansen was the veteran of record as far as the VA was concerned. Mrs. Brown's offer to sign an affidavit stating Bodeen and Hansen were the same person did no good. So Lucy's marriage certificate and Bo's death certificate were of no value in proving she was the wife of a deceased veteran. "I'm sorry, ma'am, if those documents named Borick Hansen, you might have a claim, but without that, there's nothing I can do."

Mrs. Brown tried to encourage Lucy as they rode home on the El and streetcar. "I'm sure we could get a lawyer and work this out." But Lucy didn't have any fight left in her. She began staying on the streets for longer and longer periods, until one day she went by the apartment building where she and Bo had lived and saw all of her and Bo's belongings piled by the garbage cans out back. She picked through the stuff but took only a small packet of letters from Bo, tied with a faded pink ribbon. They were the ones he'd written while in the service. They brought to mind that last envelope from him, the one in his pocket at the hospital with two tickets in it. He'd said, "*For our honeymoon ... sorry it's so late.*" She wondered what had happened to it in all the chaos. Oh well, didn't matter. What was a honeymoon without Bo? What was life without Bo?

Something in her died that day.

After that, she never went back to the Browns' house. Living on the street helped shut out the memories of the life she and Bo had shared. *Survive.* That was all she had to do. But occasionally, she and Jigger made their way between bushes and trees and stones to a little concrete bench where Lucy sat and stared at the name James Bodeen.

Chapter 48

WILL NISSAN BOUNDED UP THE STEPS of Manna House two at a time and rang the bell. Once he was buzzed in, he asked at the desk if Lucy Tucker was ready.

"*Hmm* ... haven't seen her for a while." The Asian-appearing receptionist spun the logbook around and ran her finger down the names. "But she's not signed out. She's probably in there waiting for you. I heard you were taking her for Thanksgiving dinner."

"Yeah. We're going over to her sister's. But I don't know ..." He drew a long breath through his nose, eyebrows arching. "Smells pretty good here. Maybe I should just go get Grandma and come back to join Lucy here."

They both laughed as Will went through the double, swinging doors.

In the lounge where he and his grandmother had met Lucy the first time, several residents were milling around, some playing table games, some watching TV, some talking.

"Excuse me. Has anyone seen my great-aunt ... Lucy Tucker?"

Most glanced at Will, shook their heads, and went on with whatever they'd been doing, but a pale woman with thin brown hair pulled back in a limp ponytail turned from arranging books in the bookcase. "I saw her upstairs earlier. Repacking her cart. Had everything she owns spread out on her bunk."

"Ah, good." Will held his hands out to his side in a helpless gesture. "I came by to pick her up … but men aren't supposed to go up there, are they?"

"Nope!" The woman plunked a stack of books on the floor. "But I'll go get her."

While waiting, Will paced around the room, trying not to intrude on the space or activities of the other women. He studied the mural on the wall. "The Shepherd's Fold." Interesting! Jesus held a tiny lamb in His arms, but the sheep around Him were scraggly and dirty, some thin and starved looking, some with bleeding or bandaged wounds. *"Hmm …"* thought Will, *"a shelter for the homeless, very apropos."*

"I'm sorry, sir," said the woman when she returned, "but Lucy doesn't seem to be around. Her cart's gone too. So I'm guessin' she's 'out and about,' as she always says. Did you check at the front desk to see if she signed out?"

"Yeah …" Will looked around the room again, as if he'd merely missed Lucy among the other women. "She said Lucy hadn't signed out. Are you supposed to sign out every time?"

"It's one of the rules … unless you're just steppin' out front for a smoke."

Will rubbed a hand through his hair. "But I was supposed to take her to my grandma's—her sister's—for Thanksgiving dinner."

"I don't know about that, but she's not upstairs. Check downstairs. Estelle might know."

Will found Estelle and Harry Bentley putting the finishing touches on a Thanksgiving feast, but neither had seen Lucy all day.

Will no longer worried about invading the residents' space and started asking everyone when they'd last seen Lucy. The most he learned was that Lucy often disappeared like this, "So what's the big deal?"

Frustrated, he pulled out his cell phone and called Gabby Fairbanks at the House of Hope.

"Will, I don't know what to say," Mrs. Fairbanks said after hearing Will's tale of woe. "I'm so sorry. She probably got scared. Someone from her family showing up after so many years, the whole idea of coming off the streets and living in an actual apartment ... it's probably overwhelming to her."

Will was silent for several moments, then said, "Yeah, I know. I just hate ... I hate having to go back to the condo to tell Nana that her sister's disappeared again. She's been cooking for two days. It's going to break her heart."

"Oh, Will ... Will, listen to me. Are you listening? *Don't give up.* Keep looking for her. I can't help you look for her right now, we've got all sorts of guests over here, but we'll find her. Or she'll show up. She always does, eventually. If anything, I know one thing is true. *Lucy needs you.* She may not know it. But God does. He's the one who helped you find her, and He's not going to let you down."

It was slim compensation to Will, but when she agreed to help him actually look for her the next day, he was somewhat comforted. Someone understood how he and his grandmother felt.

For so late in the fall, Friday was another moderate day— some clouds, some sunshine, a sprinkle now and then, upper fifties—which meant, Mrs. Fairbanks said, that Lucy could be anywhere. But after searching the lakefront, including the pavilion where they'd previously found her, the parks, and a couple of other shelters on the north side, they returned to Manna House. "I'm so sorry, Will," Mrs. Fairbanks said. "Some miracles take a little more time than others. I'll get in touch with you the moment I know anything."

The next day, Will called Manna House in the afternoon, but still no one had seen Lucy. So on Monday he skipped classes and drove Nana's car to the shelter. He had a plan.

As soon as Mrs. Fairbanks opened the door to welcome him into her tiny office, Dandy rushed up to greet him, tail wagging wildly. Will stooped down and ruffled the neck of the yellow dog. "Hey, boy, you're just the one I want to see." He glanced up at the red-haired program director and grinned. "You, too, of course, ma'am."

"And hello to you too, Will. Have you heard anything from Lucy?"

"No, and I take it you haven't either. But I have an idea. Do you have a leash for Dandy, and would it be okay if I took him for a walk? I might be gone for quite a while, but I'll bring him back before … well, you name the time."

I WATCHED THROUGH THE BLACK BRANCHES of the old oaks in Graceland Cemetery as the clouds in the west began to break up. They had no silver lining, but the sun pierced their dark bellies like platinum girders to prop them up.

Off in the distance, I saw a figure, almost in silhouette, making his way across the distant lawn, zigzagging first one way and then the other as a dog pulled him steadily toward me. I would've skedaddled had it been a groundsworker—they don't like me sittin' on that little stone bench—but I'd never known one of 'em to cotton to a dog. So I waited …

As they came nearer, the dog started lungin', makin' the man run to keep up. *Wha—?* I couldn't believe it. "Dandy! That you?" Saw who it was then—that Will Nissan! He'd tricked Dandy into givin' away my special place.

412

When he got close enough to see it was me, a big grin spread across the boy's face. "Whew! This dog sure gave me a run, but I'm glad I found you Aunt Cin— I mean, Aunt Lucy." He looked around at the various headstones. "What are you doing sitting here in a cemetery all by yourself?"

I scowled at him. "Thinkin', recollectin'."

"But why ...?" He spread his hands and gave me a puzzled face. "Why here in a cemetery, of all places?"

"'Cause *most* people in here don't bother me." He caught my drift but still looked bewildered. "Also ..." I pointed to the small, level stone a few feet in front of me.

Young Will stepped to my side and bent over, hands on his knees, to study it. "'James (Bo) Bodeen, Sep. 24, 1924—Apr. 25, 1946,'" he read aloud. He straightened and took a respectful step back. "That must be your husband, Bo."

Bo ... yes. My husband.

"Oh ... I see. I didn't know he, uh ... that he was buried here."

I said nothin'—what was there to say?—while Dandy nosed around behind me at the gate into the crypt, that little stone house where we'd spent more'n one night together. Finally, Will broke the silence. "You missed Thanksgiving dinner with us."

I sighed. "Yeah. Sorry 'bout that. Shoulda let ya know, I guess."

"But why, Lucy? You know Nana has spent a long time looking for you. She never gave up, knew you had to be alive. And ... to be honest? She really needs some company, and I can't be that to her. I'm trying to go to school, and I've got my own life to live. It'd sure mean a lot to her if you'd come live with her."

I sighed again. "Yeah, but maybe not. Not if she knew ..."

"Knew what?"

I turned and looked up at him, good-lookin' young man without a care in the world. Frustrated, I dug down into the basket of my cart, tired of what I'd carried for so long. "This, for one thing!" And I shoved The Purse at him.

He jumped like it was a snake, then reached out and cautiously took it. "What is it?"

"Open it, you'll see."

His eyes widened as he opened The Purse and started flippin' through the old bills. "Money?"

Could feel my lip tremblin' and I looked away. "Money I stole, that's what."

"*Stole*? From who?"

"Pa and Ma and Maggie and the whole family," I muttered, "an' who knows who all else."

He handed it back to me. "What are you talking about?"

Huh. What did it matter anymore? If I didn't tell him how I'd come by The Purse, he'd hound me till kingdom come.

When I'd finished the whole sorry tale, he shook his head. "Scoot over on that little bench. There's room for two of us." I scooted and we both sat there starin' at Bo's gravestone. Dandy came over and sat down in front of us, leanin' against my legs.

Finally Will sighed. "Aunt Lucy, I don't know what to say to you. Great-Grandpa Lester and Great-Grandma Harriet are dead, and so is everybody else you think this money might've belonged to. I don't think Nana would lay claim to a penny of it, because she's got her pension, enough to be comfortable."

Dandy laid his chin on my knee, as if tryin' to help some. I thought maybe that was it from young Will.

But a few moments later he spoke again. "But I think I do know what Nana would say, 'cause she's said it to me plenty of times when I felt like I'd messed up. 'Seek the Lord, son,' she always says. 'Tell Him about it. He's faithful to forgive.'"

"*Hmph,* heard that one before." Fact was, in all my eighty years, seemed like every time folks talked to me 'bout God, they was quotin' verses like that. *"Seek the Lord while He may be found. Call on Him while He is near."* Well, maybe He had been near a time or two, but now …?

"Ah, Aunt Lucy, why don't you just come home? Look …" He began pattin' his jacket and pants pockets until he pulled out an old, yellowed envelope and thrust it at me. "Have you ever seen this before?"

I took it and turned it over. It had an address and a canceled stamp on it. I shook my head.

"Go on, open it! Grandma Maggie said it might mean somethin' to you."

Inside were two tickets … an' I got a funny feelin'. They looked like the same two tickets Bo had given me the night he died. "What're these?"

"Train tickets, from Chicago to Detroit. Nana said they came in the mail a couple of weeks after …" He pointed at the gravestone. "… after Bo phoned and said you two were coming home to visit them."

"But he said they were for our honeymoon—"

"That's right. Nana said the same thing. He was bringin' you to visit the whole family … for your honeymoon. It was supposed to be a big surprise."

"But how …? I thought I lost 'em the night he died. Never went back to look for 'em. Didn't much care. What good would a honeymoon be without … without my Bo?"

"But don't you see, Aunt Lucy? He wanted you to come home! He loved you so much, and that was his last wish!"

Go home? Young Will's words went down deep. Bo had wanted me to go home!

I bent over and laid my cheek on Dandy's silky head so Will wouldn't see the tears that made ever'thing go blurry all of a sudden. Was the boy right, this great-nephew of mine, that Maggie wasn't holdin' nothin' against me, just wanted me to come home?

But … could I forgive myself?

You're a stubborn old fool, Lucy Tucker. Who did I think I was? If God was willin' to forgive me, why was I refusin' to let Him shine His light into those dark corners I kept carryin' around with me?

Reaching for my cart, I fished out The Purse once more and handed it to Will. "Give this to Manna House or somethin' where it might do a little good."

Maybe it was me reachin' for the cart. Or a dog's sixth sense … but Dandy bounced up, danced on his feet as if eager to go, and gave a little bark.

Will stood up, too, and held out his hand. "Come on, Aunt Lucy. Let's go home."

Acknowledgments

Our sincere thanks goes to ...

Julian Jackson, our son and the Director of Experience Design at the Adler Planetarium, for his expert advice concerning the cover design. **Chad Johnson** for the background cover photo of a carnival. **Chris Edgell** for modeling as Lucy.

Lee Hough, our agent, for believing in and supporting this endeavor from beginning to end.

Pam Sullivan, Julie Pferdehirt, and **Sue Mitrovich** for their content review and substantive edits. **Jennifer Stair** for her professional copyedit. **Lelia Austin, Michelle Redding, Erin Redick, Millisa Neal, Shondra Brown, Krista Johnson,** and **Janelle Schneider** for their very welcome proofreading.

... And (Neta here) to **Dave**, who took my passion for doing "Lucy's story" as a follow-up to the House of Hope series, adopted the storyline I'd created, and ran with it as primary writer. We even survived those "moments of intense fellowship" when we disagreed about how the story should proceed. (Hey, honey, thanks for signing us up for ballroom dancing lessons so we can celebrate! Who said old dogs can't learn new tricks?)